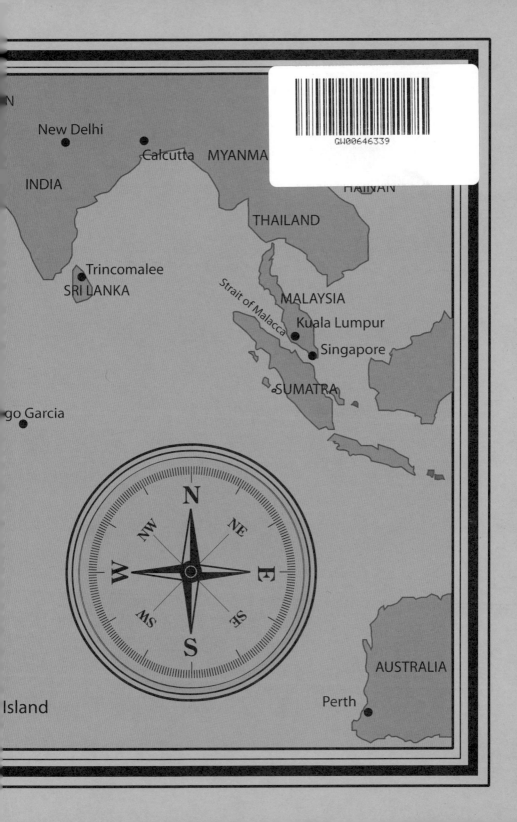

The Chinese Ocean

Christopher Meakin

THE GOODCHILD PRESS

LONDON   WASHINGTON DC   WELLINGTON, NZ   OSLO

2014

First published 2014 by

THE GOODCHILD PRESS LTD

London, United Kingdom

Reg. Off: Redwoods, 2 Clystworks, Clyst Road, Topsham, Exeter EX3 0DB
email: publisher@thegoodchildpress.co.uk

A catalogue record of this book
is available from the British Library
ISBN 978-1-897657-91-1

Set in Garamond 12.5 on 15pt by the author
Book and dust jacket designed by Christopher Meakin
Portraits, endpaper maps and dustjacket execution by Guido Miccoli

Printed and bound in Great Britain by
The Short Run Press Limited, Exeter
www.shortrunpress.co.uk

CONTENTS

Acknowledgements

Anne Billard, Docteur ès Lettres, Sorbonne
James Cumes, former Australian ambassador to the EU
Col. Nandu Koregaonkar, former commanding officer, Indian SAS

Christopher Meakin
London
November 2014

Chapter One

Overture

Central Beijing

EVERY CAPITAL CITY has an embassy district and in Beijing it lies north east of the city centre, between the second and third ring roads. The city's global importance merits some of the world's most seasoned and professional diplomats. Many years ago the Chinese government built a large signals intelligence centre to listen to the confidential messages of all those foreign embassies. Captain Zhou Man of the People's Liberation Army (Navy) was now heading for that unremarkable building for an unexpected and unusual appointment.

There was a sprightly spring in Zhou's step as he walked along the Xindong Road. He was tall and slender with pointed features and the keen eyes of a sailor. Although little had been explained beforehand about his meeting at noon, it was not every day that a middle-ranking Chinese naval officer was summoned to a confidential briefing with vice-premier Liu Fun. What else could the news possibly be but good?

A mystery to many outside Beijing, vice-premier Liu was regarded by those who knew her as an intellectual star. Behind the scenes she was China's leading strategist, almost certainly one of the most influential women anywhere in the world. Even further from the limelight, she was also a prominent member of a group of reformists called the Beijing Patriotic Association. They met in secret. A tightly-knit group of politically motivated men and women holding many influential positions in and around Beijing, they were bent on creating a powerful, efficiently-run and globally dominant China.

The BPA accepted, with reluctance, that the way forward had to include market capitalism in some form. As a compromise its members wanted the market regulated for the exclusive benefit of their country. Regulated, that is, as far as they could possibly get away with it. Their solution would be "Capitalism With Chinese Characteristics", but no-one was keen to spell out precisely what those characteristics might involve, least of all to the international media. Lots of international busy-bodies might well have raised objections to the unvarnished truth.

Not every intellectual in Beijing agreed with Liu Fun and her circle of influential friends by any means. Many took a more Western view that China was just one huge player in a global process and that mankind would best be served if all the world's principal countries moved forward in as much unison as they could collectively muster.

But not the Beijing Patriotic Association, which is why they kept their nationalistic thoughts and as far as possible their very existence out of sight. In their collective view the growing economy of China was not a step toward the harmonious wealth of nations. It was a semi-military weapon and philanthropic global free trade was nowhere near the top of their distinctive agenda. China's individual prosperity and dominance in the world most certainly were. That was about as much as Captain Zhou could find out about the Beijing Patriotic Association when it had first been hinted it might help him to join.

Two alert receptionists at the signals intelligence centre, which people were nowadays invited to believe had been converted into a normal office block for the use of senior Government figures, recognised Zhou Man immediately as he walked in from the street. The navy had supplied uniquely recognisable pictures as well as complete biographical detail from his birth onwards, including his education, his career, the assessments of his senior officers, surprisingly intimate detail on his social circle and comprehensive lists of his family, classmates and colleagues. No-one left anything to chance whenever they knew that vice-premier Liu Fun would be involved.

The receptionists promptly directed Zhou Man to a separate elevator which went only to the top floor. There a smartly-dressed secretary led him into a large office boasting extensive views over Beijing. Without any delay, the vice-premier welcomed the captain warmly and pointed to a conversation area with comfortable sofas.

No officials remained in the room and it was clear that no record would be taken of the meeting. Rather this was planned to be a highly confidential discussion, the vice-premier indulging her favourite activity of unrecorded skullduggery. She was neither tall nor short, with a fullish figure, a striking face and a penetrating look in her eyes. Her undemonstrative manner was measured, inscrutable, very Oriental. Yet even just sitting on a sofa her presence alone filled the entire room. After a cup of introductory tea she came straight to the point.

"Captain Zhou : I have selected you personally to undertake what could be the most important military and strategic task in China for many decades. You should see it as a great honour which will reflect well on your distinguished family. Now tell me: just how familiar are you with the unfortunate continent of Africa?"

Zhou Man admitted he had never been to the dark continent and was soon cut short. It had been a rhetorical question, for the vice-premier was now in her natural element. With a minimum of words yet a maximum of insight, she proceeded to analyse Africa with a deadly and unsentimental precision. Its ramshackle politics were dissected with a scalpel. Its endemic corruption held no mysteries for Liu Fun. African history was sketched with a racial cynicism which would have raised innumerable eyebrows in the West. She referred to no notes. Liu Fun seemingly knew Africa off by heart as she alluded briefly to its failure to produce great scientists, architects, education, literature or art. In her

Liu Fun

view it was a primitive and pathetic continent crudely infiltrated by generations of patronising and generally unwelcome Europeans.

For all that, Africa also had great strengths and even greater potential. It was a cornucopia of almost every basic commodity China would ever require. As Liu Fun expanded her analysis the captain was listening to the outcome of many hours of painstaking research. The Chinese diplomatic service could be exceptionally good at that. The message was abundantly clear. For all its shortcomings and infelicities, Africa was now firmly on his nation's radar.

"Captain Zhou Man: with full agreement of our Central Military Commission, you are now being asked to head an entirely new planning team here in Beijing. It is a naval post of the highest family honour, the highest status and the highest secrecy and if you accept you will be promoted immediately to the rank of admiral. Before you accept, consider this: we have assessed over thirty potential candidates for this post and you are the naval officer I have chosen. Perhaps it should be added that your desire to become a member of the Beijing Patriotic Association has also been taken into positive consideration."

Zhou Man realised he was about to win a leapfrog promotion over several hundred fellow officers in the Chinese navy. It seemed no more than courteous to sit for a moment and contemplate the prospect. No matter what it could involve, the offer was the kind of career advancement any serving military officer might only dream about. The vice-premier ordered more tea. By the time it arrived, Zhou had already made it quite clear he wished to accept. It had hardly been an offer to refuse and the vice-premier continued with her proposal. She had taken Zhou Man's acceptance as a foregone conclusion. Liu Fun had chosen her new acolyte and proceeded to explain his new mission.

"Good. Now I'm sure you will also wish to know what your rôle will involve. You are a top graduate in mechanical and marine engineering from Beijing University, while your naval career has concentrated on weapons and communication systems, you have served with distinction at sea where you were highly respected by your comrades. You have worked as a junior military attaché at our embassy in London. You read, write and speak good English. All that is valuable experience for the command I am about to explain. Your main task will be to lead a team to design a fleet of warships of an entirely new type. The Military Commission requires you first to determine their size, their speed, their armament, their general specification. However your immediate task will be to learn what the People's Republic has been creating, in secret, for over two years."

"Which is, comrade Liu?" Liu Fun smiled. "The world's most advanced jet engine factory. Without suitable power plants, your new ships will never go anywhere. We are not prepared to rely on the West to supply the principal equipment we need for our strategic military assets. That way they would know our capabilities and we wish to keep such valuable knowledge to ourselves. And only when you understand those engines will you be able to proceed with the rest of your mission.

"The cost of the new ships is not to be a major consideration. We simply want the very best, a fleet of high technology fighting machines which are more than sufficient to beat the West at their own military games. Once you have all the necessary information your task will be to inform us how large our fleet of warships should be, where and how it will be supplied, what bases you will require.

"In view of our strategic interest in Africa, your target is of course to be the so-called Indian Ocean. You are to claim it for the benefit of China, primarily to protect the umbilical cord of our trade with Africa. It is the general view of our military and of our political analysts that, in marked contrast to the Atlantic and the Pacific, those two highly militarised oceans washing the shores of the United States, the Indian ocean east of Suez has been abandoned by the West. That generous omission suits our purposes down to the ground.

"The West effectively chose to do so voluntarily back in the 1960s. Until then they had it all sewn up and even Singapore had been one of their major naval bases. Then a very helpful British politician called Harold Wilson simply slashed their government spending on defence and they all walked away, something we would never begin to contemplate. The British simply said they were abandoning "East of Suez". As I believe they would express it themselves, it was all handed to us on a plate by their Harold Wilson. In my personal view he deserved our own Hero's Medal for his conduct."

Liu Fun explained to her new recruit how an entire ocean had now become a golden opportunity and it was China's for the taking. She summarised the complacent, almost conceited military attitude of the once-mighty British. But she also made complimentary reference to their remarkable collection of strategic naval bases scattered round the world, something Zhou Man would need to study and emulate.

"The British needed to protect their trade supply routes round the globe, but mainly in the Mediterranean and the Atlantic. They held Gibraltar, they held Malta, they held Aden, they had access to India and what they called Ceylon. In the South Atlantic beyond Gibraltar they held Ascension, the Cape of Good Hope and the Falkland Islands, or the Islas Malvinas as Argentina prefers to call them.

"In the nineteenth century the British feel for global geography was impeccable and you can learn much from them. Yet in more recent times they have surrendered almost everything they ever owned without even a fight. The entire Western military presence in their 'Indian Ocean' west of Australia has been reduced to a modest airbase on a small island in the middle of nowhere. In Liu Fun's view it posed no significant military threat to Chinese ambitions.

"You might just as well ignore it. It is run by the British and used by the Americans somewhere they call Diego Garcia. When they first established the base they ruthlessly expelled the entire native population. Never be fooled by the cheap propaganda of the West at the United Nations. They always consider themselves to occupy what they call the moral high ground, but in truth they are no better than anyone else. They advocate philanthropy, typically for other people to pursue, only when it suits their own global purpose."

So that was it. The Chinese navy had at long last decided to move well beyond the coastal waters of the Middle Kingdom and out into the world's oceans. The shortest sailing distance from Shanghai to the Straits of Malacca, the natural point of entry into the Indian Ocean, was five thousand kilometres. For the first time in history the People's Liberation Army (Navy) was about to become a global force.

*   *   *   *   *

Dartmouth, Devon

THE FURTHEST PENINSULA of south west England has gradually tilted into the sea since the last ice age. The original river valleys on its southern coast have sunk and flooded to become broad and picturesque estuaries. The Dart estuary is one of the loveliest, and two miles inland from the English Channel is the town of Dartmouth. High on the hill above the town is the Britannia Royal Naval College, for a century the training centre for future officers of the Royal Navy. And for the future officers of other navies too.

Over dinner, officer cadet James Heaton of the Royal Navy was deep in discussion with his latest friend, officer cadet Warwick Sydenham from Australia. The dining room at the College is known as its Senior Gunroom. Beneath its barrel-vaulted ceiling the two earnest young men were discussing a speech made the previous day by Alan Stanley, a British trade unionist turned think tanker with a strong line in pacifism. He had declared that the Cold War was now over, that Britain's defence expenditure could be cut, the armed forces largely

Chinese dragon be about to take a Russian bear's place? Try running that awkward thought past some of the Australian naval establishment next time you are in Sydney."

The two earnest young men were deep in conversation as they left the Senior Gunroom and headed for the bar. They were both unusual in being university graduates. James's father had warned him that Oxbridge was not considered the ideal training-ground for Dartmouth, but he had wanted to remain loyal to family tradition.

At university James's first love had been the Officer Training Corps. That and his work for a demanding degree left little time to pursue the more usual Oxford undergraduate pastimes; dabbling with politics or debating or erecting homes for lost causes. The Heatons came from Dorset, a county awash with naval families. At an early age had decided on a career in the Royal Navy, just like his father and grandfather before him. Could he rise as high as his grandfather, who had made it to admiral?

The two young cadets had already joked about the 'Dartmouth Principle' once explained to James by a fellow undergraduate in an Oxford junior common room. "Look, James, there were these two cadets at Dartmouth, neither of them very bright, but both steeped in the traditions of the Royal Navy. So they agreed a lifelong pact.

"These two future naval officers," the laconic Oxford politico had maintained "both knew from their families that throughout their military careers they would be asked from time to time to name the most impressive cadet in their own year at Dartmouth. Apparently that was the standard conversational opening gambit at Navy cocktail parties.

"So their simple pact, probably agreed in this very bar, was they would each undertake on all such occasions to name the other, a travesty of the truth, and the adjective they would invariably apply would be 'sound'. Thanks to their lifelong practice of mutual back-scratching and despite their intellectual limitations, they both eventually made it to rear-admiral." Evidently it was possible to devise a career route to the top. Perhaps James and Warwick needed a pact of their own, one which had rather more substance than trotting along to naval cocktail parties and describing each other as 'sound.'

Quite unlike those two future rear-admirals, neither James Heaton nor Warwick Sydenham fitted the usual mould of young military officers. They were both free-thinking mavericks and in a conformist world that was hardly the best formula for career success. Yet the whole idea of coping with the completely unanticipated appealed to them both enormously. They were being trained for a mindset they had anyway.

So that was the enduring pact James Heaton and Warwick Sydenham agreed over the bar at Dartmouth Royal Naval College that evening. They solemnly agreed never to disbelieve what the one told the other, no matter how implausible or unanticipated the news may be, and never to attempt to mislead one another either. It would become a rule both of them stood by throughout their naval careers.

Neither Cadet Heaton nor Cadet Sydenham could possibly know it in the 1990s, but they had just established a friendship and a mutual line of communication of great power. Little could they imagine that within twenty years, their own Dartmouth pact would play a global rôle. Even less could James Heaton imagine that less than a week previously his future naval adversary had been secretly recruited in Beijing. Least imaginable of all were the fortunes in world politics and naval power which would eventually bring them into direct and personal conflict.

*　　*　　*　　*　　*

Charles de Gaulle airport, Paris

IT WAS A SULTRY afternoon as the Air France airbus from Saudi Arabia made its landing. Violaine Khalifa peered out of her window at the half-familiar country of France. It was to be her home for the next eleven years. Her mother Louise hurried her through immigration and into a taxi. It did not take nearly so long as it might have done. Violaine had a French passport, even though she had been born in Riyadh.

If her twelve year old daughter simply found Paris intriguing, Louise Khalifa found the whole experience much more emotional. It was a homecoming after almost a quarter century of first global excitement and then of Islamic tedium. It was difficult to leave her husband Malik behind in Riyadh, but they both agreed this was much the best thing to do for their beloved daughter.

Louise Khalifa had been born into a noted French family, the Comtes de Chambons. She had been brought up on the exclusive Île St Louis, an island sanctuary in the Seine just upstream from the more popular Île de la Cité. Over several centuries it had evolved into an enclave for the French aristocracy, or at least its survivors, well away from the tourist throngs around Notre Dame.

No-one could buy a family hotel particulier on the Île St Louis any more. They hardly ever came on the market and had to be inherited. Which is exactly what Louise was now doing. Her mother had died three months previously at the respectable age of eighty-three. The Hotel de Chambon had been left in trust to her, to her two elder brothers and her sister; none of the siblings had wanted it sold.

So by general agreement Louise was now to live in it and look after it on behalf of them all. She would surely find it a refreshing change after the oppressive life of a European wife in the Saudi capital. The Islamic states around the Indian Ocean were not ideal for a sophisticated woman from Paris to try and lead an enjoyable and full life. Violaine wanted to model herself on her mother. All her life, Louise de Chambon had been attractive. She had grown accustomed to it and instinctively expected male admiration wherever she went. With dark Titian red hair and blue-green eyes, she had the perfect slender figure and the natural stature of her class. For his part, her husband Dr Malik

Khalifa was an enlightened and understanding man. In Riyadh his adored wife was a misfit. He did not share the oppressive Islamic attitude toward women of his countrymen. Khalifa was a noble name too, in the Arabian Gulf, and Malik was a gentleman.

When they married, the beauty from the Parisian haute monde had known the suave Malik Khalifa for just three months. Their wedding set the gossips twittering furiously in exclusive social circles of that class-conscious city. Louise had thoroughly enjoyed her widespread, albeit brief, notoriety as she promptly embarked on a whirlwind existence around the world's diplomatic capitals. She and Malik first met by chance at an embassy reception, when Louise had only lately returned from completing a doctorate at Oxford. In those three years she spent on the other side of the Channel, the more liberal lifestyle of the Anglo-Saxons had captured her soul. Not for her, any longer, the stultifying prospect of being married to some mechanical civil servant. Nor married to some conceited rustic enthusiast who simply grew grapes.

When they had first met, her Arabian prince charming was already considered to be a man of mystery, a man of experience. Marrying Malik Khalifa at unseemly short notice was her own way of telling the Paris charivari precisely what she thought of it. Her circle of Anglo-Saxon friends at Oxford were much amused and understood her underlying motives immediately. Louise and Malik had organised a double wedding in both Paris and Riyadh in two very different ceremonies in 1972. She was just twenty-four years old. For the next ten years they became the beautiful people on the world diplomatic circuit, as he served the Saudi cause in first Paris, then London, then Beijing and finally in Washington.

Ten years her senior, disturbingly good looking, clever and quite rich, Malik swept the young Louise de Chambon off her feet and around the world. Then things changed quite suddenly. When he reached forty-four he was summoned back to Riyadh and required to settle down.

Malik Khalifa was now far too valuable a Saudi diplomat to be left swanning around the cocktail party circuit of the world's leading cities. His salad days were over and so inevitably were Louise's. She soon discovered that Riyadh with its quaint and hypocritical attitudes toward women was not to her liking.

As a distraction and with Malik's enthusiastic approval, she tried for a family. Malik already had his son by an earlier marriage; his first wife had died a year or so before he met Louise. Hamad had been brought up by an aunt. Now he was just fourteen and the birth of his step-sister had created a new family around his father. Hamad doted on Violaine. Louise Khalifa became absorbed in her new family life and in her step-son's continuing education. At least having a child of her own had put her beyond reproach.

Now Violaine was beginning to grow up. Aged twelve, she sat beside her mother as they drove towards the Seine. "Maman, why are we coming to live in Paris?" her daughter asked as the taxi took them along the Autoroute du Nord. Louise turned to look at her beloved daughter, the early signs of puberty budding in her blouse.

So it was time for her mother to be serious. "Darling, your father and I have discussed it for a long time. There are four reasons. The first is your education. You have spent seven years at the international school in Riyadh and you speak good Arabic, but it is now time for our small family to move on. Your father sees us as an international family. For the first ten years of our marriage he and I worked all over the world. That is why your brother Hamad was educated in London as an accountant and why he now works in Dubai. Both your parents want you now to grow up as a woman of Europe, not as one who has only ever known the Middle East.

"The second reason is the situation in Saudi Arabia. Neither your father nor I consider an attractive European woman can have a pleasant time in a Moslem country, least of all one dictated to by the

Wahhabis. I am not prepared to see you grow up with black cloth wrapped round your lovely face, simply to fend off the lecherous attention of uncivilised men. The third reason is that Bonne Maman died three months ago. Your uncles Charles and Antoine and your aunt Isabelle want us to live in Bonne Maman's beautiful house on the River Seine. You have been here several times. It will be a far more pleasant place to live than any home we could ever find in Riyadh.

"Fourth and most important is your father's job. When you are older you will learn more, but he now works for the Saudi government doing things which expose him to new dangers. The last thing he wants is to put his wife and daughter at risk. We will be safer here in Paris - and never forget your father can and will visit us whenever he can."

Violaine sat quietly as she took all this in. Her mother had never been quite so direct before. Perhaps this was what it would be like to live in Paris. What was her father doing that could possibly put her mother and herself at risk? In the distance she could just see the top of the Eiffel Tower. That was good. It had been her favourite Parisian building for years. She suddenly thought about all her friends back at the international school in Riyadh. Precocious girls from various countries, for them her move to Paris had been the gossip of the term. In most cases it was driven by envy. They assured her she was going to live in the most romantic city in the world, surrounded by the sexiest men.

She was, they assured her, bound to fall in love and meet her future husband. They were already knowledgeable experts on all of that, they unanimously agreed. Violaine could not quite imagine marrying anyone in particular, not yet awhiles, but she did not need to plan. The fates had quite different intentions. Like her mother before her, she would not marry a Frenchman anyway. Her future husband was an Englishman, at that very moment talking to an Australian naval friend in Dartmouth where they were planning their supper.

Chapter Two

Two of a Kind

Lanzhou , North West China

JUST HOURS BEFORE Violaine and her mother touched down at Charles de Gaulle airport in Paris, Admiral Zhou Man of the Chinese People's Army (Navy) touched down at the city airport of Lanzhou, capital city of Gansu Province in central China. It had taken him several days to obtain the official documents for his trip. The precise activities of the factory he was about to visit were a state secret.

Two security guards were waiting for him at Lanzhou airport. They recognised his naval uniform and rank immediately and his face fitted photographs already in their files. Without a word being spoken he was shown to a waiting car. Zhou Man was impressed. It was a Hongqi Mingshi, in effect an Audi 100 with a Chinese badge on its bonnet. Even in Beijing this was still quite the latest thing, the car of choice for anyone who ranked an official limousine.

Whoever was managing this Yellow River Industrial Research Facility certainly knew how to pull strings in this unexciting region of China, far from the nation's capital. Yet not all was quite what it seemed. The authorities in Beijing had chosen Lanzhou to build their 'research facility' with great care. Although it was a railway junction and a polluted industrial city with a population of two million, Lanzhou was unlikely to attract much interest from foreigners. It was just one of many such uninteresting cities in China. That was now its great virtue. It had little about it to stimulate anyone's attention.

Nevertheless it boasted a university dating back to 1909, ranking among the top six in China. Admiral Zhou had checked all of this before leaving Beijing. He knew Lanzhou university had a fine school of engineering, and another for information science.

Most important of all, the university had a world-ranking testing centre, generously financed in 1982 by the World Bank. It was ideally suited to support the top secret work being done by the Yellow River Industrial Research Facility. So far as the rest of the world was concerned, it looked like two incomprehensible institutions working in tandem. There was no doubt some sort of synergy in there, somewhere, but they generated not a flicker of curiosity even if no-one had the faintest idea what they were doing.

And so in Beijing's eyes Lanzhou was an ideal place to conceal from view one of China's most important strategic factories. The nation's leaders left nothing to chance. Much thought had gone into making it inconspicuous, a scheme with vice-premier Liu Fun's fingerprints all over it. As his car approached the factory complex it suddenly struck Zhou Man that there was nothing anywhere to indicate what the Yellow River Industrial Research Facility actually did. Even so the security procedures at its main gate were surprisingly tight. Not only was every official scrap of paper Zhou brought with him from Beijing examined in minute detail but several received a resounding chop of solemn bureaucracy.

Once inside the gates it was clear the research centre was all very new and he could see much of what later proved to be its manufacturing area was still being built. His smart Mingshi saloon drove straight past a large construction site to the research centre's laboratories, a three storey building which would never have won any architectural prize. It could not have been more anonymous if it tried and that, of course, was the point.

Standing at its entrance to welcome him was the senior research manager who had arranged all his documentation. He knew this to be a woman called Antonia Foo and she now proved to be decidedly attractive and probably younger than forty. As they exchanged the usual introductory courtesies he soon discovered she had chosen her western name with much care, after thorough research in the gossip columns of England's smarter newspapers. Antonia had taken this important lifestyle decision while studying in London for a degree at the Imperial College of Science. 'Antonia' seemed to be a very English name favoured by the very best English literary ladies. It had since proved a rewarding way of introducing herself at the international conferences and seminars which she regularly attended.

"Welcome to the select elite, Admiral Zhou Man." said Antonia Foo as she showed him to her office. "And why do you say that?" he asked. "Because everyone involved in this whole exercise I have met so far has been individually selected by vice-premier Liu in person. You were so chosen less than a month ago, I was chosen two years ago and you are going to meet a few more of us just like that. There has never been any competition for these posts and, perish the very thought, there was certainly never any advertising. So welcome aboard the good ship invisible."

It was obvious from her accent that Antonia Foo did not come from Gansu nor anywhere near. She was Shanghainese, a sophisticated woman from quite the most sophisticated city in China. "And how do you like working here in Lanzhou?" he asked her, half knowing what her answer would be. "I cannot stand the place," she responded, "but my pay is astronomical and the perks are extensive. You saw my car. I have a lovely house out in the country and I travel

Zhou Man

all over the world, provided of course I stay tight-lipped about what we do here at our factory complex." Zhou Man knew already but asked politely "Which is what, precisely?" Both were aware China had decided to produce the world's most advanced jet engine. This research facility in Lanzhou was where it was being developed.

"You already have security clearance, Admiral Zhou, or you wouldn't be here to begin with, so let's get straight down to business. Here at Yellow River we have successfully adapted Britain's Rolls-Royce RB 211 engine which they first announced with great publicity in 1972. It had already taken them six years to develop. We are now developing it ourselves, far away from the attention of anyone else. Exactly what goes on in this factory is top secret. It took Rolls-Royce in England a further eighteen years to develop the Trent version from their original engine and they are still working on yet more powerful versions which may not appear for another decade. We aim to do all of that in twelve years."

Zhou Man was most impressed, again. It was clearly going to be one of those eye-opening days. "How do you manage that so quickly, when it took even the British so long?" Antonia smiled. "They have been most generous. Our national airline bought its first Airbus ten years ago and one of them has since been stripped to its basic components. Then five years ago Airbus set up a sales operation in Beijing, most conveniently so. We have in effect an undeclared alliance between the Middle Kingdom and the United Kingdom, one which neatly avoids involving either Russia or the United States of America. Without knowing it, everyone is proving to be most co-operative. We estimate it has saved us a total of ten years' development work on our jet engines here in Lanzhou."

"How far have you got?" Even in his first few weeks work it had soon become obvious to Zhou Man that suitable engines for his ships would take longer to perfect than anything else. "Before I answer that, I would like you to change out of that handsome naval uniform and put on this laboratory coat. I see no point in advertising to all and sundry that China's navy is already interested in what we do here. If you wish you may use my private bathroom through there."

Once he was dressed as an engineering technician, Antonia led him into her laboratories. The newly-civilian admiral watched as her staff finely adjusted a turbine blade on a test rig. She explained. "Those blades are the critical component. We need to make certain that every single one of them will survive billions of revolutions without fracture. It is going to take us several years more work yet, but we are working with some excellent analytical and testing centres right here at Lanzhou university.

"One of the biggest challenges with all jet engines is making sure its turbine blades are strong enough to be up to the job, yet still light in weight. The British have developed some extremely sophisticated ways of manufacturing them, making them partially hollow. That also reduces stress at high rotational speeds, what some might call centrifugal force." As she talked him through the finer details of turbine blades and the broader principles of jet engine design, Zhou Man could see exactly why Antonia Foo had been chosen for her job. She might be forty, feminine and decidedly fetching but, for the moment anyway, she was very clearly a thoroughbred expert on jet turbine engines.

Antonia led him away from the areas where her staff were working. "The first thing you should understand is that you and I, alone in this building, know just about everything there is to know about the wider purposes of the Yellow River Industrial Research Facility. Although I'm its chief executive I'm not sure even I know all of that. When it suits her, vice-premier Liu Fun can play her cards very close to her chest. I cannot over-emphasise just how secret the real purpose of this centre must remain.

"Just to confuse matters, there will be three distinct versions of our engine anyway. The main one is for civil aviation and that is also the most difficult. There will be another version for generating electricity and then there is the one you want for marine use. Engines for aviation have to be as light as possible and they also have to survive the possibility of a bird being sucked into them. That doesn't do the bird very much good, I would readily agree, but it doesn't exactly improve my jet engines either."

Admiral Zhou appreciated her dry English understatement, clearly a habit acquired during her years as a student in London. Antonia Foo was enjoying herself thoroughly, flirting her femininity and flaunting her technical virtuosity side by side. "Of course you will not exactly be sucking many seagulls into your engines at sea, let alone pigeons which are always the greatest risk at airports. It was a test which wrecked Rolls Royce early development of the RB 211, when their original lightweight turbine blades were shattered.

"Weight will not be such a concern for you either. I suppose that could simplify the design but in practice we cannot afford the luxury of developing three quite different engines. As it is we need to develop them for different fuels; aviation gas for airliners, diesel for yours. Let us say every Yangtze engine which leaves this plant will be basically the same as all the others no matter what its eventual use nor what gadgets we bolt onto it. That makes for much better security all round. It all adds to the security smokescreen."

Zhou Man had approved of the name chosen for the engine, the first time he heard it. The British had renamed the most recent variant of their original RB 211. It was now known by a name shared with one of their largest rivers instead. Antonia Foo had decided to adopt their unassertive example; nothing sensationalist, no self-admiration either. More importantly, he wanted to know how long it would take before the engines would be ready.

"We started from scratch here in Lanzhou two years ago. If all goes to plan we will have our first fully working prototype in about three years. But then work really starts. Here at our Yellow River Facility I will have a two-year testing programme. It's not just engines themselves, it's all the components. We need to find out which component is going to fail first.

"We then need time to go back to component manufacturers and make them retool their systems. That all takes years rather than just months. Liu Fun has decided we should not be dependent on foreign component suppliers for any of them.

"Quite the opposite. She is deliberately using this project to develop China's high technology capabilities across the board. The task is no less complicated than our space programme and infinitely more valuable. That is for international propaganda. This is for real. Once we have perfected all the components, we then need to bring our own production line up to speed and get all the bugs out of it. At Rolls-Royce the British have had years of practice, just like the Americans have at General Electric. Here at our research centre we enjoy none of those important advantages. But we will."

"So when can I have my first engines from your perfected production line?" The admiral's mind was churning through the huge project which vice-premier Liu had given him. Every day that passed the task ahead seemed more and more daunting.

"In about ten years time. Is that going to fit with you main programme?" As Antonia spoke, two of her staff knocked on her door, anxious to talk. Zhou Man was understanding. "Look, Antonia. I can see you're busy. Let me not take up any of your time. Leave me to wander round the rest of the site and talk to people. If I've time may I use your car and visit the university? What time do you finish work? Let's have supper this evening away from inquisitive ears, somewhere we can talk more freely."

As it turned out the supper was not exactly what Zhou Man had expected. When he returned to her office as the working day ended, Antonia had changed out of her professional scientist's white coat and into a black silk cheongsam. She looked exquisite and she knew it. A touch of Shanghai's finest in boring Lanzhou. Her plan for the remainder of the day was sophisticated too.

"So far as this evening goes, I've had a better idea. I don't like the restaurants in town anyway, not the ones I have tried so far and in any case, as you've no doubt discovered this afternoon, downtown Lanzhou is about sixty kilometres away. Instead let me take you home with me and cook supper for the two of us. Then we can talk business without being overheard by anyone."

By the time supper had been cooked and eaten, it was too late for Zhou Man to return to his hotel, which seemed to have been Antonia's plan all along. After all, they were both divorcees and inside the professional exterior of the chief executive of the Yellow River Research Facility he discovered a lonely woman. But not lonely tonight. The cheongsam had served its glamorous purpose over supper and now put up little resistance as Man removed it. Nor did Antonia Foo resist either. She was maybe forty years old, maybe a little younger and, quite apart from her former husband, had evidently known numerous men very well indeed. Practice makes perfect.

Antonia Foo had honed her bedroom skills as finely as they honed a rotor blade in her factory - perhaps an odd thought but one which struck him anyway. Man had long held the view that the cleverer a woman, usually the sexier she was and over the next two hours Antonia Foo did nothing to make him change his mind. He found her something of a bedroom virtuoso and she clearly expected him to admire her expertise. Antonia Foo had been born in 1957, the Year of the Rooster. In Chinese folklore roosters are honest, direct, blunt even. They are happiest when surrounded by others, the centre of attention. Zhou Man was doing his best. For roosters, September is their finest month. It was September. A naked and now very satisfied Antonia curled appreciatively alongside him and rested her head on his shoulder. "Now are you prepared to take some advice? And how much are you really prepared to tell me?"

"What advice?"

"Security. You've seen my factory. No-one in Lanzhou knows what we do here and that goes for most of the people who work in the complex itself. If they are only working on components they know nothing about the total project. Those who know the whole story have high level clearance. They are told to keep quiet, and those few are monitored individually. As no doubt I am."

"Why all this obsession with secrecy?"

"I'll tell you why. The Americans in particular. And possibly the Australians. Maybe even the Russians. Never forget just how nervous other countries are becoming about China's industrial strength. If they ever hear about something like this we can wave goodbye to peaceful tranquillity, working anonymously in Lanzhou. Far better just to keep them in the dark and that means keeping as many as possible of our own people in the dark as well. America's CIA operates with a very large cheque book.

"I'm not telling you anything vice-premier Liu won't tell you herself in the next few months. China is thankfully a very large country with many dark corners in which to disappear. Unless foreign intelligence agencies are told where to look they are not very likely to come searching for us.

"Your task will be more difficult building entire ships, but it is worth considering just how far you might disguise what you do. And anyway you haven't really told me what you intend to do. All I have been told is to design a marine version of the Yangtze engine which can be built here in China."

Zhou Man looked down at his new mistress with the first shoots of genuine affection. She was very clever, yet a very lovely woman and she was beautiful, especially naked. Like almost any man he was tempted to impress her by telling her just how important his new job was . . . but no. Just tell what she needed to know and no more. Lovely though Antonia Foo was, he had known her for less than twenty-four hours, who knew who her friends might be? So he decided to give her his cover story instead.

"You've already worked out, from who I am, that the People's Navy has decided it is going to need much more sophisticated warships in the decades to come. My job is to design a fleet which will look after our interests in the Yellow Sea and perhaps the Sea of Japan. No-one in Beijing really trusts either side in Korea not to do something stupid. Beyond that it is always possible our occasional friends the Japanese will produce a new generation of politicians who do not share the pacifist attitudes of those who experienced the Second World War at first hand.

As always the people to watch are the Americans. They set the standards and only fools ignore them. It's almost eight years already since they sponsored some studies calling for a complete re-think of warship design. They've called it Group Mike and it's pretty obvious they are going to adapt the Stealth technology they developed for the Nighthawk F-117 fighter plane - and that's already fourteen years old.

"Just you watch. They will use it on one their warships and so must China. We would simply be throwing our money away if we build ships which are not state of the art."

They talked into the early hours about China and world politics as seen from Beijing. Antonia Foo enjoyed her new boyfriend's ability to lift a curtain over wide horizons well beyond the tedium of Gansu. He stimulated her intellect. But there were other parts of her anatomy which had been stimulated also and they were now asking for second helpings. Admiral Zhou Man was only too pleased to oblige. Antonia Foo and Zhou Man had discovered just one more interest they had in common.

*   *   *   *   *

Portsmouth, England

THE FRENCH sub-lieutenant, an ensign in his own navy, noticed the three men only moments before they reached him. They were wearing quite soft shoes, his boots clattered noisily on the pavement. Xavier de Kerguelen had allowed himself an hour or so ashore to look at the old naval town of Portsmouth.

"Are you a Frenchie?" they challenged. He was. That was sufficient. "Well it's payback time, sunshine. We lost our jobs because of you. Welcome to England, Frenchie."

The three men were sailors who had worked on the ferries to France. Or they had been until a recent change in the demands of a French trade union and the British had all lost their jobs. They knew there was a French warship in port. After a good night on the town they were looking for trouble and pushed the Frenchman against a brick wall. He pushed back and easily deflected a clumsy swinging fist. More jostling, but it was his knee in the groin of another that really started the trouble. One of them produced a large knife.

James Heaton was also returning to his ship, walking along Queen Street, when he spotted a flash of steel in the dark. Three against one was over-doing it, but three against two would be an entertainment, while the opposition looked to be fairly drunk. He thought he half-recognised their victim anyway. His well-aimed run across the street sent one of them flying, while he smashed the knife arm of the other with his left fist.

With commendably quick reactions Xavier used his left knee once again to good effect and within seconds all three assailants were stumbling around shouting profanities. James Heaton picked up the knife and asked them to explain what they proposed to do next. It did not take them long to decide. They stumbled off, cursing navies in general and the French in particular.

The two naval officers introduced themselves and agreed to walk together to the French ship. She was on a courtesy call after operations in the Channel. The La Fayette was the latest and finest the French had to show. First of her class, she was a Stealth-shaped frigate commissioned into service only eighteen months previously. La Fayette had been taking part in Operation Sleeve, an exercise in Anglo-French co-operation in policing the English Channel.

In the distant past the English and French had fought across it many times, but now they were working together closely. Those busy waters were all too popular with boatloads of illegal immigrants, drug traffickers and too many captains of very large ships who had far too much drink inside them.

In the French frigate's wardroom the two naval officers realised they had already noticed one another at the briefing for Operation Sleeve. They had met. Like most of his generation, Xavier spoke good English, but with that particular French accent which is incurable. After the military manoeuvres in the Channel it had been the French officer's first experience of Portsmouth. He was not impressed, but James did everything to reassure him it had just been his unlucky night.

"I'm afraid you always risk pugnacious drunks late at night in a port. Sadly it could happen anywhere. To anyone. It just wasn't your night." Neither of them had any bruises. Their opponents had been too drunk to land a serious punch. James Heaton's training in unarmed combat as a cadet had paid off. Xavier de Kerguelen was also extremely capable of taking care of himself. He was simply grateful for the way James had crossed the road to redress the odds.

As they drank their medicinal brandies in La Fayette's ward room, they found other things in common too. They were the same age, they both came from naval families. Neither of them took many things on trust, least of all the respectable future of their navies. They both wondered whether their futures would mainly involve chasing drug-runners, pirates and illegal immigrants. It was not an exciting prospect. Serving in the navy of either country was surely not intended to become a subsidiary of some commercial security firm.

"What does this new government of yours think about the Royal Navy?" Xavier asked. "The French and the British are supposed to have the two most powerful navies in Europe. We have a great past - I could see the masts of Nelson's magnificent HMS Victory as we came alongside. I grant you won that one, just. But will either of us have a great future?"

People in France had heard about a new Prime Minister called Tony Blair. "What should we make of him? He seems to think your Margaret Thatcher is wonderful. In France we never understand the difference between your Labour and your Conservative."

"You can never tell with British governments. It all depends who can grab the television cameras next." James explained. "We get mixed messages. Especially with a new Labour government like Mr Blair's. One moment they argue the Cold War is over, that we should reduce spending and shrink our armed forces. The next moment they are sending British forces to sort out the world.

"I don't know what happens in France. Everyone seems to remember some chap called Charles de Gaulle, François Mitterrand seemed to last a long time until he died last year. Apart from that the picture gets more confused." Xavier smiled. French politics was a little more complicated than that.

"Here in Britain the arrival of a socialist government always encourages the pacifists. We have a noisy one at the moment, name of Alan Stanley, who seems to think our armed forces should be disbanded. He has quite a following, but I'm relieved he isn't in the new Government. The Alan Stanley's of this world are lovely people. They honestly believe that if they are kind and understanding then everyone else will be just as kind and understanding as they are.

"As I said, I don't know about France, but it doesn't work quite like that here in England. As you've just seen for yourself." Xavier agreed the Cold War was over, but others would surely follow. "When I studied history at school it always seemed that as soon as one enemy was beaten, another one would always pop up somewhere else. I wonder who we will have to face in our careers. The Chinese perhaps?" They both wondered if having met through a fight, they would yet face a bigger one in years to come. They would.

The two naval officers talked into the early hours. Xavier found James was unlike many naval officers, more naturally an academic. They agreed to keep in contact with one another. They both went skiing when they could and like many in the navy they sailed. They both followed five nations rugby, they both followed Formula One. All thanks to three drunks in Portsmouth's Queen Street, they had established their very own Entente Cordiale.

*   *   *   *   *

Central Paris

Across the other side of the Channel, Violaine Khalifa had been living on the Île St Louis for two years. After some difficult months among bitchy teenage girls at the Lycee la Tour, she had steadily made her mark as a talented linguist and historian. They were impressed she lived at one of the smartest addresses in Paris, not just another

immigrant Arab after all. Steadily the questions moved from her life
in the past to shared hopes for the future. At length she was totally
accepted, and her friendship was now sought. The girls read all the
elegant magazines and watched all the television shows telling them
the right clothes, the right shoes, the right make-up to make
themselves attractive and were experimenting whenever they could.
For Violaine Khalifa, life was very different from her time in Riyadh.
The smart shop windows of the centre of Paris were an education.

It had taken Violaine a full two years to grow accustomed to
living in Paris, she knew to be one of the most sophisticated cities in
the world. Now she knew her way around on the Metro, she knew all
the best shops. She could saunter down the Rue St Honoré with her
friends à la mode and flash her eyes at the boys. She had no brothers
or sisters of her age in Paris, but the three Kerguelen brothers, sons of
her godmother Tiphaine, had cheerfully taken her under their wings.

Living within walking distance of the smartest parts of the city
was exhilarating. The family mansion stood in at very centre of the
city, where once a Celtic tribe called the Parisii had built themselves a
small fishing village on an island in the Seine. As she had been taught
at school that was how Paris began, well over two millennia ago. This
was a very proud city, a very stylish city. To many, it was still the
centre of the universe.

Only Paris could resent the international decision of 1884 to
put the Prime Meridian of the world through Greenwich rather than
an observatory near Paris. Only the French could resent the way the
English language was rapidly replacing what had once been the
language of international diplomacy, their lingua franca. A coterie of
very old men at the Académie Française, known to all as The
Immortals, were fighting a rearguard action to keep unwelcome
Anglo-Saxon intrusions out of their beloved French language. It was
a losing battle. Le sandwich or le weekend or le parking were the only

way to say it whether you were down, or out and about in Paris or in London.   As Violaine had done on her visits to the Hotel de Chambon as a child, in a quiet moment she sat at her bedroom window high above the Quai Napoleon and admired Paris by night. A long black barge was slowly chugging its way along the Seine. She wondered where it had come from, where it was going, what was inside it. Long black barges were mysterious, just like people.

The view was totally unlike the dusty landscape of Saudi Arabia which had been her first home. Two very different ways of life, she wanted to balance them in her mind. And in the minds of others. Violaine Khalifa was a Libran after all. How very civilised it now seemed to be living in the West. She understood exactly why her parents had brought her here and suddenly she had a first glimpse of what she wanted to do with her life.

It was an idealist's dream, but it was possible and idealism is the privilege of the young. Could she help teach the West of her adoption and her ancestry to understand the Islamic world into which she had been born and reared? Neither understood the other. In their mutual ignorance they were two of a kind.

Chapter Three

The Three Planes

North Eastern USA, September 2001

EARLY ON THE morning of Tuesday 11 September 2001, four American passenger jets were attacked. These included two consecutive aircraft leaving Logan Airport, Boston: American Airlines Flight 11 at 8.11am and three minutes later United Airlines Flight 175. The others were American Airlines flight 77 which took off from Dulles Airport, Washington six minutes after that, and then United Airlines Flight 93 which took off from Newark, New Jersey 22 minutes later still.

They were all deliberate hijackings and by later calculations nineteen men were involved. They led to terrible events on Manhattan and in Washington known to the world ever since simply as 9-11, that distinctively American way of recording a date by identifying its month first. Almost 3,000 people were to die that morning as a result. Al-Qaeda, or sometimes al-Qaida, 'the base' in Arabic, the gang identified as the perpetrator, has since been designated a terrorist organisation by the United Nations Security Council, by NATO, by the European Union, the United States, Russia, India and several other countries.

Al-Qaeda had relocated from the Sudan to Afghanistan in 1996. That was about that same time the idea of hijacking civilian airliners and using them as flying bombs was first suggested to its unknown leader Osama bin Laden by his equally unknown lieutenant, Khalid Sheikh Mohammed. It was Israeli intelligence who passed on the warning to their American opposite numbers. With the wisdom of hindsight one may perhaps wonder which privileged Americans then latched onto that diabolical idea at the time.

Until 9-11, few people had even heard of Osama bin Laden. Unknown no longer. That day he was to become America's number one bogeyman, and eventually that dubious accolade was to cost him his life. The events of 9-11 carried international terrorism into a diabolical new dimension. Instead of bombs being concealed onto a plane, the entire aircraft was now to be used as a bomb. Because the only 'unusual' things on board were the terrorists themselves, there was no way such lethal potential could be detected at an airport before takeoff.

In December 1998, within just two years of the idea originally put to bin Laden, the director of the Central Intelligence Counter-terrorist Centre warned President Bill Clinton that al-Qaeda was planning attacks in the USA, and that it was training people to hijack aircraft. So clearly the proposition was already known in some quarters of Washington. Who took heed of it then becomes an interesting question.

In the event, the calamities of 2001 all became the nightmare, not of President Clinton, but of his successor George W Bush who had been sworn into office less than eight months previously. It was not an auspicious start to his presidency, nor did he distinguish himself in his forensic management of the subsequent enquiry. He appeared to be far more concerned with pointing a deadly finger of suspicion at somebody, preferably somebody foreign. Three of the planes were recorded as hitting their targets on that infamous Tuesday. Two buildings were destroyed almost immediately; a third was destroyed, quite suddenly, a number of hours later. The first to go was the south tower of the World Trade Centre in New York after being hit by United Airlines flight 175. It suddenly collapsed at 9.59am after burning for a mere 56 minutes. Most Americans were far too shocked by the appalling death and destruction to spend much time wondering about the astonishing speed with which it all happened. The one person who did not look at all shocked or surprised when first told about it was President Bush himself. The television coverage made that amply clear.

The first target to be hit was the north tower of the Trade Centre which American Airlines flight 11 crashed into at 8.46am. It suddenly collapsed after burning for just 102 minutes. By any standards those two buildings appeared to have been mere packs of cards. Barely anything was left standing, even though the impact zones had actually been closer to the top. In the aftermath to 9-11, more and more people did begin to ask why they had collapsed so quickly and quite so comprehensively. There was nothing left to salvage. It was never, however, a question of major concern in the White House.

Altogether 147 passengers on the two flights died instantly, while 2,606 people in the twin towers also died. The investment bank Cantor Fitzgerald whose offices were on floors 101 to 105 of One World Trade Centre lost 658 employees, more than any other firm, while the insurance and finance firm Marsh & McLennan on the floor immediately below Cantor lost 355 employees. At least 14,000 people had been in the twin towers when the aircraft first struck; more than 11,000 of them escaped. In the rescue effort the New York City Fire Department lost 341 firefighters, the Port Authority Police Department lost 37 officers and the New York Police Department lost 23 officers.

Some twenty-six minutes before the south tower collapsed, it was claimed hijackers had flown American Airlines flight 77 straight into the Pentagon building in Washington, this time right down at ground level. Amazingly so. A total of 59 passengers died as did a further 125 employees working inside the building, of whom 55 were military personnel.. Passengers on the fourth flight, United Airlines flight 93 were said to have fought a battle with their hijackers once they learnt through their mobile phones what had happened in New York. Full details of what actually happened on that flight will never be known because all 40 passengers died when it reportedly crashed into a field near Shanksville, Pennsylvania. Its intended target, believed to have been the Capitol in Washington, was about 100 miles from the crash site, just about ten minutes flying time away.

In all of this, someone somewhere had clearly achieved a major and terrifying objective. In the process the awful nature of global terrorist acts was taken into a new dimension. If that had been the objective of Osama bin Laden and his lieutenant Khalid Sheikh Mohammed, they had succeeded beyond their most extravagant dreams.

Quite what they gained personally from it other than global notoriety is more difficult to assess. The second was imprisoned in Guantanamo Bay. Bin Laden was to spend the rest of his life in hiding until he was killed in a surprise attack by US Navy Seals on his supposedly secure compound in Pakistan on 2 May 2011. Many people we led to believe he had been hiding in caves in the mountains. It turned out he had not been hiding anywhere even near but wherever and whenever they are killed, dead men tell no tales.

In the events of 9-11 the United States of America suffered its worst premeditated shock since the attack on its naval base at Pearl Harbour. That surprise attack in December 1941 had required over 300 Japanese fighters and bombers, not just nineteen hijackers using American civilian airliners. At Pearl Harbour 2,402 Americans died and a further 1,282 were injured. The first attack led directly to the United States entering World War Two. So the global question in September 2001 was how would the United States react to this latest outrage, over half a century after the world-changing events in Hawaii?

So that's the official version of what transpired on 9-11, roughly speaking. And it also fits the recorded facts, roughly speaking. That said there are nevertheless one or two logical gaps and probable discrepancies which were duly noted in various capital cities overseas.

*   *   *   *   *

Tel Aviv, Israel

IT WAS ALREADY five in the evening and Prime Minister Ariel Sharon had been glued to the television in his office for well over an hour. He and his closest staff were watching with horror what was unfolding by the minute in the United States. Sharon was a former soldier who had entered politics in 1974; among his early tasks as a politician, he had been the architect of a Memorandum of Understanding with the United States. He had also served as security adviser to the former prime minister Yitzhak Rabin. Now his own security adviser was watching the television alongside him, equally transfixed.

The private line telephone rang. It was former prime minister prime minister Benjamin Netanyahu, the man who, although twenty years younger than Sharon, had promoted him to high positions in the Israeli government. So the two men had kn own one another a long time and understood one another well. Netanyahu was obviously very shaken by the events unfolding in New York and rather reciting the obvious.

"Ariel, this is one hell of a mess. Not only are innocent Americans dying by the thousand, but it hurts me personally. Dammit I spent my high school years in the United States. I served as deputy ambassador in Washington for two years and have been in and out of the Pentagon dozens of times. I then did four years as our ambassador to the UN so I know New York even better. It is almost impossible to comprehend that the twin towers will never be seen again."

It did not take long for the highly experienced politician in Netanyahu to gain control once more. "You'd better call our embassy in Washington right now and make certain Israel is one of the first countries to offer condolences to President Bush and the American people as a whole."

The call was put through to Washington immediately, then the Prime Minister's private secretary called his wife and cancelled all their social engagements for that evening. It was going to be a long night.

"Benjamin, what the hell do you think the Americans are going to do? This is probably even worse than Pearl Harbour, and that was sufficient to drag them into World War Two."

" I'll tell you one thing, Ariel: George W Bush is no Roosevelt. My best guess is they will dither, and then dither again. Then when they have stopped dithering we will all have to watch out. Do we yet know who was responsible for what has happened? Do the Americans?"

"According to the official view in Washington, the number one suspect is al-Qaeda. We got wind that their leader Osama bin Laden was planning something very much along these lines years ago. We told the Americans at the time, and Clinton knew well enough what was likely to happen. Pity he's not in charge now. I would have rather more faith in the soundness of his judgement than I have in this new guy of theirs. An appalling situation like this calls for very cool, very decisive, very accurate political judgement. It is no place for beginners. There is nowhere in the world you can gain that kind of political experience in just as few months.

"Well one thing you can rely on, Ariel, whatever they choose to do eventually it will be an oil industry strategy. Bush is a Texas oil man through and through. The last thing the Americans will want to do is cross swords with the Saudis. And for that reason if no other, comparisons with Pearl Harbour are irrelevant. If it is al-Qaeda, then they hardly constitute an invading force bent on occupying a chunk of the United States. And if they are as I suspect funded with oil money, and some Saudi connection is not very hard to find, you can be quite sure Washington will see its latest enemy in a totally different light from the light in which it saw the Japanese sixty years ago."

"So what's your best guess?" asked Ariel Sharon. Netanyahu had the most machiavellian mind of any politician his senior colleague had ever met, with the exception of Deng Xiaoping. "And is there anything we should be preparing for now?"

Let's think it through one step at a time." his old friend replied. "First, let's assume the Americans do nothing. Then they have to do something. Their traditional response is to send in the cavalry before they even understand the problem properly. They shoot first and then ask questions afterwards. Vietnam may have cost them many lives and given a huge boost to the global drug industry, but even then America didn't really learn the obvious diplomatic lessons.

"So let's assume next that they eventually come round to Uncle Sam's knee-jerk 'send in the cavalry' technique. Just remember that in a year or so's time George Bush will start looking to the presidential election of November 2004, once the Democratic primaries begin. And there is nothing quite so good as a small winnable war to boost a leader's popularity by 100%. Bush knows that, they all do: look what the Falklands did for Margaret Thatcher."

"So where is all this leading?" asked Sharon. Benjamin Netanyahu paused for a moment for thought before continuing. "I think the odds are that American will find an excuse to go to war with one of the lesser Islamic states, in what amounts to a proxy war against Saudi Arabia. A war they believe they can win without too much trouble. And then George W Bush can go before his electorate in three year's time and romp home as the triumphant victor, or so he calculates. In a sense it would not be all that different from classical Rome, to which empire I must say the modern United States does often bear an alarming resemblance. Our forebears knew all about that from the other side. But no matter how stupid the Americans sometimes may be, let us not proclaim that in the streets of Ashkelon. Whatever happens next, we will continue to need American support internationally for the very survival of the Israeli state."

"But Benjamin, would the Saudi authorities just sit on their hands and let the Americans roll over one of their Islamic bedfellows, hand-picked by Washington as the diplomatic alternative to themselves, in some publicity-minded military confrontation and retaliation?"

"Hardly. Especially with the diabolical Wahhabis breathing right down their necks. The very fact that they are allowed into Riyadh at all means some attention is being paid to their hopelessly primitive views. However there is more than one way of not sitting on your hands. The foolish thing to do would be to confront the USA head on. The clever thing for the Saudis to do, the thing I would do if I had their money, would be to create a powerful military alliance among the Islamic countries around the Indian Ocean. It would be designed to terrify the Americans into submission. It would change the world balance of power. That way the Saudis would get the best of both worlds."

"Ouch." Sharon grimaced, as Netanyahu responded "my thoughts precisely." Several hours later, premier Ariel Sharon was speaking to a senior Israeli military officer and this time the conversation was quite different. "So you are telling me there are certain thing about these atrocities at the World Trade Centre that simply don't add up?"

The Israeli soldier, himself an engineer in civilian life, was adamant. Three buildings, not just two, had collapsed that day. He explained that there was no visual evidence that anything of any sort had dropped on World Trade Centre 7, and certainly not enough evidence of fire to explain its collapse. Rather it had gone down like a pack of cards, in what looked to all the world like a controlled demolition. That particular sequence of events had been captured on television and broadcast time and again. Such concrete evidence watched by hundreds of millions of people was not exactly a conspiracy theory. Sharon's military adviser explained something else, not so much what had happened as what should not have done.

From an engineering point of view, what had happened identically to the twin towers themselves verged on the incredible. They should have been able to withstand a fire without suddenly collapsing in a huge cloud of dust. That was not what he, as an engineer, would have expected at all. On the contrary they should, albeit significantly damaged, have remained standing. There was no valid reason for them to collapse suddenly as a precisely matched pair, simply because aircraft had flown into them. They were designed to take that. It all looked quite artificial, and orchestrated, and rather unconvincing.

Ariel Sharon remembered his engineer's comments four years later when a comparable tower block in Madrid was similarly engulfed by fire. Although the fire was much more extensive than ever seen in either of New York's twin towers, it nevertheless remained standing. Although he was no professional architect or engineer himself, Ariel Sharon did wonder exactly how that could possibly be.

*   *   *   *   *

Riyadh, Saudi Arabia

IT WAS SIX in the evening as the heat of the day began to subside, and noteworthy figures of the Saudi government and civil service were gathered round a television watching events unfold in New York and Washington. Theirs was a mood of anger and another of dissent, a classic example of the hawks versus the doves.

Leading for the doves was Dr Malik Khalifa, recalled to Riyadh from a globetrotting diplomatic career six years earlier. At 63 years old he was almost reaching Grand Old Man status in the very hierarchical echelons of the Saudi administration. Malik Khalifa was in heated discussion with a young director of the intelligence services. "Are you telling me we knew all about this outrage in advance? That Osama bin Laden is a Saudi citizen? Why did we do nothing to prevent it?" The director ducked the question, merely muttering something about "A higher authority than you, Dr Khalifa."

There was little doubt in Malik Khalifa's mind that the latest events in New York would now make his own mission far more difficult. He was supposed to be building diplomatic bridges between the disparate Islamic countries of the Indian Ocean and beyond. That was how the old British Empire had transformed itself seamlessly into the modern British Commonwealth. It was a transformation which had attracted more interest . around the global diplomatic circuit than perhaps London imagined. There was not much chance of an Islamic commonwealth at the moment. Even less so, if Saudi Arabia was to make little more than international tut-tutting noises about the appalling tragedy which was unfolding by the minute in the north eastern United States. Malik turned to his immediate boss, one of the several foreign ministers. "For the past five years my job has been to build bridges between our country and other Islamic states. Many of them are decidedly disenchanted with the huge influence our Wahhabi mentors appear to exercise here in Saudi Arabia.

"The anti-Western attitudes which the Wahhabi constantly espouse are precisely summed up in the outrages we are watching right now on the television in New York and Washington. If the moderate Islamic states have the slightest suspicion that because of our attitudes, Saudi Arabia is in any way connected with this terrorist outrage, they will drop us like a hot brick.

"So exactly how much did we know in advance, and how much did we support it, no matter how covertly?" The foreign minister was quite evidently uncomfortable with the question. "So far as your contacts

Malik Khalifa

around the Islamic world are concerned, Malik, the fact of the matter is that Saudi Arabia had nothing whatever to do with the these attacks and totally disapproves of them. Make sure on your travels you get that message across loud and clear.

"If the noises coming out of America's intelligence sources are right, those buildings were destroyed by a terrorist group based in Afghanistan. So who was supporting them geographically? There is no clear reason why it should be ourselves.

" Just bear in mind that it is Iran and Pakistan which are the two Islamic countries sharing a common border with Afghanistan. You can probably forget the country's other borders to the north. Just remember, and remind people, that we don't have any common border with Afghanistan and that is key. If anyone is wondering where external support for those terrorists is coming from, I suggest they start there."

"But it's not just this latest outrage, is it?" Malik Khalifa continued. "It's the general ambivalence toward such terrorist activities which constantly radiates from Riyadh. Look, I've served in both Washington and New York. I know those places extremely well. What is happening on that television screen over there is almost personal to me. And the same goes for many of the people I am constantly dealing with in other countries. They are members of the same diplomatic circuit, most have them have served in the USA at one point or another in their careers. Any worthwhile career diplomat should have taken a turn in Washington. They will be just as unnerved as I am by those appalling attacks on the Pentagon and on the World Trade Centre.

"Yet there are people right here in this room, senior people, who have never set foot outside Saudi Arabia in their entire lives. They are now cheering the onslaught against the United States, as it is seen around the world. What do such xenophobes know of the big world beyond? All they know is the hysterical nonsense fed them by extremists who do great damage to our religion, to our global cause. As they watch that television you can almost hear them cheering each time another ordinary American jumps to his or her certain death rather than be burnt alive. Anyone might think they were watching a football match, and applauding the goals."

Malik Khalifa could see from the Foreign Minister's eyes his message was beginning to get through. "Look. Saudi Arabia is far and away the richest, and potentially the most powerful country in the whole Islamic world. We set the tone. Right now we appear to be trying to run with the fox and hunt with the hounds. Do you think international diplomats are stupid enough to be taken in by that? We need to make up our minds what this country really stands for on the world stage, and then proclaim it forcibly in both word and deed."

The foreign minister bridled at this. "And what exactly do you think Saudi Arabia should stand for in this godless, materialistic, militaristic, immoral world, Malik?" he asked. "Is no-one going to face up to the infidel United States of America? Do we all have to roll over before them in a sea of Coca Cola, a world awash with tempting alcoholic drinks? Do we all have to eat bacon sandwiches or visit the Oyster Bar at Grand Central Station? Do we all have to watch American television all round the world? Do we all have to accept that the entire world counts its years from nought BC?"

"No we don't." Malik Khalifa responded. "But if we are going to counter American influence around the world, we do need to go forward with something much more plausible, something much more positive than primitive Wahhabism. We are hardly seen as rational and progressive if even by implication we pat on the back people who use fully laden American civilian airliners as bombs. That is hardly the intelligent way for us to try and win friends and influence people internationally." The foreign minister was curious. "So exactly how would you go about winning their respect, Malik?" The urbane diplomat sensed he was beginning to win through. "We need to portray Saudi

Arabia as the embodiment, not of terrorism, but as the embodiment of the finest aspects of Islam. We need to revive the great Islamic traditions of the past. A thousand years ago the Arab city of Cordoba, capital of what we called El Antilles, and what they now call Iberia, was the greatest cultural centre of humanity, the largest centre of civilisation on the entire planet.

"Even today there are many Europeans who readily acknowledge that. All we do is confuse them. Yet our greatness was already manifest at a time when the United States of America was not even a glimmer on the horizon; it was still over six hundred years into their future, a non-existent state in an unknown continent far beyond any possible scope of their imagination. We were there first, and we were the best, and that is the message we need to get across today. We invented universities. The Europeans copied us in Bologna, then Paris, then Oxford. There are probably few Americans today who realise our universities in North Africa were the distant ancestors of their Yale and Harvard.

"We invented the highest levels of the education system. The professor's chair was our idea originally. It was our forebears who invented alchemy. We were the great astrologers and astronomers. We were the great philosophers, the great mathematicians and historians. It was us, not a bunch of primitive medieval Europeans, who rediscovered the wisdom of Plato and Aristotle and brought it back to the attention of the civilised world. If that were still the visible nature of 21st century Islam, my global selling job would be simple."

"Dr Khalifa, you are merely talking about ancient history, which is perhaps where you should belong." said the young firebrand from the intelligence directorate, as he now muscled in on the conversation. "The rest of us need to live in the 21st century, not the eleventh, if we allow ourselves on this occasion to adopt the Christian calendar. America is the great Satan. How can we possible counter that by becoming part of the Western culture ourselves, and celebrating people like Plato and

Aristotle? We finish up playing their game for them." The two men exchanged glances of mutual incomprehension. "So exactly what game are we playing?" Dr Malik Khalifa challenged his young companion.

The following day Malik Khalifa received an intriguing telephone call from an old friend who now held high rank in the Saudi Arabian military. The group captain had been examining in greater detail the photographic evidence of what had supposedly happened on 11 September. " Two things simply do not add up, Malik. I will leave the illogicalities of what supposedly happened to the twin towers on in Manhattan to others. Right now, I'm much more interested in the other two supposed aircraft crashes. After all, flying is supposed to be my particular expertise.

"First of all, let's look again at the hole in the outside wall of the Pentagon. It is evidence of the most amazing achievement in flying since the Wright Brothers and probably surpasses even that. First the pilot managed to skim along right down at ground level without disturbing a single blade of grass on the lawns outside the building. Supposedly in an aircraft with a huge wingspan, they did not even bend a single lamp-post. Even our top military pilots could not achieve that, flying our latest fighter jets. Yet supposed amateurs flying into the Pentagon achieved it with a lumbering civilian airliner. If you find that far-fetched fairy story convincing, you would believe just about anything.

"Second and even more remarkably the pilot made his wings disappear into thin air in the moment before impact. There is no wing-shaped hole in the Pentagon wall either side of the hole made by the supposed fuselage. Contrast that with the wing-shaped holes made by the aircraft flying into the World Trade Centre, an impact which was filmed. The two holes bear no resemblance to one another in shape. How very convenient there was no camera trained on that part of the Pentagon, or if there ever was the film has disappeared for good. And if the wings somehow snapped off before the plane hit the building -

then where are they now? There is no evidence whatever of them on the lawns of the Pentagon either. So that just doesn't add up. The whole thing looks to me far more like the result of a wingless missile.

"Next, let me turn to the crash site in Pennsylvania. Where was any convincing aircraft debris? Above all where were the remains of the engines - engines that actually related to the ones on that particular marque of aircraft? They were nowhere to be seen, yet invariably in such crashes, aircraft engines are virtually indestructible.

"Cast you mind back to that terrorist attack less than three years ago which dumped a Boeing 747 onto the town of Lockerbie in Scotland. It left a huge long gash in the ground. This one in Pennsylvania apparently made a helicopter-like vertical landing. As with the Pentagon impact, it would have taken an incredibly talented pilot to achieve that, not just some amateur with a couple of hours' flying time. Is that really supposed to be credible?

"I tell you, Malik, whatever made that hole in Pennsylvania was certainly not a civilian airliner in distress with no-one in control as its flight crew fought with its passengers. The hole shown on the television footage looks far more like the clean crater left by a large quantity of explosive." Malik Khalifa listened without comment. But it was definitely interesting food for thought, and gave him good cause to wonder exactly who was running the United States of America. And whose international friends were whose.

*   *   *   *   *

Beijing, China

IF THE MOOD in Tel Aviv was machiavellian, and the mood in Riyadh was a cultural dichotomy, the mood in Beijing was on a quite different plane from either. It soon grew into one of political philosophy, a lengthy reflection on the true nature of American capitalism, as seen from the Chinese point of view. Vice-premier Liu Fun had left a meeting followed by a most private dinner of the Beijing Patriotic Association somewhat early, and was home in time to watch the ten o'clock late evening news on television. Towards the end of the bulletin there was a sudden extra item. Reports were just coming in of a major airline incident in the United States of America.

Almost incredibly, one of the towers of the World Trade Centre in New York had been hit by an aircraft shortly before 10 pm Beijing time, and it was already feared there would be many casualties. The newscaster explained that the television station was changing its schedule because reports, many of them conflicting, were now being received every minute. Liu's close male companion brought some much-needed tea and joined her nervously on the sofa.

"I find it impossible to believe that the Americans could allow one of their aircraft to fly accidentally straight into the tallest building in New York." said vice-premier Liu Fun. "They have the most sophisticated air traffic control systems anywhere in the world, and they manage the traffic into and out of three major airports around New York City. I've flown in and out of the international airport at J F Kennedy more than once. There's something entirely wrong here. It doesn't ring true. I find such aircraft or pilot error quite incredible."

By now the television was showing footage of a modern Boeing 767 belonging to American Airlines ploughing straight into the south tower of the World Trade Centre. "Look. That puts the whole thing beyond credibility. That is no accident," said Liu Fun. "The pilots made no effort whatever to save themselves or their aircraft. That is a deliberate suicide attack, quite the most horrendous I have ever seen. No-one could have survived it."

By now the television news channel had determined that a second aircraft had ploughed into the remaining north tower of the World Trade Centre, and earlier confused reports that it was all the same aircraft had been dispelled. "Appalling though it is, that just proves my point. This is no air traffic accident" said the vice-premier, as much to herself as anyone else. It appeared that a new and appalling chapter had opened in the history of terrorism, and that ordinary Americans citizens, going about their normal business, were becoming its victims.

By eleven o'clock it was reported that a third aircraft, another American Airlines flight, had crashed into the Pentagon building in Washington DC. Fun began to wonder just how many more there might be before the day was out. Whoever had organised and coordinated the events was going for a spectacle far more ambitious than any ever conceived by the capitalistic moguls of Hollywood.

Liu Fun was now on the telephone, while her partner continued to watch the appalling events unfold. The television showed the footage of the aircraft ploughing into the tower of the World Trade Centre over and over again. The programme producers seemed oblivious to the true horror of what they were showing, and in a morbid way far more interested that it was gripping television. The Chinese ambassador to the United Nations in New York was keeping senior government officials in the Forbidden City as up to date as he could, but in reality he could do little more than watch the same television broadcasts they were watching themselves.

When the towers themselves collapsed one by one, Liu Fun could see for herself that many thousands of people must already have died that morning. It was America's most appalling experience since Pearl Harbour. Analysts at the intelligence division of the Central Military Commission had been summoned from their homes and theories were beginning to emerge as to who was responsible. As a vice premier, Liu had access at the highest level to their thinking. "Who did it?" asked her companion. "The CAC is awash with theories" she replied "but the current favourite is some well-organised Islamic terrorist organisation. We knew of them already, but they would not have been our lead suspect, at least not until now. We are constantly watching many such organisations, and until now this one was no different from the rest. But if it is them, I think they are going to become everyone's favourite suspect from now on." At midnight Liu Fun was joined by Admiral Zhou Man, who had telephoned half an hour earlier. The two were anxious to think through how the latest developments in America rebounded on their Indian Ocean strategy, which despite all was still moving ahead methodically.

It was now over four years since Zhou Man had given vice premier Liu his preliminary assessment of the project. After many months of political consultation and analysis the admiral had set himself the objective of a Chinese warship being able to reach anywhere in the Indian Ocean within two days, preferably less. This dictated both the number and location of the naval bases they would need, and also the speed of the ships.

The speed of the ships and their eventual size in turn determined the power of their engines. Zhou Man's ever closer friend Antonia Foo was in charge of all that. Vice premier Liu had been well aware of their intimate friendship and did not disapprove. "You might as well keep all the secrets within the family. Pillow talk can do less damage that way, Zhou. In any case she is a very sexy woman."

When she wasn't busy keeping the admiral comfortable in bed, Antonia Foo was standing by her promise professionally. A first prototype Yangtse engine from her Yellow River Industrial Research Facility had been fired up over two years ago, and her promised programme of ultra-thorough testing and modification was well in train.

Yet the ships themselves were only half the answer, and they were the easy half. They simply cost money, all of it spent within China itself under strict security. Admiral Man had eventually determined that even with fast ships capable of at least 55 kilometres an hour, they would need six well located naval bases, and none of them on Chinese soil. In turn the number of bases determined the number of ships they would need on active service at any one time. The master calculations were confidential between Liu Fun and Zhou Man and would remain so almost for a further four years. When Liu eventually took her completed naval plan to her government colleagues, it would no longer remain secret. The longer she could keep it all under wraps the easier its preliminary stages would be.

"So what does this latest twist in relations between the Americans and the Islamic world do to us?" asked Liu Fun with her habitual rhetoric. "If it is the terrorist group the CAC think it is, then we are straight into the politics of the Indian Ocean littoral. That means us, it means you and me, Admiral Zhou."

It was now well turned midnight, and the dreadful news reports from New York continued to emerge by the minute. Both towers of the World Trade Centre had collapsed, bringing death and destruction on a vast scale. It was not yet known how many people were still in the buildings when they fell to the ground, and guesstimates varied wildly. Liu Fun produced a very fine bottle of vintage cognac, and poured a generous glass for each of them. "It used to be a tradition of the British Navy to drink rum before they went into battle. Here we have much the same general idea, but I think you'll agree this stuff tastes rather better."

Zhou Man was watching the television contemplatively, thinking out the wider implications. "Let me give you some first guesses." he said to his boss. "We know from Korea to Vietnam that the Americans find it very difficult to stand back and simply be philosophical. Sooner or later their hawks demanding military retaliation will win.

"Their obscene military-industrial complex has all the money, and so has all the greatest political influence in Washington. And if it is who we think it is caused all that mayhem in New York this morning, that calls for attacking a Moslem country." Liu Fun chipped in. "Whatever you say, comrade Zhou, the Americans will never attack Saudi Arabia. They daren't. The effect on world oil supplies would be catastrophic.

Never forget their new President is a Texas oil man. From the days of President Lyndon Johnson it has always been in the best interests of Texas oil to have their own man in the White House."

"I wasn't thinking that. I agree the world's largest oil supplier would be their last conceivable target. I think the Americans will go for a proxy war instead. Attack someone smaller. All they will want to do is show the Moslem world who is still boss. But the point is this: whichever country they attack, the Wahhabis in Saudi Arabia will interpret it as an attack on the whole of Islam. They are bound to do so."

"Which would of course mean a stiffening of attitude in Riyadh. Perhaps that is what the terrorists were seeking all along; they thought it up all by themselves. I wonder . . . is it not at least as likely the Saudis themselves want to provoke America into a military response, so their hawks in turn are empowered to respond to whatever the Americans feel obliged to do next? Tell me, Admiral Man, do you share the Russian enthusiasm for playing chess?"

The following day Vice-premier Liu Fun's mood changed considerably after a further briefing from one of her intelligence experts. In his professional view there were certain things which simply did not add up. The first concerned the showers of sparks which had been filmed falling from the twin towers near the original fire. They were evidence of far higher temperatures than could ever be achieved by burning jet fuel, most of which would probably have exploded anyway in an incendiary cloud within moments of impact.

"There was something else inside that building causing the fire. We think it was tergite, and we believe the building had been pre-prepared for the explosions long before the aircraft hit them. We have reports from some Chinese building workers in New York that for many weeks those two buildings were being stripped of asbestos. When that happens the area involved must be cleared of all but properly-protected personnel. If you wanted to instal some incendiary and explosive devices that would provide the perfect cover to do so." Liu Fun thought back to the firemen who had been talking on camera in the basement of the twin towers before they collapsed. They had several times reported hearing explosions going off a considerable time after the moment of impact. Firemen were well trained to recognise what they were hearing, for in such circumstances their own lives were at risk.

It was surely impossible that bits of the aircraft could have reserved themselves for subsequent explosions, explosions so delayed there was enough time to summon firemen and deploy them throughout the twin towers. Liu Fun realised the hijacked aircraft themselves would have been entirely destroyed in the first massive explosion. So the explosions heard by the firemen much later must have been caused by something else.

Liu Fun then wondered about a comment from an engineering colleague in the Beijing Patriotic Association. He knew a lot about buildings. "Those two towers did not simply collapse. They exploded in a huge cloud of concrete dust, exactly the sort of thing you can see when a building is demolished by explosives placed deliberately.

"The whole thing collapse looks more like a carefully-timed set piece, while the crashing aircraft merely served as a melodramatic overture to the main event. And it is most strange that the lower sections of the twin towers well away from the impact zone exploded as well. What explosive force caused that, exactly? Certainly not an ordinary civilian aircraft." The Chinese engineer was adamant.

The intrinsic nature of American capitalism regularly attracted the curiosity of members of the Beijing Patriotic Association. It was their bête-noir. Liu Fun had long ago learnt that, under such mysterious circumstances as the twin towers disaster, the wisest course was to follow the money and see where it led. Who benefited financially and most profitably from the collapse of the twin towers? In the suspicious anti-capitalist mind of her colleagues in the Beijing Patriotic Association the answer was a simple one: the sort of capitalists who would have collected on the insurance. Such people were too often at the centre of apparent accidental fires and other catastrophes. But to collect their payout the events would have to look like a terrorist act, the sort of disaster covered by insurance policies. A simple controlled collapse caused by pre-installed explosives would not have served such a financial objective at all. Liu Fun knew enough about the ways of western insurance companies to realise any such claim for a planned collapse would have been pushed aside. To collect any insurance money an unmanageable and terrible catastrophe would be the requisite first step.

After some further reflection, Liu Fun concluded that her strategic quest to challenge the might of the capitalistic United States was now more justified than ever. After a hundred years trying to run the world, that large country had fulfilled any purpose it was ever intended to have in the upward progress of humanity. Recent events had exposed some appalling weaknesses in its moral architecture. So now was time for the world's peoples to move on and to start afresh.

It seemed entirely obvious to Liu Fun that the cradle of the next great level of civilisation, as humanity moved upwards in its intelligence and sophistication, would of necessity be devised somewhere other than the United States of America. The first upwards step by humanity towards civilisation had been the creation of agricultural societies. They were simple structures, providing only a very basic material standard of living. That had been humanity's first, most primitive civilisation.

Then the West had inadvertently devised its capitalism, epitomised by the brash prosperity of the United States. America's economic progress had been an unprecedented step forward and upward. Yet it was just the temporary second phase, the next plane, it was never destined to become anything more important or permanent or desirable than that. In Liu Fun's assessment, a heartless inhumanity poisoned the capitalism of the West. It had been revealed by the terrible events of the last few days. It was the final indictment of capitalism. Worthy civilised people in their thousands could be ruthlessly sacrificed without a second thought, merely for financial profit by a secret few. Rather than be burnt alive, many well-paid, highly-educated American bankers and investors - beloved sons, treasured brothers and sisters, essential fathers and mothers - voluntarily threw themselves to their deaths. Karl Marx had been right philosophically all along.

In her personal view true humanity now needed to move to a higher and better civilisation, even if there would be some inevitable bumps and scrapes along the way. Change was never easy. It would gradually shift humanity to a middle way developing the best aspects of poor but honest agriculturalism and those of rich but corrupt capitalism. And the natural country to find that middle way, that next and higher plane of civilisation, was inevitably the Middle Kingdom. The Beijing Patriotic Association had read the geopolitical charts wisely.

Chapter Four

The Fourth Arrondissement

Central Paris

IT HAD BEEN A vintage afternoon at the Stade de France and after a journey right across central Paris James Heaton was enjoying several congenial drinks at a bar in St Germain de Prés with Xavier Kerguelen. By now the two rugby fans had dissected the England-France match in minute detail. The two of them had known one another for years, but as serving naval officers their meetings were inevitably fewer than they wished. Fortunately a regular flow of emails kept them in contact even from opposite corners of the world.

Now an opportunity to meet had arisen and Xavier had suggested they celebrate it with a long weekend in Paris, watch the England-France friendly and then meet the Kerguelen family. James had grabbed the opportunity and obtained a few days much-needed leave from the Royal Navy. Ever since those atrocities in New York three years previously, the military had been on a semi-constant state of alert. It was time to relax. And in the view of James Heaton there was nothing better than being taken round a stylish city by someone who knew it like the back of his hand.

On the Sunday evening they would drive down to Xavier's family home on the coast. James knew the Kerguelens to be an old naval family, rather like his own, while Brittany's far west was definitely worth a visit. It would be an interesting comparison with his days at Dartmouth now almost nine years ago. Was the rocky coast of far western France anything like the rocky coast of Cornwall he had explored so many times?

Xavier was keen to impress James with the manifold pleasures of his native France and with the high life in contemporary Paris. He considered himself an archetypal and thoroughly modern European. "Oh and while you are here in Paris, James, we have another surprise. You are coming to a very smart birthday party tonight. That's why I said you should bring your mess uniform. I know it's not required normally on leave but this one is special."

"Whose birthday party?" asked James. "I suppose I should know your style well enough by now, Xavier de Kerguelen. Always full of surprises; all very Gallic and a touch exotic."

"You can definitely say exotic." Xavier explained. "It's a twenty-first birthday party for a girl my brothers and I have known since she was twelve. She is virtually a sister to us, half French, half Arab, very much out of the usual. You'll like her, James; stunning looking, fabulous figure and loads of self-confidence whenever she's around men. The three of us, my two younger brothers in particular, have trained her well. You're about to see the French aristocracy at its most stylish best. She's called Violaine - we would consider that a super first name here in France. Our mother Tiphaine originally met hers, Louise, years ago when they were both girl guides together, for God's sake. They've known one another for ever.

"So our dear maman Tiphaine is what you English would call Violaine's godmother, or as we say it in French her marraine. It will come as no surprise to you that upper crust parties like the one tonight, especially in Paris, are always keen to invite eligible young men: you are exactly what they are looking for. Tiphaine, bless her, fixed your invitation the minute she knew you could visit from England. She is never slow off the mark."

"I can smell it a mile off. You've been plotting again, haven't you, Xavier Kerguelen?" His French companion smiled broadly. "I suppose you could say that. Anyway she wants you to look the part, our very tailor-made version of Commander James Bond. That will go down very well in the Fourth Arrondissement, you believe me."

"Steady on, Xavier. Arguably I might be irresistibly handsome in a suitably darkened room, there's no denying I am an officer in the Royal Navy, but I have nothing remotely like his capacity for booze. I'd be under the table. Nor does anyone nowadays have a licence to kill, whatever that means exactly. I fear the gay Mr Fleming rather got carried away with himself over that one. So I hope your friends won't be too disappointed. Oh yes, of course, he and I do have one other thing in common though; we both definitely approve of women."

"All sounds good to me, James, I doubt Tiphaine will be disappointed, she's much more likely to make cooing noises. Anyway, as an Englishman you should definitely approve of the venue. We're going to a very exclusive club in the Rue du Faubourg St Honoré. It's called the Cercle de l'Union Interallié and it was originally founded for the military. It's a bit like all those gentlemen's clubs you Englishmen seem to enjoy so much in London. I believe there are lots of them around Pall Mall, is that what you call it? You must agree that's a very strange name for a street, even in London.

"Apparently Louise's grandfather was something very distinguished in the First World War, so be became a founding member of the club, or something like that." The two sailors discussed the finer points of London and Paris gentlemen's clubs for a while, until Xavier suddenly looked at his watch.

"Better drink up, James. We need to go home, smarten up and get across central Paris before eight. It doesn't do on these occasions to be late. We're off to the Fourth Arrondissement, don'tcha know and things can't get much smarter than that." Xavier's command of colloquial English was getting better by the week and he loved to try it out when he could.

Violaine Khalifa scrutinised herself in a mirror. Her new dress, tailor-made and close-fitting in gold silk, made her feel quite excited. Even she reckoned her figure looked pretty good and her brown hair had been brushed to perfection by her mother. Her shoes were in matching gold, her make-up and perfume the finest which Paris could provide. Today was her official twenty-first birthday and to celebrate a large family party had been arranged.

After four hard years studying at the Sorbonne, it was time for Violaine to discover a wider world. She now had a Maîtrise de Langues Étrangères Appliquées, a degree in English and Arabic. Not only that, she had come high in her class in both subjects. With her tutors' help, in just two weeks' time she would be going to Oxford University in England to study for a doctorate in Islamic history. That had brought much joy in the Hôtel de Chambon. Some thirty two years on, Violaine would be following in the footsteps of her very successful mother.

But tonight it was her party. After a row with her mother it had been agreed it would not take place at home, for Louise Khalifa had originally insisted on using the Hôtel de Chambon's ballroom in keeping with a long family tradition. Yet no matter how grand it was living in the Fourth Arrondissement, Violaine considered it hopelessly uncool for a thoroughly modern girl to hold a twenty-first birthday in somewhere as passée as the family home. o at considerable length she and her mother had finally compromised on a private club, the Cercle de l'Union Interallié. It was very grand, a venue of choice for the

Parisian elite. For several years Louise Khalifa had been a member of its ladies' committee, the Comité des Dames. Her grandfather, a senior French officer in the First World War, had been one of the founder members. Becoming involved in such exclusive pursuits was almost expected of the chatelaine of a renowned hôtel particulier. And as virtually an hereditary member she was welcome to use its premises any time she wanted for a private family party.

Once she had agreed on the party venue in the wake of the steely determination of her daughter, Louise had thrown herself into the event with gusto and lavished five star treatment on its planning. It was going to be an event which Paris's haute monde would find hard to forget. Some eighty friends and relations had been carefully selected and invited, the ladies would all be wearing their party finest. Paris was, after all, still the world centre of fashion as they all constantly reminded themselves.

Punctuality was considered polite. At eight o' clock everyone sat down to a formal dinner in the salle à manger, followed by live music. The food was very imaginative, an unusual combination of classical French and classical Arabic. On that at least, Violaine and her mother had been in early agreement. It was a touch of originality which won much approval from the somewhat jaded palates of the Parisian haute monde. Something different to eat at last.

Once the banquet was finished and the music began, by convention Violaine's first dance was with her Papa. Malik Khalifa, who had flown in specially from Riyadh. As soon as family formalities were over and Violaine had dutifully worked her way round tables talking to the older guests, she went to find the Kerguelen brothers. As an only child, she had been brought up with the two youngest, Frederic and Vincent. Now they were all in their twenties; while the eldest brother Xavier was almost thirty-one with a promising career in the French navy.

She found the brothers in their shirtsleeves in the billiards room playing some sort of complicated game. There were four men in all and she soon found out the stranger was English, another naval officer. A few years ago, apparently, Xavier had met him in a side by side fight in Portsmouth. The two of them had won and celebrated their victory on Xavier's ship. They had been good friends ever since.

It took Violaine little time to discover that Xavier's handsome English friend was called James Heaton and he was a lieutenant in the Royal Navy. She had caught a glimpse of his rather gorgeous uniform over dinner and now was her chance to meet him properly. He was trying to teach the Kerguelen brothers the complicated skills and rules of snooker. They had often heard about this strange game played with balls of many different colours, even watched it played on English television from time to time. Actually playing the shots was proving really difficult, even for James, after several glasses of the quality wines which the Chambon family considered de rigueur on such auspicious occasions.

By eleven o'clock Violaine had successfully detached James Heaton from her god-brothers, looped her arm through his and walked him out into the cool air of the Parisian night. For a twenty one year old this was definitely a winning move, strolling stylishly through the decorated gardens of the club on a balmy evening with a handsome man who must have been ten years her senior. Her girlfriends from the Sorbonne watched with ill-concealed envy as she swished along elegantly in her silk dress, on the arm of some gorgeous new man in his smart uniform.

James soon learnt that Violaine was about to go up to Oxford University for her doctorate and was delighted. "Which college?" he asked. He had already discovered why her English, after five years at school in Paris, then four years at the Sorbonne, was quite so fluent. Violaine Khalifa was a natural linguist with a fine ear for accents.

Violaine Khalifa

James Heaton

James Heaton quickly concluded this was not just an extremely attractive young woman but an extremely clever one too. "It's somewhere called Keble College," she answered "and is that good or bad?" Better than just good, it was music to his ears.

"Violaine, you have at least thirty colleges to choose from these days and you have managed to choose my own. Okay it's almost ten years since I was there, but you will find that unlike other British universities, at Oxford or Cambridge you belong to your college for the rest of your life."

Violaine was definitely in luck. Her mother had many fond memories of Oxford and she wanted to know if it would still be the same. "Do you think I am going to enjoy it?" Her life until now had been shaped by the rigid academic discipline and competitive stress of the Sorbonne. She had been told that Oxford would be much more relaxed and apart from encouraging supervision every now and then, how she actually went about her studies would be her own business. That would be a very new experience.

Violaine talked about her future work. She wanted to write a doctoral thesis on Islamic history, specialising in its greatest period. It was soon clear to James Heaton this was a woman with a mission. "I want to show that Islam is not just a breeding ground for terrorism. It is vital to rediscover the importance of places like Cordoba or the old Arab cities of North Africa."

She was appalled by the modern image of her peoples. James was slightly taken aback by this forthright twenty-one year old Frenchwoman talking so seriously, holding forth even at her own birthday party. "Well, Violaine, I'm merely a down-to-earth sailor and all that sounds quite awesome. I just did an ordinary undergraduate degree in engineering. But the important thing is to have chosen something you enjoy doing anyway. If it's fun and you feel at home with it, that makes the work far easier."

Violaine explained that for the first twelve years of my life she had been educated at the French school in Riyadh. She spoke and read Arabic with ease and wanted to read its historic texts in their original form. "What might seem off-putting to others of my age will be relatively easy for me. Does that count as enjoying myself ?"

James took her point immediately. "I think Oxford will welcome you with open arms. It's hardly my field, but I do know that the Bodleian Library's collection of Islamic manuscripts is one of the finest in Europe. You should be in your element. And you're also in luck. Unusually the head of your new college is a woman, a don called Averil Cameron. She's a leading professor of Byzantine studies, an expert by any international standards, but she doubles up as the person leading the College.

"I imagine she will thoroughly approve of a woman doing a doctorate in classical Arabic manuscripts. Right up her street. Often Oxford Colleges are headed by pensioned-off civil servants. Its cloisters can become so introverted they often think an outsider will help shake things up. But Averil Cameron is shaking things up like a good 'un anyway. You'll like her."

"James, I have been looking for someone to explain to me what my life is going to be like at Oxford, when I am not working that is. I have heard so many stories, I don't even know which ones are true. But before you tell me that, tell me something else first. Did you enjoy your own time at Oxford?"

He was keen to impress this young woman with his dark blue knowledge and was delighted she wanted to know. His explanation was detailed. She was not really surprised to learn that most undergraduates either worked or drank, although some did both. A few headed out of their colleges and made for the heart of the university, seeking stardom in places like its debating society, the Oxford Union, or in undergraduate journalism, politics or theatre.

"Then they leave and that interest often becomes their career. Half the top names on British television started that way." James took a distant view of the literati and glitterati of his old university. Their world had not been his. "In many of those non-academic pursuits, Oxford is the world's leading university. Cambridge is good at theatre. Far from anything people might learn from its formal teaching, many simply go to Oxford to focus on those non-academic pursuits instead. You will meet them constantly, yet studying for a doctorate you will be senior to them; they are usually undergraduates. The Oxford Union debating society is the club on which Britain's House of Commons was modelled. Most of Britain's Prime Ministers since 1900 have gone to Oxford in their youth.

"Including Margaret Thatcher? And Tony Blair?"

"Definitely including Margaret Thatcher. And yes, even Tony Blair. He was one of the long-haired beer-drinking fraternity at the university. She took her time there rather more seriously." James then explained about the university's sportsmen, almost a world apart. hey seemed to train all the time. Every year the university's most senior eight rowed against Cambridge University along a gruelling course along the River Thames in London.

James told his fascinated new companion how, throughout the Summer, Oxford played cricket against the professional English counties. "That's a weird British pastime, but you'll eventually grow used to it. The cricket ground is straight across the road from Keble in the University parks. My tutors used to abandon our tutorials in the Summer so they could stroll across the University Parks just to watch the cricket matches instead."

"Did you do any of those things at Oxford, James?" Violaine asked, her eyes wide open, as she rapidly weighed up her social and romantic prospects. "No. I did something rather different. The university also has its own officer training corps, especially for those planning a career in the military. Nowadays the university even has a specialised naval unit complete with its own patrol boat, but not in my day. What with that and quite a lot of socialising and studying engineering, that took up most of my three years at the University."

James looked back. He had enjoyed the academic work. It came naturally. The officer corps had taken him away from Oxford itself. In many ways he had been an outsider - but that often happened to scientists at Oxford anyway. It was the people in the humanities like Violaine who made a bee-line for the non-academic activities. They seemed to have much more spare time on their hands.

"So how should I spend my time apart from working? I'm twenty-one and it's about time I had some real fun in my life." James weighed her up; she would be much in demand. "Well, Violaine, remember you will be older and rather more mature than most undergraduates. Nowadays there is a large contingent of post-graduates, more every year, but a lot of them will be working hard, especially the ones aiming for an academic career, God bless them."

The trick for Violaine would be to balance the time she spent on academic work with the time she spend socialising. Getting to know Oxford contemporaries was half the reason for being there. The contacts lasted for life. "The important thing is to stick with it and stay in Oxford all the time and not be tempted to drift back home to Paris at the weekend. I realise that the Eurostar service will be starting in about six weeks' time, in your first term and it would be all too easy to catch the train from Waterloo every Friday afternoon and be at the Gare du Nord in a couple of hours.

"Try to resist the temptation to keep coming back to the familiar. Enjoy the university instead. Let the men take you to places a woman is unlikely to try on her own. There are some super pubs out of town up the river; places like the Trout Inn at Godstow. It's an easy cycle ride from college - good idea to have a bike. Keeps you fit.

And if you win yourself a serious boyfriend out of it, then all I can say is he will be a lucky man." Violaine smiled with more than normal pleasure at the neat compliment; maybe she even blushed. It was a pity James would be away in the Navy rather than at Oxford. He would make a very good boyfriend. They agreed to keep in contact anyway, swapped email addresses and telephone numbers. Then there was always their matched college connection to bring them together. James reckoned he was bound to revisit the old place several times while Violaine was there.

It was long after midnight and Violaine thought perhaps she had better be seen once again around her own birthday party. It was all very well disappearing to talk to a handsome new stranger, but she also felt she had to circulate. Then again it was her party and she'd even cry if she wanted. Not that she wanted to cry tonight. Quite the reverse. But he was 31, already with a career. Violaine Khalifa decided that evening as she joined the world of adults that she definitely preferred older men. She wanted to meet James Heaton of the Royal Navy again. Definitely. And as soon as possible.

"Who was that remarkably handsome naval officer you were with half the night?" asked her mother over a meal that was doing duty as breakfast, although by that late hour of the morning it was more déjeuner than petit. Both women were still in their nighties. "Do I gather he is English? Apparently Tiphaine de Kerguelen arranged it - he's some friend of Xavier's. Do tell me more."

"Maman, his name is James Heaton, Lieutenant James Heaton of the British Royal Navy. That's how he met Xavier." her mother smiled knowingly. "Your eyes are glowing, child. Did you like him that much? Are you smitten, my dear? And how old is he? Does he have a girlfriend? Are you going to see him again?" Violaine blushed. "Patience, Maman, patience. Yes I thought he was super. And anyway you said yourself how handsome he is. He's clever and he understands me. He went to Oxford, he even went to the same college as mine is going to be and apparently that's very important. He told me all kinds of things I should expect once I get there. And I do agree he is ten years older than me. And although I will be in England, he probably won't be. Certain to be on a ship on the far side of the world I expect."

"Oxford and the Royal Navy too? We do have to be impressed. And I can hardly complain about you chasing after older men, they're always more attractive. I was exactly the same and after all Papa also is ten years older than me."

"Don't rub it in." said Dr Malik Khalifa making an appearance from his study at precisely the opportune moment. "And I think I am just about old enough to deserve a cup of coffee. So, daughter mine, did you enjoy your party?"

"Darling she met an absolutely gorgeous naval officer and guess what? He's ten years older than she is and he went to Oxford University as well. Apparently he's been telling her what to expect." Louise stopped as she saw the expression on her husband's face. "Did I say something wrong?"

Malik paused. "I'm probably just being over-cautious but given my job in Riyadh, a close family connection with the British navy might not be considered entirely wise."

"Oh, come on, Papa." Violaine replied. "He's just a man I met at my party and much that I fancy him I'll probably never see him again. And anyway he is really just a friend of Xavier de Kerguelen who's in our navy and your job in Riyadh can hardly dictate to Xavier who his friends should and shouldn't be."

Malik shrugged and then smiled at the two women. "Okay, Violaine, I'm sure there's no real harm done. Now you're older it is perhaps important that we all understand the people you might bring into this house." Many people living on the Île St Louis in the very heart of the Fourth Arrondissement would have said much the same.

"Okay, Papa, but wouldn't it perhaps help a little if you explained to Maman and me exactly what we need to understand about your job in Riyadh? And by the way, thank you both, that was a brilliant 21st birthday party, much, much better than I was expecting and I owe it all to you and Maman. Thank you both. I think I chose my parents very well."

Dr Malik Khalifa stared at his wife and only daughter for a moment, then slowly nodded, then asked, "Tell me Violaine, exactly what do you want to achieve at Oxford with your doctorate in Islamic history? I suspect you will be half-way to answering your own questions before you even get there."

Violaine explained her shame at the way the great religion of Islam was labelled by the rest of the world. Its disreputability had been put to her forcefully time and again since she first came to live in Paris. She wanted to change the image of Islam by digging into its past. The Bodleian library at Oxford had one of the finest collections of old Islamic manuscripts anywhere in Europe. It was time to put her fluency in Arabic to good use.

Malik Khalifa listened enthusiastically as his beloved daughter set out her ambitions. They were impressive. "Violaine, now listen to me carefully. What I am about to say is strictly between you, Maman and me. If my private opinions about what is happening in Saudi Arabia today were public knowledge, my diplomatic job could be in jeopardy and perhaps your education could also suffer as a consequence. So let's all be discreet about my views but you are now an adult. That's exactly what yesterday evening's party was all about.

"Perhaps I should not keep so many secrets about my work, especially when you and I are in such agreement anyway. Yes, there are times when I listen to colleagues in and around the Saudi government and they make me wince. My job as an aged diplomat is to build bridges with other countries in the Islamic world. The extremist version of Islam being promoted in some quarters in Saudi Arabia makes that job ten times harder. Sometimes I even think there are those at home who suspect my loyalties."

Father and daughter agreed on the achievements of Islam's past. They agreed on the difficulties caused by its modern image. If it were different, Malik's job would be easier and Violaine would be pushing at an open door with her Oxford thesis.

"So I suppose you and I are really fighting the same battle, Violaine. I will give you all the help I can with your doctorate. There are some great academics of Islam who privately agree with me and they will be very supportive when I tell them what my daughter is trying to do. Even if our modernists have difficulty coming to terms with the idea of a highly-educated woman, strangely enough our traditionalists will not. To them the whole idea of a female Islamic intellectual is totally right. That's the irony."

"Papa, one of these days will you introduce me to some of the real traditional intellectuals of Islam? Not yet, but say in a year or so when I am digging into those ancient manuscripts and really need some help. I'm sure that if Oxford thought I had family contacts like that it would win approval. And if I could convince Islamic academics in Saudi Arabia I was doing a good job at Oxford I would win approval there too."

Louise listened to her daughter talking to her father with much admiration and delight. Sharing their Arab roots they were rapidly building an intellectual bridge across a generation and here they all were on an island right in the middle of the Seine. It had relied on bridges for its very existence. "Violaine," she said. "It's becoming abundantly clear to me you are definitely better off with older men. Don't worry about that darling, it runs in the family. The James

Heatons of this world will make perfect boyfriends and who knows beyond that? But you are now also exactly on a wavelength with your own father. To me the whole idea of an intellectual alliance between my husband and my daughter makes me feel very proud and not a little thrilled. I suspect the great days of this family are still to come."

Louise had been brought up a Roman Catholic and was still an outsider to the tradition her husband had known all his life. She intensely disliked the way her religion of adoption had been spoiled by awful people. She knew Islam was worth far more than that. "If my husband and daughter can do something between them to put matters right, then a powerful chapter in the history of the Chambons will have been written in the 21st century.

"Malik, darling, you know you can count on the absolute discretion of both of us about your private doubts. Never forget that here in France especially a degree of uncertainty is a mark of a truly intelligent man. He never quite takes everything around him at face value. Why even our greatest philosopher René Descartes invented his 'method of doubt'. And I do vaguely remember that was based on an even earlier Islamic philosopher. Any educated Frenchman would correctly raise a glass in honour to that."

Dr Malik Khalifa looked at his wife and daughter and a huge sense of relief swept through him within, while a much encouraged smile broke out without. The contrast between his acceptance at home in Paris and the undertow of rejection in Riyadh was palpable. It all seemed a million miles from the horrors of Islamist atrocities. He had never before felt bound quite so closely with his immediate family in a common intellectual cause.

It was a fine feeling, especially when they were normally separated by a whole continent. He decided it was time to celebrate. So Malik swept aside any lingering Islamic disapproval of alcohol, strolled to the fridge and found a bottle of champagne. "I was really saving this until supper this evening but, no matter, I think this is the right moment. This is a 1983 vintage, Violaine, a special birthday treat for a very special daughter." And with a resounding pop and three glasses, Dr Malik Khalifa celebrated as he reflected that his trip from Riyadh for his only daughter's 21st birthday party had suddenly brought a reward even greater. He was steadily discovering there was something both exciting and reassuring about the aristocratic way of life in the Fourth Arrondissement.

*   *   *   *   *

Pointe du Raz, Brittany

"YOU RATHER FELL for our little Violaine, didn't you, James?" Xavier asked as the two of them peered down at the turbulent Atlantic over a vertical cliff edge on the Breton coast. James Heaton agreed, yes he had. She was lovely. And if there were any such thing as his type of woman, she would almost certainly be one of the few.

Paris seemed a million miles away as they scrambled over the rocks, looking across the strait to the Île de Sein. James had decided there was after all a refreshing similarity here to the coast of Cornwall, even if there was nothing quite so impressive as the massive grandeur of Land's End. That said, coastal Brittany had a splendour all of its own. In the process he had also soon discovered that the Kerguelen 'home' was in fact a castle and it had been in the family for centuries.

A distant Breton ancestor of Xavier, one Yves-Joseph de Kerguelen, had discovered the eponymous, if decidedly inhospitable, island in the southern Indian Ocean over two centuries earlier. 'Ker' was a common enough prefix on both sides of the western sea and as James had pointed out, the Cornish name for its tiny and rather unsuccessful nationalist party was Mebyon Kernow.

From his days at Dartmouth, James recalled how the Devonian locals living east of the River Tamar regarded them as an intermittent half-way house, somewhere between a joke and an irritant. There never was much love lost between England's two westernmost counties.

As they strolled in the fresh Atlantic air, Xavier talked about his seagoing ancestry, something he shared with James Heaton. They talked about Violaine and her family background. Xavier explained just how powerfully the Chambons ranked in Parisian society - any alliance there took one straight to the social summit. James wanted to know more about her father's exact role in Riyadh but Xavier's knowledge of that soon ran dry.

They talked about Oxford, something which Xavier rather envied and both of them agreed that, with her Arabic family upbringing, Violaine had made a superb choice for her doctorate. That came to four good reasons why just a single evening and early morning spent in Paris's smartest club had probably changed James Heaton's life and changed it for good.

Chapter Five

The Five Elements

Glasgow Airport

DHENG TURKU WATCHED the passengers streaming into the arrivals lounge at Glasgow airport. It would not be very difficult to spot a Mongolian face in Scotland and he soon picked out Iqo Zontang, who was pulling a large grey bag. Though the two men had not met before, helpful photographs had been supplied by their controllers in Beijing. Dheng Turku gave Zontang a hand with his luggage. After thirty hours of flights from Beijing and a four hour flight to Beijing from Urumqi before that, it had been a tiring journey.

This was Iqo Zontang's first trip outside his native China. He was impressed that here in Scotland his new colleague could afford to drive a Mercedes. It was not exactly the latest model but even so, Mercedes of any vintage were a rare sight in his home province of Xinjiang. Iqo soon felt weary as he relaxed into the unfamiliar luxury.

While he dozed, Dheng drove down the M8 to Junction 25 then took the northbound Clyde tunnel under the river to Scotstoun. Traffic was heavy and the journey was slow. Their destination was the Flying Dragon Chinese restaurant, one of hundreds in the city, in Inverness

Avenue off the Dumbarton Road. The establishment had opened quite recently and, unusually, it was also an internet café which specialised in access to all the most popular Chinese websites. Its hourly internet fees were negligible and the café had rapidly become a mecca for Chinese nationals in Glasgow.

Most of the Flying Dragon's regular customers were lonely young men far away from their families back home. The café had quickly become their social venue of choice, while its waiter did not seem remotely concerned whether they bought any food or not. They were welcome to stay all day if they wished. Their continual flow of internet traffic was exactly what Admiral Zhou Man wanted when he had originally financed the business.

Their innocent internet chatter was infinitely more valuable to China than any profit to be had from selling portions of sweet and sour pork, fried prawns with bamboo shoots and water chestnuts or the occasional bottle of Tsing Tao beer. The internet activity was a smokescreen. From a back room marked "Private: Mah-Jong Club Members Only" much more intriguing internet traffic was generated, little if anything of it involving Mah-Jong.

The five men living in the flat above the Flying Dragon restaurant were a cell of Chinese spies. Apart from Dheng's son Zhuang there were the brothers Mong and Tonghu Zizhiku. Despite appearances all four were knowledgeable naval engineers, now to be joined by Iqo Zontang, an expert in data systems and communication. Nor were they the ubiquitous Han Chinese. They were Dzungars and they all spoke a language which bore little relation to Mandarin, or to the Cantonese of Hong Kong much more familiar in Britain.

The five of them spoke Uyghur, a variety of Mongolian, more closely related to Turkish than anything heard elsewhere in China. The language might well have made more sense to Genghis Khan. Above all it was a language which Zhou Man reckoned would be very difficult to understand in a coded email, even if the opposition could crack the primary cypher. In his studies at Beijing University, Admiral Zhou had learnt how the United States would recruit Indian speakers for its coded military communications. It was an attractive idea. The Navajo language had been used among America's Navajo marines as a code the Japanese could not break. Meskwaki was used to confuse the Germans in North Africa, just as Choctaw was used in World War One. Admiral Zhou had decided to do something similar. He took the view that a rare and difficult language such as Uyghur was ideal for his espionage purposes.

The Flying Dragon restaurant was an easy bicycle ride from the Scotstoun shipyard on the banks of the Clyde. Its five residents took carefully-chosen jobs there such as fork-lift truck drivers and general labourers, jobs which enabled them to observe most of what was happening. The first of Britain's new class of Type 45 destroyers was being built at the yard and Admiral Zhou wanted to know its exact method and sequence of construction.

The Royal Navy's Type 45's were not being built by the usual method of first laying down a keel then assembling a hull on it bit by bit. Instead they used a technique first seen on the Type 23 frigates called block construction. This latest class of destroyers was assembled from pre-constructed modules. These reached Scotstoun, sometimes from as far afield as Portsmouth, readily fitted with electrics and plumbing. Britain's Type 45 destroyer was expected to be the most advanced warship in the world and was costing the British taxpayer a fortune.

Much useful information had already been passed to Beijing. The admiral knew the specification and equipment of the large boat-building shed. He already knew the technical equipment of the ship in considerable detail. Iqo Zontang had been recruited for his skill at discovering what was on computers. A vital element of the admiral's plan was to find out exactly how the destroyer was being assembled by the British, a section at a time. It could save many months of trial and error in China's Dalian shipyards. The five Dzungar spies were working to a practised routine. Many plans of detailed components of the Type 45 had already been sent to Zhou Man's team, disguised as assembly instructions for flat-pack furniture. It was not immediately apparent what such drawings depicted and that was vital to efficient espionage.

Companies such as IKEA bought huge quantities of flat-pack furniture from China for onward sale in European markets. Their multinational business required pictorial instructions to be included with the flat-packs and these instruction leaflets were shipped from Europe in bulk. By avoiding written language and using diagrams instead, in principle they could be understood in every country where the flat-packs were sold. Whether they could be properly understood in any of them was a frequent bone of contention. No matter. Large consignments of such unexceptional literature being shipped from Europe to China were most unlikely to arouse suspicion.

None of the furniture companies ever had much chance to examine what was in the consignments of instruction leaflets anyway. Well-trained Chinese packers knew how to insert material which had certainly not originated from the leaflet printers. This additional material had been prepared instead by a small team of experienced Chinese engineering draughtsmen ostensibly working at a Glasgow design studio. They reckoned that if the inserted diagrams looked sufficiently ordinary, no-one would bother to examine them all that closely. Information about many critical components on a Type 45 had already reached the admiral's team in Beijing by such means.

Meanwhile coded reports about shipyard activity were transmitted each day from the Flying Dragon's Mah-Jong Club. Its computers contained a programme which converted an already difficult language into a near-impenetrable cypher. The Zizhiku brothers, father and son Turku and Iqo Zontang were all well paid. Their modest pay packets at the shipyard in Glasgow - modest by Scottish standards, anyway - were being quadrupled. Over the two years Zhou Man permitted each spy to remain on station they would accumulate a sizeable nest-egg by the time they returned to China.

It was Zhou's policy to keep his team of watchers in Scotland rotating steadily. They were each required to stay long enough to understand what was going on at the shipyard, but not long enough to integrate into the local community. Well before they ever left Beijing all of them were coached on how to live among the Scots and other nationalities at the shipyard without becoming too friendly.

Although all five of them had more than a smattering of English when required, it was politic to converse most of the time in Uyghur. The restaurant Cantonese from Hong Kong, even, could not understand a single word of that and rather left the five Dzungars to their own devices. That was exactly what Admiral Zhou Man wanted.

* * * * *

Doyle's Restaurant, Sydney Harbour

THE HARBOUR FERRY to Watson's Bay departed from Wharf Four at Sydney's Circular Quay. It made three stops en route and the journey took 25 minutes. Lieutenant Warwick Sydenham of the Royal Australian Navy had arranged to meet Captain William Boyce for a late lunch. Appropriately the senior officer had chosen to eat at Doyle's restaurant on the Sydney Harbour waterfront. For over a century it had been one of the most popular and probably the best-known seafood restaurants around Australia's pioneering city. Where better for two officers from the Royal Australian Navy to exchange military confidences?

The retired captain was an old shipmate of Warwick Sydenham Senior and he had known Warwick Junior almost all his life. He reckoned now was the right juncture in the career of his shipmate's offspring to put him in the picture. He needed to understand both the possibilities and the shortcomings of the Royal Australian Navy. Bill Boyce had requested, and obtained, a secluded table beyond the earshot of other diners. Even half-way through a fine bottle of Hunter Valley pinot noir, the well-seasoned old salt was already in his element. He was waxing lyrically. His lyrics, to a familiar melody of financial constraint, were those of well-honed naval insight with a traditional refrain about chronic political myopia.

"The silly bastards have all forgotten why we need a navy, Warwick. They choose to overlook the fact the Japanese actually shelled Darwin in the Second World War. We were brilliant in the Battle of the Coral Sea, but dammit that was in May 1942, now over sixty years ago. Today they turn a political blind eye to naval power. Yet Australia depends on its overseas trade more than ever and that means command of our seas. I tell you, young Warwick, it's not exactly rocket science."

Warwick Sydenham pondered. His personal experience in the Australian Navy so far had been really rather encouraging. "I can understand your feelings, Bill but today we still have the most powerful navy in the Southern Hemisphere. Let's not lose sight of that either, before we beat ourselves up totally."

"Ah yes, but just remember, Warwick, so far you've personally had a golden career in a ramshackle enterprise. You went to one of Australia's top private schools. That's hardly the norm in the Navy. You then went to university, that's not the norm either. You were packed off to Dartmouth naval college in England. It really doesn't get much better than that, believe me. You were posted on an Anzac almost straight away, virtually as new as it came out of the box. That's jumping straight into one of the best seagoing jobs the Australian navy has to offer. But let's not kid ourselves it's all like that, because it isn't.

"We need to take a leaf out of the Brit's military manual. The poms might not be as good as Australians at cricket or rugby, but they are a whole lot better than us when it comes to running a navy. In

Britain their Royal Navy has always been the senior service, with tremendous kudos and respect. You must have seen that for yourself at Dartmouth and probably in your fleet time in England afterwards.

"Here in Oz you will discover, if you haven't discovered already, that the Royal Australian Navy always plays second fiddle to the army. I'm quite sure your father told you that. Complete opposite of London. It gets starved of funds. The Anzac frigate you served on is a pretty good piece of kit, or they will be when we've finished building them, but let's keep that in perspective. Okay, we are going to have ten if you count the New Zealand ships as well, but they're still only frigates."

Bill Boyce knew about naval power and the facts about world navies were at his fingertips. All told there were about twenty aircraft carriers, mainly American. There were just thirty or so heavy cruisers, shared between the Americans and the Russians. There were about fifty ballistic missile submarines in the world and twice that number of nuclear attack submarines.

Stabbing his index finger on the table in emphasis, Bill Boyce went on: "Warwick, the salient point is this. We have nothing, absolutely nothing in the Australian Navy which comes anywhere near that heavyweight class. They're right out of our league. So let's come down a notch or two and talk about destroyers." The discussion already required a second bottle of wine, liberally poured by Bill Boyce before resuming his theme. Analysing the many shortcomings of the Australian navy was very thirsty work.

"Remember, Warwick, I do know the navies of the Pacific. It was my job for long enough. Everyone else seems to be expanding. Our navy is on the decline. So let's start with the basics. Take the Japanese. They've been building destroyers ever since their economic boom in the 1970s. They've at least forty-five of them in their so-called Self-Defence Fleet and although some of them are starting to leak at the joints, their latest Takanami class are state-of-the-art and they've already

Bill Boyce

got five." From memory Bill Boyce ran through the Chinese navy's strength in destroyers; the fifteen-strong Luda Class, the four massive Kee-Lungs built by the Americans. He counted off three newer classes all around 6,000 tons. "Their Luyang Class only came into service last year and they are state-of-the-art too."

He next turned to South Korea with its ten home-built destroyers and a more advanced class already in the pipeline. "I'm not sure whose allies any of them would be when push came to shove, but that tots up to about seventy destroyers just on this western side of the Pacific. This is not exactly a demilitarised zone. Are you still sitting comfortably?

But then there are the Russians. They are quite different, at least they are fellow Europeans. They have a large fleet based in Vladivostok, and we do share with them some definite concern over the intentions of the Islamic world. You could draw a few crumbs of encouragement from that. They have assisted the Indian Navy, which is a very positive move, but they are a very long way to the north. I agree the Indians have the three modern Delhi Class destroyers they've built in the last ten years and they're pretty big too. So at least there's at least one other Commonwealth presence in the Indian Ocean, but it hardly constitutes a full-size maritime police force."

Bill Boyce refrained from making the obvious point. As Warwick and he both knew, the Australian navy did not possess a single destroyer. Bill found this a disgrace. In the retired Captain's view, it was not the job of politicians to design warships for navies, or to say how many ships would be needed, or to tell the professional sailors how to carry out a mission. Such decisions should be left to the naval professionals who knew what was what.

Captain Bill Boyce was an old sea dog. His recital of Australia's naval severe limitations was deliberate. He wanted a younger ally to continue his long-standing battle in Canberra and Sydney. Warwick Sydenham was his best hope for the future. "A country's military works best when its politicians keep to the things they are supposed to be good at; assessing the global situation and working out what the overall challenges and threats are likely to be. Then they tell the military the challenge, but leave us to work out what assets we need to respond. In my view, the bastards have got that all wrong here in Australia."

To Bill Boyce it was a matter of geography. Australia was one of the few major countries in the world with potential naval challenges on two oceanic coastlines, arguably three. "For deep sea naval challenges, even the Brits only ever needed to watch seas to their west and perhaps to their north. Nowadays they have friendly nations in most directions but it was not always so. They have been facing naval challenges since the Spanish Armada over four hundred years ago, arguably since the Vikings arrived over six hundred years before that. Since long before Captain Cook they have never doubted the need for a first class navy. Here in Australia we no longer see the need.

Now it was submarines which Bill Boyce had in his sights. "We've been building the Collins Class since the 1990s and the latest was commissioned only a couple of years ago. But we can't man them, they've been plagued by problems. At the end of the day they may be big but they are still diesel-electric. And they shoot nothing larger than torpedoes. That's no way to run a navy.

That raises the next issue. Who are our potential friends and who are our potential enemies? Who can we rely on if things start to heat up? The Americans? Rather you than me. Look what they did to the Brits and the French over Suez: dumped them straight in it. So much for their NATO alliance. Then they stood back and merely observed while the Brits threw the Argies out of the Falklands, no matter how many American desk admirals were whistling Rule Britannia or singing like Rod Stewart around the corridors of the Pentagon or Norfolk, Virginia. The retired captain had a long memory and he was not too sure about the British either. "They're a somewhat better bet, but even then, they rather dumped us in it when they pulled out everything East of Suez in the late 1960s. Six years later they doubled the punishment by joining the Common Market, as it was at the time and abandoned the old system of Commonwealth Preference. We caught it both ways and Australia was rather left to its own devices. You should have heard your father on that subject."

Warwick Sydenham had indeed listened to his father on that very subject on a number of occasions. Bill Boyce had a particular habit of emphasising his points by staring intently across the water at Sydney, tilting a wine glass toward the metropolis and squinting through the refractions it created, rotating it gently as he did so. This method of contemplation could not be performed satisfactorily with an empty glass; the refraction did not work properly.

With his absent-minded lenticular experimentation in full swing Bill Boyce continued his peroration. "To be fair, the Pacific has never really been of prime concern to the British anyway. They have always had their work cut out in the Mediterranean and the North Atlantic, particularly in the Cold War.

"They rather left the Pacific alone. It has not been a real theatre of conflict or confrontation since the Japanese were defeated in 1945, so they leave it to us. You could say we should be flattered but given the size of the ocean, even just our western corner of it, I think that is being a trifle optimistic. The New Zealanders are our closest allies, sure, but their navy is no great shakes either."

"The Indian Ocean? Until now it's been peaceful enough, but of course nature abhors a vacuum and so does military strength. Just you watch the Indian Ocean. Only last week, I'm sure you read, a shipping line in Hong Kong handed over about three hundred thousand dollars to the Mombasa representatives of some Somali pirates, just to release one of their natural gas tankers, the suitably-named Feisty Gas. It was time to replenish their glasses. Again. Bill Boyce paid scant attention to his medical advisers. "If the Somalis can get away with that kind of piracy once, you can bet there will be plenty more of it. Even Caribbean piracy only died out in the 1800s. By then the British navy had been fighting the pirates with guns blazing and it still took them the best part of two hundred years. Things were simpler then. Nowadays any modern warship chasing pirates off the Somali coast would be swamped with diplomatic paperwork long before it even fired its first shot."

Bill Boyce doubted whether the problems in the Indian Ocean would be confined to piracy. The Indians were already alert to a wider challenge. They now had an aircraft carrier, admittedly about fifty years old and obtained secondhand from the British. The Thai navy had a pocket aircraft carrier built for it by the Spanish less than ten years earlier. There's hardly any naval strength in Africa worth spitting on any more and, apart from India, that just leaves a bunch of Islamic countries and Singapore. Militarily, from our point of view the Indian Ocean is has to be seen as completely wide open."

Warwick Sydenham had been listening to his father's old shipmate in silence, as he worked his way through a further supply of soft-shell crabs. The restaurant was right on the beach, looking almost due west into Sydney harbour. The late Summer sun was gradually swinging round from the north. If they stayed talking long enough it would be pointing just about straight toward them, illuminating the skyscrapers of central Sydney in perfect silhouette. The pattern refracted perfectly through a glass. Darkly or otherwise, the city of Sydney was a very beautiful place.

Captain William Boyce was the voice of naval experience and certainly knew his ships. Warwick was thirty-two years old and had been in the navy for almost a decade. He had served on a modern frigate as a junior officer. He had done a couple of postings driving a desk at fleet headquarters, Pott's Point right here in Sydney Harbour. He had served on a Paluma Class survey ship in the shallow northern waters, done a liaison job with the New Zealand Defence Force and a couple of staff courses. He was learning his trade. The real agenda of the lunch with Bill Boyce, so far undeclared, was what Warwick should seek to do next. "That all sounds devastatingly practical and rather depressing, Bill, but let me ask two questions. What sort of navy should Australia have and what should I be trying to do in it?"

"Warwick, as to the first part, we need to recognise what we are up against. We need to be able to defend our home waters and your guess is as good as mine how far offshore that extends. Arguably, they extend five thousand miles west of Perth right to the shores of Africa. As said, there's not much help from the other end. Even if the Southern Ocean is off-limits to most, we also need to think carefully about what we and the New Zealanders, will be up against here in the western Pacific. Who will be our friends and how far can we rely on them.

"I would always err on the side of caution and that should mean a fleet of medium to large destroyers which pack a lot of firepower. Again, we have a lot of islands to our north, they could cause trouble at any time and that calls for amphibious landing craft. We might need to land Australian marines in any one of a hundred different locations with all their kit and we would need to do it quickly as a kind of pan Pacific fire brigade. This is the most powerful country in the region.

"The Brits have built themselves a couple of beauties, largest of their kind in the world. Hardly surprisingly the first is called Albion and the second is called Bulwark. The newest big ships in the Royal Navy. They can each land a complete Marine force, complete with several Challenger tanks if need be. That adds up to one very superior fire extinguisher. Those ships are exactly what we need here in Australia.

"And on top of that, I think we need to do what the Brits do and run a small fleet of nuclear submarines, ships which could pack a very large punch indeed, a nuclear deterrent in fact. It kept the peace, remarkably so, in the NATO theatre when that was important.

"The Russians and NATO have chased one another's nuclear submarines around in circles for about thirty years but they never in fact fired a shot in anger. Almost looks like a gentlemen's agreement. But a fleet like the British have - half that size would do - would also put us on a much more equal footing with the Americans, just as it does for the Brits. You then have some chips to play at the table. That's leverage worth having in all sorts of places - military, political and diplomatic. You are suddenly treated as important at the United Nations."

Warwick Sydenham looked across at his dinner companion with palpable respect. This candour was a revelation: no serving senior officer had ever spoken to him like that before. He contemplated the career prospects in an under-resourced service. "Tell me, Bill, why did you never make it to the top in the Navy? Why just captain - why never commodore or even admiral?"

"Warwick, we don't even have a full admiral running the entire Royal Australian Navy. The last admiral was Chief of the Defence Force, Chris Barrie, and he retired nearly three years ago. Our top purely naval man is a vice-admiral. As for me and my career, I tend to speak my mind far too freely. I mean what I say and I say what I mean. That doesn't go down too well in Canberra. Too many people in the defence business regard me more as a military irritant than as a military asset and I often wonder how I made it even as far as captain.

"As to you, my friend, you have reached the stage in your naval career where you should benefit from and contribute to, the wider picture. It's all very well everyone singing about Australians being young and free and rejoicing in the prospect, but ultimately to keep things that way Australia is going to depend on people like you.

I am in no position to pull strings formally but I still do know a lot of people. I think it's about time you were posted into naval intelligence." Bill Boyce was not a prophet. He could hardly know that within less than ten years everything he had said to Warwick Sydenham would come to fruition. Even less could he know that the future Commander Sydenham would be in the very the thick of it, or that his homily on strengthening the Australian navy would be the trigger. Least of all could he know that by then, he himself would be dead. Fortunately his naval tour de force over soft-shell crabs and fine Australian wine at Doyle's would echo in Warwick's mind for many years to come. As the country's national anthem had it; "With courage, let us all combine to advance Australia fair." Commander Warwick Sydenham of the Royal Australian Navy would need every ounce of that.

*   *   *   *   *

West London

DR CHRISTOPHER CUNNINGHAM watched the crowds passing through the arrivals gate at Heathrow airport. It should not be too difficult to spot Martin Barraclough, a tall and balding man he had known for years. Carrying only a large black briefcase, Martin was one of the first passengers off the flight from Tel Aviv. He shook Christopher warmly by the hand, glad to be home. Dr Cunningham looked curiously at the briefcase. He knew it contained a crucial piece of equipment which could transform their company's fortunes.

The two men were the two senior scientists of the Sharava Corporation. Theirs was a deliberately obscure company which developed and manufactured computer software for, well, just about anyone who could afford it and who actually understood what the product could do. The global customer-base of Sharava Corporation was not a large one.

Even fewer people knew where the company was based. Formally it was registered in Willemstad, capital of the former Dutch Antilles colony of Curacao, an island at the southern end of the West

Indian archipelago. Sharava Corporation was only visible to the world at large through its technical sales offices in Dubai, Geneva, Hong Kong, Willemstad and London and through its discreet stands at international exhibitions of military hardware. Its working language was always English, as were all its manuals. However its prices were always denominated in Swiss Francs and its name had been derived from the Sanskrit word for 'arrow'.

There was little more to be learnt from investigating the ownership of Sharava either. Any research into its shareholder register merely exposed a string of nominee holdings scattered across the globe, none of them apparently having a controlling interest. The nominee holdings were also totally opaque, a string of unhelpful names generated by computers, rather like the names of Japanese cars. At Sharava Corporation, calculated obscurity and total anonymity were paramount at every stage.

The real operational headquarters of Sharava Corporation was buried in an unmarked London technical centre, one apparently called 'Reception'. Its visible postal address was just a box number in its office in Geneva, which forwarded mail to another unhelpful box number in Great Britain. Sharava's security was complicated, deliberately so.

The company was actually located in Park Royal, a sprawling industrial estate around the M40, the London to Oxford motorway. Sharava did business with equally discreet customers in many countries and it radiated a carefully-nurtured image of political and global neutrality. Neither its multinational name nor its multinational style gave any clues about its domicile.

Everything about Sharava Corporation was calculated to show it owed allegiance to no-one, that it was only interested in its improving its profit and loss account. The skeletal company returns filed in Willemstad revealed a consistent but far from excessive flow of profits. This, too, was deliberately ordinary. Sharava's ultimate paymasters were wizards of the inconspicuous, of the unexciting and of the boringly routine. Christopher Cunningham's Mercedes drove along the M4 to Junction one, where he then turned north onto the A406 towards Ealing. The traffic was heavy and the journey took about forty-five minutes. This was an important day for both men. His companion had in his briefcase the patent software drives for the Bijali Encoder, named after the Hindi word for lightning.

The Bijali was a device designed in Israel which converted a huge volume of data into an almost instantaneous bolt of transmission. The data was highly encrypted. Its code depended on a prime number with over 10,000 digits and was virtually unbreakable. To any untutored ear, when the Bijali worked its magic it sounded like a transmission blip of momentary interference. Yet it had in that instant transmitted more data than had been needed to drive an Apollo spacecraft for a whole day.

Among various other civilian computer systems, the anonymous Sharava Corporation also designed tracking and fire control systems to be used in the world's most advanced warships. The company prided itself on its computer software being the most sophisticated in existence. The systems were extremely expensive but, surprisingly, Britain's Ministry of Defence took a fairly relaxed view about the permitted customers.

Unknown to anyone at Sharava save its founders, Christopher Cunningham and Martin Barraclough, the company's naval tracking and fire contol system had been built from the outset to contain an undetectable spy. The device being imported from Israel today was the critical component which would make that spy technology effective. Shavara's software for warship operations kept a full log of all military information and activity as it happened. There was nothing unusual about that. An electronic record of operations room activity was needed for subsequent analysis, just like the black box flight recorder on an aircraft. However the Bijali device meant that all that military information could be sent, undetectably and instantaneously, somewhere else. Communications away from the warship would be simplicity itself. All ships were in continuous communication with satellites anyway for the benefit of their Global Positioning System, GPS. The Bijali gizmo meant that a complete record of military information could now hitch a ride into the sky and back down to earth to be analysed by more Sharava technology.

From now on all Sharava's tracking and guidance systems would contain the Bijali, but none of them would be operative. Only two people, Christopher Cunningham and Martin Barraclough, would have the electronic codes needed to activate the electronic spy. And they would only do that if a customer paid them to do so. And the price would be high. And that customer would never be the same who had bought the original Sharava tracking and fire control system for their warship in the first place.

"How did you get on with the guys in Tel Aviv?" asked Chris Cunningham. "Pretty well." replied his companion. "I knew Moshe Davis well enough when were at Durham together and we have kept in touch ever since. I think he was pretty pleased to discover that after all these years I am working for a company which could become a customer of his, one that pays instantly through a bank account in Switzerland. Good honest Jew that he is, he does prefer to see cash on the nail. I like doing business with him: you always know where you stand with Moshe. Not only that, he really knows his stuff. He never gives you any bullshit. Always straight to the point."

"Exactly how curious was he about our intended use for his Bijali?" Martin's boss was already wondering about security. "Not much at all. It made perfect sense to him to be told we are developing a new system for the corporate treasurers of big multinationals to keep real-time track of their company funds around the world." Christopher Cunningham had spent quite a long time wondering what the most innocuous cover story could be for Sharava's interest in Bijali. Preferably it would be a strictly commercial use. Heaven forbid it should be a military one. As he now explained to Martin Barraclough, "Corporate treasurers have a perfectly plausible use for the device, the sort of thing Moshe's company had in mind when they developed it, a use which could not be further removed from anything to do with defence. And of course once the Bijali is suitably buried in our operations room software no-one, not even Moshe Davis, will know whether it is in there or not."

*   *   *   *   *

Saudi Foreign Ministry, Riyadh

IT WAS THE HOTTEST TIME of day in the hottest month of the year. The air conditioning was going full blast as outside temperatures reached well above the heat of the human body. A group of senior government officials, Dr Malik Khalifa among them, sipped fruit juice as they watched a television showing some horrific events as they unfolded that day in London.

Little more than an hour earlier, at about 8.50am London time, 11.50am Riyadh time, three suicide bombers had exploded devices on the London underground. As it later emerged, Mohammad Sidique Khan, aged 30 and of Pakistani extraction, had exploded his bomb as his Paddington-bound train left Edgware Road station. He immediately killed seven people including himself. Shehzad Tanweer, aged 22 and also of Pakistani descent, exploded his bomb travelling eastwards on the same Metropolitan Line. It went off between Liverpool Street and Aldgate, killing eight people including himself.

Both men, Mohammad Sidique Khan and Shehzad Tanweer, had lived in the north of England, in Leeds. The first had worked as a mentor in a primary school and left behind a wife and child. The second still lived with his parents in a fish and chip shop. Germaine Lindsay had been born in Jamaica and exploded his bomb on the Piccadilly Line between King's Cross and Russell Square. Like the other two trains it had passed through King's Cross-St Pancras station only minutes before the blast. In the restricted space of the deep tube line, Lindsay's bomb killed 27 people including himself. Aged just 19, he had lived in Aylesbury Buckinghamshire with his pregnant wife and young son.

Dr Malik Khalifa watched the television in horror. In his own late twenties he had served in London as a junior diplomat and knew all these places well. Russell Square was the station for much of London university and the British Museum. That was where he had spent many hours studying the great cultural roots of classical Islamic philosophy. Sometimes he wondered whether, along with the British Library, the Museum was his favourite place on the entire planet. In due course it emerged that the bomber who exploded his device at Edgware Road had virtually travelled beneath the Library.

The London outrages were far more personal to him than to many of the other men standing around him at the foreign ministry. At that stage no-one knew the exact cause of the three explosions, let alone the identity of the suicide bombers, but he could make an intelligent guess. Then came reports of a fourth explosion on a bus in Tavistock Square almost an hour after the others. Later it transpired that the suicide bomber had been Hasib Hussain, also of Pakistani descent, also from Leeds. The double-decker bus in the open air had not been as confined as the underground trains, but Hussain's bomb still killed fourteen people including himself. In the space of less than an hour some fifty-two innocent Londoners, most of them simply on their way to work, had died instantly. Many more had been injured.

Less than four years after suicide pilots had supposedly flown their hijacked planes into buildings in New York and Washington, it was not difficult to see a connection. The London bombings had all the apparent hallmarks of a bid for worldwide publicity by Al-Qaeda and its leader Osama bin Laden. He had deliberately organised bombings and murderous carnage in three of the most powerful cities of the western world. And Dr Malik Khalifa had in his overseas diplomatic career served in all of them. The foreign ministry complex of Saudi Arabia is one of Riyadh's modern architectural landmarks. It occupies its own island site at the junction of An Nasiriyah Street and the King Saud Road and is surrounded on three sides by groves of carefully-tended trees in an arid and naturally treeless land. It was a natural place for government officials, diplomats and ministers to gather on dramatic and appalling occasions such as this.

A young Saudi official standing next to Malik seemed almost excited. "That will teach them. The West cannot look down on Islam any more. We are the masters now. We have shown today we can take the holy war to anywhere in the world."

"And what war is that, my young friend?" asked Malik Khalifa. "Have we actually declared war on the United Kingdom? Did I somehow miss an official announcement? Have you ever worked out who our real allies are? Who are our potential foes?"

"God does not require a formal declaration of war, Dr Khalifa. Allah does not deal in scraps of diplomatic paper. The Prophet himself declared war on the infidel and we are simply obeying his orders. It has been our struggle for centuries and it is not finished yet." The young Saudi official seemed unconcerned that the perpetrators of the London bombings were Al-Qaeda terrorists.

"So in your view these terrorists led by Osama bin Laden are just some irregulars serving with the Saudi military, are they?" Malik Khalifa's hoped his irony would not be lost on his young and enthusiastic compatriot and told his companion to watch his tongue. Talking about 'we' meant the Kingdom of Saudi Arabia.

"Perhaps when you have served overseas yourself, when you

have seen the world, when you have come to understand the world a little better, you will realise the sheer stupidity of what you have just said." The young Saudi was unrepentant. Apparently it was Dr Khalifa who misunderstood. He himself had been brought up a good Moslem like his father and grandfathers before him. He had watched how the godless materialists of the West had raped this planet. He had seen depravity, alcohol-fuelled excesses, extravagant waste of the world's resources. "Is it our destiny merely to follow in their footsteps? Is that how our religion, our morals, our culture would have us all behave?"

"Young man, you are of course entitled to your doubts about the culture of the West, although in passing I might observe it has achieved a greatness far beyond anything we ever did even at the height of our Caliphate. Have you ever flown out of Riyadh airport? Just how many of those jet aircraft were designed, or built, anywhere in the Arab world? Would you rather the Moslem was known around the world as someone who hijacks such aircraft and uses them as flying bombs to destroy the buildings of New York and Washington? Is that your idea of a superior religion? Is that really what the Prophet taught us to do?" Malik Khalifa could sense his opposite number was beginning to wilt.

"Tell me, do you honestly believe there has never been any blood on our hands, never been any waste or depravity in our past? Did you ever watch wealthy young Saudis jousting with American-built Cadillacs out in the desert? Would that be your idea of teaching the materialist Americans a lesson they will never forget? Do you honestly believe women deserve the degrading treatment we give them in Saudi Arabia? Did not the Prophet teach that all human beings are equal?"

The young diplomat did not recognise a voice of experience. He could not understand how Malik Khalifa had risen so high in the Saudi diplomatic service. He spoke his mind too freely. "So what would you have us all do, Dr Khalifa? Simply roll over and let the West run the entire world in its own way?" Malik Khalifa knew what he should do.

His mission had been set by his prime minister. It was to build diplomatic bridges with other countries, especially in the Islamic world. "We may all share the same religion but we are nowhere near a commonwealth of like-minded nations. There is no equivalent in Islam of the Vatican, or even the international leadership of Anglican Christians by their Archbishop of Canterbury." The young Saudi looked blank at the mention of names and institutions which only appeared in foreign newspaper articles he never bothered to read.

"And that is our great weakness, a weakness you might care to ponder before you go much further in your career. Seen from afar we look more like an ill-disciplined rabble lurking in some worthless desert than an ordered gathering of the great and the good. You talk about the Prophet. He wanted to unite the world, not to destroy it, not to smash it to pieces like Osama bin Laden."

To Malik, terrorism was certainly not the true way of Islam, although he often despaired that too many people in high places thought it was. "That is the fundamental dilemma we face. Bin Laden may think he is in his natural element, surrounding himself with death and destruction but somehow never detonating a suicide bomb himself. In the West that would be considered the mark of the coward. Its military officers are expected to lead from the front. They are expected to expose themselves to the same dangers as their soldiers, just as it was the great Islamic armies of the past.

Osama bin Laden was no great hero. "He leads his pathetic bombers from thousands of kilometres away, using a mobile phone. Never for him the certain prospect of being blown to smithereens in pursuit of some contrived holy war. That is a bloody fate he saves exclusively for his brainless and eminently disposable infantry foot soldiers, fobbing each of them off with some absurd promise of seventy-two virgins to care for their every whim in an early afterlife.

"Even at its very worst when the West used its infantry as

cannon fodder, at least it still giving them a fair chance of surviving the conflict. In the name of Islam, bin Laden now uses his infantry as the ammunition, giving not a single one of them the merest prospect of surviving their one and only experience of waging war. Every last one of them is guaranteed instant death the second they enter battle. Like Japanese kamikaze pilots in the second world war, every one of them is instantly reduced to a few scraps of mincemeat or even worse. Have you the vaguest idea just how idiotic, inhuman and cowardly that Islamic military compact sounds to the rest of the world?" The young man shook his head in total incomprehension.

For Malik Khalifa the terrorists were painting a terrible picture of fanatical madmen, for all the world to observe, as the frontline troops of Islam. "He might believe those bombs in London strengthen his cause and there even might be a few men in this very room who actually agree with him. But in the eyes of the world at large Osama bin Laden has set the cause of true Islam even further back from civilised acceptability. The only lesson he is teaching anyone and everyone is that a devout Moslem should be utterly beneath their contempt."

Dr Malik Khalifa realised he was rubbing salt in a wound. He was also creating some enemies. He nodded to the young diplomat and turned away from the television. He looked out of the window at the mosques and government buildings of central Riyadh. The difficulties of his global mission were increasing with every outrage perpetrated by Islamic terrorism. He was seeking to build diplomatic bridges with moderate Islamic countries such as Turkey or Malaysia. The alternative as he saw it was an axis of violence and manic corruption. That meant countries such as Libya, a nation led by a diplomatic gadfly called Muammar Gaddafi, a man who supported global terrorism, yet still sought to win back his international respectability. The Libyan colonel was the Janus of North Africa, hoping his great wealth from oil could buy him the ability to face both ways at once. The contradictions expected of his work concerned Malik Khalifa more as each day passed. The international respectability he sought was not in his gift, nor even that of King Fahd. It was not helped by the views of zealous young diplomats either. Global credibility was something that had to be earned and that was a very long journey down a very hard road. At best Dr Khalifa was the guide on behalf of his country and perhaps on rare occasion he might even be its policeman. But he could not drive every vehicle on the road all by himself. Nor could anyone.

* * * * *

The Peak, Hong Kong

ADMIRAL ZHOU MAN had not visited Hong Kong before. His flight from Beijing landed at Chek Lap Kok airport, an expanse of international commerce which had opened just seven years previously. According to the Guinness Book of Records the airport had been the most expensive ever, costing twenty billion US dollars. Construction had been started by the British and completed under Chinese control after the handover in 1997.

There was much self-congratulation about Chek Lap Kok to be found in the in-flight magazine of Air China. With great pride the writers explained how it had grown to become the world's second busiest cargo airport, handling more freight than Shanghai's Pudong International and London's Heathrow combined. The Chinese authorities were extremely proud of that. It was evidence that Hong Kong's economic miracle had barely faltered following the political handover by the British in 1997, as so many Westerners and even local residents had feared it might.

It was proof that China was leading the world. Yet Zhou Man saw little of the airport's ceaseless cargo activity as he passed rapidly through the huge passenger terminal building, also proudly described as the world's largest when it was built, eventually to find vice-premier Liu Fun's chauffeur waiting for him in the arrivals hall.

Nor had Zhou Man ever ridden in a Rolls-Royce before. Silently and effortlessly it took the North Lantau highway, swung into the Tsing Sha highway, then under the Nam Wan tunnel towards Kowloon. "All these new roads built since British time." the chauffeur said with obvious pride. As a Cantonese he did not speak the mandarin of the Admiral, nor anything like it, so resorted to his Hongkonger's variant of English. "In British time, this part of Kowloon no good place. Soon we have tallest hotel in world on new land, all built in Chinese time." The post-1997 propaganda machine powered by Beijing had been working hard.

The driver continued his well-rehearsed patter for the journey from the airport into the centre of town. Zhou Man looked across to Kowloon's notorious congested apartment blocks near the old Kowloon waterfront. Not the best legacy of the British. In their day they could boast the highest density of population anywhere in the world. Researchers from the Guinness Book of Records must have had a field day in Hong Kong.

The Rolls-Royce soothed its way past shiny new apartment buildings along a new waterfront then left the Chinese mainland as it dived into the tunnel of the Western Harbour Crossing. The tunnel surfaced on more new land, a part of Hong Kong Island reclaimed from the harbour. They swung round a half circle into the old Connaught Road then ran eastwards along the island's old waterfront. This led to the long climb up Cotton Tree Drive and Magazine Gap Road to the Peak, the highest point on what the British had called Victoria Island.

Vice-premier Liu Fun's autumn retreat was a relaxing apartment on Plantation Road. In November the air up here was exceptionally clear. She welcomed the admiral courteously and proudly showed him the view. The apartment's verandah provided a panoramic vista of Hong Kong's superb harbour, the view then stretching right across the

Kowloon peninsula to hills far beyond. On the distant horizon was a conical peak which, as Liu Fun pointed out, was in true China itself.

Do you know of a British politician called Harold Macmillan?" she asked Zhou Man in her rhetorical way. The admiral was not entirely sure, but no matter. He was about to be told. "Over forty five years ago, this prime minister Macmillan made an important speech to the South African parliament in Capetown. It has been quoted a thousand times since. Harold Macmillan famously said "The wind of change is blowing through this continent. Whether we like it or not, this growth of national consciousness is a political fact".

"With all the wisdom of hindsight, Zhou Man, we know that Macmillan was signalling the end of old western colonialism in Africa, the colonialism of the nineteenth century. That all died out again in the twentieth century. In the twenty-first century, a new wind is blowing through Africa. And that wind is our Chinese wind. The Beijing Patriotic Association is taking a lead in helping that process of African revival. That is one of the main reasons I chose you for your job.

"Just look at this magnificent view. I chose this apartment because it takes me away from the political intrigues of Beijing. Had I wished I could have lived down there in mid-levels or in the government district.   But that would have defeated my purpose. Up here on the Peak I have my privacy. I have my study, my internet, my sitting room, two guest bedrooms, my servant's quarters at the back and a swimming pool. It is my chance to be almost anonymous, to live alone with just my thinking and writing.

"Many is the time I lean against this balustrade and look over Hong Kong to China beyond. I think of the millions of people crammed into the territories before me and then I think of the wide open spaces of Africa. When the British first came here in the 1840s they took this land from us by force. At the time it was little more than a backwater, its greatness long gone, merely a haven for pirates preying on the shipping of the Pearl River delta. Just as there are pirates today off the coast of Somalia.

Liu Fun recalled how the British had transformed some almost uninhabited islands into one of the greatest cities of Asia. Even the Japanese invasion of 1941 failed to halt their progress and were quick to recover after the war. "Two great bronze lions were found in a Japanese scrapyard and returned to their proper job, guarding the money in the Hong Kong and Shanghai Bank. They are there still. The local people are very suspicious about their good fortune, you should see how they celebrate Chinese New Year. This is still a great financial centre. Our own Bank of China has expanded enormously."

For Liu Fun, history was always important. It was the only way to understand the realities of the present, or find a basis for realistic plans for the future.   She was talking about the very origins of Hong Kong itself, how it grew from a small quay, the fragrant harbour, and Heung Gong was as close as the occidentals could pronounce it. "There is a new fragrance wafting over the whole territory today, Zhou Man and it is the delicious fragrance of money. Our money. Do you like my Rolls-Royce? It is my one indulgence. The great city of Hong Kong is not the only thing we may acquire from the British."

Liu Fun returned to Africa's prospects. China's new empire in that continent would be commercial, not political. "In the nineteenth century the British built the greatest empire the world has ever seen, but they built it with armies, bullets and the bible. That was their greatest mistake and in the second half of the twentieth century they had to dismantle it all once again.

"So remember your history, Admiral Zhou. At least the British must have thought the number seven was their lucky number, because they began dismantling their empire when they left India to its own devices in 1947. They completed the job when they sailed out of Hong Kong half a century later in June 1997. Their so-called treaties ended after ninety-nine years. They were never more than an unworthy lease, signed under duress, between militaristic Great Britain and the pathetic remnants of China's Qing Dynasty. It was all very proper of them, all very legalistic, but remember their Margaret Thatcher was a lawyer herself. For our part we never recognised those unequal treaties in the first place. If the British had chosen to stay, then we would have had a real problem. We could only have thrown them out by invoking treaties we did not recognise. Mrs Thatcher kindly solved the problem for us."

Liu Fun took great pride in her jigsaws of events in history and of places in geography. "The British sailed out of here on a large blue yacht, with all its flags fluttering, one built especially for their royals. They named it Britannia, the old name for England when it was just a part of the Roman empire. That was how they learnt their colonialism; the British had once been a colony themselves. After their ship sailed home to England they promptly turned it into a museum. What better epitaph could there have been to mark the end of the British empire?"

"In Africa they began dismantling their empire in the Gold Coast forty years earlier. It was most revealing. They handed power to a crook called Kwame Nkrumah who renamed it Ghana. He only survived nine years in power before being deposed, he amassed a fortune in his private banks in Switzerland of a hundred million dollars. And yet the West rewarded him for his efforts with the Nobel Peace prize. How ridiculous their sentimentality can be. Even in the money of the day, far more valuable than it is today, he was taking money out of his country and putting it in his own pocket at a rate of more than ten million dollars a year. That was far more than the Nobel Peace prize brought him, and he did it every single month he was in power.

Almost certainly he made much it from corruption in the cocoa trade. Mere cocoa; an unnecessary indulgence for the fat women of the West. The continent of Africa is full of much more valuable raw materials and remember, Zhou Man, it is also full of politicians who will sell them and who are for sale themselves. That is our Chinese interest today and how we shall build our new empire. In Liu Fun's mind the ending of western colonialism had presented a great opportunity to China. The colonial nations of Europe - the Belgians, the French, the Portuguese but most of all the British - had left their former possessions to their own devices, or rather to corrupt local potentates. The result, if not a power vacuum, was a demonstrable shortage of political competence. For forty years, the Middle Kingdom had been moving in where the United Kingdom had been moving out.

Admiral Zhou Man was still on more or less familiar territory, although his vice-premier added much detail. After admiring the view they had retreated from the verandah and were sipping a cognac served by a silent manservant. The vice-premier wanted a new kind of colonialism. "My reasoning is simple. We modern Chinese have no desire to run other countries on behalf of their inhabitants. Let them have their petty revolutions, the more the merrier. Nor have we any desire to challenge their religious beliefs. Let them believe whatever they wish, just so long as their corrupt leaders believe first and foremost in delicious money for themselves."

For Liu Fun and the Beijing Patriotic Association, there were in principle three ways to meet China's requirements. The British method of trying to take over the supplying countries and run them politically was not efficient. Another method would be to buy what China needed in world markets, but the ability of Africans to sell effectively, honestly and efficiently was almost non-existent. In her view they were just too corrupt. "So the best way forward, admiral, is to set up our own companies locally, but we do want to be invited in by the inhabitants. Otherwise it could look like neo-colonialism.

Already European companies such as de Beers or Lonrho have carved out huge niches for themselves in the mining and production of African resources. I think the time has come for them to be accompanied, taken over or even replaced by Chinese companies. If we present it wisely, we can be seen to be doing Africa a favour, a further break from its colonial past." They both smiled at the gentle irony. "The way forward is to weaken political resistance. We do not share the fervent Christianity of the Europeans with their selective moralising. Why seek to impose morality on a continent which has none of its own? More wisely we simply look to the realities. Why send a thousand missionaries, when it is far easier to send twenty container loads of machine guns? All we need do is select them from arms manufacturers all around the world and ensure there is nothing to suggest they come from China. Then we generously donate them to both sides in a conflict and leave them to get on with it.

"You can normally rely on African tribesmen to decimate one another over a decade or so. Wonderful. Another cadre of black troublemakers is buried beneath the red soil of the dark continent. In some countries we have been stupendously successful - keep that useful idiot Robert Mugabe in power in Zimbabwe for another ten years and with luck what was once one of the most advanced countries in Africa, when it was in British hands, will have been reduced once again to a wide open tribal reserve.

"Just think. We could then control it with a minimum of effort. In some cases we can probably do it just by sending a lot of Chinese chicken farmers. Much cheaper than soldiers. Treat native African leaders the right way and they will come running with their wallets wide open. They are a twenty-first century variant of what was once said of European communists. They were our Useful Idiots of the West. So we have invented the Useful Idiots of Africa."

Admiral Zhou Man was listening to a plot hatched by the Beijing Patriotic Association. It had little room for sentiment. An American called Dale Carnegie once wrote a very useful book called 'How To Win Friends And Influence People.' The vice-premier recommended it.

"One day, when I retire, I might even write a sequel. I think my version will probably follow a real western philosopher called Niccolo Machiavelli. I'm sure you will have heard about him. A very wise man. Even though he was European he at least would have approved of our strategy." The vice-premier took the machiavellian view that if an African warlord was smart enough to seize power, a supply of weapons should be sent to his opponents. Within a couple of years another despot would be deposed in another bloodbath, another gang of potential troublemakers would be eliminated. It was all very different from the friendly noises about Africa which China made in international theatres like the United Nations. China wanted African friendship in public, in private it wanted African resources.

In some places such as Kenya the locals were more resistant, traditions of the old British military surviving well. "They had a British rail route through Kenya to Uganda, but why fight over it? So in 1970 we chose to build our own railway through Tanzania to Zambia instead. Our railway can export copper. Their railway led to farms. Did you know Uganda could feed the whole of Africa if they farmed it properly? What the British can do, we can do better. It is interesting, isn't it, how Tanzania has been much more politically stable than Uganda ever since.

The Machiavellian arithmetic were simple. In principle China could afford to give every man, woman and child in black Africa a gun and invite them to shoot anyone and preferably everyone else. Given several decades of such unregulated carnage, Liu Fun argued, and the dark continent would murder its own populace eventually to be almost as lacking in population as Antarctica.

Unfortunately that method would not win many friends at the United Nations, especially when people eventually realised who was behind it. "Far better to arm the troublemakers and their enemies a few at a time. They can shoot one another well away from the gaze of journalists and photographers, in what Western media choose to call a 'civil war'. You and I both know it is really a war of extermination by proxy. I don't suppose for one moment that China is the only country supplying arms to Africa, but we are the cleverest." Admiral Zhou sipped appreciatively at his brandy. It was interesting to learn how the Beijing Patriotic Association saw the world. The vice-premier's assessment of the African opportunity was ruthless and seemed foolproof. In her rapidly expanding view the average African was not going to acquire six centuries of political sophistication in six months, or even in six years. So long as they believed they could make the greatest personal progress by killing one another, China was in business in Africa. It was in control.

Liu Fun was disdainful. "Even in the second half of the twentieth century, gorillas like Idi Amin of Uganda still thought it a military advantage not only to kill their opponents, but to eat them as well. With cannibals like that in charge of entire countries, who can blame us, the most sophisticated race the world has ever known, if we regard them and treat them as if they were animals? They deserve nothing more. Treat them as they wish to be treated."

In the vice-premier's view, twenty-first century China had an unmatched advantage over nineteenth century colonisers. Misguided Europeans had been burdened with a conscience driven by Christianity. Their first thought was to change, not ownership of mineral deposits of a country, but rather the religious beliefs of its inhabitants. "We can succeed without any such moralising nonsense, let the local baboons enjoy any religious belief system they like. So long as their leaders desire material wealth on Mondays to Saturdays, who gives even half a grain of rice which kind of songs they all prefer to sing on Sundays?"

So that was the Chinese view of Africa. Zhou Man might have guessed half of it, but even he did not realise it would be quite as ruthless. No wonder the vice-premier was so keen to strengthen naval presence in the Indian Ocean, which was fast becoming a strategic artery. Liu Fun moved swiftly on. "We have talked enough about the wind of change and about the red earth of Africa. Let us build our wisdom on my five traditional elements. So let's consider water. Now it is your turn. Tell me about navies and the so-called Indian Ocean. Admiral Zhou Man stared into his brandy and took a mental count of twenty before he spoke. It added to the solemnity and it gave him time to think. His mentor Liu Fun was hardly a woman to appreciate prolixity. Rather it was his own turn to articulate some highly rational Beijing Patriotic Association ruthlessness.

"Let's begin with those Somali pirates." Zhou Man said. "If they demonstrate anything at all, they demonstrate that western naval power is so weak they cannot even catch and eliminate a few criminals in pathetic fishing boats. We should be massively encouraged by that. The British were ruthless enough with the Pearl River pirates when they arrived here in Hong Kong. How times have changed. They are no longer ruthless, they are now merely toothless."

The admiral set out his own rules. He wanted to be able to put a warship anywhere in the Indian Ocean within less than two days. His destroyers would travel at an absolute maximum of forty kilometres an hour over long distances, anything quicker would burn too much fuel. That was almost a thousand kilometres a day. So in terms of strict geometry, a network of naval bases four thousand kilometres apart, perhaps somewhat less, would be enough to put a Chinese warship anywhere within his target time.

"We are still a long way from that and it is beyond my powers to create the military presence we need. I can only provide the assets. However I can now tell you what is required and then it is up to our government in Beijing. The British had the right answer when they created naval bases in places like Gibraltar, or Malta, or Aden or the Falkland Islands. The Americans had much the same idea when they built Pearl Harbour in Hawaii. China now needs to do the same, but in the twenty-first century we cannot do it, as the British did, by military force. We will need to do it by diplomatic stealth."

Vice-premier Liu Fun nodded. The naval logic was obvious although any political implementation would be ambitious. There were very few empty islands left. "So tell me Admiral Zhou where, exactly, do we need to make new friends?"

The admiral ticked off the countries round the ocean's coast. He assumed India would be uncooperative. It was more friendly with the Russians and the West. Sri Lanka had a superb harbour at Trincomalee which would serve China's purposes to perfection. "Perhaps we should be watching their Tamil Tigers more closely."

He dismissed Myanmar, as Burma was now called and wondered about the Islamic states of Malaysia and Indonesia. Although Malaysia had a large Chinese ethnic minority they were overseas Chinese by choice. Their homeland could not automatically count on their support. Australia was beyond reach. The best plan was to keep them quiet. They had domestic arguments about the size of their navy, which in principle should be the most powerful in the southern hemisphere. "Let's just hope they keep on arguing among themselves rather than doing anything about it. I trust our embassy knows what we want monitored and the right soothing noises to make. Let the Australians feel secure without any military might."

In the admiral's view, China's best hope for naval bases was in Africa and perhaps some link with the Moslem countries. That left the middle. Following the British technique for finding useful mid-ocean bases, he was looking closely at the French possession of Amsterdam Island. Few people had even heard of it. Apart from about thirty scientists living at a research base, it was uninhabited with no local politics. "In geographical terms it is almost ideal, but I leave that one to you. It could become our Malta or Falkland Islands, perhaps even our

Hawaii. Who can tell what its popularity will be?" Liu Fun smiled. "There is a fine precedent, Admiral Zhou Man. When the British first arrived in North America, today's city of New York was originally called New Amsterdam, but they very quickly changed that.   What an entertaining thought about your mid-ocean island: perhaps when we arrive we should announce it has now been re-named New Shanghai."

Zhou Man grinned at her parallel and moved on to the ships he needed, a fleet of twenty high technology destroyers. "Do I gather you have decided on the design of destroyer?" asked the vice-premier. She half knew the answer but was keen to be brought up to date. The admiral had the facts at his fingertips. "Next Spring, if all goes to plan, the British are launching the first of a new class of destroyer, the Type 45. I've been studying the options and their Type 45 seems by common consent to be just about state of the art. That's the ship I want."

"And how are you going to get it? You can't exactly go to a supermarket in London and buy one, can you?" Zhou Man smiled. "No I can't, but I can obtain all the plans - which I already have. My agents have been collecting those for several years. I also know the techniques of building. Another group of agents have been supplying those for two years. And of course we have the engines. So with approval from our government in Beijing I am, as of this moment, in a position to build the fleet you requested. My construction facilities are already complete. We now have all the shipbuilding sheds and will never be quite clear to anyone else what we are building inside them. For as long as it lasts, we will encourage a rumour that our new fleet will just be small ships to patrol our legitimate interests in the Yellow Sea or the Sea of Japan. That shouldn't make too many waves."

Vice-premier Fun nodded at the little joke in return and asked for the proposals in writing, in a more comprehensive form, and to be marked Top Secret. The proposals should reach her personally to ensure he obtained the right authorisation. Liu Fun then moved on.

"That's enough about water. Another element. Let's talk about fire. I gather you have already been to see our activities in Jiuquan? Jiuquan was in the remote Gobi desert, a thousand miles west of Beijing. It had virtually no population except those who ran China's huge rocket testing facility, known in the West as Shuang Cheng Tzu. In 1970 it had launched China's first earth satellite. More recently in October 2003 it had launched China's first piloted spacecraft, proof indeed of the quality of Chinese technology.

With astronaut Yang Liwei, China became the third country able to launch a man into space. Jiuquan also tested missiles, the reason Admiral Zhou Man had made the long journey. "They were a bit surprised when I told them their ground-to-air system needs a sea-to-air version as well. In fact I told them Beijing will probably require maritime versions of all their missiles. They told me they would wait until they received official authorisation and resources from Beijing, but thanked me for my advance warning. The very least I could do. BI also reminded them that maritime versions would be even more secret than land or air-based versions. They understood that as well."

Liu Fun nodded in approval. Her master plan was beginning to take shape. She now wanted to know about missile guidance hardware and software. Admiral Zhou was not quite so optimistic about that. "We have some technical problems. No matter how much fire you can squirt out of one end of a rocket, if the other end is not entirely certain where it is supposed to be going, you haven't achieved very much. We also need to find the targets in the first place. That's quite tricky."

The vice-premier took Zhou's news without visible concern. Instead she waxed philosophical. "Ah yes. That elusive fifth element, ether, subtler than light. The core of wisdom, the base of understanding. Also the world of computer software. Leave it to me. I might even put your old girlfriend Antonia Foo onto the task. Her engine plant in Lanzhou is about to come on stream - she has done what she was asked to do. It is time for her to earn her reward. Let's see what guidance software she can buy commercially. I believe the Sharava Corporation of India has highly advanced software they would be prepared to sell to us on the right terms. And Antonia is in her element on the diplomatic circuit. It would be a pleasant change from her exile in Lanzhou."

"And now I have a small surprise for you, Admiral Zhou. Have you by any chance read a curious book called 1421? It was published three years ago, the work of a helpful British submarine captain. He had done much research into something we were vaguely aware of, the treasure fleets sent around the world by emperor Zhu Di, third emperor of our Ming dynasty. You may recall he was the Yongle emperor, the fourth son of Zhu Yuan Zhuang.

"An imaginative British naval officer has kindly brought him back into the world's limelight, almost six hundred years after he died. A remarkable public relations success, and one which is now most convenient to us. It does not matter two hoots whether it is true or not, just so long as enough people read it and believe it could be

"To begin with many people in the West dismissed it all as merely preposterous. How on earth could the uninquisitive Chinese have possibly beaten their maritime heroes such as Colombus and Magellan by a whole seventy years? The West is always much too conceited. Now our academics in Beijing reckon that sufficient of the book is true to warrant a research institute looking into its suppositions. It is all most convenient and timely.

Liu Fun gently tapped the arm of her chair, as she did so frowning at her own finger. "Perhaps we should inform the French that there may be some very interesting archaeological remains to be found on Amsterdam Island. May be. Their great leader Napoleon was always fascinated by archaeology. Let us therefore tell his modern descendants just how much China admires their cultural tradition. Not only that, Amsterdam Island is close to a key rupture in the earth's crust. That could interest us too. I think the Middle Kingdom could shortly have some very friendly and very constructive discussions with those old European colonialists from Paris."

The admiral nodded wisely, exactly as he was expected to do. With her five simple elements, vice-premier Fun had reduced her African strategy and her plans for the Indian Ocean to a classic Confucian philosophy. She had eliminated the ludicrous religious and democratic sentimentality of the West from her grand calculations. In Africa such old-fashioned moralising had failed totally. What remained was a simple architecture of economic exploitation, a construct to provide China with almost of the raw materials it needed.

So that was to be Africa's new, true function. Liu Fun's ineluctable logic could only be admired. No wonder she was regarded by her colleagues in Beijing as one of her country's most brilliant strategists. It was a privilege to work for her. Zhou Man wondered how many western politicians, bedevilled by the constant demands of uninformed democracy, would have had the freedom to do the same.

Although he had scarce understood it to begin with, the admiral was now beginning to fathom the fundamental rationale, the inmeffabloe subtelty, of the Beijing Patriotic Association. Rather like the manufactured excitement over the book 1421, it was ultimately a matter of strategic public relations. In its democratic excesses, the West was hidebound by the attenuated wisdom of its thronging, barbaric, unthinking voters. What an unrecognised asset they were to China.

On a previous occasion, and over several glasses of very fine cognac, Liu Fun had explained the underlying sense of Plato's guardians. As she saw it, the intellectual constraints imposed by western electorates could not apply to the Forbidden City. On the contrary the Beijing Patriotic Association, no matter how shadowy, no matter how deniable, was ruthlessly exploiting that remarkable advantage. At stake was the unbound admiration of those countries the West called the

Third World, admiration lavished while at the same time China was ruthlessly acquiring their bounteous raw materials in profusion. It was not so much rape, more an amorous seduction. Antonia Foo suddenly flashed into his mind. The technique was far more satisfying all round.

Zhou Man marvelled at the way his country knew precisely how to sympathise with Third World countries about the much-vaunted iniquities of the old colonial powers of Europe. Yet it simultaneously contrived to become a ruthless modern colonial power itself.

Confucius might well have approved of the duplicity. The Italian philosopher Machiavelli would certainly have done so. Today's Chinese potentates were his princes. The nomenclature might have changed but his underlying concepts were universal, eternal. There was more than one way for machiavellian countries to succeed in the material world, and it was China's good fortune that the West had failed to do so.

Today's world was full of greedy, ill-educated warlords and bullies all ripe for the taking. Machiavelli could see straight through any of them. They would become the pliable pawns of the modern China. The admiral's first-ever visit to the exciting city of Hong Kong, really a small country which despite its material success had never experienced democracy either, was indeed proving to be most instructive. Perhaps Hong Kong had succeeded simply because it had never been infected by Western sentimental philosophy, although its protestors would doubtless have none of that. The Forbidden City, on the other hand, could afford to take a more enlightened view. Or so concluded Admiral Zhou Man.

Chapter Six

The Six Ships Sail On
The Ally-Ally-Oh

Scotstoun, Glasgow

THE MOOD WAS ONE of celebration and pride. The largest warship ever built in the Scotstoun shipyard in Glasgow was about to be launched by Sophie, Countess of Wessex, wife of Prince Edward. Amid the shouts and cheers of a large crowd and with the strains of Rule Britannia played by a band, the first of the Royal Navy's D45 destroyers took to the waters of the Clyde.

HMS Daring, her pennant number D32 painted in white on her side, slid stern first into the water as was tradition on the river. The launch was timed precisely to meet the peculiarities of the tide. In the next five years, five more Type 45s would be launched from Scotstoun and from the Govan shipyards on the opposite bank. The final ship HMS Duncan, D37, launched in October 2010, was probably the last for the navy ever to be launched stern first.

They were also six of the best ships ever to enter service with Royal Navy. Building them had given a huge boost to the Scottish economy, a benefit much welcomed by the Chancellor of the Exchequer, Scotland's very own Gordon Brown who had originally approved the programme. After all, his own parliamentary constituency of Kirkaldy and Cowdenbeath was just forty miles away.

Anyone watching closely might just have noticed, standing quietly at the back of the crowd, five self-effacing Chinese. They were Dheng and Zhuang Turku, the brothers Mong and Tonghu Zizhiku and the most recent arrival, Iqo Zontang. They were celebrating a quite different achievement. Their painstaking espionage meant that everything they were watching would now be replicated to a high level of precision in north east China. Thanks to them the task facing the shipbuilders of Dalian would be simplified greatly. It was a fine example of technology transfer, one of which its inventors were wholly oblivious. Neither cheers nor shouts, just quiet smiles of satisfaction and pride adorned the normally impassive faces of the five Mongolians. The Flying Dragon restaurant in Inverness Avenue had certainly lived up to its name.

The military significance of everyone's achievements, one way or another, was spelled out the following day to the press by Commander John Woodland. He was the Royal Navy officer now charged with supervising the fitting out stages of HMS Daring. "When she comes into service in 2009, we're going to have the most a©dvanced warship in the world. Her combat system is the cutting edge of technology. Daring will have more firepower than the combined fleet of our earlier Type 42 destroyers.

"Her main weapon, the Principal Anti-Air Missile System will monitor the airspace for hundreds of miles around the fleet she is protecting." In his thoughtfully-scripted explanation the Commander pointed to great improvements for her crew, making her a posting of choice throughout the fleet. "The old-style messes accommodating thirty or forty men have been replaced by cabins which sleep six. Each berth will have its own internet connection. Nowadays the crew can write home on their laptops and their messages can be with their loved ones within hours rather than days, as it used to be."

Quite unknown to Commander Woodland, the internet had already been used to send many thousand messages about Daring, most of them in an impenetrable code. The following morning in Beijing, Admiral Zhou Man also read the press reports from Glasgow with pride. His choice of the British destroyer on which to base his own fleet for the Indian Ocean had been vindicated. He saw to it that an accurate translation of Commander Woodland's most helpful remarks would land on several important desks in the Forbidden City.

Now was the time to begin replacing the men living above the Flying Dragon restaurant. To ensure the switch was unobtrusive, the replacement would last several months. Iqo Zontang would remain behind to instruct an incoming team and they too would be Dzungars speaking their unusual language of Uyghur.

Then father and son Turku and the brothers Zizhiku would retrace their route broadly along the old Silk Road, ancient pathway of rich merchants. They would be reunited with their families in Xinjiang. Once home they too would be rich men like the Chinese merchants of old, to be reunited with two years' most generous back pay in a Chinese bank account. Their transcontinental merchandise had not been valuable textiles, but even more valuable intelligence. In the icy calculations of Admiral Zhou Man, the five Mongolian spies had earned every single one of those yuan.

*   *   *   *   *

Lanzhou , North West China

ANTONIA FOO watched with pride as the first completed Yangtze jet engine was lifted off her production line. It came out of its cradle and was slotted onto a waiting truck without a scratch. The engine would now be taken for thorough testing. Nothing could be left to chance. Antonia's engineers had found problems with many component manufacturers around China. They had all been resolved. Her team of traveling experts, every one of them a graduate engineer in an appropriate discipline with extensive grounding in manufacturing technology, had been trained to have eagle eyes for mistakes. They were there to ensure no-one was cutting any corners.

The Yellow River Industrial Research Facility had lived up to Beijing's expectations. Its jet engines would be every bit as good as, if not better than the English Rolls-Royce Trent engines from which they had been copied. Unlike Antonia's Hongqi Mingshi car, her Yangtze jet engines exploited a peculiarly Chinese technique of badge engineering which required no licence fees to be paid.

Behind the cradle now vacated by engine number 2006001 she watched the chassis of engine 2006002. She knew it would be completed in about two weeks' time. Beyond that she could see the cradle awaiting the largest components of 2006003. She smiled with satisfaction. Her baby was born. Production would be speeded up as her assembly teams became more familiar with their tasks.

Once the testing centre confirmed the engines were performing as intended, she expected production would exceed forty a year, maybe more. Antonia Foo had shown people, some very select people, exactly what women engineers could achieve in the modern China. She thought of the many men at university she had left trailing in her wake to make it as far as she had come in her career. There was much paperwork to complete in her office, but it would have to wait. Tonight she would celebrate. Standing at her side was a visitor from Beijing, Admiral Zhou

Man. For old time's sake she went to her private bathroom and changed out of her white laboratory coat into a cheongsam. Her perfume was Parisian and seductive and when she had finished preparing herself not a hair was out of place.

As was her custom she took Man back to her house in the country, where she then put the finishing touches to their meal for two. After they had eaten, as was their other custom they spent a passionate night together in bed. It had been their preferred routine for almost ten years, on his rare yet welcome visits to Lanzhou. There were no other men in Lanzhou to arouse her interest, so when the admiral arrived in town she always made up for lost time.

Yet even Antonia Foo and Zhou Man eventually reached a point where their passions were spent and where they could start talking about their other great interest, their work. In the early hours of the morning he asked Antonia "What has Beijing told you about the future for your engines?" as he stroked her hair in a ruminative way. It was not the usual kind of question a man would ask in bed of his lover, but then Antonia Foo was certainly no ordinary lover.

Antonia switched back effortlessly into her engineer mode, just for the moment. "The first twenty or so are the aviation version. They are earmarked for a new airliner which they hope to see tested in a couple of years' time. Beijing wants to become much less dependent on Boeing or Airbus now that a modern air transport network is so vital for the health of the Chinese economy."

Admiral Zhou was more interested in engines for his warships. "Don't worry," she reassured him. "I have a team working on your marine version as well. The difference is we need to burn diesel in them, not kerosene. Just like the British. The batch from number twenty-one onwards will be mainly for you and I expect those to be rolling off the production line from the end of the year. When are you expecting to launch the first of your warships?"

Antonia Foo

The admiral was planning for about five years' time. "Just like you, I also want a period of thorough testing and assessment. Anyone can develop a prototype with mock-ups to a certain point, but after that you need the real thing. I will send a sample engine to train our teams at our maintenance facility. We will dismantle it a component at a time. So all the good work being done by your teams here will be patiently undone by my teams there. I trust you can lend me some expert engineers to make our learning processes as smooth as possible. And once we start launching the ships, our demand for engines will speed up considerably."

"How many ships is that?" she asked. "The rumours from Beijing are that it will be a huge fleet. The admiral gave her the most accurate answer he could. "To begin with I will need six ships. Anything fewer would be militarily ineffective. Beyond that I cannot speak for Beijing's plans, but I have agreed with vice-premier Liu that I will eventually need twenty ships to complete my own naval mission. They could well be planning another ten beyond that for the right customers in exchange for certain diplomatic favours. And it may be they will also adapt my design for further fleets elsewhere. Who knows? They only ever tell us what we need to know.

"If that sounds a lot, remember the Americans launched their latest Arleigh Burke class destroyer, the Gridley, back in December. That already makes fifty-one in the class and another is expected in September this year. Beijing will have taken full note of that. I don't suppose for one moment Uncle Sam will stop there. And those are big ships, over a thousand tons larger than my Advance class."

Antonia switched out of engineer mode once again. "So that's what they are all going to be called, darling. I see. Why don't you roll over this way, stop all this boring talk about other people's ships and give me another lesson in your own advance class? It's far too long since we spent time together like this. Would you perhaps kiss me again in just the same way you were kissing me before?" As each year passed,

Antonia Foo became more self-confident, more imaginative, more proficient and probably more demanding when she went to bed with a man. And so it was tonight, but there were some clouds ahead. "Do you realise this may be our last chance to be together for a very long time? Liu Fun has been talking to me as well. Like yours, my life is really just another of her little planning exercises. It now sounds as if my next job is going to be in somewhere far more desirable. I think it may thousands of kilometres away in London."

*   *   *   *   *

Royal Navy Fleet Headquarters, Northwood

THE DRIVE down the M4 from Oxford to Fleet Headquarters usually took less than an hour even at legal speeds. James Heaton had driven that route for four weekends, but this occasion had been Violaine's final few days in Oxford. Her doctoral thesis was complete and she would shortly be heading back home to Paris for good. The traffic was helpful and he returned to work in excellent time.

His advice in Paris several years ago to choose herself a new boyfriend while at Oxford University had worked. Her rapid decision had been entirely straightforward. She had chosen James Heaton of the Royal Navy, even though his travelling around the oceans as a warfare officer on a frigate meant she had seen him somewhat less often than she would have wished.

Whenever his ship returned to its home port in England he had rushed to Oxford to see her and they had spent some romantic holidays together. After twelve years in the aridity of Saudi Arabia, the sea had beckoned her also. They had been sailing on the north coast of Minorca, they had sailed in the West Indies. Their favourite island was St Lucia. To her own astonishment she had even become a trapeze expert hanging precariously over the water. In less than three years their relationship had blossomed, they had grown close. A combination of academic work she found fascinating, at a level of freedom she had not known before, of clever people around her in the university and a man she adored had made Violaine's three years at Oxford quite the happiest time of her life. She told herself that the way the Royal Navy rationed it, their time together had been more precious than ever.

Now the newly-promoted Lieutenant-Commander James Heaton was going to be based near London for months on end and Paris was less than three hours from London on Eurostar. Later the following morning, James knocked on the door of his superior officer. He had only been in the Royal Navy intelligence division, N2, for a month. By eleven that Monday morning there was already something vital to report.

"As you know, sir, we have been tracking a Russian naval group supporting the carrier Admiral Kuznetsov since they left Murmansk. There are six ships - the carrier, a cruiser, three frigates and a supply ship. So far so good; they are perfectly entitled to sail the high seas. They're a little over six days out of their home port and they're currently somewhere around 50° north, 20° west."

I can't see any immediate problem with that, Commander. It's approximately four hundred miles west of Ireland. That's just about the course I would steer myself out of the Norwegian Sea for an exercise in mid-Atlantic. Is there anything else?"

"Yes sir, there is." James Heaton replied. "It's what they've done next which is rather unusual. We've been watching them over the weekend. They've turned just about due east and seem to be heading straight for the British Isles. That's a new one on us. And they've slowed down. Previously they were rattling along at the best part of twenty knots. It's now down to about ten."

"Well I still don't see anything to worry about. What do you want me to do about it?" James Heaton looked at his senior officer with a keen eye. "Sir, I would be happier if we could send a frigate from

Devonport just to shadow them. See what they're up to. I suppose if there is one anywhere near, we could even send a nuclear sub and take one or two periscope photographs just to show we are on the ball. In fact just do something to let the world that we know what the Russians are up to nowadays."

"I'm none too sure about any of that, James. I do understand your concern, but the old days of the Cold War are behind us, thank goodness. The days when we burnt vast quantities of fuel chasing one another round in oceanic circles are a thing of the past, thank goodness. In any case it might seem unnecessarily provocative on our part. Leave them alone for the time being; they are sailing on the high seas perfectly legitimately. Let's just see what they do next."

In the event that was to prove rather difficult. For two days naval intelligence lost sight of the Russian carrier group altogether. With no Nimrod surveillance aircraft that far out in the Atlantic, nor a tailing frigate from Devonport, there was not much else Northwood could do. Three days later, James Heaton knocked on the door of his commanding officer again.

Yes, James? Have our Russian friends now disappeared into the way blue yonder? I do think you have been making a drama out of nothing significant. " James Heaton had more serious news. "I have to confess that in N2 we are not exactly ecstatic. We lost sight of them for two days and now they've popped up again just south-west of Ireland. We haven't a clue what they've been up to in the meantime." It was a primary task of naval intelligence to watch what the warships of all other navies were doing. "Now that they're practically in home waters, sir, can I suggest we do run a Nimrod training exercise and inadvertently keep tabs on them, as it were?"

"I grant you that's a bit close to home for a Russian carrier group. Let me have a word with the RAF, tell them what's happening, see if they will put us some eyes in the sky. But I still don't think it amounts to a diplomatic incident. If anything those Russians ships are still in Irish waters rather than ours. I don't think we should over-alarm the Ministry of Defence either. The last thing we need is a whole boatload of desk admirals hopping up and down in their cages with unbridled excitement."

Over the next two days the Russian carrier group was tracked through the Celtic Sea and into St George's Channel. It sailed neatly half-way between St David's Head in Wales and Carnsore Point in Ireland, the fifty mile gateway to the southern Irish Sea. It then continued heading north. Then west of Holyhead, east of Dublin, it executed a steady 180° turn and headed back whence it had come. Yet Whitehall never knew anything about it, nor did the Secretary of State for Defence. It was considered there was nothing to report. The only record of it was an N2 file note prepared by James Heaton, setting out excactly who had done what, or not done at all.

There was no announcement to the London press and the Russians said nothing either. It had been a non-event. Merchant ships which made chance encounters in the Irish Sea did not realise they were looking at a Russian carrier group. Moscow had succeeded in testing Britain's military response protocol. Its high command in Murmansk was fully aware the British military had kept a watchful eye on the carrier group, but also that it had not reacted in any other way.

In a Moscow restaurant conversation between an official in Russia's defence ministry and an assistant Chinese naval attaché, the news was received with polite interest. Yet within hours it had been analysed and reported to Beijing. There the reaction was much more enthusiastic. If that was what the British did, or rather did not do, about foreign warships deep into their own home waters, what would they ever bother to do about warships in the far distant Indian Ocean?

*   *   *   *   *

Westminster, London

ALAN STANLEY had been a British Member of Parliament for just over ten years. He was staunchly Labour, sat steadfastly on the party's back benches and was an unflinching pacifist. Twelve years earlier in 1995 before he became MP for Pennine South, he had made a tenuous reputation for himself by declaring, as had several others but not quite so vociferously, that the Cold War was over. He had announced to anyone willing to listen that Britain's armed forces could be largely demobilised and that the British people deserved a massive peace dividend instead. He had decided that was an easy vote-winner, a route straight to the top in British politics.

His analysis had been given a lukewarm reception by the Conservative government of John Major, which had other more pressing things to worry about at the time, particularly its own survival. Then it had been Labour's turn. Tony Blair won a famous parliamentary victory over the waning Major government in May 1997. His first task had been to assemble a cabinet, always a tricky balancing act for the Labour Party, especially for a party which had been out of power for eighteen years.

Tony Blair could not have been a greater contrast from the previous Labour Prime Minister James Callaghan. The old boy had once been a seaman and a stoker in the Royal Navy, 'Stoker Jim' Callaghan was already turned 64 when he had entered Ten Downing Street. He had only survived in the job for three years before being overwhelmed by Margaret Thatcher. Yet he lived on long after that, becoming the grand old man of the House of Lords. Lord Callaghan had died just two years previously, the day before his 93rd birthday.

Stoker Jim's political balancing act had been precarious throughout his thirty months in Ten Downing Street. On one occasion he had taken the unusual step of promoting the number two at the Foreign Office straight into the Cabinet. It meant David Owen had leapfrogged many more senior colleagues. This however avoided disrupting the political balance of Callaghan's cabinet. The sudden death of Callaghan's Foreign Secretary Tony Crosland had prompted desperate measures. That was in 1977, yet six years later David Owen and three colleagues abandoned the Labour Party to set up a new one, the Social Democrats. Their Limehouse Declaration had been made from David Owen's own home on a curve in the river Thames.

It was always like that in a Labour cabinet, and even more so in the parliamentary party. Dissent and friction were always just round the corner. Policy ideas and factional groupings took as many twists and turns as the Thames as it, too, flowed through the capital. Alan Stanley was a prominent member of a party faction now. It was highly unlikely there would be a welcome place for him anywhere in the Blair government. His face did not fit, nor did his politics.

Unlike Callaghan, Tony Blair had been one of the youngest British Prime Ministers ever. He entered Ten Downing Street almost on his 44th birthday, the first British Prime Minister to be born after Queen Elizabeth succeeded to the throne. His was a different generation; a generation of Labour politicians who had never experienced any military service. Alan Stanley had watched the power struggle in his party with a mixture of quiet amusement and even quieter ambition. The controversy over 'New Labour', a novel concept he found quite absurd anyway, had been moved centre stage thanks to Mr Blair and his scheming henchman Peter Mandelson.

Alan Stanley never experienced a time when the Labour Party had been out of power at Westminster. He sat for a seat in the north of England. He was avowedly, narrowly English rather than British and held little enthusiasm for the mafia of Scottish MPs supporting the new Prime Minister, Gordon Brown.

One of them was at the Despatch Box now. Des Browne was a tough Scottish lawyer and had become Labour member of parliament for Argyll and Bute, spending his first five years in opposition. Then in

1997, just as Alan Stanley came into parliament, Des Browne had moved to the safe Labour seat of Kilmarnock and Loudoun and won it with a majority of 7,000. The magical tap of promotion on the political shoulder had come Des Browne's way in Tony Blair's final year. Perhaps it was intended to appease the Scottish Tendency in the party, yet another Labour cabinet balancing act. Mr Blair had made Des Browne secretary of state for defence. Now the Scots were firmly in control with the accession of Gordon Brown, he had given the fortunate Mr Browne the additional rôle of Secretary of State for Scotland.

As Alan Stanley listened from the obscurity of the back benches, he smiled, but it was a smile of scepticism rather than amusement. Within a month of appointment Des Browne had managed to combine his two rôles. He was explaining that two new aircraft carriers were to be built for the Royal Navy in, surprise, surprise, Scotland. They would cost £3.9 billion apiece, the Queen Elizabeth and the Prince of Wales. At 65,000 tons displacement, they would be two-thirds the size of an American nuclear Nimitz class aircraft carrier, but half as large again as the French nuclear-powered aircraft carrier, the Charles de Gaulle.

It was not entirely clear to Alan Stanley what military purpose either of the two British aircraft carriers would serve. He would make that clear in his speeches. They would have been a useful asset in the Falklands War, but that had been won over twenty years previously and was unlikely to be repeated. In any serious future war involving aircraft carriers, the Americans with their ten massive Nimitz class carriers would take charge and the two British ships would simply be a sideshow. No-one in Whitehall or Westminster, least of all Alan Stanley, knew that just a month previously a Russian carrier group had penetrated up the west coast of Great Britain, right into the Irish Sea.

To Alan Stanley such military manoeuvres were of limited significance anyway. They amounted to little more, in his oft-voiced opinion, than men playing with boy's toys. Very expensive toys. Far from any military purpose, he concluded the two aircraft carriers being announced today served a cynical political and electoral purpose instead. They would provide a major boost to the Scottish economy, just as the six Daring class destroyers being built on Clydeside were doing at present. They would create many jobs in important constituencies.

Alan Stanley did not like warships at the best of times. The latest announcement seemed a one-sided deal to use English taxpayers' money to buy Scottish votes for the Labour Party. North of the border his party was locked in permanent combat with the Scottish Nationalists. Yet no matter how popular those Tartan Tories became, they would never match the financial largesse which could flow from the coffers of Whitehall. Come the next hustings, no doubt Scottish voters would be reminded of that frequently.

It was all rather distasteful. In his view there were better things to spend taxpayers' money on than warships, or indeed on anything to do with the armed forces. And if such spending on naval power was really necessary, he would much prefer it to be spent in the north of England, on Merseyside or even on the Tyne and the Tees. That was his growing power base. Together with the grand old man of northern Labour, his hero Tom Booth, Alan Stanley's small group of like-minded English members of parliament now numbered six.

As he listened with grim fascination to the plans laid before Parliament, he was beginning to hatch plans of his own. Tony Blair had said the way to the top in politics was to smile a lot and have other people deal with your enemies. All Alan Stanley had to do was wait for the pendulum of democratic sentiment to swing his way. He needed no grand global strategy. Here in democratic Europe that was a job for philosophers, not politicians. In the event he would have to wait another seven years before he could do much about the febrile moods of the British voter. Patience would be his key to success. Ordinary people admired patience like his, they distrusted flash in the pan cleverness. So in the meantime all he needed to do was practise his political smile. The observant Alan Stanley had spotted something else. Tony Blair, like John Major and Jim Callaghan before him, had all been tall men. So had Alex Douglas-Home. The way to the top in politics, as it often was inthe board room, seemed to be measured in feet and inches. That suited the 6'2" tall Alan Stanley just fine.

*   *   *   *   *

Riyadh, Saudi Arabia

SEVERAL COPIES OF Violaine Khalifa's thesis were already doing the rounds of ministries and the intelligentsia in the Saudi capital. Her three years at Oxford University studying Islamic history had proved most fruitful. In the best traditions of that university she had argued a case which was original, powerfully researched and controversial. She had started with the six articles of belief of Islam. Muhammad had explained that faith had to be affirmed in Allah, in His angels, in His books, in His Messengers, in the Day of Judgement and in destiny. Beyond that Violaine had gone farther than most others dared. She had opened up some deep divisions in the Arab psyche.

In Violaine's writing there was no place for either Islamic terrorism or even Islamic fundamentalism of the modern kind. The sooner Islam rediscovered the greatness of its Fatimid dynasty, which in the modern Christian calendar had come to power in 945AD, the better for everyone. Her researches into old manuscripts in the Bodleian Library had strengthened an already powerful case. She found countless examples of achievements in Islam's greatest intellectual era, some of them previously unknown.

That era had been both militaristic, certainly, but even more important it had been enlightened. Its brilliant general Jawhar had led a victorious army as far as the Atlantic. Under an Islamic umbrella of political security, overseas trade had flourished and was actively encouraged by its rulers. The trade went in many directions, to Italy and the western Mediterranean, as far as India thought the Red Sea. The Islam of the Fatimids enjoyed profitable dealings with the orthodox Christian Byzantines in Constantinople. Violaine drew the contrast vividly. There was no religious antipathy.

At a time when the continent of Europe was riven by petty rivalries, when the Anglo–Saxon kinglets of England were fending off incursions by Viking raiders, Islam was at its most glorious. At a time when the very thought of anything like higher education was unknown in Europe, Islamic universities were flourishing. In its ignorance, western Europe had labelled such cleverness magic, the work of magi. At its universities Islamic scholars had devised the notion of a professor and the chair from which he taught.

Although Cordoba was fundamentally Islamic, its outlook was also enlightened. Many of its most able scholars were not Arab at all. Rather, and despite Christian Europe's belligerence toward the Islamic presence in Iberia, many of them were drawn from all corners of Europe, selected for their knowledge and their intellect. This cosmopolitan insight and originality made much more sense to her audience in Oxford than it did to many modern audiences in Riyadh, where too much Western cleverness was nowadays distrusted.

Not until 1088 had the first glimmerings of any European university emerged in northern Italy, in Bologna. Even then it would be a further two hundred years before the earliest signs of a university in England, with Merton College at Oxford. The oldest buildings of that now very rich college dated from 1288. Violaine's own college of Keble dated from as recently as 1870. She gently reminded her readers that the intellectual traditions of Islam were far older than those of this western world, and she was working and studying in the English-speaking world's oldest university.

Some of the numerous viziers of classical Islam had been Christians, some even converts from Judaism. How strange that seemed in the twenty-first century, when Israel and Islam were permanently at loggerheads. How much more civilised things had been a millennium previously. Violaine's thesis pulled no punches in its criticisms of modern Islam, nor even of Israel. And that was not wildly popular in Saudi Arabia, whose doctrine of Wahabbism was deeply entrenched.

Violaine's examination of Islamic history highlighted the importance of Cordoba in Spain. Its caliph had been acknowledged as one of the most important men anywhere in Europe, a view shared by local rulers in north Africa and even by Christian princes in the north. The Islamic province of Andalus had been in the van of learning and of progress. In 990AD a college in Baghdad held about 10,000 manuscripts in its library. The collection in its contemporary library in Cordoba was at least ten times as large.

The Fihrist, an index written by Ibn-an-Nadim in 988 listed the titles of a huge number of books, many of them now lost forever. It was one of the most valuable of all surviving documents, an insight into the breadth of Arab wisdom a century and more before the Crusades. Three years after it was written the Anglo-Saxons of England made their first payment of Danegeld to Viking invaders, who came and went as they pleased. The contrast between the fortunes of northern and southern Europe had never been greater.

There was always more than one audience for controversy. Some in the Islamic world suggested that Violaine's father, Dr Malik Khalifa, had exerted great influence on what his daughter had written. It was even suggested by some he was using his influence to promote his personal vision for the future of Islam. A father seeking rapprochement among the many different countries of the Islamic world, a daughter seeking explanation of the greatness of Islam. They had reached very similar conclusions.

If Violaine's thesis had generated a mixed reaction in the country of her birth, at Oxford it had been received with great enthusiasm. She had put forward the principles of a powerful 'road map' for ending so many of the conflicts and pressures of the Middle East. Her analysis hinted strongly at an Islamic renaissance and reformation which might even find some favour in Tel Aviv.

She had pointed out that the Christian reformation of Martin Luther had begun in 1517, about 1,400 years after the origins of Christianity. Luther had published ninety-five theses each challenging the stultifying orthodoxy of the medieval church. The prophet Muhammad had completed writing his Koran in the year of his death, 632AD in the Christian era. So Islam, too, was about coming up to its 1,400th birthday. It was a parallel of history which her thesis hammered home. In Violaine Khalifa's acid assessment, Islam was about due for a historic makeover.

The acclaim given to her academic achievement generated an even more practical response at home. Louise was delighted by her daughter. Her three years' work seemed strictly intellectual, far removed from the tough world of power politics. When she first moved to Paris she had warned her daughter that her father could be in danger. Neither woman was to know it, but Violaine's pursuits in Oxford had now made his peril even worse. But before that her efforts in Oxford brought her a new job in Paris.

* * * * *

The Sixth Arrondissement, September 2007

IT WAS TIME to celebrate a new job. Violaine Khalifa strolled with her parents Louise and Malik along the Boulevard St Germain. It was a balmy evening and they were on their way to number 166, the Rhumerie which specialised in Martinique's most potable product. Even better, Violaine had arranged for the recently-promoted Lieutenant-Commander

James Heaton to join them. By the time they arrived James was already well into his first rum cocktail, much appreciated. This was, he concluded, one of the better things to do in Paris's Sixth Arrondissement, the gastronomic hub of the universe. As he sat on a high leather chair at the brilliant multicoloured bar, he looked around to see Violaine arrive with her parents. Once again, in his honour, she was dressed in gold silk. Such calculated sentiment was broadly permitted, while punctuality was compulsory among the haute monde of Paris.

At more than one of their many meetings in Oxford over the previous three years, Violaine had warned James about her father. Dr Khalifa was a senior Saudi diplomat and wary of the Royal Navy. But there was none of that caution this evening. Moslem he may be but Malik bought a round of rum cocktails with the aplomb of a seasoned drinker and congratulated James on his naval promotion. On that he had been well briefed by wife and daughter alike. Over the next two hours, to the delight of both men, they were to develop a new friendship which surprised them both. It boded well for the future. Tonight was the first time they had ever really spoken together seriously. Another meeting of minds.

After all the usual courtesies and greetings, Malik Khalifa raised his glass. "James, Louise, I wish to raise a toast, to that consummate expert on Islamic History, Violaine Khalifa and to her new job in Les Renseignements Generaux." As James was to learn shortly, this was the official name of the French Secret Service.

"James, I'm sure you will be as delighted as we all are that Violaine has been given a challenging research job in the Section Nationale de Recherches Opérationnelles. "She will be researching the Arab world. Obviously I can help her on that, behind the scenes of course, but in my personal view the sooner the Quai D'Orsay and all its tentacles understand the Arab Islamic world far better than they do at present, the better for everyone concerned. Santé."

The conversation moved seamlessly across the Channel, for the Khalifas were keen to learn about James's naval career. The comings and goings of the Royal Navy became the centre of attention. In their many conversations in Oxford and London over the previous three years, Violaine knew all the details of James's successful rise through the ranks. Progress had been reported back to the Hotel de Chambon in detail; Louise seemed almost as enthusiastic as her daughter on the subject.

For his part, Malik Khalifa listened to the British officer with quiet approval. He respected the way James analysed both the strengths and the weaknesses of Britain's senior service. It was just the kind of candid analysis he would have welcomed more frequently from young men of that same generation in Riyadh. It was also a measured performance in another way too. James did not consider this the right time to give too many details about his new job in naval intelligence.

The drinks to celebrate Violaine's new job and the progress of James's career made them hungry. Malik had booked a table for four at the oldest restaurant in Paris, Le Procope. As explained to James, it had been founded in 1686 and had entertained such distinguished diners as Voltaire, Danton, Moliere, Robespierre, Molière, Diderot, Thomas Jefferson and Benjamin Franklin. Tonight its diners included a prominent Parisian aristocrat, a leading Saudi diplomat, a member of the French secret service and a rising star in the Royal Navy. Even if Napoleon Buonaparte might have raised half an eyebrow at the last, he would surely have approved of the others.

It was a short stroll down Rue Mazarine. Conversation drifted back through Oxford and to the impact Violaine had made with her doctoral thesis. James was able to report on its very favourable reception in Oxford, from his own college, which pleased Malik and Louise. They had planned their gourmet itinerary with care and were welcomed by the restaurant as old friends. Louise was particularly pleased with the menu, because in September Le Procope specialised in Breton dishes. "Shame the Kerguelens aren't here," she observed, "I'm quite sure Tiphaine could steer us through this list of delights like Escoffier himself and request dishes which aren't even on the menu."

James Heaton was rapidly discovering a level of eating out in Paris far above anything ever experienced by a tourist. He was willing to learn. The fish soup brought a magic still rarely encountered in London, let alone Portsmouth or the other ports of call of the Royal Navy. The wine was an inspired choice, produced in Burgundy by an exclusive vintner whom Louise seemed to know in person.

Traditional Breton lobster rose to new heights in the Sixth Arrondissement and as they savoured the food conversation moved to the castle on the coast far to the west. James and Xavier had known one another for almost ten years. Louise was delighted by the friendship, James was becoming part of their extended family. They all agreed Xavier de Kerguelen was nobody's fool, that he was doing very well in the French navy. There were rumours he, too, might join the Direction du Reseignement Militaire, the combined intelligence service formed after the Gulf War.

Malik Khalifa steered the conversation to Violaine's achievements. "James, I gather we have you to thank for pointing her so early in the direction of the Bodleian Library. She took me to see for herself and I could easily have spent a week there. The manuscripts, to anyone who reads Arabic, are astonishing. You British certainly know how to collect things. And I'm very glad you have done so. At least that priceless material is in the hands of people who respect and cherish it.

"If you don't know already, James, Violaine has really put the cat among the pigeons in Riyadh. And I agree with her entirely. I used to be guarded in my criticism of the present regime, but as I grow older I don't see why I should." Father and daughter alike shared a pride in the greatest achievements of Islam. They took turns over dinner to explain the important parts of Violaine's thesis. "You might imagine, James, that the powers-that-be in Saudi Arabia would be delighted by the new spotlight my daughter has shone on the greatness of her culture. Some people do. Yet there are many there who seem to share a taste for the new global militancy instead. I am not one of them. She has opened up a gulf between opposed philosophies in Riyadh."

Once the meal was over, the four of them strolled through the Sixth Arrondissement towards the Seine. It was a pleasant walk down the Boulevard Saint-Germain and over the Pont de la Tournelle, back to the Hotel de Chambon. Louise gently steered her daughter into the salon and left James to talk quietly with her husband. She had a fair idea what was about to take place.

In his study Dr Malik Khalifa poured two glasses of fine armagnac and gave one to James. Without a further word he looked expectantly at his younger companion. Since everyone seemed to be pregnant with suspense, James went straight to the heart of the matter. Royal Navy officers did not shilly-shally. "Dr Khalifa, I would like your permission to marry your daughter."

Malik Khalifa stared into his brandy glass for a few moments, nodded gently and then said "I think that would be an extremely good idea. Violaine lights up in your company. Your own career prospects are quite excellent. You already make a very fine couple and thanks to Oxford University you have many things in common. Even if you are differently French and English, your minds seem to match. That is very important in a marriage. So you do have my full permission to marry my daughter and my permission is given with great gladness of heart. When is the happy event likely to take place?"

"First let me tell Violaine the good news, sir, but I would not expect the wedding for several years. She needs to settle down into her new job, to make her mark. She will bring a great talent to their efforts and I want to give her every chance to shine. Again the Royal Navy has a frequent habit of sending our ships to the four corners of the globe.

And anyway I think Violaine and I should spend some time getting used to the idea. Our lives are going to be complicated."

"She knows you are going to ask me for her hand?" asked the doctor. "Yes, sir, she does but she did not know what your response would be. Should we not bring her in and tell her?" Malik went to the door and called out, "Louise, Violaine. Can you both join us for a few moments?" There was something unmistakeable in his tone of voice.

It was clear from Louise Khalifa's facial expression she knew what was coming, a mother brimming with joy. "Violaine," said her husband with mock solemnity, "James has asked me for your hand in marriage and with much pleasure I have given him my permission." His daughter, latest member of the French secret service, managed to stammer "Oh Papa, oh James" before bursting into tears.

They were happy tears of delight. Within a few moments her mother had joined in. There was no better way of signalling acceptance of Lieutenant-Commander James Heaton into the family. While the Khalifas celebrated, he smiled, accepted their congratulations and pondered. He was a British naval intelligence officer who would be marrying into the French aristocracy, into the French secret service and now with his personal hotline to whatever Malik Khalifa, that self-avowed maverick of Arab diplomacy, was doing in Saudi Arabia.

Later that evening, Violaine sat and stared out of her bedroom window at the River Seine, just as she had done since she was twelve. Her life now seemed quite perfect. She reflected on her good fortune since she flew out of he first home in Saudi Arabia with her mother to Paris all those many years ago.

She now had a wonderful home in central Paris where she was part of a distinguished family. They were rich. She had enjoyed an outstanding education at two of Europe's oldest universities. And now she had a demanding and intellectually fascinating job. Best of all her father had just agreed that she could marry the greatest love of her life, the Englishman James Heaton of the Royal Navy. No woman of her age could possibly ask for more. Violaine Khalifa could not even conceive of anything more to ask.

As she stared into the Parisian night, almost invisible black barges chugged quietly down river, their riding lights alone marking their path through the enveloping gloom on the river. They were her mysterious, almost silent, invariably comforting, gently unobtrusive, totally undemanding friends. Just as they always had been. It must have been a busy night on the River Seine because, by the time she grew drowsy, she had already counted six of them.

Chapter Seven

The Lucky Seven

Westminster, London

THE MOST OBVIOUS   building in Whitehall is the Ministry of Defence, finished in white stone, standing in its own open grounds which reach to the Thames.   There was a spring in Christopher Cunningham's step as he left the building and walked down Whitehall to Westminster underground station. The station's concrete cavern formed the basement of Portcullis House, a spacious and rather ugly office block for Members of Parliament and opened six years earlier. For many years before that, Britain's parliamentarians had squeezed shoulder to shoulder in the cubbyholes and corners of the old Houses of Parliament.

From Westminster station Christopher Cunningham took the Circle Line to South Kensington, from where it was another long ride on the Piccadilly Line to Park Royal. There, lurking inconspicuously in a large industrial estate, were the global headquarters of the Sharava Corporation. Strictly speaking Christopher Cunningham was the managing director of Sharava but it often suited him to imply he was not. As he rode the Piccadilly Line to Park Royal he looked back on his morning's work with considerable pride. It was not often he was invited to a meeting with one of the most influential and least visible officers in the Ministry of Defence. Captain George Gould liked to keep well out of the limelight, for among other covert activities he was the Royal Navy's leading expert in military disinformation.

The Ministry had been involved, as far as possible invisibly, in Sharava's development of military software from the very outset. It was a carefully-concealed arms-length relationship known to as few people as possible. There could be many advantages for a company such as Sharava being free from apparent links of any kind to any political or military authority anywhere.

Rather the company presented itself to the world as an avowedly commercial operation, entirely free to do as it wished in an industry usually festooned with political red tape. Nor was there a scrap of tangible evidence it was even British. If Sharava had any sign of nationality at all it was possibly Indian, or maybe it was Swiss. Who could tell? Who wanted to know? None of its multifarious activities could be traced to the totally anonymous building in Park Royal. It was an unheadquarters. The apparent absence of any link to the British military had been George Gould's idea from the start, and he was about to exploit all that carefully-nurtured independence to spring a trap.

Some non-military software was deliberately produced by Sharava to titivate its brochures and train its young boffins. It all looked convincing enough. The real effort however, was almost entirely military. One of the company's key products was a tracking and guidance system for warships. Over the past two years this system had in turn been fitted with a piece of software which transmitted details of what was being tracked and what was being guided.

It had been Christopher Cunningham's idea. Captain Gould was intrigued by the Bijali device which could deliver the result. He had been thinking about it, and that morning at the Ministry of Defence he

George Gould

told Christopher Cunningham the outcome. "I think, Chris, this time around we will break every rule in the security manual and sell this particular military software to all-comers. Especially to people we don't fully trust. If any of their ships ever popped up on the other side in a military conflict, it would be extremely useful for the Royal Navy to know exactly what was afoot."

The two men also agreed to let it be leaked publicly that Sharava's system was being fitted to Britain's Type 45 destroyers under construction in Scotland. The first of these, HMS Daring, was due to join the fleet in two years' time. The careless revelation would appear in a little-read technical journal, where it could appear to have surfaced unintentionally. Captain Gould reckoned that would attract the maximum degree of interest. "The smarter the intelligence operation, the more likely they are to spot it, and such clever countries are the ones most likely to have a navy which could become a customer." George Gould had a distinctive smile, Christopher had realised, which he saved for his more machiavellian proposals. It was a smile partly disguised by his semi-military beard.

It was not entirely true that the Royal Navy's own destroyers would have the standard version of Sharava's tracking and guidance system, but who was to know the difference? However creating a worldwide impression that it was quite good enough for the finest ships in the Royal Navy would be extremely valuable to the Sharava Corporation. It was an enviable product recommendation.

Other countries might generally expect the British to design their own tracking and guidance system, but on this occasion they had apparently gone into the commercial marketplace instead. Or that was to be the general impression. Any resulting overseas orders could hardly do other than boost Sharava's profits, which would be most welcome. As he counted the stations along the Piccadilly Line, Christopher Cunningham reflected upon the huge slice of commercial good fortune that morning had brought. He had also discussed something else with George Gould. In their experimental tests of the Bijali system, Christopher Cunningham and his colleague Martin Barraclough had used themselves as the first guinea pigs.

It had proved quite difficult to play both sides of the warfare game simultaneously in real time, watching one's own tracking and guidance system as well as that of one's opponent. The two scientists had rapidly agreed it would require a quite unusual, and certainly very clever, mentality. Captain Gould had taken this on board too. It meant that any naval officer expected to make simultaneous use the Bijali feed of data from the other side as well would need to be equally exceptional.

The ingenious George Gould had immediately suggested to Dr. Cunningham that the Sharava Corporation might build a testing programme to work out which naval officers were best suited to the task. For security's sake the work on the new aptitude tests should be kept quite separate from Bijali. Ostensibly Sharava should confine the tests to the ordinary tracking and guidance system. George Gould always liked to keep defence-related pursuits in separate boxes; one never knew who might be watching.

From his guinea-pig efforts with Martin Barraclough, Christopher Cunningham had already started to imagine what the testing programme might require. When he reached his anonymous office in Park Royal he pulled out an English-Sanskrit dictionary. It was not a volume one might normally expect to find in the desk of a scientific entrepreneur. Even so Christopher Cunningham wanted a new brand name, and he soon found it.

He decided the new brain testing programme would be called Kundalini. That was a Sanskrit concept of coiled-up energy at the base of the spinal column. Through practice of Raja Yoga, this energy could be released up through the spine to the brain to reach the inner brain and produce super-consciousness. Or so it was argued. Some people could do it naturally, some learnt it the hard way, some would never be able to achieve it. The general idea matched Sharava's covert plans for revealing tracking and guidance plans using Bijali rather well. So Christopher Cunningham opened a new computer folder, labelled it Kundalini, and protected it with an extremely unlikely password.

*   *   *   *   *

Rotherhithe, London

ANTONIA FOO pushed open the French windows in her new flat and stepped out onto its verandah. She had arrived in London three weeks earlier, and spent much of the time finding somewhere to live. Her rôle back at the Yellow River Industrial Research Facility in China had finished once the production line of Yangtze jet engines was up and running. By the time she left Lanzhou all three versions, those for aviation, marine and industrial had been tried and tested. Antonia was ready for her next assignment, which she had been promised would be somewhere preferable to the industrial backwaters of China. Between times she had completed a master's degree in defence electronics at China's military academy and a demanding course in the English language. Vice-premier Liu Fun never left anything to chance.

After the arid tedium of China's western desert, London was the ultimate in cosmopolitan and exciting. Antonia Foo was a Shanghainese, a stylish woman from quite the most sophisticated city in China. Now she had been sent to the cultural heart of Europe and she felt instantly at home. In her view London was the most stylish city in the world, yet apart from an occasional flying visit she had not really had chance to explore her dream in twenty-five years. If there was one place outside China she would love to live, it would have to be London.

In her early twenties, Antonia had studied for a doctorate at London University's Imperial College and was now inbtrigued to discover how much London had changed in the years since. The

evidence of that was visible all around her. She had chosen a flat down
the Thames in Docklands, none of which modern development had even
existed last time she lived in the capital city. Her third floor verandah in
Trinity Wharf looked straight down the river almost as far as Greenwich,
a perfect vantage point from which to observe the numerous and
fascinating comings and goings on the river.

Less than a mile upstream, although she did know it, and almost
within sight was the home on the River where David Owen had
composed the Limehouse Declaration, the birth of the breakaway Social
Democratic Party led by a gang of four rebels in 198. Antonia knew all
about gangs of four political rebels. She was after all Shanghainese.

She was looking across the river's Limehouse Reach now. With
every tide clumsy barges carrying yellow garbage containers put in an
appearance, while steadily throughout the day the bright red tourist boats
churned to and fro, even at this late time of the year. Occasionally the
Royal Navy would send a frigate to moor alongside HMS Belfast in the
Upper Pool. Antonia particularly liked the fleet of sleek white
catamarans, a hop on, hop off passenger service speeding straight into
central London. Nothing like that had existed last time she lived here.
The graceful boats raced and up and down the river faster than a car.

Antonia had soon discovered she could stroll along the tree-lined
riverside walk to the Hilton hotel and from there catch a five minute
ferry across the river to Canary Wharf pier. That was where the large
catamarans stopped before they ran upriver as far as the London Eye.
That was something else new to her. London's huge ferris wheel had
opened in 2000 for the Millennium.

One of Antonia's first treats for herself had been a trip around
it. That took her as high as almost every building in London, and opened
up views right across the city and beyond. Like almost all Chinese, she
had an excellent head for heights. Antonia's encrypted email link with
the department of vice-premier Liu was installed and secure. She held

several briefings with the assistant military attaché at the Chinese embassy and with the economic and commercial counsellor's office. Her basic task was commercial but its military requirements made it far more complicated than that. She was to negotiate the weapons software for Admiral Zhou Man's ships.

A signal from China's ever-alert intelligence directorate had confirmed what Beijing already suspected. Britain's brand new Type 45 destroyers were being fitted with a commercial tracking and guidance system manufactured by the Sharava Corporation. The vital snippet of information came from a department in Beijing which rarely missed anything. She already knew the discreet electronics company had a sales office in London, and China was well aware they offered their software at defence exhibitions. The technology could be bought freely on the open market. And if it was good enough for Britain's Type 45, then it was probably good enough for any warship in the world. It was just her good fortune the email from Beijing had arrived when it did.

Now an equally welcome email confirmed she was to meet one of the senior salesmen from Sharava's London office, a man called Christopher Cunningham. He had found her most impressive on the telephone. The idea was they should say hello informally at a wine bar in the centre of town, one which she would easy to find right beneath Charing Cross Station. It was called Champagne Charlie's. They did have something to celebrate, after all, and new customers for Sharava were always most welcome. Not many people understood the potential of its products, but those who did could bring substantial business.

A few days later she took the clunky ferry across the Thames to Canary Wharf, and caught the sleek Thames Clipper catamaran into central London. Christopher Cunningham had sounded very intelligent and masculine, and she hoped he would prove to be good-looking too. After several weeks living by herself in the big city, Antonia Foo was starting to feel lonely. Her outfit for the introductory meeting had been chosen with considerable care. Like vice-premier Liu Fun, she never left anything to chance. Her straight dark skirt was exactly the right length, just above the knee, her heels were high while a mildly revealing neckline beneath her jacket showed cleavage judged to within a millimetre.

Her hair was immaculate, her stocking seams were precisely straight - she never wore tights on principle - while her French perfume was very expensive and she wore an exquisitely-carved jade dragon pendant. She was determined to make a favourable impression, one to be remembered. Dr Cunningham sounded as if he might be worth it; Antonia Foo had always believed in mixing business with pleasure.

As she walked uphill from the catamaran pier at Embankment, Antonia was quietly pleased by the way, shortly after her fiftieth birthday, she could still attract appreciative stares. At least that had not changed since her days at Imperial. She made her way up the busy street beside Charing Cross Station, then turned left into a lofty arching passageway then left again down into the chosen wine bar. Its website had been easy enough to find on the Internet, and it was exactly the kind of rendevous where London's politicians, civil servants and young entrepreneurs would meet over lunch. No-one would pay much attention to a woman dressed smartly for business meeting a man in a dark suit.

Christopher Cunningham turned out to be tall, dark and really rather handsome. Antonia's luck was in once again. They shared a bottle of pinot grigio and began by talking generally about London, then about international politics. They then moved to the building of commercial links between Britain and China. No-one else within earshot was likely to understand what a tracking and guidance system did, and in any case Dr Cunningham seemed fairly open about it. Perhaps that was the cleverest way not to attract much attention to their conversation.

He made it clear enough that so far as the Shirava Corporation was concerned, sales to China would pose no political or strategic problems. Although he was often in London that was simply because it was one of the best places in the world to do business. Otherwise the company had no particular links with Britain. The technical centres where it actually manufactured its software were invariably unrecognisable, almost always disguised, and it owed no particular allegiance to any single country.

Christopher Cunningham was impressed by how much Antonia Foo already proved to know about the system. Better still, price did not seem to be a significant issue. Sharava's military electronics systems were never cheap. He made it clear that no special export licences would be needed from any country to make the transaction permissible. What Sharava sold to its international customers was no business of the British authorities nor of anyone else. Sharava Corporation was its own commercial master and acted alone.

It was not entirely clear to Antonia Foo just how high up the organisation her new companion ranked, but he seemed to exude natural authority. She liked that in a man. She definitely liked Christopher Cunningham from the moment they first met. After many brief and unsatisfactory encounters with the male of the species, it seemed she could be in luck at last. She wondered what he might be like undressed; there was something about Englishmen which had intrigued her for years, especially the ones with large feet. She had taken due note as they first met that Christopher Cunningham possessed very large feet. After her work, men had always been the next highest priority for Antonia Foo and easily her second greatest expertise.

The broad principle of the deal agreed, they took out their diaries and planned a series of more technical meetings in what he described as the unmarked Sharava UK sales office in Baker Street. With luck the deal would be completed and the software on its way to China some time in the following year. Antonia assumed that assembly of what was essentially pre-designed software in a box would not take too long. That same afternoon Christopher Cunningham telephoned George Gould to say they had snared a potential customer for Sharava's tracking and guidance system. The man at the ministry was most intrigued when he learnt the likely customer was the People's Republic of China.

The following day in Beijing, Admiral Zhou Man was equally pleased that the Sharava Corporation was willing to do strictly commercial business without asking too many questions about the exact purpose of the warships being built. If the end user was not in much doubt, at least the end use was still clouded in mystery. Had it been connected with, say, Britain's Ministry of Defence even indirectly, Sharava would surely have been much more curious. Antonia had done well in making contact with the secretive company so quickly; they did not exactly advertise. Although she was many thousands of miles away she was bringing him luck.

*   *   *   *   *

Dar-es-Salaam, Tanzania

THE ONE-STOP British Airways journey from Beijing, calling at Heathrow *en route*, touched down at Julius Nyerere International airport. His excellency Zei Huang collected his few belongings and was one of the first off the aircraft, the usual privilege accorded to passengers in First Class. He was met by an official from the foreign ministry and taken to a waiting limousine. So the plenipotentiary from China had arrived safely in Tanzania.

It had been a long trip and Zei Huang was weary. The Mercedes took him along the Pugu Road, past the palm beach and down the Haile Selassie road onto the Msasani peninsula. He was driven straight to the Golden Tulip hotel in Oyster Bay. It was a modern four star establishment with architecture inspired by the Arabic influences on this, the Swahili coast. Like most Chinese diplomats, Zei Huang wanted to understand the country he was visiting, no matter how fleetingly. The

Swahili culture and language of coastal Tanzania, like that of neighbouring Kenya, was a mixture of African and Arabic. The dual influence dated from the days when the Arabs of the Middle East had collected African slaves for sale in Oman. Their ships had brought back wood and other valuable commodities, and it had been a most profitable trade. Zei Huang was optimistic he could do something very similar over the following week even if slavery was, officially anyway, now firmly a thing of the past.

The Chinese diplomat was pleased to find that his room in the hotel overlooked the Indian Ocean, for that was the real purpose of his visit. Ostensibly he was there to offer Tanzania some generous foreign aid, but there was a subtle rider to be added to the package.

The friendly relationship between China and Tanzania dated back some forty years. In the late 1960s, negotiations had led to construction of the Tan-Zam railway, still one of China's largest-ever projects of overseas aid. Tanzania had something which Beijing now wanted, which was the excellent port facilities of Dar-es-Salaam. With just a few thousand tons of concrete and some warehouses, the banks of a broad estuary could be transformed into China's principal naval base on the East African coast.

The time zone difference between Beijing and Dar es Salaam was five hours. Under Chinese rules Zei Huang was forbidden to undertake any serious negotiations until he had enjoyed two nights' sleep. So the following day was spent lazing around the outdoor swimming pool at the hotel. An expensive glossy brochure explained it was the largest in the city, and even in January, the outdoor temperature was around 27^0 Celsius. To a visitor straight from the chilly Beijing winter, that was more than sufficiently warm.

Two days after his arrival the Chinese visitor paid his first call on the minister, Tendaji Tajirika. They had known one another several years previously, when both worked at the United Nations and both spoke

good diplomatic English. That was precisely why Beijing had chosen Zei
Huang for the mission. After fifteen minutes spent catching up on old
times and mutual friends, they got down to business. Mr Tajirika poured
them a glass of government whisky apiece.

Zei Huang explained that Beijing has decided to make Tanzania
one of its principal trading partners in Africa. The deal would include
foreign aid. There was plenty of money available, for China had
accumulated great trade surpluses with the West and because of the
ineluctable logic of finance the money could only be spent outside China
itself, unless China used it to buy yuan on the international currency
markets. Such transactions could only harm the yuan and benefit the
American dollar. So the People's Republic was now looking for overseas
investment projects on a grand scale.

In Beijing's publicised view it was far better to spend the
mountains of money on foreign aid supporting needy countries. The
proposals Zei Huang brought to Dar-es-Salaam would help to increase
the prosperity and success of the East African country to which Tendaji
Tajirika had devoted his whole life.

Beijing also predicted a substantial increase in shipping traffic
through the port to handle expanding trade. In the Chinese view it
would need to be enlarged, and as another major project of overseas aid
China was willing to pay for it. "We saw years ago when the oil boom
transformed Nigeria's fortunes how international shipping could not find
docking facilities in the port of Lagos. There were even shipments of
cement which solidified while they rode at anchor for months on end
waiting for berths. The ships simply had to be scrapped. I think we can
agree that Dar-es-Salaam and Tanzania deserve better than that."

Both men smiled wryly at the misfortunes of West Africa, and
at a huge country whose principal commercial activity appeared to be
inventing internet scams. On behalf of Tanzania, Tendaji Tajirika
welcomed the proposals set out by his old Chinese acquaintance with

enthusiasm. The deal could gain him influence among fellow members of the Tanzanian government. His star would rise high. The two men next studied a map of the harbour and its surrounding road and rail connections. It was not too difficult to work out where to undertake the port expansion in Dar-es-Salaam.

The Chinese diplomat seemed very well briefed on the likely cost. A little over two years earlier the post of Sydney in Australia had embarked on a similar project to expand its facilities. Together with earthworks and land reclamation, dredging deeper channels and providing new railways and roads, Sydney's Port Botany expansion would cost a billion Australian dollars and take seven years to complete. The minister gleamed with anticipation : a billion dollar's worth of contracts was a bounty indeed.

So it became a simple matter of drawing up heads of agreement, which the minister could then present to his Cabinet colleagues. He expected no major problem with anything discussed so far. On the contrary, Tanzania had just achieved most favoured nation status in the eyes of Beijing. The contracts and legal team at the ministry would be instructed to draw up the outline documents over the next few days.

"Just two other points need to be mentioned in private between us," the wily Chinese murmured to his old diplomatic friend. "The first is that we might require in future to bring the occasional naval ship into the harbour. China has no military presence here in the Indian Ocean. But as trade between our countries develops, circumstances could change. I think you and I would both agree it would be advantageous to be able to protect our mutual commerce should the need arise." Both men were well aware of the piracy further north on the African east coast. The Tanzanian minister nodded sagely and asked exactly what the Chinese diplomat had in mind.

"We would wish to add a confidential protocol to the agreement, one which is seen by as few people as possible. There is no need to alarm anyone with something which is purely hypothetical. I take it you would, as I have, sufficient authority to sign such a protocol on behalf of our respective governments."

"I think that could be arranged." said the Tanzanian minister. "As you rightly say it is entirely hypothetical. The occasional visiting warship can hardly do much harm. You mentioned there was one other thing; what was that?"

The Chinese smiled; when in Africa do what the Africans do. "There is also of course the conventional issue of commission on the deal. Shall we say ten per cent payable into a bank account of your own choice in Switzerland?" The Tanzanian smiled broadly, for it was his lucky day. With the shake of a hand his personal fortune had been totally transformed. The difference was that while the Chinese understood Tendaji Tajirika's pleasure completely, his own equal delight was somewhat more discreet.

*   *   *   *   *

Jakarta, Indonesia

THE FLIGHT WITH Garuda airlines from Singapore had taken little more than an hour, as Malik Khalifa's plane landed at Jakarta's Soekarno-Hatta international airport. As with most international airports, it was named after politicians, in this case modern Indonesia's first two presidents. The first had given the country its full independence following world war two. By the time he landed Malik was becoming quite an expert in all this. He always believed in doing his homework before diplomatic trips. Soekarno was the man who had rescued his country from the Japanese occupation, but decided to retain the name given its capital city by the northern invaders. It had once been known as Batavia, but that was all too reminiscent of the long colonial era of the Dutch.   President Soekarno had wanted to stake a visible claim to permanent independence. Dr Malik Khalifa collected his few belongings and was one of the first people off his aircraft, the usual privilege accorded to passengers in First Class. He was met by an official from the foreign ministry and taken to a waiting limousine. The Mercedes drove along the Jalan Tol Profesor Sedyatmo toll road towards the centre of the city, then swung south onto the Jalan Tol Letnan Jenderal S Parman before its name became something else. Dr Khalifa struggled with the long road names. Although they were written in the Latin alphabet, the language was a standardised form of Malay which seemed to involve many if not most of the surnames to be found in the Jakarta telephone directory. So he gave up the linguistic struggle and sat back in comfort to enjoy the ride.

On the flight from Singapore, Dr Khalifa had studied the history of Jakarta with interest. He had long held the view that a smattering of accurate knowledge would serve him well in delicate diplomatic negotiations. This was the largest city in south east Asia and the tenth largest anywhere in the world. With a population well in advance of nine million, it was twice the size of his home city, Riyadh, and larger even than London. It was over four times the size of Paris, where his wife Louise and daughter Violaine both now lived in safety by the Seine.

Jakarta was also old; its origins traced back to a fourth century Hindu settlement. The city sat on a strategic trade route, and had changed hands many times through the centuries. The mouth of the Ciwilung river had been the port of choice for spice traders. It had attracted merchants from both the Indian and Pacific oceans. Although beyond the sphere of interest of medieval Europe, it had fascinated the sub-continent of India. So had its spices.

A Hindu regime in what became Indonesia had lasted over a thousand years until the Portuguese arrived in 1513. Malik Khalifa recognised the familiar colonial sequence of events after that instantly. The Portuguese presence did not last long. Twelve years later they were thrown out by Moslem conquerors who changed the town of the town from Sunda Kelapa to Jayakarta, the Sanskrit for 'Great Victory'. The name had been restored over 400 years later by yet more invaders, the Japanese. When he re-gained Indonesia's independence, President Soekarno had wanted his city to live up to its name; to move onwards from the colonial memories of the Portuguese, the Moslems, the British and the Dutch who had called it Batavia. For him, the city of great victory deserved some great monuments. Among his many public works he had built magnificent highways which, with their equally magnificent names, now led through the heart of the city.

The official Mercedes drove Malik Khalifa straight to the Dharmawangsa Hotel, in the swish residential district of Kebayoran Baru. Since leaving home he had crossed four time zones. It was always tougher travelling from west to east, so he decided to allow himself at least a day to recuperate sensibly from the jet lag.

The tourist literature explained that his hotel was named after a fourteenth century Hindu king from east Java. King Dharmawangsa had laid the foundations of the great empire of Majapahit, the golden age of Java before the European colonisers arrived. It illustrated as well as anywhere the remarkable mixture of cultures - Hindu, Buddhist, Confucian, Islamic and Christian - which had intermingled to create today's Indonesia. The hotel's facilities were designed to be the perfect place to unwind after a demanding journey. Dr. Khalifa would after all be seventy later in the year. His private suite had a verandah overlooking the city, and like every guest he had a personal butler, an expert in the art of Javanese hospitality.

There was a reason Malik wanted to be sure of his cultural understanding. He had arrived in the country with a delicate, complicated and mainly secret mission. After years of ducking and weaving in the political turmoil of Saudi Arabia, he had at length scored a philosophical victory. Now it was being put to the test. His plan to build significant links between Islamic countries around the Indian ocean had been acknowledged. Indonesia's religion was now primarily Islamic, divided between the modernists of Sumatra and Borneo, and the traditionalists of Java. There were still pockets of Hinduism, Buddhism and Christianity, both Catholic and Protestant, while the Indonesian constitution guaranteed freedom of worship for all.

Well, for almost all. After a political coup in distant Portugal in 1974, its former colonies in the far east were released from the final vestiges of European imperialism. This release included the island of Timor, at the eastern extremity of the Indonesian archipelago. A group called FRETILIN had declared Timoran independence in November 1975 in its capital city of Dili. The Indonesian army moved in to occupy the territory the following month. Amid much bloodshed East Timor had been ruled from Jakarta for a quarter century.

Then in 1999 two Timorese, Carlos Filipe Ximenes Belo, and José Ramos-Horta had been awarded the Nobel Peace Prize for their persistent efforts to end the occupation peacefully. A plebiscite three years later had voted overwhelmingly in favour of full independence. Three years after that the Indonesians departed. It was estimated that the violent occupation had claimed the lives of around 150,000 people out of a total population of 700,000. Few would regard it as one of the finer phases of Indonesia's long history. Perhaps now was the time to change the country's international image from repression to progress. Would its government therefore take the Saudi bait?

In principle Indonesia was a rich country. Then its economy had taken a severe battering from the tsunami which had been triggered by an earthquake in the seas off Sumatra just three years previously, wreaking havoc along the coast of that island.

For many years Indonesia had also been a member of the oil producers' cartel OPEC. Then with declining production in Sumatra's oilfields, with the absence of new discoveries and the demands of a booming economy, the country had ceased to be an oil exporter. It seemed inevitable Indonesia, OPEC's sole member in south east Asia, would withdraw from the organisation once its membership expired later that year. All in all Malik Khalifa had a delicate balancing act ahead of him. He met the minister two days after his arrival. The two men, academics both, knew one another quite well although Dr Khalifa had never visited Indonesia before. They were both veterans of the diplomatic circuit. With a shared interest in Islam both ancient and modern, they greeted one another warmly. It had been a long time.

The Saudi diplomat's refresher course in Indonesian history had paid off. Most of their initial discussion was spent rehearsing the country's virtues, and the minister was impressed and flattered by Malik Khalifa's familiarity with Indonesian history and culture.

The stakes were high. His few allies in the Saudi foreign ministry reckoned that if Malik Khalifa could pull this one off, other Islamic countries would follow. So he had been given a free hand. It was make or break, and his objective was straightforward. He wanted to build a naval alliance around the Indian Ocean, and his dream was something he privately called INA, an Islamic Naval Alliance. The eventual objective was was massive. The trick was to begin with a simple and practical achievement, and choose what seemed the easiest target first.

In his political studies Malik Khalifa had noted how in Europe, a simple alliance once concerning just steel and coal had evolved gradually into the European Community, and then into the European Union. It was a precedent which appealed to his cosmopolitan mind. The British often talked about the inevitability of gradualism and that was an idea he greatly admired.

The European Coal and Steel Community had originally been proposed by the French foreign minister of the day, Robert Schuman in May 1950, when Malik's wife Louise had been less than two years old. The European community which grew from it had been the story of her life, and she had worked through the diplomatic logic with him many times. It was a vision of history as seen by a globe-trotting diplomat. There were those in Riyadh who thought Malik Khalifa paid far too much attention to the history and culture of other countries. This was the many stranded-background to the conversations between the two Islamic experts in Jakarta, and they lasted many hours. It was clear to the Indonesian that his Saudi counterpart saw the alliance as a way of creating an axis of moderation within the Islamic world. It would be a practical counterweight to the terrorist excesses of Al-Qaeda, and the negative image of Islam which that had created. But after fighting for so many years for its own independence, Indonesia would be wary of anything even hinting at a loss of its sovereignty once more.

For his part, Malik Khalifa stressed that the security of Indonesia depended more than ever on safe passage at sea. There was piracy in the Malacca straits between Malaysia and Sumatra, while Indonesia would become more and more independent on imported oil. Its era of political independence was giving way to an era of economic and military interdependence. Malik Khalifa expressed adroitly his personal view that Riyadh's traditionalists were approaching the future posterior first. He was keen his Indonesian opposite numbers should not do the same.

It was a persuasive argument to an educated academic mind. Even more so was the practicality of Khalifa's proposal. His naval alliance would be a pact which encouraged Islamic countries to come to one another's aid in times of difficulty. In the aftermath to the tsunami in December 2005, Indonesia would certainly have welcomed that.

Dr Khalifa then pointed to the way the nations of Europe and North America had created the North Atlantic Treaty Organisation after the second world war. Was it not time for the nations of Islam to show their political maturity by doing the same? Once he sensed the Indonesian's support, he explained what was needed. "My team of analysts and geographers have decided that three ports in Indonesia are crucial to the plan. Two of them were already established, but the third will require massive investment." Malik Khalifa had been canny enough to see the positive advantages of that. "The two principal headquarters of the Indonesian navy, Jakarta for the Western Fleet Command, Surabaya for the Eastern Fleet Command, are not part of the plan. It would be better if our visiting warships were out of sight of inquisitive foreign diplomats."

And that was the plan the Saudi plenipotentiary put forward. In the far west of Timor, the existing small Indonesian naval base at Kupang, the provincial capital, could be expanded to create a control point for the main sea route into the Western Pacific.   On the north east coast of Sumatra, the excellent port facilities of Belawan could be developed to give a strong military presence in the Straits of Malacca. That was a potential solution to the regular problem of piracy, on which Malik Khalifa lay heavy emphasis. He was somewhat less emphatic that it would also command the northern route into the western Pacific.

There remained the exposed eastern coastline of the Indian ocean. Malik Khalifa proposed a major development at Singkil on the west coast of Sumatra. It was accessed by deep water and its location was protected by a natural headland. Offshore the small island of Pulau Tuangku offered further shelter, in much the same way that the main British naval base at Portsmouth was sheltered by the Isle of Wight. With suitable naval facilities established in Singkil it would be possible to police a large area of open ocean.

The minister pulled out a map and quickly acknowledged Malik Khalifa's logic. It was a poor part of his country and the proposal would be an economic bounty. He wondered how much the development would cost. The Saudi offered a useful comparison, based on the port of Sydney in Australia. That expansion would cost a billion dollars and take seven years to complete. The minister gleamed with anticipation : a billion dollar's worth of contracts promised a bounty indeed. All that remained was to draw up heads of agreement, which the minister could then present to his Cabinet colleagues. He foresaw no major problem with anything discussed so far. On the contrary, Indonesia had just achieved most favoured nation status in the eyes of Riyadh, without compromising its independence. The contracts and legal staff at his ministry would be instructed to draw up the outline documents over the next few days; his government colleagues should be most impressed.

"Just one other point needs to be mentioned in private between us," the sophisticated Saudi murmured to his old acquaintance. The minister nodded sagely and asked exactly what the Saudi diplomat had in mind. Dr Khalifa smiled; when in Indonesia do what the Indonesians do. "There is then the conventional matter of commission on the deal. Shall we say ten per cent payable into a bank account of your own choice in Switzerland?" The Indonesian smiled broadly, for it was his lucky day. The difference was that while the Saudi understood his colleague's pleasure completely, the delight of the potentate from Saudi Arabia was somewhat more discreet.

*   *   *   *   *

Rotherhithe, London

ANTONIA FOO had been living in London for over six months and had decided it was time she did something about her love life. Since they first met in October she had been working closely with Dr Christopher Cunningham of the Sharava Corporation. Despite its international structure he did seem to be based in London a lot of the time, and she liked that. Since they first met for a drink in Champagne Charlie's, the two of them had put in a lot of hard work together on the electronic software order for new ships in the Chinese navy.

Over the months, Antonia had decided that Christopher Cunningham was her kind of man. So today he was going to be in luck. Antonia had been born in 1957, the Year of the Rooster and that meant she was destined to be proud and aggressive. It would be interesting to discover which sign of the zodiac explained Dr. Cunningham. She hoped it would be something sociable. For this special occasion, Antonia had resorted to her favourite cheong sam. After meeting Christopher for the first time at Charing Cross she had wandered along the Strand into Covent Garden. In the craft market in its Jubilee Hall she found the stall of a little Chinese lady with a splendid collection of cheongsams for sale, two of which she purchased.

But today she would be wearing her special one, her seduction dress, brought lovingly all the way from Shanghai. It was thick black silk with sprays of lilies embroidered tastefully across its front and round its hem. The slit at the side went almost to her waist. Her carefully-chosen underwear was minimal. She knew she would be irresistible in her outfit because her stockings, shoes, hair, jewellery, make-up and perfume were exactly right too. Antonia Foo was leaving nothing to chance.

The day had been chosen with considerable care too. Her neighbours had told her that from the early summer onwards the ocean-going cruise ships came up the Thames, right past her flat, to tie up alongside HMS Belfast on the Thames. Their timetable was available on the web. They also explained you could always tell when one was about to arrive on the flood tide, because Limehouse Reach in front of her was where the large tugboats would hover. Apparently it was always either the Shorne or the Cobham. Today it was the Shorne already on station, which meant the cruise ship was probably approaching the Thames Barrier at Woolwich. Antonia anxiously checked the flowers, the wine and the crudités.

With immaculate timing the buzzer from downstairs rang. It was her guest. She released the remote door lock and told him to take the lift to the third floor where she would meet him. Less than five minutes later they were both sipping a cocktail on the open verandah as a Caribbean cruiser, the 'Ocean Countess' came slowly and majestically into view round the river bend from Greenwich. She was the first big ship to come right up the Thames that year. The tugboat Shorne slipped into position behind her and a cable was attached for the tricky right angle turn upriver at Limehouse. As the cruise ship slowly disappeared from view towards Tower Bridge, Antonia and Christopher talked about the great buildings opposite at Canary Wharf and the amazingly fast expansion of that high-rise business district from the derelict East and West India Docks. That led to their chatting about ships. The cruise ship had served its conversational purpose. Antonia wanted to talk about nothing in particular. Not tonight.

They had after all spent the previous months, on and off, designing electronics for a new fleet of ships which, according to Antonia, would be deployed by the Chinese in the Yellow Sea and the Sea of Japan. Christopher Cunningham was none too sure about that, but for the time being said nothing. Rather he slid an appreciative arm round Antonia's shapely waist and was delighted by her immediate and powerfully positive response. He had often wondered what she would be like in bed and he was shortly to find out.

A couple of hours later Antonia had found out quite a lot about Christopher Cunningham. He had been born in 1960, the Year of the Rat. According to the Chinese zodiac that made him charming, creative and sociable, and apparently keen to gossip. They had got that right on all four counts. She also discovered that like her he was divorced and, away from work, was finding life lonely. That May afternoon they were both discovering, simultaneously, a welcome physical cure for that. The other things she had found out about him strongly suggested that second helpings, and many future romantic encounters, would be a good idea.

What she had not discovered was anything much about the Sharava Corporation. She knew it was registered in the Dutch Antilles, that it worked in swiss francs, named its products with Hindu or Sanskrit names and had sales offices in key cities around the world. Once again he left her with the clear impression although it probably had a large Indian shareholding, the business owed national allegiance to no-one. Sharava was simply in it for the money.

By mid-evening they were both hungry and she suggested a good Chinese meal would be in order. Antonia changed into something less dramatic than a black silk cheong sam with a slit up the side and they then walked along the riverbank to the Yun Hai. It was a quiet and stylish Chinese restaurant, several cuts above the noisy tourist traps in Chinatown. Rather than the chef being a hireling of some absentee proprietor, the chef of the Yun Hai owned the establishment himself. His menu was clever, the restaurant service efficient and disarmingly friendly. The staff obviously knew Antonia Foo and her knowledgeable Chinese food preferences well.

After a starter of minced mixed meats served on lettuce with plum sauce, the meal moved away from the printed menu completely. Antonia had negotiated quite different dishes beforehand with the chef. While she drank white wine, Christopher Cunningham stuck to Tsing Tao beer. He did not wish to diminish his amorous prowess for the remainder of the evening and, ideally, through the night as well.

Back at her apartment they loved into the early hours. Christopher was discoving a new level of expertise and enthusiasm in a woman. His alcohol management had succeeded too, and by next morning Antonia decided that she wanted to stay in London longer than her work for the software order would allow. Then over coffee Christopher chose his moment and gradually steered the conversation round to the Chinese navy.

Antonia now wanted to impress. He was interested to learn that her factory had built not conventional diesels, but high powered jet engines, and that each ship would need two of them. Christopher Cunningham knew enough about naval ships to realise these would not just be coastal patrol craft as Antonia had been told. He confirmed her suspicions that there was more to it than that. Antonia was puzzled. Had the admiral and vice-premier Liu been misleading her all along? No matter what she had been told in Beijing, everything Christopher Cunningham told her now made far better sense. But why had she been misled? They both wondered what secret Beijing was hiding. This troubled Antonia Foo. On her next visit to Beijing she would try to find out what was really going on, but right now it was far more enjoyable to wrap herself in the strong arms of her amorous occidental. Perhaps London was where she belonged after all. Antonia was enough of a romantic to wonder whether this very satisfying evening would be the delightful overture to an entirely new phase of her life.

* * * * *

Westminster, London

IT WAS GOING TO BE a very important lunch for Alan Stanley MP. He had been in parliament for over twelve years, but only now was anyone beginning to pay him much attention. The spacious dining room in Portcullis House was noisy with political chatter, but everyone was far too preoccupied with their own little world to pay much attention to the five Labour plotters. The political tower of babel failed even to notice Graham Crowfield's lapel badge saying 'CLYND' - although it was still hot off the press, and no-one else would have a clue what it meant.

It had been Alan Stanley's speech on defence policy shortly before the recess which had done the trick. Suddenly he was emerging from the shadows as a notable left-leaning thinker and orator. He had celebrated his forty-third birthday by spelling out what needed to be done to Britain's over-large defence sector. "We started dismantling the British Empire in 1947 with the independence of India. It took five whole decades of democratisation until we set Hong Kong free in 1997. We no longer have a British Empire. So why do we need to keep up the pretence that we still have an empire to defend? So, colleagues, ask yourselves: why do we still need a Royal Navy?" It had been inspiring stuff to some, extreme stuff to others - but that was always the privilege of a back-bencher. Anxious Labour members who depended on some naval dockyard vote to put them into Westminster were not his problem. That was what party leaders were elected to worry about.

Among Alan's new admirers was Graham Crowfield, who sat for the safe Labour seat of Sheffield Meadowhall. His lapel badge stood for 'Cheshire, Lancashire, Yorkshire, Nottingham and Derbyshire' and he was explaining why.

"Our once-great party is currently in the grip of a Scottish mafia. Before that it was in the grip of a gentrified pseudo-Geordie mafia. The Welsh have had a crack at running it. London has always been willing to give it a whizz. It's high time we brought our party back to its roots in the north of England. Let us never forget, comrades, that the Labour Party started with a railway trades union in Doncaster. The co-operative movement really began in Rochdale." It was not difficult to spot that Graham Crowfield had studied politics at university. At Ruskin College, Oxford such crucial knowledge of the origins of his party was served with the Weetabix and cornflakes at breakfast.

"If the Labour Party is anything at all, it should be a joining of hands across the Pennines. The Scots and the Welsh are preoccupied with their ersatz nationalism, the party in the South is just too effete. Alan here sits for Pennine South. We are talking the north of England. We could not ask for a more perfect geographical centre for the rebirth of a genuine English Labour Party. Let's get back, not so much to our intellectual past, but back to our true geographical roots."

Graham flashed his CLYND lapel badge round his comrades with pride. For the moment it was their secret society, but not for much longer. The doyen at the lunch was Tom Booth, a veteran from the Lancashire Labour Party until he had retired from the fray in 2005. He had a powerful agenda all of his own. "We also need to get back to the great days of the Worker's Education Association - far better than pretending to be middle class by sending everyone to university. 'Education, education, education' - and what was that all about? Tony Blair was out of his tree.

"But what on earth can you expect of a posh public schoolboy from Scotland and Oxford, a poofter pirouetting with the likes of Peter Mandelson? They both think the working class is something you can just about spot out of your Jaguar's window as you sweep into your constituency for a couple of hours' show time. Education? Lads and lasses from industrial families getting degrees in television awareness and flower arranging? And what kind of Socialism is that, exactly?"

As if Tom Booth's heretical views on education were not enough, he then moved on to housing. "We have had fifty years building rubbishy flats for the working classes. Ronan Point? Do me a favour. Now go and look at the proper council estates of the inter-war years. Then look again at the post-war council estates all around us. They are being built at vast expense one year and demolished again twenty years later. Better even to have Margaret Thatcher's owner-occupiers than that sort of cheapjack rubbish."

The name of the Westminster Witch made them all twitch, but the wine flowed copiously so they soon recovered their natural composure. By the time their puddings had been eaten the five Labour parliamentarians had cooked up a real Socialist agenda which covered housing, the social services, health, education, pensions and defence.

Alan Stanley was delighted. His friends Steve Wilson, who held the safe seat of Liverpool Toxteth and Brian Potter, with the safe seat of Runcorn in Cheshire, completed today's Famous Five. Between them they were writing the agenda for a Labour Party renaissance, one which was firmly rooted in the party's heartland. "Just look at a map of England," the rising star of true Labour values explained enthusiastically.

"Look at our Labour heartlands. Look where we can always count on voting support. Draw a line linking Birmingham, Hull, Leeds and Liverpool, embracing the great cities of the north of England. Just remember that inside that line you can find all the history, all the power, all the common sense and the founding supporters of our great party. Everything else is peripheral. That is the people we represent. It's about time we took back control."

"Yes, I agree with that," said Tom Booth. "But not yet. First look what's happening today. We face not one but two bloodbaths. The party conference at Brighton in September will be a disaster, and then we will have a general election before this time next year. If Brown had any sense he would go to the country this Autumn, but political common sense is in very short supply at the moment, and they never manufacture very much of it in Glasgow even at the best of times.

"They're all far too busy getting pissed in Sauchiehall Street. You watch - he'll hang on to the very last possible minute next May. Mark my words. And then David Cameron will walk all over him. So we will have two bloodbaths in eight months. By next summer, put any money on it, what's left of this party will be reeling. That is our best chance.

"Just look what has been happening lately. Only last month we were hammered into third place in the European elections behind UKIP, for God's sake. Heavyweights from the party have been deserting Gordon Brown and his Scottish mafia in droves. We are fast losing some good women.

"First we lost Mo Mowlam. Clare Short has gone, Jacqui Smith is a gonner, Hazel Blears has told him where to get off. Look how Caroline Flint gave Brown both barrels last month. What did she say? 'He treats female ministers as window dressing.' Then she quit because she was not being promoted. Now Beverley Hughes and Patricia Hewitt have decided to stand down at next General Election. And that's just the women - remember once upon a time we had the Blair Babes? All that now seems a very long time ago. Mark my words, we are going to have ourselves a Labour revolution against our Scottish Labour mafia. The last time Westminster had one was a Tory revolution after their Scottish leaders Alec Douglas-Home and Harold Macmillan. And just like us, their skilful Scottish wheeler-dealer got out of it while the going was good and put in another Scottish stool-pigeon to succeed him to face the music, or rather the cacophany on the hustings.

"You probably don't remember but two very clever men, Iain Macleod and Enoch Powell, both refused to serve under Alec Douglas-Home. You don't have to agree with their politics but you should respect their principles. We are about to suffer exactly the same fiasco in our Labour Party. And it will have exactly the same result. A young party leader opposite will walk all over us just like our Harold Wilson walked all over their Alec Douglas-Home. No-one ever really learns, but perhaps today we just might."

"Okay, Tom, so that's all the negatives. So what are our positives? How should we proceed? Are you saying that we, the members of CLYND, should do what this Macleod and Powell did and keep out of the fray?" Steve Wilson asked the sixty-four thousand dollar question, while Graham Crowfield, Alan Stanley and Brian Potter all nodded wisely in agreement. Well-choreographed nodding is the very essence of political intrigue.

Once again, Tom Booth's hard-won knowledge of British politics came into play. "Well first of all I suggest we learn from the Tories. They are, after all, the experts at getting it wrong. After John Major was wiped out by us in 1997 it took them not one, not two, not even three but altogether four attempts to find a Tory leader who might actually win a general election. So let the five of us learn from other people's mistakes. The odds are that whoever takes over when we dispense with Gordon Brown next summer, as the party surely will, is not going to be the same leader who takes Labour to victory over the Tories when we eventually get round to beating them. So let's try thinking ahead a bit. I'm quite sure Alan here will have his lucky day, but I would prefer not for the time being. Let the Milibands and the Johnsons and the Balls and the Abbotts fight it out tooth and nail next summer, while we just stand on the sidelines. Then just you watch. The honeymoon period for whoever takes over from Gordon Brown will be extremely brief, if there is one at all. Then the bloodbath will begin all over again. The Tory government will go on and on about all the messes Labour left behind, and blame us of course for everything that goes wrong.

"Then will come the political autobiographies, as our defeated heroes each try to prove it was everyone else's fault but their own. We will have the traditional passing-out parade of literary post-mortems, leaving our new Labour leader spinning like a top. After Gordon Brown he or she will have the impossible task of trying to justify our track record from when we were in office, and will be crucified in the process. And after he or she has been crucified, that's when Alan here steps in. He will be a brand new Labour leader facing the future who takes over from a God-foresaken Labour leader facing the past."

The small gathering of CLYND members rejoiced at these words of experience and wisdom from their spiritual leader. Tom Booth could read the Labour Party well. For his companions, listening to him was like listening to a Delphic Oracle from the profound depths of Lancashire; they would definitely drink to that. And in that moment of sublime truth Graham Crowfield, Steve Wilson and Brian Potter discovered the bottle was now empty so they headed for the bar.

While they were out of earshot, Tom Booth gave somewhat different words of advice to his talented protégé. Then he added "They may be cheering you now, Alan, but just remember this. The policies and arguments which will sweep you to the leadership of the Labour Party, and should sweep you into Ten Downing Street, are not necessarily the realities you will discover once you are in office. That has been the bane of Labour leaders every time. Too often it all looks very different once you are in power. Most politicians discover the floating electorate would much rather listen to a comfortable lie than an uncomfortable truth. That's how you get elected but the lies soon dissolve in Whitehall and only uncomfortable truths remain. I've seen it happen too many times - to the Tories as well. More often than not an election-winning manifesto becomes a government's epitaph.

"Sometimes a genuinely Socialist manifesto doesn't even make it as far as that. Just think back to Michael Foot's disastrous leadership of the party in 1983. He was well and truly hammered by Margaret Thatcher in that general election. Many thought he deserved it, thoroughly nice guy though he was in person. And what did that thoughtful Labour politician Gerald Kauffman have to say on the subject? He explained that Michael Foot's election manifesto had been the longest suicide note in history. Like it or not, Alan, you must accept that Gerald Kauffman was absolutely right.

"Down the years many good honest Labour MPs have been unable to hack it. Just look at the number of incurable old alcoholics this party has produced. One of our most accomplished piss-artists of all times, deputy leader George Brown, resigned from the party overnight. Remember too the Labour men who defected to the Tories, only to be vilified by the party for deserting our cause. Too often they had simply disowned a world of comfortable political fiction once they were forced into the world of uncomfortable political fact. Mark my words, Alan - don't tie yourself down to a string of vote-winning non-retractable promises that one day will come back to haunt you. They are the most addictive of all do-it-yourself political elephant traps."

"Come on, you pair of miserable sods, this is a time for celebration." chorused the trio of hardened drinkers as they returned with a brace of fresh bottles from the bar. "For God's sake have a drink and let's look to the future. Stop going on about the past. Let's bury it."

So the five of them did exactly that, and once glasses were held aloft the wine then tasted sweet. As they drank to all those future victories, Alan Stanley quietly did his sums. By 2012, he would be forty-six years old. It was the perfect age at which to stage a party coup, with young Turks behind him and admiring supporters in front. He would become a youthful emperor of the Labour Party, one born aloft in triumph.

The last two men to lead the party to success had also done it in their forties. Harold Wilson had been 47 and Tony Blair had only been 41. And as he pondered the hard-earned wisdom of Tom Booth and rejoiced in the unquestioning support of his closest friends, the lofty Alan Stanley reached a personal decision. Their conspiratorial lunch in July 2010 would become the foundation stone of his future leadership of the Labour Party, making that leadership a hat-trick for the successful forty-somethings - Harold, Alan and Tony; a hat-trick indeed.

Yet totally unlike Graham Crowfield, Steve Wilson or Brian Potter, Alan Stanley realised that history was the only window through which anyone could observe and understand the present. They could neither understand nor manage the present just with their surreally optimistic dreams about the future. It was a personal philosophy which in years to come would prove to be the eleventh -hour salvation of Alan Stanley's own leadership of his own party.

Chapter Eight

The Rowing Eight

Canberra, Australia

THE RUSSELL DISTRICT in the Australian capital city of Canberra is not over-abundant with interesting, congenial bars. The neighbourhood is mainly occupied by the headquarters of the Australian Defence Force, buildings equivalent to the Pentagon in Washington or the Ministry of Defence in London. For those who are thirsty it is necessary to go somewhat further afield to find a drink. After a wholly frustrating morning in the office, Lieutenant-Commander Warwick Sydenham of the Royal Australian Navy was much relieved to discover that Captain Bill Boyce had come up from Sydney and was right here in town. Bill was a world expert when it came to finding somewhere suitable for a congenial drink.

He met the curmudgeonly old sailor for lunch in a bar which was, without doubt, both congenial and interesting. It was the choice of an expert imbiber, not a bar which Warwick had visited before, but he was always willing to learn. Bill was not in the best of health but that minor hindrance diminished neither his drinker's impressive omniscience nor his alcoholic intake, even in the middle of the day. His medical advisers were not Bill Boyce's favourite people.

Warwick Sydenham was in high dudgeon. "Bill, tell me, why does the Australian Defence Force specialise in recruiting people with nothing between their ears?" Captain William Boyce smiled. His old shipmate's son was learning fast. "Warwick my boy, I see you are rapidly discovering that here in Canberra the Navy plays second fiddle to the Army. I have never known why. Perhaps it's because bureaucratic Canberra prefers to see Australia as the world's smallest continent rather than the world's largest island. And according to that convenient logic, oceans should be someone else's problem.

"It's all a question of mindset. Those of us who understand warships and the high seas know better, of course, but here in Canberra professional sailors are a beleaguered minority. Quite the opposite, for example, of the way it works in the Great Britain. The Poms have always seen themselves as an island race. The English Channel is their most treasured geographical asset. You have to hand it to the Brit who once wrote that fabulous headline 'Fog In Channel: Continent Cut Off.' Definitely my kinda guy."

Bill took a healthy swig of numbers, as Kronenbourg was known among his dedicated drinking companions. Over the rim of his glass he scrutinised his companion. "Okay, Warwick, I can see you're going to explain what happened. You're in the right company. Give it to me with both barrels."

For the next twenty minutes, Warwick Sydenham detailed the furious row he had endured that afternoon. He needed to unwind, to debrief, to unload. His strategy paper on the resource requirements of the Royal Australian Navy had been roundly rejected by his senior officers, an army colonel and his assistant. Warwick had been working on it for months.

"Bill, I took them right through the obvious logic you explained to me five whole years ago when we had that long lunch at Doyle's. It was stark logic then and the stint I've had since on an Anzac has simply confirmed it in even starker detail. I told them as much in my report, yet they just threw the whole thing straight out of the window. Our navy is hopelessly under-equipped should any of our Pacific neighbours start getting frisky. And if anything starts to happen in the Indian Ocean, God save us all here in Australia, we could find ourselves in one hell of a mess."

Warwick was smarting particularly at the calumnies heaped on people like him who were graduates of Dartmouth. "The problem with you, Lieutenant-Commander Sydenham," the army colonel had said somewhat tartly "is that you have become as gung-ho as the Brits. That's what they always do to you at Dartmouth. The Royal Navy has been throwing its weight around the seven seas ever since it was created by that lecherous old bugger King Henry VIII. That is so long ago that Australia wasn't even Australia.

"In this modern country, Lieutenant-Commander Sydenham, we are actually aware that the cold war is over and that our proper military task is to take care of our own back yard. Britannia can still try to rule the waves if she insists, but Australia has much better things to think about and many much better things to spend the people's money on."

The colonel and his assistant had been quite adamant in rejecting Warwick's paper and that, unfortunately, was that. At which point the independent-minded naval officer had cleared his desk and gone in search of a necessary drink.

Bill Boyce listened carefully and nodded wisely. "You have to understand, Warwick, that the men right at the top of the Australian military are soldiers, not sailors. Take Duncan Lewis, National Security Adviser. A perfectly good fellah but ultimately a veteran of

Warwick Sydenham

the campaigns in East Timor. Or Richard Wilson, head of the Defence Intelligence Organisation, another veteran of East Timor and another soldier. The British seem to rotate their top military jobs through their three armed services. Perhaps one day we could adopt that sensible principle here. From time to time we could do with a man at the top who has the sea in his blood. There are times, probably all times, when we should start to see ourselves as another island race, just like the Poms always have done."

Warwick went on to explain the more detailed contents of his paper. In his view, too many ships in the Navy were little more than rust buckets. He had been to inspect HMS Tobruk, twenty years old and in theory the spearhead of the navy. As a sailor himself of fifteen years' experience, Warwick doubted if she was even fit to go to sea. In theory the Tobruk could land eighteen Leopard tanks. In practice Warwick Sydenham doubted she could even land one and in his report he had said as much. That had won him no new friends among the military top brass.

Bill Boyce's advice was still uncompromising. "Stick to your guns, Warwick. One day they will believe you. It will probably be by force of circumstances than by force of logic, but you will at least be able to say it was you who got there first.

"Or rather you will not say anything of the sort. Few people ever feel comfortable with a professional 'I Told You So' and nowhere are such people less popular than here in the Australian armed forces. Remember I spent most of my career in the Navy being regarded as a military irritant rather than a military asset, but in the end it's always the likes of you and me who will be proved right." Warwick Sydenham grimaced and took a savage swig of his drink.

*   *   *   *   *

Westminster, London

DAVID CAMERON'S coalition government had been in power for about four weeks, but the rows at its Ministry of Defence were already growing fast and furious. His new defence secretary Liam Fox had been asked by the new Chancellor of the Exchequer George Osborne to examine the defence budget meticulously and such scrutiny was not to the liking of the senior people in his department. The Secretary of State for Defence explained "Every single bit of the operation must come under scrutiny. Every single thing must be justified."

So one weekend in June witnessed moves of rare savagery even by Whitehall standards. They claimed the scalps of the two most senior officials running Britain's armed forces. The Chief of the Defence Staff, Air Chief Marshal Sir Jock Stirrup and the Department's most senior civil servant, the Permanent Secretary Sir Bill Jeffrey were both told they would have to go. It was brown envelope time and perfectly obvious that there had been a huge row in Whitehall. Military specialists in parliament were quick to put the boot in as well. Their turn had come at last after too many years being forced to wait in the wings.

Patrick Mercer, a Conservative MP and former soldier, said the change at the Ministry was desperately needed. "The last regime allowed our men to go into Helmand Province in Afghanistan improperly prepared, while huge sums of money were squandered on projects such as the refurbishment of the Ministry of Defence."

Another Tory backbencher, Adam Holloway, a former Guards officer, said: "There was a tendency under the Labour government to promote 'politicians in uniform' rather than officers willing to give frank advice about the strategic drift in Afghanistan." It was the general view on the Tory back benches and beyond, that Mr Blair had been a prime minister who preferred cosmetic style over military substance. Another member of parliament put it succinctly, "Given the key choice between an attractive untruth and an unattractive truth, Mr. Blair always chose the saleable lie by congenital instinct." Colonel Tim Collins, who had quit the army over the lack of funding, said: "Jock Stirrup was a well-known apologist for Labour's muddled thinking over Afghanistan."

In the wake of such obvious discord, the guard had been changed by Liam Fox. Perhaps it had been unkind to ask a career RAF officer to take command of a ground war in such awkward terrain and conditions as Afghanistan. That impenetrable country had already defeated a British army in the nineteenth century and a Russian army in the twentieth. It was not looking all that good for a combined American and British army in the twenty-first. Nor was it entirely clear what they were fighting, but Uncle Sam felt obliged to fight somebody, somewhere about something following the events of 9/11. Who, where and what seemed more or less secondary.

The incoming government asked for a radical review of Britain's defence requirements and resources. Again there was criticism that Sir Jock Stirrup, "a lame duck", would be in charge of it for the next few months. Liam Fox wanted "the best people to be in the appropriate posts" once the review was over. "We have to be able to maintain full stability and the full confidence of the people who work for us, not least because we're in a very dangerous armed conflict," he said. Sir Jock Stirrup has been criticised for not doing enough to support front line troops.

Labour's back-bench MP Alan Stanley treated the entire Department of Defence pantomime with disdain. He had never been particularly impressed with the way defence had been run by the last two Labour prime ministers, Tony Blair and Gordon Brown. Nor was he sympathetic to the priorities of the new coalition government either. Alan Stanley was an unrepentant Little Englander, permanently of the view that Britain's armed forces should keep their noses out of other people's business. He had much sympathy for the way Australia's armed forces, despite being the largest in the southern hemisphere, managed to keep themselves to themselves.

For Alan Stanley the proper place to be on that Melodramatic Monday, as news of regime change and ruthless decapitation at the Ministry of Defence emerged, was in Annie's Bar. It was the thinking and drinking establishment of choice in the Houses of Parliament for MPs of a gossipy disposition.

As he downed a pint of good northern bitter with his good northern friend Graham Crowfield, the Member of Parliament for Sheffield Meadowhall, they found themselves at a considerable distance from the cut and thrust of the debate. "The Tories have always been un controllably gung-ho when it comes to the armed forces." said Graham "What has interested me was the fascination Tony Blair also had with going to war. He never carried a rifle in anger in his entire life, but he was still a wannabe general."

Alan Stanley, the battle-hardened MP for Pennine South, took a further sip as he scrutinised his old friend. "That probably explains it of course. Give a man a box of toy soldiers for his birthday and, if he doesn't know any better, he will probably find it irresistible to play with them sooner or later. I know Blair was born in Yorkshire but that didn't make him a real Yorkshireman. Or a real Lancastrian. He's just an effete public schoolboy from the poshest school in Edinburgh and Oxford University, where he apparently he got a First Class Honours degree for his consumption of beer, with a special paper in playing the guitar. Badly."

The increasingly wily politician from the other side of the Pennines agreed. "I tell you, Graham, we have all come a long way from the days of a real Yorkshire soldier like Denis Healey. He served with the Royal Engineers in North Africa, Sicily and Italy. He was a beachmaster at Anzio. That generation knew exactly what they would be letting our lads in for. So did Jim Callaghan. Or indeed Ted Heath, who was also a major in World War Two. Ultimately it's not even party political. It's all a matter of generations. Heath and Healey were born in the same year, 1916, the middle of world war one. So for that matter was Harold Wilson, although he spent most of the war working for people like Beveridge right here in Whitehall. By contrast those former soldiers in parliament knew from first-hand experience what it was all about.

"Did you know that Enoch Powell, whatever you thought of him subsequently, climbed all the way from private to brigadier during World War Two? Whatever their politics it doesn't matter. You've just got to admire someone as able as that. Such men learnt their military stuff the hard way, not by playing computer games. They knew exactly what it meant for their friends to die.

"Contrast our recent lot, who didn't seem to give a toss. I reckon that's one of the reasons we got kebabbed in the general election. We gave the distinct impression from Ten Downing Street that warfare is just some thrilling computer game. You know, just "Bang, bang you're dead" but they can all get up again and go home afterwards. Except in a real war, they can't. Instead we flew them all back to Brize Norton in wooden boxes. Gordon Brown couldn't have cared less, he didn't even know how many soldiers had been killed. My round, I think."

As his parliamentary colleagues listened to Alan Stanley set out his wider thoughts on the logic of military activity and the nature of international diplomacy, they were all attentive. It was clear Alan was nobody's fool, in an era when political foolishness was an all-too common Westminster characteristic. Nor had he been tainted by the simmering row over parliamentary expenses, an important asset for the future. Alan Stanley had been careful to keep his parliamentary expenses claims to an absolute minimum. In the midst of a parliamentary fracas the group of friends drinking with him in Annie's Bar were among the first people in parliament to see a substantial political future for Alan Stanley, the very tall and increasingly impressive member for Pennine South.

*   *   *   *   *

Shanghai, China

ANTONIA FOO was in two minds, at the same time feeling both excited and slightly guilty. For the first time in three years she was back in her home city of Shanghai and it had changed. Much for the better and that was exciting. She had booked into the five star Pudang Shangri-La Hotel and her room was one which overlooked the Bund. To help overcome the jet-lag from London, she had treated herself to tuina massage treatment and an amber facial. She had tested the hotel's various restaurants and bars. She had taken the courtesy bus to the World Expo which was running through the summer and had a good look round. Shanghai was doing just fine, especially when it was free of automotive pollution.

She had taken a long walk along the Bund, still with the old headquarters building of the Hongkong and Shanghai Bank amid its attractions. The bank's old building dated back to the 1920s but it had stood up well. At one point it had even served as the headquarters of Shanghai's notorious Gang of Four.

China may have gone through many political contortions but its architecture lingered on. Antonia reflected how, when she looked out from her flat in Rotherhithe, she was looking straight across at the modern headquarters of that very same bank, HSBC as it liked to call itself nowadays. But that might not last much longer either. The bank also had a splendid headquarters building in Hong Kong itself, an architectural triumph of its day when it had been completed in

1985. Perhaps one day the strength of the Chinese economy might persuade the bank to return to its true home in the Orient. Her Shanghai batteries suitably recharged, she was ready to meet Admiral Zhou Man for the first time in those three years. That prospect was making her feel vaguely guilty, not an emotion she often experienced. The two of them had been in contact many times by email as she sorted out the electronics for his fleet of warships. Yet she had not seen him face to face since she left behind the unappealing Yellow River Industrial Research Facility in Lanzhou.

Suddenly it all seemed a very long time ago in a very distant place, as she explored her native city once again. Since she had left China, Antonia had been working closely with Christopher Cunningham of the Sharava Corporation in London and she had come to like him rather a lot and grown more and more fascinated with finding out what Sharava did. The little she knew had opened up a whole new world to her, one which pointed to the world's future and her own. Her real problem was whether to tell Zhou Man about her new romance.

In the event he solved the problem for her. In the years since they last met it now emerged he had married. He broke the news to her quite gently over their second drink in the Jade On 36 bar, while they admired the splendid view across the city. Antonia was astonished. In his numerous emails he had not said a single word about such a major change in his life. Now it turned out he even had a baby daughter. Under China's one-child policy, that would be the limit, but it was still far better than none.

In that instant she decided there would be no need to say a single word about Christopher Cunningham back in London. On the contrary she could move from defence to attack and to cover her tracks. Antonia determined to attack with gusto. They were both Chinese, although from different parts of a huge country, so to begin with the row was decidedly taciturn. But the anger within was simmering and growing. It continued to strengthen as they had a supper in the ultra-smart Jade On 36 restaurant, where the taste of excellent food did very little to mollify her.

The real row erupted when they went up to her room for a cocktail. By now she was almost apoplectic and for once the seduction cheongsam was going to stay on her lovely body. She rather wished she was wearing jeans instead, although her admirers told her she looked pretty good in those as well. "How could you do this to me?" she exploded. "I thought you and I were friends, good friends, good lovers. Now you have just thrown me aside like some tramp, without even mentioning a single word."

For his part Zhou Man was unrepentant and that made it worse. His viewpoint was so simple, the very last thing she wished to hear. As he saw it, Antonia had immersed herself in the thrills and attractions of London, by all reports one of the most exciting cities in the world. How was he to know whether she might find herself a new boyfriend amid all those possibilities, all those excitements, all those tall handsome occidental men? He was getting no younger either and wanted a child. How much longer should he wait? He was already 48 years old when he married. That did not please Antonia very much either. Her child-bearing years had already come and gone.

"Why did you not tell me you wanted a family when we first met? I could have done something about it then. Did it ever occur to you I might have wanted a family as well?" All the Admiral could do was bluster. "Antonia, you were a divorcee. I just assumed you wanted to have a decent sex life and to leave it at that." Antonia promptly moved the argument a notch further. "Well you were wrong. You and I both had a job of work to do. In any case you were a divorcee too. And Lanzhou was hardly the sort of place anyone would ever want to bring up a child."

As Man pondered this onslaught, Antonia shifted tack. "And why did you lie to me about your fleet of ships? You told me we were building them to patrol the little seas on the Pacific rim. That wasn't true, was it? They are going to be a new fleet in the Indian Ocean. People have guessed, or worked it out for themselves. You knew all along that the Middle Kingdom is hell bent on a twenty-first century version of old-fashioned colonialism, in Africa of all places. It's all so obvious now. I should have seen it at the time."

Admiral Zhou's protestations that China would need to guard its supplies of raw material cut no ice at all. Antonia was on the home straight. "Perhaps that is so, but what I object to is the blatant hypocrisy. How can we smooch with the anti-colonial forces at the United Nations, when we intend to become the next great colonial power ourselves? I tell you Admiral Zhou Man: I want nothing whatever to do with it. Any of it. I am a scientist and an engineer, not some double-dealing politician."

There was little more to be said. Zhou Man made a courteous farewell and left the Pudang Shangri-La Hotel as quickly as he could. He knew immediately he was walking right out of her life, finally and absolutely, never to return. It was the end of a potentially great relationship. Hell hath no fury quite like a scorned Antonia Foo.

* * * * *

Paris, France

IT SHOULD HAVE BEEN an enjoyable 27th birthday for Violaine Khalifa, but it was one of the least enjoyable she could remember. Her problems at work had been the cause of that. Her strategy paper on how to develop relations with the Arab Islamic world had been summarily rejected by her security department. As soon as she left the office, almost in tears, she telephoned James Heaton for sympathy

and support. Her fiancé quickly picked up on her mood and asked
what was wrong. "I'm not supposed to discuss my work at the
Section, darling, but since my paper has been rejected outright I don't
exactly see how it can still be considered top secret. It was simply an
assessment of trends in the Arab world generally and Islam in
particular and explaining how we should deal with them. I can't
believe it. They simply threw it out of the window. They didn't want
to know." She gave James a quick summary of what her paper had
contained. James was familiar enough with her views already and
supported them whole-heartedly.

"Well, Violaine, I can assure you of something. You are not
the only one to suffer that fate." James replied. "I must surely have
mentioned my Australian friend Warwick Sydenham before; you
know the chap I mean. I had some emails from him quite recently
explaining that he had also written a strategic paper, in his case for the
Australian Navy and that too was thrown straight out of the window.
Perhaps it's the fate of our generation.

"You should meet Warwick. It's high time he saw some of the
wonders of Europe once more. You could show him Paris, I could
show him London. And you could then both sympathise with one
another about having serious professional rows at work."

"How do you know him?" Violaine wanted to know. She
wanted to know everything about her future husband's life. "I first
met Warwick about fifteen years ago when we were cadets at
Dartmouth. We became close friends right there and then. I suppose
that's one of the purposes and effects of going to Dartmouth in the
first place, rather like the lifelong contacts you form at Oxford.
Although the two of us have been on opposite sides of the world
much of the time since, we have never lost touch. I know this might
sound strange, talking about Australia, but he really is one of my
oldest friends in the navy.

Violaine thought that all sounded very reassuring. However the future Mrs Heaton was understandably keen to be at the side of her husband-to-be. In times of adversity she always wanted him with her, his arms wrapped comfortingly round her. She had met him on her twenty-first birthday in Paris and now she was twenty-seven. "James, when can you come over to Paris?"

He was as positive as he could be. "Look, I can't get over for a few days at least and I don't suppose you can get over to London either. Is your father around? He's one of the wisest men I have ever met on the comings and goings of the Islamic world. Just talk your report through with him. At least you'll get the feeling that you are right and they are wrong, no matter how many are ranged against you.

"Remember that every great original idea the world has ever known always began as a minority of one. Yours is probably the same. Remember also you understand the Islamic mind from the inside and you've had the rare opportunity at Oxford to spend three years researching it and analysing its history objectively. That is something I bet none of your work colleagues in Paris could ever claim no matter how senior they may consider themselves."

Violaine had already thought of her father. "I think Papa may be coming home this weekend. If he does I'll corner him then. Right now I feel if they all carry on as stupidly as this, I would rather throw in the job, marry you, have some children quickly and live happily ever after." That sounded pretty good to James Heaton too.

Her father arrived in Paris on Saturday morning, on an early flight from Riyadh. She and her mother Louise were equally delighted to see him and the family celebrations went on right through lunch. But then it was Violaine's turn for a serious discussion. In his study over a coffee she told her father exactly what had happened earlier in the week. She had endured a huge row with her superiors in her department at the Renseignements Generaux.

"Exactly what did you say in this paper?" Malik asked his daughter.
"To be honest, Violaine, I suppose I could guess quite a lot of it, but
your views may have moved on from your Oxford days. After all that
was three years ago and you've had plenty of time since to adjust to
the changing realities of what is happening now."

Violaine was pensive for a moment and then explained. The
problem as she saw it was that the old guard in her department were
still living out the challenges of their youth. Back in those days,
French politics had been dominated by the Algerian problem. Anti-
Islamic attitudes had become ingrained. Problems with Moslem
immigrant workers from Turkey had simply strengthened the
prejudice. Then every time Al-Qaeda or some other terrorist group
committed another atrocity, it merely gave further confirmation that
those prejudices were right. So far as her senior colleagues at work
were concerned, any Arab was a bad Arab, especially if he was also a
devout Muslim. The job of the department, as they saw it, was to
oppose such cultural inferiority every inch of the way.

"They don't seem to realise that the only way to deal with the
problem is to understand the divisions within Islam itself. To
understand the difference between Sunnis and the Shia would be a
good start, many of them haven't even grasped the essentials of that.
How can they be so stupid? Any soldier or diplomat would tell you
the right way forward is to divide and rule the opposition. They just
don't seem able to grasp that." Malik nodded in sympathy. He had
heard too much of this before, throughout his own diplomatic career.

"Look, let me explain something which might even encourage
you." he offered, "I get exactly the same problem with many
colleagues in Saudi Arabia, but seen from the opposite end of the
telescope. It happens. Even in the mild and modulated manners of
Islam, we have our rows too. Believe me. There are those in Riyadh
who see nothing but evil in everything the West stands for. They are

quite blind to reason. Before you were born, before I married your mother even, I spent the early part of my career travelling round the world. The English say that travel broadens the mind and they are right. I carried on travelling well after I married.

"Your mother and I served in some of the most educated cities on this planet. I know from first hand that for all their problems, those great cities are something the entire Arab world has so far failed to equal. We can put up huge glamorous skyscrapers by the dozen, but that is not quite the same thing as the positive hum of stylish cosmopolitan civilisation that should surround them. Where exactly are our Shakespearian or West End theatres, our stylish bars and restaurants selling every kind of cuisine in the world, our Versailles, our Place du Tertre in Monmartre, our Bank of England, our British Museum, our Louvres, our many centuries of superb architecture, our stunning galleries like the Royal Academy or the Wallace Collection with priceless collections from all over the world?

"Violaine, just remember always that your colleagues at work are also talking utter ignorant rubbish. When they start to sound persuasive, always pinch yourself. It's just the same for me. You would scarce believe some of the arguments I have had to endure, arguments with self-acclaimed experts on the entire planet, men who have never experienced any other part of it in their whole lives.

"And now a serious piece of advice from your father. Never forget that the real world constantly moves on, people change, important jobs are re-filled, while most good ideas become lodged in the brickwork. No matter how crudely it has been rejected this time round, still make certain your paper is correctly filed and recorded. One day you will be proved right. There is always a little satisfaction to be gained from being the person who can eventually say 'I told you so.' In the meantime, having rows with inferior people is an essential part of your continuing education."

Chapter Nine

The Nine Lives

Nairobi, Kenya

IT WAS SEVERAL YEARS since James Heaton and Warwick Sydenham had last met and they greeted one another warmly. Ever since their earliest days at Dartmouth, now fifteen years ago, they had always been in contact by email and telephone. Now, just as it had been when they first came face to face as naval cadets, it was instantly a meeting of minds. Sometimes their conversation seemed almost telepathic.

Nairobi was a convenient half-way point for them; one flew in from London, the other from Sydney. They were part of a three-day conference to discuss Operation Atalanta, the multinational fleet chasing pirates off the Somali coast. The venue was the Nairobi Serena Hotel on Kenyatta Avenue, round the corner from Uhuru Way, just along from Haile Selassie Avenue near Moi Avenue and Tom Mboya Street. Central Nairobi was a concrete catalogue of the names of top African politicians.

Only the finest thoroughfares were named after them. If such political and diplomatic immortalisation persisted, it would only be a matter of time before central Nairobi needed a substantial civic makeover. A twenty-first Baron Haussmann would become essential, or in his continued absence some very important person indeed would eventually feel slighted by urbane exclusion.

The Atalanta Conference followed a familiar pattern. Military and diplomatic experts explained how numerous the pirates were and what they were achieving. There was a description of their semi-military tactics and how they had steadily evolved. The speed and range of pirate boats was discussed in much detail. There was an analysis of the number of hi-jacked ships and crew members currently being held for ransom.

In rather more private sessions naval officers exchanged ideas on joint tactics which could be used to counter the pirates. Then there was a plenary session led by unidentified British intelligence officers on who was almost certainly arming, controlling and benefitting from the piracy. That led to the issue of which international terrorist organisations had moved in and were now using native Somalis as a convenient smokescreen. Ransom money was by-passing the nouveau riche of Mogadishu and finding its way straight into Swiss and other secret bank accounts. The accounts were known to bankroll some of the world's most ruthless terrorist groups.

The general advice supplied to merchant shipping was to give the African coast a wide berth, with a recommended minimum transit distance of 300 miles. This was not feasible in the Gulf of Aden to the north. At some points, the Gulf of Aden between Africa and Asia was only 100 miles wide. There a different strategy of hugging the Yemeni coastline and setting course through a series of agreed waypoints was in operation, allowing warships to patrol a much smaller area.

Maps were circulated while a naval analyst explained where the pirates were based. The port of Bosaso on the African coast was the centre for the northern Somali pirates. They could all pronounce that, but as the description moved south the place names became more taxing. Beyond the Horn of Africa the pirates were operating out of Eyl in

Puntland, out of Hobyo in the Somali region of Mugdug and out of Hararardhere in Galmadug. Meanwhile the Somali capital of Modgadishu was a favourite port for re-supplying pirate motherships.

After all boat-spotting, high finance, unfamiliar geography and strange-sounding names, James Heaton and Warwick Sydenham definitely needed a drink. They homed in on the hotel's Maisha health club, whose swimming pool lent some style. It looked inviting but after an assessment the two officers agreed to take their liquids internally. As they raised their glasses in a mutual toast, James pointed out that, most appropriately, the word Nairobi meant 'sweet water'. The city's name had little to do with human refreshment however. It had everything to do with railways.

The engineer in James Heaton had always been fascinated by trains. To while away the off-duty hours at the conference he had been doing some homework. Kenya's railways were known the world over as a steam locomotive enthusiast's dream but they were also a key part of political strategy. Railways had changed the nineteenth century map, not just of Africa but of the whole world from transcontinental Canada, to the whole of India, to the trans-Siberian. As he studied Africa's more recent history and politics James had quickly spotted a pattern. There was a new player in the game.

"First," he told Warwick, "Let's just rehearse a spot of history. A pioneering railway was built by the British to connect their main port on the Indian Ocean with the highlands of central Africa. Their destination was Uganda, which was at a high enough altitude to suit Europeans, rather like Simla in India."

Warwick Sydenham knew all about that. Australians were instinctively aware of climate extremes, especially from the days before someone had invented air-conditioning. James had his facts at his fingertips. "Of course it gets cooler as you climb higher, so Uganda is in principle lovely, in many ways the pick of Africa. Go higher still and even right on the Equator, not far from here, there is permanent snow. Just go and look at Mount Kenya. You find exactly the same thing further south on Mount Kilimanjaro; equatorial jungle at the bottom, snow at the top. That said as something to climb the mountain is a disappointment, more of a long walk. Unlike Mount Kenya.

"So the Brits started building the railway inland from Mombasa in about 1896 and it took them five years to reach Lake Victoria. They eventually reached their destination, the Ugandan capital Kampala, as late as 1931. It was a final fling of British imperialism."

"We had exactly the same thing in Australia." agreed Warwick. "A railway was only reason the western provinces like Perth and Freemantle ever signed up to join our commonwealth of Australia. If it hadn't been built they would have become a separate country.

"The trans-Australia railway to Perth across the Nullarbor plain was a purely political project, including three hundred miles of dead straight track running through the middle of nowhere. You can see the same pattern in other countries too. Look at America as it expanded from its eastern beginnings across the Mississippi. Its Wild West was opened up by the railroads and the banks and they weren't all that scrupulous about how they went about it either."

"Warwick, remember what you've just said." replied his English companion. "You can begin to see just how pioneering railways and political skullduggery have always gone hand in hand since the nineteenth century and it is no different today in the twenty-first. It's just that one of today's players is new, ambitious and really rather threatening from our point of view.

James Heaton explained that Kenya's remarkable railway was the main artery of British colonial policy in East Africa, a steel highway linking Kenya and Uganda with Tanganyika. Once the British left, any neighbourliness between Kenya and Tanganyika rapidly evaporated. Old tribal loyalties stepped into the power vacuum left by the British. The railway link between the two countries round Mount Kilimanjaro was abandoned. "So what had turned itself into Tanzania was once again isolated from the other railways of East Africa. That's key too."

"Remember power vacuums, Warwick. I think that is the lesson we are actually learning at this conference. The Somalis spotted an opportunity in the Indian Ocean. I suspect the Chinese spotted another one from four thousand miles away. And they want all the raw materials Africa has to offer. And that's why I am talking about railways. It's something far more significant than trainspotting nostalgia."

James continued his history lesson. Nairobi was modern, built from scratch in the middle of the African bush, a place with a reliable water supply for locomotives climbing six thousand feet into Uganda from the coast of the Indian ocean. Just like England's Crewe or Swindon, it was a railway town created in the middle of nowhere and soon had workshops for repairing locomotives. "Out of that has grown the largest city in Africa between Khartoum and Johannesburg. All because it had sweet water. Building railways is as powerful as that."

With the further mention of sweet water, the two thirsty naval officers simultaneously flagged down a waiter and ordered two more beers. In no time at all, James Heaton was back with his history lesson. "So, Warwick, we can hardly be too surprised if the Chinese decided to build a railway of their own, all the way from Dar-es-Salaam on the Indian Ocean, right across Tanzania into Zambia. They've obviously been studying carefully how we British originally built our empire.

"China was simply claiming for its own benefit the same territory we had abandoned, as something called a wind of change apparently blew through Africa. Or that was the melodramatic phrase concocted by a British prime minister called Harold Macmillan, about fifty years ago, in some grand declaration of his to the South African parliament. In fact he was grandly mistaken. It wasn't a howling wind of change at all. The sound Macmillan thought he heard was merely the hissing of a respray job on African railway stations. The Chinese called their brand new investment the Tan-Zam Railway and it is over 1100 miles long. That's a whole lot of railway, but it now provides a direct link for the Chinese economy from those strategic copper mines straight to the sea. Thank you very much.

"The Chinese did not exactly hang around either. Tanzania only won independence from Britain in 1964 and the railway was already being built by 1970. Then it took only about five years, a damn sight quicker than the British sixty years before. Apparently the Tan-Zam Railway was the greatest engineering effort of its kind after world war two and it was far and away China's largest chunk of what they fondly called overseas aid. Evidently they reckoned what the British could do once, they could do much better second time around."

Warwick nodded. It was obvious politics and he had more to add. More recently the Chinese had been given permission to expand the port of Dar-es-Salaam. But before James could ask any questions, he suggested they continue their conversation somewhere else. "Let's reconvene in an hour or so and I will take you to Carnivore. It's years since I've been there. None of its other diners will ever guess we are both naval officers, unless of course we make it blatantly obvious."

The Carnivore restaurant outside Nairobi is renowned far beyond Africa. It is about four miles south of the city, next to the airport. In the good old days it was allowed to serve wild game from the bush. As they arrived Warwick explained, "When I was last here you could eat giraffe, wildebeest, probably elephant and more exotic species still. The general idea was that you should continue eating different varieties of bush meat until you just about burst.

"As you can see the waiters are the cooks as well, using that charcoal grill. Those chunks of meat on their swords are not the sort of stuff you'd buy at your local butchers. There's no menu to speak of. As it passes your table the general idea is to try a slice of everything.

"Nowadays genuine bush meat has been banned, but we can still eat camel, ostrich and crocodile. You can also have ribs and kidneys and ordinary stuff like that, but that's really not the point. I tell you, James, this is no place for vegetarians. But it does get a lot of tourists and for once that could be rather useful. Fewer wagging ears. Did you also hear what I learnt yesterday from the Tanzanian observer at the conference?"

"No. Do tell."

"As we know the Chinese are expanding Dar-es-Salaam, all at their own expense. They signed a major development contract just over three years ago. On the face of it the aim was to improve commercial shipping facilities linked to their railway. I imagine that's what you'll see from satellite reconnaissance, and nothing more. Diplomatic staff on the ground would quickly confirm it."

"Go on." Warwick was delighted to impart such fresh and important intelligence. "Apparently there was a secret protocol in the agreement. The Tanzanians have agreed to give the Chinese navy full access to the Dar-es-Salaam port facilities to use as a naval base."

"Christ! They *are* getting ambitious. Mind you, only last month the Chinese sent a frigate into the Mediterranean to rescue their civilians from Libya. That was a first. It had them all hopping up and down at NATO headquarters, I can tell you. Our Fleet HQ in Northwood wasn't exactly over the moon either. So the People's Navy wants to come all the way across the Indian ocean on a regular basis, do they? That is interesting to say the least. I don't suppose it's because they just want to be better informed on the tourist sights either."

"James, my old friend, it gets even better. Or worse, depending on your viewpoint. You remember our pact at Dartmouth sixteen years ago? We agreed neither of us will ever be shocked into contradiction by what the one of us tells the other, no matter how implausible or unanticipated? Well, James, here I am in Nairobi and I'm invoking that pact right now. I've found out the Chinese are building a large fleet of destroyers copied exactly from your latest British Type 45s. Putting two and two together I now reckon they are aiming to create their very own Indian Ocean fleet."

"That definitely counts as worse, my friend. And how do you know all that? Are you absolutely sure? It was our understanding they are simply building a fleet of workaday frigates to patrol the East China Sea and the Sea of Japan. Mind you, some people did rather wonder why they needed such sophisticated electronic kit just for a fleet of basic coastal patrol craft. Your version does make a whole lot more sense."

"They only announce what they want you to know. There's no free press in China. Fortunately we too have our sources and one way or another we've been watching China for years. The latest intelligence has split the Australian political establishment in two - those few that know about it, that is. Until now the watchword in Canberra has been 'Forget the Australian navy'. At long last some of them are starting to change their minds. As to our sources? I'll say this much. The Chinese have always been instinctive traders and for the right price they are as keen to sell military intelligence as willingly as they sell flat-pack furniture. They would probably quote the going market price for grandmothers if you were to make them a half-decent offer."

James was unsure about the customer benefit of trading in second-hand grandmothers. It was probably much more sensible to purchase naval intelligence. "Do you mind if I put in a report including all that as soon as I get back to Portsmouth? It meshes with something else. Our Type 45 is becoming extremely popular. I gather we might be selling several to Saudi Arabia.

"But then again we might have to think about which side they might be used on. Just think of all those revolutionary goings-on in Tunisia, Egypt, Libya, Bahrain and Syria, fighting against their dictators. The Islamic unrest is spreading like wildfire and the last thing we want is to be accused of arming the wrong side. All too easy unless you do your homework first. Suppose Saudi is next on the list? I know more about all that than perhaps I should comment, Warwick. Just wait till you meet my fiancée and find out who she is."

"You've mentioned her before. You said her name is Violaine, sounds rather pretty and upmarket. French, isn't she? Lives in Paris, did you say? Sounds quite a sheila." James Heaton smiled at that. "I'm not sure she'd like 'sheila' exactly. That's sounds just a bit too Antipodean for her taste. But if all goes to plan she and I are getting married in Paris next year and you, sir, will be there. There's nothing quite like globalisation nowadays.

"So let's hope you meet her before that. More to the point let's hope you also meet her father, Dr Malik Khalifa. The two of them are a father and daughter axis of constructive Islamic controversy. You'll enjoy that. Violaine has been having problems with the French secret service, which is where she works. I told her that her problems exactly mirror yours with the Australian navy."

So it was Warwick's turn. "And that, James, is precisely why I am telling you about all this. It's why I wanted to come to an anonymous out-of-town restaurant. Even if a few people in Canberra are starting to hop up and down, as matters stand our Navy is in no position to do anything about a strengthened Chinese naval presence around the Indian Ocean. So it's up to you Brits, possibly the French in view of what you've just said, probably the Indians and perhaps, but only perhaps, Uncle Sam if he has the guts to do anything about it at all.

"But in view of what Obama said last month about abandoning America's role in Libya as soon as they possibly can, the odds are the Fifth Fleet will stay at home at its base in Bahrain until the last possible moment and longer even than that. We have already suggested privately that they negotiate with Sri Lanka and shift it to Trincomalee, get it out from under the Islamic sphere of influence, but you might just as well talk to a brick wall. The Indian Ocean is the exact antipodes to the

United States of America and they treat it as if it is on the other side of the world." James Heaton smiled at the dry irony as Warwick Sydenham continued "Okay, now let me tell you something else. I have another contact in Australia and he's a senior policy adviser at Brisbane University, specialising in Sino-Australian relations. Last year he visited about ten universities in China.

"He recognised exactly the same pattern after he had visited a relatively unknown university in the central province of Hubei. It was the China University of Geosciences and it was the *alma mater* of their current premier Wen Jiabao. My chum noticed during his visit a conspicuously large number of African students wandering around the campus, more so than usual. So he made enquiries about the number of overseas students at the university."

James Heaton offered no comment and instead urged Warwick to continue. This was a very new perspective on African post-colonialism. Warwick needed little encouragement. "Of course most universities in China nowadays have an international programme and the students are mostly from Korea or Japan, perhaps from European or American countries. But the China University of Geosciences in Hubei, I hear, has around four hundred international students. Quite exceptionally around half of them are Africans, most of them on Chinese government scholarships. Nearly all are reading engineering or the geological sciences of course. Not for them the broad-based humanities.

Warwick looked expectantly at James, who promptly started to sketch in the gaps. "I have little doubt these African students at Chinese universities are being coached deliberately to become key technocrats and bureaucrats, part of China's long-term plans for Africa. They are being shaped in Wen Jiabao's own image. Beijing is deliberately educating the future technocratic leadership of this dark continent to think in Chinese. It's a whole lot cleverer than educating them to be argumentative, rule-bending lawyers at the London School of

Economics, as we stupidly did with Robert Mugabe. There's something else. Only last Summer I read that a whole squadron of Chinese archaeologists turned up right here in Kenya. That triggered a few thoughts, I might tell you. Meantime the BBC reported just a couple of months ago that there are now a million Chinese chicken farmers in Africa and in places like Lusaka and they are driving the locals out of business. Our British farmers in the whole of Africa never numbered more than a few tens of thousands."

Warwick was thoughtful as he listened to James Heaton, then started ticking each point off on his fingers. "Okay. So we now have a Chinese policy for Africa which embraces military, cultural, economic infrastructure, mass immigration, educational and diplomatic initiatives. Put all that together, James my friend and we are looking at the new colonialists of the twenty-first century. I think we both need another drink." James flagged a waiter. "Better make that a whole bottle, Warwick. It seems the two of us really do live in interesting times."

* * * * *

Park Royal, London

EVENTUALLY JAMES HEATON had found the unobtrusive laboratories on the Park Royal industrial estate. He left his car in a parking slot marked Visitors, although none of the other slots in the half-full car park were allocated to anyone. He was deliberately dressed in civilian garb. He strolled into Reception, where a clever-sounding middle-aged woman seemed to know exactly who he was. "You're here to see Dr Cunningham, I believe. Despite the plain clothes it's really Lieutenant-Commander Heaton, isn't it?"

James was invited to sign in, supplied with an electronic identity badge, then waved towards a lift and told to go to the fourth floor. As he walked out of the lift Christopher Cunningham was waiting for him and led toward a spacious and quite luxurious office, one which offered nothing better than an unexciting view of other nondescript factories around the industrial estate. "Well, Lieutenant-Commander Heaton, welcome at last to the Sharava Corporation. Not that many people on these premises call it by that name, however. As you no doubt know already, I'm Christopher Cunningham and I'm its managing director. I've been hearing quite a lot about you. We have, I believe, a mutual friend at the Ministry of Defence in Captain George Gould." That was technically true, although James Heaton had met the elusive captain only one month previously for the very first time. It had introduced him to a very different aspect of the Royal Navy.

Christopher Cunningham continued "I also understand that you produced a paper a couple of months ago about potential military developments in the Indian Ocean which made quite a few hairs stand on end at the Ministry. I also know that as a knock-on consequence of your paper, you're going to be posted in HMS Daedalus as her Executive Officer. And now you are here at Sharava to learn what is so special about her." James Heaton looked up sharply at Christopher Cunningham. This was already promising to be yet another different aspect of the Royal Navy.

"By the time you and I have talked everything through, you will be the only man on board that excellent Type 45 who actually understands what is going on. I take it you have already signed the Official Secrets Act, or you wouldn't even be here. Let's have some tea. I promise you an interesting morning."

Christopher Cunningham was an engaging man, tall and quietly impressive. James put him at about fifty years old; very English; very self-possessed. He was a boffin, but a boffin with very evident political acumen as well. Over the next half hour, Sharava's managing director explained the unique tracking and fire control system being fitted in the Ops Room of HMS Daedalus. Superficially it was the basic Sharava system, although it had been developed to a level of sophistication not available to foreign navies. "We have made no secret of the fact that Sharava's standard system is apparently being fitted to the British Type 45s, if you read the right technical journals, it's all in there. Indeed we hope several observant people in other countries will have taken the trouble to read those technical journals too.

"In fact that's exactly why we placed the article in the first place, because we are rather keen for other navies to buy the basic version of our system to equip their own warships. You might be interested to know we are even selling them to the Chinese."

James Heaton looked surprised at that, in view of Warwick Sydenham's recent intelligence. Christopher Cunningham smiled. "We - that's George Gould and myself - reckoned that once they learn it is good enough for the Royal Navy, they might conclude it's good enough for them. It worked. Not only will we make a considerable pile of cash that way, but we will then also know exactly what their military capabilities are likely to be. It's a little wheeze in on-going military intelligence cooked up by George Gould and myself. Rule number one: understand the opposition."

While James Heaton admired his plot of commercial acumen and military subterfuge, there seemed to be a small hitch in the logic. "But won't people be just a bit wary of buying such a system from the British, when they can work out for themselves we then have an exact measure of the fighting capability of their ships?"

Christopher Cunningham pursed his lips, steepled his hands and frowned. "But how will they even know they have bought the system from the British in the first place? One of the several reasons you have signed the Official Secrets Act before you even came to this laboratory, is that you are have the rare privilege of knowing the true identity of the Sharava Corporation. Very few people share that knowledge. As you came into Reception, you will have seen nothing to identify the building or the company. If you look at our literature, if you look us up on the Internet, if you do a search for our shareholders, you will encounter a very carefully-created impenetrable smokescreen. Hardly anyone here knows these are the laboratories of the Sharava Corporation, or has even heard of that elusive organisation.

"We don't exactly put Sharava nameplates on our products in this factory. Most people around here imagine they work for a company called Park Royal Advanced Electronics Limited, which signs their contracts and pays their salaries. We even have a PRAEL logo, discreetly displayed here and there around the premises. It only takes a screwdriver to change a nameplate."

Cunningham explained that a lot of the work in the laboratory looked rather like development of difficult computer games, nothing whatever to do with military software. Serious computer geeks would have been astonished to discover how their favourite game originated.

He went on "so far as Sharava itself is concerned, it is a world far distant from almost everything you see here. Its intended military customers know it only as an elusive and amorphous global company, possibly based in Switzerland, possibly owned by Indians. If they go looking they will find it is registered in Willemstad, capital of the former Dutch Antilles island of Curacao, in the distant West Indies. Sharava is only visible to the world at all through technical sales offices in Dubai, Geneva, Hong Kong, Willemstad, in a different part of London and through discreet stands at international armaments exhibitions.

"Customers never come here. It is true our working language is English, although that is universal practice nowadays for any multinational worth its salt. Our operating manuals are also all written in English and English alone, but you will look in vain for a printer's imprint on any of them. They are actually printed in Hong Kong where hardly anyone understands them and they are always warehoused anonymously in Rotterdam. You will never see any copies of brochures

anywhere in this factory. God forbid. Our prices are always
denominated in Swiss francs and our name had been derived from the
Sanskrit word for arrow. Our sales staff are about as conspicuously
multicultural as you could possibly recruit. Deliberately. And they only
understand what our products do. Not one of them knows where the
equipment is manufactured. So far as they are concerned everything
appears as if by magic at a warehouse in Basle. We then ensure customs
and lading information is always removed as a matter of routine.

"Almost all Sharava staff training courses take place in Lucerne
or Geneva. Their salaries are paid out of a bank in Zurich. Their
contracts of employment are all Swiss contracts. They are never allowed
to see anything to link the company they work for with this country. We
run on a strictly 'need to know' basis. The purely commercial operations
of Sharava and the technical work here at Park Royal Advanced
Electronics Limited are as separate as it is possible to make them."

That sounded like a pretty effective smokescreen to James
Heaton and he smiled a wry smile. Someone had been doing some very
thorough planning for a number of years; it was a pièce de résistance of
counter-intelligence.

That was as maybe, but Christopher Cunningham rather treated
it as ancient history. "So let's move on to the really interesting bit. Over
six years ago now, we brought in an intriguing piece of software
originally developed in Israel. What I am about to tell you is so secret
only five men know the complete story and one of them is George
Gould. You will make it six and you will be the *only* person in Daedalus
who knows anything about it.

"Your captain will be given a separate and confidential briefing
at MoD so he understands broadly what you are about. But even he
does not need to know the complete story. No-one else on board does
or should." James Heaton realised this was becoming more intriguing
by the second. How often did the second-in-command know far more

about his ship than his commanding officer? Christopher Cunningham continued. "The secret gizmo is something we now call the Bijali, a name derived from the Hindu word for lightning. It is manufactured in Israel and even they don't have the foggiest idea how we actually use it, nor that Bijali is actually one of their own products. Once the chip goes in, who the hell can interpret what it does or even where it came from?

"Nor do they really care, just so long as we pay cash on the nail. It is buried deep in the software of our naval tracking and fire control software and has been incorporated in every system we have supplied for the past three years. Anywhere. In essence it is quite simple, but none of the Bijalis, until now, has been activated. We can do it from anywhere, but only two of us here at Sharava actually possess the deciphering keys to do so. Need to know, once again.

"Bijali encrypts data and compresses it for virtually instantaneous transmission. All our tracking and fire control systems have a black box facility built into them anyway, so that the chaps in the ship's operations room can review their activities afterwards at leisure. All our customers know that as a matter of routine and fully appreciate its purpose. What they don't realise is that all the hard work has already been done for Bijali. All it does is encrypt all that Ops room data and transmit it elsewhere in a sudden electronic burst.

"But in turn that does mean that whoever is on the receiving end can listen in on everything electronic going on in a military engagement and even pick up some of the human conversation too. That could be a worthwhile military advantage." James Heaton smiled at the deliberate understatement. Knowing what the enemy was thinking about and planning second by second was rather more than a worthwhile advantage. It was every military officer's dream.

James Heaton was also thinking through all this rapidly. It was far removed from anything they had been taught at Dartmouth. "Okay, but I've served in an Ops Room in very realistic exercises at sea and even that demands some pretty fast thought processes nowadays. Are you really saying I will have to follow what is happening in a completely different Ops Room, on the opposite side in the same engagement, in the simultaneous time frame? Won't my head soon start to spin?"

Christopher Cunningham did not seem over-concerned about that. "No more than a fighter pilot has to absorb real time data about the enemy at a very high speed and do his own flying job at the same time, or for that matter the driver in a Formula One Race. Just regard yourself the seagoing equivalent of Lewis Hamilton or Jenson Button. You will enjoy it. But don't worry. You will be trained thoroughly here until it all becomes second nature. That is where Kundalini comes in."

"Kundalini?"

"That's another device George Gould and I concocted at one of our meetings. We thought it up nearly four years ago when we were contemplating the type of mind which would be able to make full use of something like Bijali. You are right that it is a mind-stretching exercise, which is why we decided to measure minds for their stretchability."

Christopher Cunningham rang a buzzer by his telephone and invited someone to step into his office. "Right. I'm about to introduce you to one of our multinational staff I mentioned a few moments ago. She is one of our top specialists on Kundalini, a quite recent addition to our security-cleared staff.

"She knows what we are trying to measure in the mind and she understands something about tracking and fire control systems. And that is the precise extent of her knowledge. She knows nothing whatever about Bijali and it should never be mentioned in her presence. She has signed the Official Secrets Act, but technically she still counts as an alien and you must bear that in mind at all times.

"I have to admit George Gould has been rather dubious about it all, but he is of the old school. As I explained, we operate on a very strict 'need to know' principle in this organisation, a rule never to be flouted. But she does know a great deal about how to stretch and adapt the human mind." There was a knock at the door, it opened almost immediately and in walked Antonia Foo.

James found himself looking at an extremely attractive, early middle-aged Chinese woman. Her face and figure were quite unlike like the Cantonese he was accustomed to in the Chinese restaurants of London or Portsmouth. Even just looking at her, it was apparent from her face that Antonia Foo came from a quite different region of that huge country.

"Antonia, I'd like you to meet Lieutenant-Commander James Heaton of the Royal Navy. James, this is one of our technical staff here at Sharava, Dr Antonia Foo. She is one of the very few who know our real identity. She knows as you do that Sharava sells various high technology products on the international market and she also knows Sharava manufactures some of its kit right here in the UK.

"As I mentioned that is knowledge shared by very few people, which is why the three of us in this room need to be discreet. As she will explain herself, Antonia is every bit as Chinese as she looks, but she does have a doctorate in engineering from Imperial and more recently she has done a very demanding course in psychology also here in London. And she has worked in London for several years. Antonia, James here is going to be one of your guinea pigs on the Kundalini programme."

Antonia Foo gave James Heaton the kind of winsome look any physically-minded unmarried woman would give a handsome naval officer in his late thirties. She could have given him about sixteen years as well, but such Chinese women do not instantly reveal their true age. "I'm pleased to meet you, James. Most of my guinea pigs so far have been civilians. You are the first British naval officer I've met, although in the past I have obviously met several officers in the Chinese navy." James remained very calm as she said that and simply looked at Christopher Cunningham who raised a knowing eyebrow. Just four months previously Warwick Sydenham had been telling James all about the likely ambitions of China's navy. It had been part of James's job at Naval Intelligence to pass on the information and it had been relayed to the Ministry of Defence in Whitehall.

Now was perhaps not quite the moment to raise the matter, but he did wonder how much Antonia Foo might know about it. He could understand George Gould's caution. Best stick to the task in hand. "Christopher has been explaining something about a system called Kundalini and apparently I am to be your guinea-pig, so can you tell me a little more about what it involves?"

"Certainly, I'll be glad to. Stop me if I tell you something Chris has already mentioned. I have joined a programme here which is doing research on different kinds of human intelligence and we have even developed a machine to identify and measure them. The aim of the programme is to see how well people can absorb and act on information from multiple sources. It is basically a civilian programme but we recognise it could also have some valuable applications in the military.

"We are now testing a variety of subjects with different cultural backgrounds, different jobs, different types and levels of education. Obviously someone with a job such as yours, a military warfare officer, could be of particular interest to us. We hope to draw up some kind of profile for measuring and predicting levels of success. I hope by this time next year we will start to have something to show for our efforts."

"Why exactly did you choose the name Kundalini?"

Christopher Cunningham rolled out his well-practised answer. "You may have spotted that, to flatter our ultimate paymasters, almost all of our products are given an Indian name. Kundalini is named after a Sanskrit notion of coiled-up energy at the base of spinal column. Indians have an exercise called Raja Yoga which is intended to release this energy through the spinal column to the brain. It is supposed to reach the inner brain and produce super-consciousness.

"I'm no expert on neuroscience, it's all just a black box to me. All we are interested in is the effect, rather than the supposed cause. That is the kind of mental energy the Kundalini software and evaluation looks for." Antonia Foo smiled. She was quite looking forward to working with Lieutenant-Commander James Heaton. She particularly enjoyed working with handsome men. He looked the perfect age. It might prove to be a life-enhancing experience for both of them.

* * * * *

Sydney, Australia

WARWICK SYDENHAM LOOKED round the church. It was an eclectic mix of people, including some top brass from the navy. Obviously children and a wider family. And some who quite clearly had been Bill Boyce's drinking chums. Bill had been a widower and it was his daughter Patricia who had asked Warwick to deliver the eulogy. "My father always spoke very highly of you, while your father and he had been the closest of friends in the navy. At least you were always on his side. I'd rather you gave the eulogy than some senior sailor who never quite agreed with dad's viewpoint. Please do his close family a favour and put in a good one for him and his often unfashionable views. I'm sure he would have wanted that more than anything."

The service of remembrance was a solemn one, but there was a general feeling Bill Boyce had lived a very full life and enjoyed almost all of it. The usual cricketing metaphors about 'a jolly good innings' set the dominant tone. Even so, Warwick decided it was a suitable occasion to ruffle a few feathers. As the organ faded gently at the end of the hymn, Warwick picked up a small sheaf of notes and walked slowly and solemnly up the steps of the pulpit. He looked up at the expectant congregation and then deliberately counted to ten. By the time he uttered his first words they were all hanging on the edge of them.

"We are all here today to celebrate the life of one of my family's oldest friends, Bill Boyce. I suppose if he could really have had his way he would have died suddenly on the bridge of an Australian aircraft carrier somewhere in the middle of the Indian Ocean. As it was, he had to settle for a sudden heart attack after a convivial evening with friends. Bill, I profoundly wish I had also been there with you for that final beer. I imagine we all do.

"Many of you will have enjoyed, as I did on many occasions, the wisdom of Bill Boyce's company. My father always said Bill had the sea in his blood, if indeed there was enough room for it. And when you talked to him about that wisdom of the sea, about the wisdom surrounding ships and talked about navies, that wisdom surrounded every syllable of his conversation."

Warwick Sydenham looked straight into the eye of a distinguished naval commodore sitting in the second row of the congregation. He twitched very slightly. Both of them knew the Australian navy had no aircraft carriers. Warwick had hit his first target.

"Bill Boyce believed profoundly in Australia. His family went a long way back, but they never found him a convict. Rather Bill Boyce was a man of convictions. And he was convinced of one thing above all others. There is no room for the indecisive optimist in a world full of bullies. And say what you will of him, Bill was never indecisive.

"It is all very well us singing about advance Australia fair, but that rather assumes other countries will then be equally as fair as we wish them to be. Bill Boyce rather doubted the practicality of that. Yes our land abounds in nature's gifts, yes we have golden soil and yes we have boundless plains to share. Do we ever ask ourselves who else might perhaps wish to share all those wonderful things with us?

"It has always been the Bill Boyces of this world, no matter how unpopular they may be in Canberra or in the political arena, who argued that to make this Commonwealth of ours truly ours and remain so, the price we must pay is eternal vigilance, not just organise military barbeques every other Sunday afternoon." The congregation rustled slightly. Any mention of barbeques in Sydney was certain to touch a raw nerve. Undeterred, Warwick Sydenham continued his theme.

"At least we do recognise that our home is girt by the sea. That's something we do at least share with our British forefathers. Great Britain is girt by the sea too and at times like the Spanish Armada, or when Napoleon or Hitler peered across the English Channel at the white cliffs of Dover, the British have been mightily thankful for that stretch of water which turns them into an island.

"The Brits sing that Britannia rules the waves, but they cannot rule over all of them. There are some things we must do for ourselves. We must ask ourselves - where are Australia's challenging Napoleons? Where are Australia's challenging Hitlers? Does any of us really believe all such tyrants have been conveniently consigned to the dustbins of history? Or that they can only ever emerge in the north Atlantic? We are brought here together to celebrate the life of a man who did ask those awkward questions, and I trust he has taught me to do the same.

"So as we all remember Captain William Boyce of the Royal Australian Navy, let us all remember exactly what he stood for. He would ask of any of us no more than that. He stood for a strong Australia, an Australia girt by the sea which needed to protect itself around its shores and far beyond. Because only then can we all be reasonably sure we can advance Australia fair. Ladies and gentlemen, I ask you all to be most grateful for the life of Bill Boyce. It was the life of a man with a turbulent intellect. May he now rest in peace."

His congregation had rarely heard the words of the Australian national anthem put to quite such poignant use. It was intentionally electric. With a further extended glance around everyone in the church, Warwick Sydenham stepped down from the pulpit and resumed his seat. For better or for worse, his task that day was done.

Warwick had given Bill Boyce a eulogy of which, as he peered down from the heavens through his telescope, he hoped his idol could be genuinely proud. Over drinks afterwards, the naval commodore drew him to one side. "That was a very brave performance, young sir, but privately, and between ourselves, there are more and more wise people in Canberra who now completely agree with you. Bill Boyce's greatest mistake was to be born forty years ahead of his time. If he had been younger he could have been running Australia's navy today. As it is, we fobbed him off with being a captain."

Warwick Sydenham smiled at the commodore and said thank you. Naval battles are normally won in the open ocean. He wondered if, today, he might have begun to win one from a pulpit. Bill Boyce's naval career was over, but Warwick Sydenham's was only just beginning.

* * * * *

East End of London

GEORGE GOULD enjoyed good Chinese food, but he sometimes had other reasons for visiting London's East End. He also took much pleasure in the devices of theatrical make-up, especially the tricks which stood scrutiny in broad daylight. Today would involve a trip across London in his guise as the slightly dishevelled Bernard Chesterton, someone whose appearance would be quite unrecognisable even to colleagues at the Ministry of Defence.

More importantly, no-one was likely to connect such an eccentric East End character with a staid ministry official from Whitehall. George Gould enjoyed constructing his anonymity. Deception was instinctive to him. In his new guise he took the lift from a floor which was not his own to the main entrance lobby of his mansion apartments. By then his tracks were already covered, someone unknown, probably just an occasional visitor. An eleven station journey along the District Line from Victoria took him to Aldgate. After that it was just a few minutes' walk to his unremarkable destination.

As Bernard Chesterton he was warmly welcomed by Joseph Choi who ran the Chinese restaurant. It was still quite early and there were few people around as he was shown to a private back room. The two men had originally met in Hong Kong, where it once had been part of George Gould's job to build lines of communication with the Chinese underworld. The disguise of Bernard Chesterton had been developed for the rôle. Joseph Choi had been called something quite different in those days. The two men used to meet at dingy bars in Hong Kong's notorious walled city, an ungovernable enclave of drugs and vice run by the Triads. George Gould had bought much useful information about their various activities from his old and much-valued contact.

Then the Kowloon criminal fraternity started to suspect what was happening. Surprisingly Mr Chesterton seemed to half expect they would and he had arranged a swift emigration for his Chinese source to London where he was given an entirely new identity. The freshly-minted Joseph Choi was unknown to anyone in Hong Kong and eternally grateful for his rescue. The mysterious, but obviously well-connected, Mr Chesterton somehow managed to transfer to London at about the same time. He seemed to have everything under control and even found some very friendly funding to help finance Mr Choi's smart new restaurant near Aldgate.

Even if the Ministry of Defence did not know what Bernard Chesterton looked like, they certainly knew what he achieved. As he became established in the Aldgate community, Joseph Choi had been encouraged to position himself as someone with useful intelligence to sell. He was familiar enough with the rules of the game. There were plenty of paying customers in London, especially for the snippets of discreet military information Joseph Choi had on offer, at the right price.

These snippets had been carefully manufactured by George Gould and a small group of select colleagues at the Ministry of Defence. They were part of a wider programme of disinformation. George Gould found it much more effective to sell the information rather than simply give it away, part of a financial deal with Joseph Choi also involving dividends on the restaurant business. The funds found their way into a secret Ministry of Defence bank account which could be used for virtually anything with no questions asked. As the Ministry of Defence hoped, eventually the Chinese restaurant owner started asking for specific information in return.

His East End customers for espionage had been fed enough legitimate information to equip Joseph Choi with a carefully-nurtured reputation for selling high quality material. The requests he fed back gave George Gould's department much helpful guidance on what the other side did not know and wanted to find out, even if it was not always possible to answer their questions completely, well not with entirely honest answers anyway.

In return, Joseph was willing to do favours for Mr Chesterton and undertake a variety of tasks which were outside the legitimate activity of the security services. That was the real purpose behind George's clandestine visit to the restaurant today. "Joseph, my friend, in all the years we have known one another you have always accepted my information with no questions asked. I thank you for that courtesy, you are wise enough to realise I have to protect my own sources.

"But now my people have a problem. There is a Chinese woman here in London who is coming under suspicion and I want to give her a fright to see what she does next. So we don't want her killed. My contacts think you could stage what looks like a deliberate attempt to mow her down. Terrify her, but don't harm her. To protect your contacts, we will supply a car which cannot be traced and it will disappear immediately afterwards."

It was the kind of messy business Joseph Choi's Chinese contacts in the East End were good at, especially given the sum of money proposed for the work. Mr Chesterton gave precise details about collecting and disposing of the car and Joseph learnt it would be an old Audi 100 with unusual number plates. George Gould had already researched its colour with care, although he made no mention of that. Joseph Choi was simply given an address in Rotherhithe at which the target could be observed, a physical description and a photograph. It was that of a good-looking woman he did not recognise and never would, nor would he ever learn that her name was Antonia Foo.

Within a week there was an anonymous Ford parked regularly outside Antonia's apartment block. Working in shifts, its apparent drivers were two very patient men who unobtrusively built up a picture of her regular habits. When the street was quiet they also did one or two test drives against a stopwatch from a parking spot round the corner. It was ideally positioned to intercept Antonia where she normally crossed Rotherhithe Street on her daily walk to Canada Water station.

Once the Chinese gangsters were satisfied with their plan, the word was passed to Joseph Choi with a simple map of their exact manoeuvres. He in turn contacted Bernard Chesterton on a rarely-used mobile phone which served no other purpose. A day was chosen and in his customary Chesterton disguise, George Gould parked a car at an ideal vantage point. A call on his mobile phone alerted him that Antonia was on her way.

As she stepped to cross Rotherhithe Street an Audi 100, disguised as a Hongqi Mingshi careered round the corner, deliberately missed her by a matter of inches, stopped to pick up the watchman and sped off down Salter Road. Antonia recoiled in horror, fell briefly to her knees then ran back to her apartment in total panic. The disguised Audi was then parked by the Pizza Hut at Canada Water for a few minutes only, carefully out of sight of surveillance cameras, while its two Chinese occupants made their way to the underground station. As they left, George Gould arrived, replaced the temporary Chinese number plates with normal ones and drove the car round the corner.

In Quebec Way a delivery truck was waiting, one of many which congregated round the local warehouses and supermarkets, also out of range of surveillance cameras. George drove the Audi straight up the sloping tail flap of the truck from which he had extracted it an hour earlier. He then strolled back to his own car at Pizza Hut while the truck driver raised the tail flap, sealed the truck and departed. The Audi was never to be seen again.

Back in her apartment Antonia telephoned Christopher Cunningham. She was distraught. "Chris. Someone has just tried to murder me." He asked for details and she described the sudden events in the street outside her apartment. "How do you know it wasn't just an accident?" he asked "Because," she replied "I recognised the car. It was the same one I had when I worked in Lanzhou. Same model, same colour, same Chinese number plates. Someone was out to get me, personally. Chris, what am I to do?"

He told her to stay at home for the morning, bolt the door, try to relax, keep away from the windows. His immediate attempts to contact George Gould with the distressing news were unsuccessful. The captain would not be available at his desk until later that morning.

When some hours later they did eventually make contact, George Gould asked for Antonia's precise description of events. He also wanted to know the time she had called. As Christopher Cunningham gave him a blow by blow account the captain at the Ministry of Defence smiled privately to himself. Antonia had passed the crucial test.

She had called Christopher Cunningham almost immediately. She hid nothing from him. He was her first and main point of refuge. George Gould knew her reactions would have been entirely different had she been secretly working for the Chinese. He suggested to Christopher that Antonia prepare to move out of her Rotherhithe flat immediately. He would help find her somewhere secure in a quite different part of London, where her identity would be unknown.

Christopher Cunningham was most grateful. It occurred neither to him, nor in due course to Antonia, that her new flat would be a Ministry of Defence special. It would be fitted with the most advanced surveillance equipment, devices of which she knew nothing and would never find out. George Gould would then have achieved his further objective of terrifying Antonia Foo, a former Chinese national, out of her commercial flat in Rotherhithe into somewhere that he had control. He was not the kind of man who ever left anything to chance.

*   *   *   *   *

St Polycarp's, north Lancashire

ALAN STANLEY had not been inside a church for over twenty years and he knew none of the hymn tunes. So he just mouthed the words on the service sheet and tried not to sing out of tune. He would not have been in church at all, except that the Booth family had asked him to deliver the eulogy at the funeral of their late father Tom Booth, a much respected former Lancashire member of parliament.

Alan looked round the church, slightly nervously. It was an eclectic mix of people. Some bigwigs from the Labour Party, lesser wigs from the local council, Tom's children and his wider family. And some who quite clearly had been among Tom's numerous drinking chums, a number of whom Alan knew well. Among them he could see Brian Potter and Steve Wilson, fellow Labour MPs. He gave them a wink, for they knew what was coming.

Tom Booth had been a widower and it was his daughter Norma who had asked Alan to deliver the eulogy. "My father always spoke very highly of you, Mr Stanley. The real Labour party members here in the

North West are always very close and I know that not everyone agrees with you all by any means. Mr Stanley, I know we would all be grateful if you would speak up for dad. At least you were always on his side. I'd rather you gave the eulogy than some distant figure who never quite agreed with him. Please do his close family a favour and put in a good one for him and his views. Dad would have appreciated some thoughtful words like that more than anything."

The funeral service was a solemn one, but there was a general feeling that Tom Booth MP had lived a very full life and enjoyed almost all of it. Inevitably in Lancashire, the usual cricketing metaphors about 'a bloody good innings' set the dominant tone. Even if it was a funeral, Alan thought it a most suitable occasion to ruffle a few feathers in honour of his old mentor.

As the organ faded gently at the end of the hymn, he picked up a small sheaf of notes and walked slowly and solemnly up the steps of the pulpit. When it came to public speaking, the tall and impressive-looking Alan Stanley was in his element, a practised orator from the House of Commons. He looked up at the expectant congregation and slowly counted .to ten. It was a favourite technique to gain their attention and by the time he uttered his first words they were all hanging onto every one of them.

Alan Stanley was possessed of a powerful voice and it echoed round the church. "My friends: we are all here today to celebrate the life of one of my oldest friends in politics, Tom Booth. When I first entered Parliament back in 1997, Tom was already my guide and mentor. Especially for us, members of parliament from Lancashire, he was everyone's guide and mentor.

"I suppose if he could have had his way he would have died suddenly in the House of Commons, having just torn the Tories to shreds for the final and greatest time in his life. But as you perhaps know, members of parliament are never permitted to die in the House of Commons. The place of death is always shown as St Thomas's Hospital just across the river and that is where Tom did indeed die. I was at his bedside holding his hand after that fatal heart attack. He managed a final epithet: "You show 'em, Alan. It's up to you now."

"Thank you Tom, for showing your faith in me. You have my promise I shall try to live up to it. So let's start right here and now. It is what Tom instructed me to do. Here in Lancashire, ably abetted by our favourite rivals across the Pennines in Yorkshire, we invented the Labour Party. It does not belong to London, it does not belong to the Midlands, it certainly does not belong to Scotland. It belongs to us, right here in the north of England. And it is time to bring it home. Tom Booth would expect no less of us.

"Some of you here today will have noticed a few of us are wearing a bright red lapel badge. It simply says CLYND and a few people have asked me what that stands for. Let me tell you what it stands for. It stands for 'Cheshire, Lancashire, Yorkshire, Nottinghamshire and Derbyshire'. It stands for the very heart of Labour England. Which is what I and other members of this congregation I can see before me stand for too.

"Here in Lancashire we might not all be royalists, but we are definitely loyalists and when Tom swore his oath as a member of the House of Commons, when I swore my oath as a member of the House of Commons, we did so with the greatest of pride. People like us go into politics to serve the great British people, not the British aristocracy, not the bankers, not the wheeler-dealers or the arms dealers, the drug dealers or the peddlers of lies. Well might the only good television soap opera be based somewhere in Manchester. It is called Coronation Street and for a very good reason.

"Manchester is being born again. It is becoming a new centre of media. Look for yourself round what used to be Salford Docks. It is the new home of the BBC. In this part of the world we constantly re-invent ourselves. Given half a chance, the peoples of the north are the greatest inventors on earth, just as we produce many of Britain's greatest radical politicians, especially those determined to serve ordinary people.

"When that brilliant northern engineer George Stephenson decided to build the world's first-ever real railway, where did he choose to build it? Between Manchester and Liverpool of course. Where else? Here in Lancashire the cleverness of our people just needs to be given that fair chance. George Stephenson's parents were illiterate. But he understood the value of education and paid out of his own money to go to night school and learn reading, writing and arithmetic. Like his parents George Stephenson was also illiterate until he was eighteen. Yet he became so important to the world, that, a hundred and fifty years after he died, the Bank of England put his portrait on our five pound note. That symbolises something and it says everything.

"George Stephenson never went to university. But two years after he retired he became the first President of the Institution of Mechanical Engineers, one of the greatest ever. Here in Lancashire we are a race of born engineers, making everything from nuts and bolts to trucks and aircraft.

"Tom Booth always had plenty to say about that, so let me repeat today what he said. It is no use sending clever but ordinary people to university in the hope of turning them into something different. Far better to do what George Stephenson did and get educated while you work. Tom Booth always said if we want to take the people of Britain forward, let's reinvent the Workers' Education Association. Let's help ourselves, not just lean on others.

"I think Karl Marx said something about elementary education by the state being altogether objectionable. Government and church should rather be equally excluded from any influence on the school." At this point in Alan Stanley's peroration, the vicar of St Polycarp's looked slightly uncomfortable, but the eulogist stuck to his guns and continued,

Rather, the state has need, on the contrary, of a very stern education by the people. I don't suppose many of you expected to hear Karl Marx quoted from this pulpit this morning, but that is the real Karl Marx, not the Karl Marx turned upside down by twentieth century university intellectuals and foreign tyrants who put words in his mouth, words which were the very opposite of what he intended.

"Who needs university intellectuals? Too often they have their heads in the clouds and their feet are no longer anywhere near the ground. If that is what is really meant by New Labour, I want none of it. Nor did Tom Booth.

"But I say this to you now. The British people have conquered the world in two ways. They have conquered it with their language and their inventions and that conquest will live forever. They have conquered it with their guns and warships and that conquest has failed. I know which I prefer. I know which Tom Booth preferred.

"So we owe it to the memory of the great man that we celebrate today to keep fighting his fight long after he died. We are gathered here today to celebrate not the death, but the life of Tom Booth. His spirit lives on with us all. It is immortal.

"So please watch over us today Tom, from your favourite pub in heaven with a pint in one hand, a cigarette in the other and thoughts of everlasting wisdom in your mind. Keep giving us those thoughts. We promise we will not fail you. May you rest in peace, my wise old friend." With that, Alan Stanley gathered his small sheaf of papers, tapped them together and as his final words lost their echo round the corners of the church, he counted to ten. Then he slowly and solemnly walked down the pulpit steps and back to his pew.

As he did so, Tom's daughter Norma in the front row gave Alan Stanley a discreet wave of thanks. As she did so, out of the corner of his eye he was watching two members of the Labour Party national executive in the congregation. They looked in his direction and nudged one another. The morning had served its real purpose. Alan Stanley had not only delivered a eulogy for his hero. He had, quite deliberately, put down an important political marker for himself.

He more than anyone knew which way the wind in the Labour Party was blowing and it was blowing his way. For once a maritime logic appealed to him. New Labour and all that sailed with her belonged to yesterday. Theirs was a becalmed, rudderless empty vessel ready to be left behind in his wake. His political career at Westminster, albeit an Old Labour career, still belonged to tomorrow and now it had the wind in its sails. Alan decided that it would shortly be the appropriate time to crank up those political winds to storm force ten.

*   *   *   *   *

Paris, France

THE MORNING EUROSTAR from London St Pancras droned into the Gare du Nord, its distinctive siren noise filling the air. From the number of people who alighted, it was clearly almost full and Violaine Khalifa stood high on her toes to try and see James in the crowd. Tomorrow was her 28th birthday and her parents had decided to make it a big family party at which their future son-in-law could meet the rest of the family. It was a party which Violaine was most anxious should succeed. The de Chambons, the Kerguelens and the Thiraults were not always the easiest of people to deal with.

It took less than three minutes before Violaine was wrapped in James's welcoming arms. She had not seen him for weeks and the next gap was going to be even longer. In a few days he had to return to Portsmouth to take up his duties on HMS Daedalaus, one of the most modern ships in the Royal Navy. James was going to be her Executive Officer and Violaine knew that would take in back to sea and she would probably not see him for months on end.

Violaine learnt from her god-brother Xavier de Kerguelen that Executive officer in the navy meant second-in-command. In his turn Xavier had been impressed. "Those new Type 45 destroyers the British are building are superb. The Americans are envious. We are all envious. When the Royal Navy gets it right, everyone is envious. James is so lucky to have been given the posting he has. You should be proud."

For James it was a welcome return to his second favourite city. After meeting Violaine seven years ago, Paris had become more and more his second home. Even more so was the family's private Hotel de Chambon on its aristocratic island in the River Seine. It was now four years since the two graduates of Oxford university had become engaged, much to the delight of Violaine's parents Louise and Malik Khalifa.

"He's here, Maman, Papa!" Violaine declared as they walked in through the door. "He's here! This train was right on time into the Gare du Nord. And I could see him almost half way down the platform. I always knew I preferred tall men." Almost immediately Louise appeared in the hallway and embraced her future son-in-law in true French style. James definitely approved of that. Louise Khalifa might have been sixty-three, but her fine figure, good looks and obviously expensive fragrance could still warm any man's heart.

"Come on in, James darling. It's just wonderful to think the Royal Navy can actually manage without you for a few days. You get more handsome every time I see you. Malik is upstairs finishing a phone call, he'll be down as soon as he can. I'm sure Violaine has told you. We've decided to make this birthday party a double occasion. Now we have you captive in Paris I want you to meet some more members of your future family. And I can assure you they all want to meet you."

Malik's phone conversation completed, or truncated, he joined them and welcomed his future son-in-law warmly. As they moved into the drawing room James was pleased to see Xavier de Kerguelen again and also his mother Tiffany whom he knew well enough. Years ago he

Louise Khalifa

had stayed at the Kerguelen residence in Brittany. Now James was standing next to Xavier's father Erwan, an old naval officer himself, just as the Kerguelens had been naval officers for generations.

Captain Erwan de Kerguelen looked approvingly at James, he had heard much about this British officer from his son. The camaraderie of navies ignores national frontiers; the sea has been the shared and eternal challenge for all of them. Erwan was interested to learn about James's global network of naval contacts. Warwick Sydenham of the Royal Australian Navy was soon mentioned.

The British still had tentacles to the other side of the world and he asked how he and James had met. "We were officer cadets at Dartmouth together almost twenty years ago. We may have been on opposite sides of the world most of the time, but we have always kept in touch. I think it is going to be very interesting when he meets Xavier. I'll tell you one thing, Captain de Kerguelen. I can already see your son leading his two fellow naval officers, one Australian and the other British, on some long voyages round the better class drinking establishments of Paris."

Erwan de Kergulen approved greatly, as he approved also of Dartmouth Naval College. "It's just only across the sea from our home in Brittany, James and over the years it has produced some of the finest sailors the world has known. If you and your Australian friend met there as young cadets, I'm sure Xavier will be in his element."

Erwan became reflective for a moment, perhaps almost envious. If only he had been able, in the prime of his naval career, to build such a personal network of fellow naval officers around the world. And had he known where the Sydenham-Heaton-Kerguelen fellowship would one day lead, his enthusiasm would have known no bounds.

Erwan had also worked alongside the Royal Navy in his time. So far as he was concerned there were only two navies in Europe worth worrying about and they were both represented in the Hotel de

Chambon today. For his part James was thoroughly enjoying the birthday party. He found himself in his element too, among Violaine's closest relations. She had warned him they might be difficult. He was discovering the exact opposite.

For the first time James met another member of the Khalifa family. Violaine had mentioned on several occasions she had a somewhat older half-brother, his father's by a Saudi wife who had died in childbirth. As a small child in Riyadh he had been her hero and mentor. Today Hamad Khalifa was there in the flesh and as it turned out four years older than James. He looked and sounded very like his father and James found that reassuring. Violaine's half-brother was already married and had two children, making her an aunt. He doted on Violaine, whom he had known since she was born and, until she left Riyadh at the age of twelve, had been the apple of his eye.

Hamad Khalifa was a banker working in Dubai, but had been educated as an accountant in London and spoke excellent English. His wife, like Violaine, was half-European, half-Arab. They had originally met in London, although they had not finally married until he was thirty. Like his father and half-sister, Hamad took a very enlightened view of Islam. Apart from anything else it soon emerged he did not share the Prophet's draconian views on rates of interest. The banking he practised in Dubai was normal by western standards, not the tortuous interest-less banking they pursued in Riyadh in a forlorn attempt to follow Mohammed's obsolete, vaguely absurd strictures.

Next in the line of introductions was Violaine's aunt Isabelle and her dapper husband, Antoine de Thirault, Violaine's godfather. He was a politician, a member of the Assemblée Nationale and represented a constituency somewhere in northern France almost facing England. James was not quite certain which. Amid the canapés and champagne Antoine de Thirault seized James by the arm and led him to one corner, intent on a more serious discussion.

The gist of it was that some members of the French Assembly were decidedly pro-British and always had been. Antoine was prominent among them, chairman of a Franco-British forum. On a clear day he could almost see the white cliffs of Dover from his constituency - well, it was a bit of an exaggeration, but the optimistic spirit was there.

He and his assembly colleagues had been delighted by the way the British and French had co-operated in March to sort out the Libyan problem, while others merely dithered. "When the British and French work together, James, the rest of the world can just stand and watch. We have the two finest navies in Europe. We should always be standing shoulder to shoulder, just as we were in two world wars. Just as we were at Suez. Between you and me, Lieutenant-Commander, the British and French are far better allies than the Germans and the French ever were, no matter what Feydeau farces they like to act out in Brussels."

Antoine de Thirault could hardly have made his position any clearer. He explained with great approval how Nicolas Sarkozy and David Cameron worked side by side when the going got tough. "I tell you, James, things have come a long way since the days of Charles de Gaulle. The great Charles did important things for France, his Fifth Republic gave us much greater stability, but after working in exile in London in the Second World War he always had a blind spot where the British were concerned. He never liked Winston Churchill, but that is now history. And watching the way things are brewing in the Islamic world and further afield, I think that a renewed alliance across La Manche is going to become very significant."

Malik Khalifa had joined them. "Between you and me, Antoine, I am inclined to agree. I know it's not politic to say these things when I am with many of my colleagues in Riyadh, but here in Paris, with discretion, I can speak my own mind. Violaine and I are an axis of Islamic moderation. No civilised man can sympathise with a lunatic like Colonel Gadaffi, just because they both happen to venerate the same prophet. The British and French were right to do what they did in Libya and I am proud the Arab League backed them all the way. That is my kind of Islam. I'm sure your god-daughter has told you her own views on that, Antoine. And having told her your views, she has told you my views as well."

Antoine de Thirault nodded wisely. "Malik, keep on fighting the good fight. You know all your family here in Paris is right behind you. Islam has a great tradition - we've all been to Cordoba. It was once the intellectual centre of Europe, just as Paris and London are its intellectual centres today. If I had my way Islam would rediscover its own true roots and do it quickly. It desperately needs what we had here in Europe centuries ago, a renaissance. There is simply too much wisdom locked away in the true traditions of your people to let it all go to waste."

Malik particularly approved of Antoine de Thirault's instinctive phrase 'your family.' After a shaky start with an elder generation, it had felt like that to him for years. He was now where he ultimately belonged. "Antoine, you must have been reading Violaine's doctoral thesis from Oxford. For all I know, you probably even helped her write it. I agree. You know, sometimes there are moments when I simply want to resign my job in Saudi Arabia and settle down here in Paris in sensible retirement, as you so kindly put it with my real family. This is without any doubt one of the most civilised cities in the world.

"It's not as though we couldn't afford it. Over forty years as a Saudi diplomat may not make you blissfully happy, but it does make you reasonably rich. If nothing else, diplomatic travel certainly shows you what the rest of the world has to offer. I would choose Paris with good reason, just as I half expect my daughter would probably choose London. They are two cities in a world league of their own."

"In that case, Papa, I can resign my job at Les Renseignements Generaux straight away, marry James and have lots of babies." Aglow with excitement, Violaine had joined them and Malik wondered what was coming next. His daughter was standing next to her future husband looking determined, while his wife Louise clucked with delight at the prospect of becoming a grandmother several times over. The de Chambons were noted exponents at that. Theirs was a proud dynasty to perpetuate and a dash of fresh blood from Britain, strong naval blood, would do the dynasty no harm at all. "So have you and James eventually decided on a specific date, darling?" Louise enquired.

"Yes, Maman, we have. We were going to tell you all later, but let's do it now. Please listen everyone. James and I have something to tell you. We've been engaged for four years and we've both decided that is quite long enough. As we drove over from Gare du Nord this morning, we have finally decided. We want to get married this time next year. James is going to arrange some leave from the Royal Navy. I am going to leave my job.

"Five years working for the secret service will have been a perfectly respectable career. But it's my life and I want it to be a good and useful life. I think there is no finer thing this almost thirty year old woman can do now than produce some beautiful and clever children. You are all invited to the wedding. We will hold it in Saint Louis en L'Ile. Then back here at the Hotel de Chambon."

Malik Khalifa was already popping open another bottle of champagne, ably assisted by Louise's brothers-in-law Charles and Antoine with the glasses. This was a great day for the family, as Violaine proclaimed "I've decided, we've both decided, that is how my life is going to be from now on. Violaine Heaton, once of the Sorbonne, then a French graduate of Keble College Oxford just like her husband, the proud wife of a British naval officer and mother of his children." Everyone raised their glasses to that. A new twenty-first century Entente Cordiale had just been sealed on the very same island which had once witnessed the very beginnings of Paris.

Chapter Ten

Machinations

Fillmore, Cheyenne

THE STATE OF CHEYENNE shares borders with Missouri, Nebraska, Iowa and Kansas. As is proclaimed by the licence plates on its trucks and its cars, it lies at the very Heart Of America. It was where the Union of the north had confronted the Confederate south face to face on more than once occasion. There may not be quite so much bloodshed nowadays, but it has remained a polticial battleground ever since. Now in the twenty-first century the battle was one of jaw-jaw rather than war-war, but every bit as ruthless.

In years gone by the state capital of Fillmore had made its name by building rear-paddle steamers and distilling bourbon. City wiseacres had long maintained the captains of the former were by far the most accomplished consumers of the latter. Their distinctive navigational techniques bore eloquent and often noisy testimony to that, as Samuel Clemens had observed more than once. Yet Fillmore's glory days were over. Until now it had been inconsequential America, not the first place anyone would expect to shape the future of world politics. Yet that was its singular fate today.

The state of Cheyenne stakes only one real claim to national significance. Its voters are very finely balanced between Republicans and Democrats. It swings obediently in America's political wind, an astonishingly accurate weathervane of party fortunes. "Whoever wins Cheyenne wins Washington." So ran one of the most frequently-cited mantras of twentieth century political America.

But now in the early twenty first century the state governor, Republican Abigail Fenceville, was deep in conversation. It was a lunch shared with her two oldest political friends and mentors, Jack Bunkerton and Ezekiel Watchman. They were in their favourite downtown Italian eatery, the Biglia Restaurant and Bar. People pronounced it Big Lear in Fillmore, Cheyenne, and it served quite the finest lasagna to be found anywhere in the state. To be seen eating at the Biglia regularly showed you had arrived at the pinnacle of Fillmorian society.

They had asked for and been given a secluded alcove table where no-one would overhear their conversation. Over two or more bottles of Chianti, an expensive imported wine for a special occasion, they were discussing the prospects for the American presidency. For the past year Jack and Ezekiel, a tarnished pair of Mississippi machiavellis if ever there was, have been observing the frantic survival initiatives of President Barack Obama, and discussing little else.

"Abby, let's face it, Barack Obama is done for." said Ezekiel. "Just read any newspaper. Just listen to things folk like Rush Limbaugh are saying. Never underestimate the radio pundits. Worse, it's only four months since the Obama administration came within an hour of being forced to close down the entire US Government. When matters get as dire as that on Capitol Hill why, even the dumbest American voter starts to take notice. "And it's not just here in the US they reckon he's done for. It's often a good idea to read what people are saying in those foreign countries. Sometimes they have clearer perspective. Let me tell you something. An old friend of mine in London, England, sent me this leading article, a leading article no less, from the London Times way back in March. That's even before Obama was dropping apart y on Capitol Hill. Just listen to this . . . "

The headline in the British newspaper ran 'Deserted by Obama' and it closed with 'Mr Obama is proving to be a brutal disappointment.' Zeke Watchman folded the clipping away carefully and grimaced. "That's what they think about him over there in London town. The British are supposed to be our oldest allies and friends. Not exactly pulling their punches, are they, in the old country? I don't need to remind you that is the country that once produced Margaret Thatcher. Never let us, any of us, forget Great Britain's Margaret Thatcher."

Abigail Fenceville was deeply impressed by such worldly wisdom. "Gee, Zeke, will people expect me to read foreign newspapers as well? How will I ever find the time? As it is I get pretty well absorbed by everything there is to learn in our Fillmore Clarion. I believe a politician needs to know what's going on in her home town. Sometimes I take a squint at the Washington Post, but I'm the first to admit most of that fancy Harvard stuff goes straight over my head."

Ezekiel Watchman smiled at the single-mindedness of his attractive protégée. He could always read the complicated newspapers for her, and leave Abigail to do what she did best. Her task was to attract votes. His task was winning elections: in the state of Cheyenne, it was in the genes. "Abby, you know full well that in November next year the people of America are going to vote for their President, and I'll tell you something right now. The American people are going to be choosing between two fresh candidates and Abigail Fenceville if I have my way, and Jack here has his way, you will be one of the two. If Margaret Thatcher could do it for the woman of Britain in 1979, you can certainly do it for the women of America in 2012. Things will have come on a long way gender-wise in those thirty-three years. When the GOP assembles in Tampa, Florida, in just over one year's time we are going to sweep the board, and here's how. We first let the front-runners exhaust themselves attacking one another, then you make your entry appearance late, you look fresh, you look untainted, and you look strong. You speak from the heart and you speak for the heart of America.

"That is what the state of Cheyenne is all about. And then you go into the Presidential election itself and you will win there too. If as I expect Glenn Silverdale tears the Democratic convention in Charlotte to shreds a week later, they will be a hopelessly divided party. Our Republican candidate will storm straight through that gap and straight into the White House. Mark my words."

With that Ezekiel tossed back an almost full glass of Chianti. It might have been an unbridled gesture of triumph but political plotting was still thirsty work. They were all familiar with the Democrat Glenn Silverdale, junior senator for Cheyenne. Despite the difference in their party politics, he and Abigail Fenceville had known one another since school. Two years her senior, it was nowadays widely rumoured that when she was seventeen she had on occasion dated the future senator. Narrower rumours even suggested the encounter had taken place in the capacious back seat of his class-mate's beat-up Chevrolet.

Ezekiel Watchman raised the fascinating prospect of two American politicians from the same state running against one another for the Presidency. Jack Bunkerton, principal architect of vulgar Cheyenne politics, relished the thought. "If you are right, Zeke, it will be a definite first for America. Both presidential candidates from the same town, and outside politics both of them very old friends. It will either be the cleanest presidential campaign in the history of American politics - or the dirtiest. You choose."

They could choose. Scheming Fillmore city bosses like Jack Bunkerton and Ezekiel Watchman were in total control of the political machinery of their state. Their power to choose who did what was invincible, for Cheyenne bred some of the toughest political fighters in the nation. Not that Abigail Fenceville looked tough at all. She was five foot six inches tall, with a shapely, matronly figure. Her face was rounded and rather good-looking, her eyes were brown. She had medium length hair, usually dyed to a vaguely authentic auburn. She wore glasses intended to convey an air of intellectual substance, trying not to look too much like just another glamorous granny.

Abby took a lot of care with her appearance, for she reckoned it was worth many thousands of votes. She had never quite worked out whether it was women voting for her out of respect for her motherhood, her handling of an unpleasant divorce, her steadfast career or the way she took good care of her appearance. Either that, or it was men voting just because they had the hots for her. Not that it mattered. She harvested their votes either way by the thousand, and an attractive physical appearance was a crucial part of her political package.

Abigail liked to see herself as a political idol, a rôle model and a standard-bearer. They bred them like that in her part of America. She was no east coast intellectual, not by a million miles. She had never been anywhere near Boston or Harvard, and would have quickly gone missing had she tried. She came from the political heartland of the nation, and her heart beat in rhythm with that of its people, the real people of America. She lived in the greatest democracy the world had ever known.

Regardless of party loyalties, another local political hero had been Harry Truman. He had been born in next door Missouri, and some eighty-eight years after that he had died in next door Kansas. The political rivalry between the adjacent state capitals had always been strong, as they fought for the spirit of middle America. Or at least the political spirit of the nation as they both perceived it. But then, as Ezekiel Watchman hardly needed to remind them, Truman had been on the other side, a Democrat. He had become the thirty-third American President and in the view of many one of the most successful, but then he was defeated by Dwight D Eisenhower in 1952. Just sixty years later, the lunch companions hoped, Abigail Fenceville would walk where her fellow Republican Eisenhower had once walked and defeat a popular Democrat for the White House. Anyway that was their plan.

Although neither of them could be certain about it, that lunchtime two political wheeler-dealers were setting Abigail Fenceville on course to become the forty-fifth President of the United States. Fifteen months later the three of them were to look back on that landmark lunch in Biglia's in downtown Fillmore with pride. It acquired the status of an historic occasion. Out of it had grown the New Republicans. They were to become a more substantial force in politics than the diaphanous Tea Party which had gripped the political imagination in several states over the previous three years.

As Zeke Watchman explained it, "The Tea Party have shown us the way. They're not the right answer, but even they revealed their power in April, when they stood at the shoulder of the main Republican party telling Barack Obama how he should run his government. Let's learn the lesson and learn it good. America is ready for some tough talking, and some tough action in Washington. That, Abby, is going to be us."

By the Fall of 2012 the Biglia Lunch had, in rarified Republican party circles, acquired the status of a hallowed occasion. Restaurant customers asked to be seated at the same table. To the friends and admirers of Fenceville, Watchman and Bunkerton - the Biglia Three - it had been one of those pivotal turning points in political history. It set the Republican party on a new course, leaving far behind the party's supposedly unhappy days of George W Bush. Others would come to regard the landmark lunch at Biglia's as a national disaster of the first magnitude. Such are the vicissitudes of political fortune.

And so the conversation that lunchtime examined in detail the life and times of Harry S Truman. Even if he was on the other side, there was still much to be learnt. He had been another machine politician, one swept to power in Washington by the premature death of

President Roosevelt. In his earlier years Truman had worked briefly on the newspaper in Kansas City, despite its name the state capital of Missouri, and the nearest state capital to Fillmore. He had never been to college. Nor had Abigail Fenceville. Instead she had worked as a junior reporter on her local newspaper, the Fillmore Clarion, before she joined a firm dispensing easily digested public relations around the state.

The combination had been a fine apprenticeship for a career in local politics. At the age of 28 Abigail had stood for, and won a seat on Fillmore City Council. A formidable political machine, one which never flinched from dubious tactics when they were effective, had swung into action behind her. One thing had led to another and by the familiar route of city mayor she had become the first female governor of the state of Cheyenne by the age of 42. Now she was a ripened 54 and ready for another great leap forward in her political career.

The three of them sensed they were plotting a transformation at the very top of American politics, a route map built on the wisdom and the success of the past. After drinking fine Chianti, none of them was in an equivocal mood, it was time to get started. Despite his alcoholic intake Ezekiel Watchman's political memory was still second to none. He reminded them: "In the very year I was born, Harry Truman said: 'I never did give them hell. I just told the truth, and they thought it was hell.' I think, Abby, we could well make that our watchword. Whatever his party, Harry Truman came from this part of the world and he understood his politics. Ideally we are going to make them think we have given them hell too.

"They, that political intelligentsia in the East, deserve it. Our Republican party belongs to the ordinary people of America, not to heads-in-the-clouds intellectuals. We are going to bring American politics back home. When you give your State of the Union address to Congress, never forget who your true audience is. At the very beginning of the American Declaration of Independence remember it says 'We, the people.' It definitely does not say 'We, a self-appointed bunch of political egg-heads from the Commonwealth of Massachusetts." Even with several glasses of genuine imported Italian wine inside him, Ezekiel Watchman's precise knowledge of American political structures was still without doubt second to none.

When Ezekiel Watchman gave vent to his patent version of political theory he could be pretty impressive, at least in Fillmore, Cheyenne. Yet his old political partner Jack Bunkerton was not going to be outdone. When Jack was thirty-three years of age, Ronald Reagan had been the thirty-third governor of California. "You and I are in total agreement about East Coast intellectuals, Zeke. It's not even a matter of party politics. It's a matter of political insight and not fearing the establishment. Ronald Reagan once said that the problems will not be cured in Washington because Washington was the problem. Something along those lines, anyway."

At that Abigail Fenceville swelled her matronly bosom with pride. As she roundly declared: "If Margaret Thatcher is my greatest political heroine, then Ronald Reagan is my greatest political hero. Nearly everyone laughed when a B-list actor from Hollywood became governor of California. There were those here in Cheyenne who didn't take me seriously either when I became governor of this state. They aren't laughing now. Well we showed them all, both of us, did the great Ronnie Reagan and me.

"No-one will ever forget how Reagan went on to demolish Jimmy Carter. I was twenty-three years old in that election and that more than anything is what made me want a career in politics. Reagan slaughtered the peanut-farming Democrat by 490 votes to 49. He became the fortieth president of the United States. The Great Ronald gave the Republicans control of the Senate for the first time since 1952. "Ronnie Reagan was almost seventy when he got to the White House but he showed them once again. He might not have been one of the cleverest himself but he could see the advantage of choosing people who were cleverer than he was. I admire that. When I get to the White House that will be you, Zeke, and you, Jack. A good politician never forgets who her real friends are." With a stylish gesture Abigail downed almost a full glass of chianti, and wiped her mouth with feminine decorum.

"I still reckon Ronald Reagan turned out to be one of the greatest American presidents of the 20th century. Then he went into partnership with the great Margaret Thatcher, the first woman to be British Prime Minister, and between them they overthrew the entire Soviet Empire and they did it without a shot ever being fired.

"If I walk in Reagan's footsteps to become the forty-fifth President of the United States, if I walk in her footsteps to become the first woman president of the United States of America, I will show them all too. And I will only be 55 when I enter the White House. Margaret Thatcher was 53 when she walked into Ten Downing Street. I can do everything she could do." It was Abigail's turn to show off her worldly political wisdom. She knew Margaret Thatcher's political biography off by heart, one of the few books about politics she had actually read.

Ezekiel Watchman smiled with approval once again at the political determination of his protégée. As Abigail evoked the names of Truman, Reagan and Thatcher he raised his glass to her political heroes. ."Let's drink a toast to the future of real America. Let's drink a toast to those who dare tackle the political establishment, rather than allow themselves to be swallowed up by it.

"Why, even Karl Marx once wrote that freedom consists in converting the state from an organ standing above society into one completely subordinate to it. I'll bet you've not heard many Republicans quoting Karl Marx with such approval before, it's probably a first, but the old scoundrel was absolutely right." His two lunch companions looked at their political memory man in utter admiration. A simple political message which evoked everyone from Margaret Thatcher to

Karl Marx looked like a comprehensive winner, especially from the perspective of Fillmore, Cheyenne. And with a further clink of Chianti-filled glasses, the fundamentals of Abigail Fenceville's presidential campaign message were agreed. What it might lack in political substance, it would certainly make up for in political style.

It was a suddenly pensive Jack Bunkerton who brought the Biglia Three back down to earth. "Abigail, for all the wonderful dreams, let's not lose sight of the fact that before you reach the White House, you have to beat the Democratic candidate. Just suppose that's Hillary Clinton? She is not doing a half bad job as Secretary of State, even if the White House sends her a load of dud policies to pursue, and her husband was definitely one of the better Democratic presidents. Hillary Clinton knows her stuff.

"Whichever way you look at it, a state governor from somewhere ordinary in America could have a tough time beating her." Abigail nodded ruminatively. It was not necessarily going to be as easy as all that. If she had to run against Hillary Clinton, all hope of harvesting most of the votes of the women of America would be dashed overnight.

"Just a minute, Jack," said Ezekiel, "Before we all burst into tears, let's first do our sums. To become the Democratic presidential candidate, Hillary Clinton has first to overturn her boss. One of the cleverest things Barack Obama ever did was to make her his Secretary of State. He might be just another Harvard lawyer but he is not a totally stupid Harvard lawyer.

"It's the same old principle. It's always better to have them on the inside of the tent pissing out, than the outside of the tent pissing in. Even Hillary Clinton can't do both at the same time. By giving her one of the top jobs in his administration Obama more or less neutralised her political prospects. Probably quite deliberately so, unless he chooses to stand aside. I don't quite see Mr Obama doing that, do either of you? Jack Bunkerton warmed to the theme. "Yes, Zeke, perhaps you're right.

On reflection I think a complete outsider is much more likely to win the Democratic Party nomination. Someone with no strings attached to the present administration. Unless some political miracle makes Barack Obama look half-plausible again. The way things are going the next Democratic hopeful will want to distance himself or herself from the Obama White House as far as possible. Someone fresh, someone new, someone just like our old friend Glenn Silverdale, in fact.

"I realise Duane Stracken's on the other side of the political divide here in Fillmore, but I've known him for years. Years ago he and I even worked for the same firm of realtors. When he was very young Glenn did a stint there too. I'll tell you about that some day. That's how he and Duane first met, and they have been inseparable ever since. One day I'll explain all that too, if it ever becomes necessary.

"Old secrets aside, what I am telling you now is more or less what Duane told me over a couple of beers a few days ago, and I think his political arithmetic is right on the ball. As they see it, Glenn Silverdale is a tough Washington senator and they reckon he has everything it takes to be the Democratic nominee. So long as no-one looks more closely than that, he could be a very convincing candidate; right age, right looks, worked his way up in a proper small business. Three kids, unimpeachable family background and sex-life. Anyone can take a look at his birth certificate. As macho as you like and a refreshing change from all those Ivy League smart-asses from New England. Someone born, bred and rooted here in the heart of America. Just hearken to me! I could be writing his platform for him.

"Better yet, we must do everything from our side, discreetly, to ensure Glenn Silverdale gets the Democratic nomination. Let it be known privately that our GOP fears him more than any of the alternatives. Because I tell you both this. If they get him, we get him. I have enough on Mr Silverdale from his days as a realtor to have him spinning on a dime, not knowing which way to turn next. That is why, as of this lunch here at Biglia's, the junior senator for Cheyenne becomes our preferred choice for the Democratic nomination. For the Lord's sake just don't tell anyone why we think so, that's all.

It was Jack Bunkerton's turn to toss back an almost full glass of Chianti as a gesture of triumph. The bottles were emptying fast. "Remember Harry Truman. Remember the Kennedy's. It's calculating machine politicians like them who always impress the Democratic party faithful. The intellectual Hubert Humphreys are the ones who come second. Glenn Silverdale is a machine politician to his fingertips. If I were a Democrat I'd probably back him myself. And whether you are a Democrat or a Republican, if you come from Cheyenne you are always someone to be reckoned with.

"We breed tough politicians in this state and we always have done. In some places they don't count the votes, they just weigh them instead. They might have an easy time of it but we never have done. We have to fight for every vote we get in our state - never forget Cheyenne is the political fulcrum of America."

Over a three-hour lunch the Biglia Three had succeeded in discussing politics non-stop, yet not one word had been devoted to the substance of policy. The name of their game was power for power's sake, not power to achieve anything in particular. Questions of foreign policy, defence or the wider world never occurred to them. In a democracy politicians existed to be elected, policies were merely something to be worked out as they were going along. Their machiavellian vision stretched no further than beating Glenn Silverdale in November 2012. Beyond that were hurdles still beyond their comprehension. Policy was just a vague range of clouded hills on the farthest horizon, political hills to be climbed on a different occasion.

*   *   *   *   *

Dalian, north east China

THE MOOD WAS ONE of great celebration and pride. The most modern warship ever built in the Dalian yards of the Chinese Shipbuilding Industry Corporation was about to be launched by China's vice-premier Liu Fun. The ceremony was traditional. Amid the shouting and squealing of a large crowd, and with the Chinese national anthem played by a military band, the first of the People's Liberation Army (Navy) Advance class destroyers slid smoothly into the waters of the Dalian Wan. The great Chinese port on the Bay of Korea was little more than two hundred miles from the coast of North Korea. Not that these latest high technology ships would ever have much to do with that particular stretch of sea.

In its sheltered bay, just five hundred kilometres east of Beijing as the crane flies, Dalian was a natural place to build a port. Its shipyards were more than a hundred years old. In the 1960s they had built China's first guided missile submarine. In the 1970s they had built China's first guided missile destroyer. In the 1990s they had introduced block construction, the technique which had lately been used to such effect by the British in Scotland to build their own Type 45 class destroyer. With some clever modifications the same methods had been used in Dalian for China's decidedly similar Advance class.

This latest addition to the Chinese military fleet was being named the Admiral Zhou Man, after a legendary Chinese admiral of the fifteenth century. More than seventy years before Vasco da Gama or Christopher Columbus set sail from Europe, he had commanded part of a huge Chinese fleet which had explored the oceans of the world, or so it was claimed. Over the next four years, nineteen more Advance class destroyers would be launched from the numerous shipyards of Chinese Shipbuilding Industry Corporation. Each of them would be named after a great Chinese admiral of history. Despite their nostalgic names, the new fleet of destroyers would be anything but backward- looking. They would proclaim a powerful presence on the world's oceans, much as the illustrious admirals after whom they were named had done in the past. They were the most technically-advanced ships the Chinese navy had ever owned, hence their name. The fifteenth century junks which admiral Zhou Man and his fellow commanders had sailed had also, in their time, been some of the most advanced ships the world had ever known. It was a tradition which the vice-premier reiterated.

The importance to China was spelled out the following day in an article in the Chinese People's Daily signed by vice-premier Liu Fun herself. "When this ship comes into service in 2014, China will possess one of the most the most advanced warships in the world. The combat system is the very cutting edge of technology with enormous fire-power. These ships are fast, powered by high technology engines built in China and we are using a fully electric propulsion system. Within a few years our people's navy will have a whole fleet of them."

It was an important part of Liu Fun's public message that China saw itself as the guarantor of world peace. No matter how great the fire-power of its new ships, Beijing did not wish to appear militaristic. Her article was a finesse of Oriental subtlety. "China is becoming a great force for comradely friendship and economic progress all over the world. Our Advance class of naval destroyer represents this, as our modern world breaks free from its dark era of colonialism. This entirely new class of ship is being built with the finest wisdom of three continents. Our Chinese industrialists have always been quick to learn from the best ideas overseas. The hull is shaped with sloping sides, our version of what America calls stealth technology.

"Her engines are not old-fashioned diesels, but extremely powerful Yangtse turbojets. These are a Chinese improvement on an engine originally conceived by the British for use in the largest civil airliners, including those operated by China. The accurate weapons have been developed by our own Chinese engineers. The electronic fighting systems are developed from the latest computer software being designed in India. The Advance destroyer is a potent symbol of technology and co-operation among many different peoples. The greatest history of mankind has been built on interchange of clever ideas among many nations and many cultures. China has played an active part in that interchange which has been more distinguished than most.

"In centuries past, our civilisation has given the world many original inventions. Over three thousand years ago we gave the world silk. Over two thousand years ago we gave the world paper. Over a thousand years ago we gave the world porcelain. Over eight hundred years ago we gave the world explosives and the compass.

"And then almost six hundred years ago it was a great fleet of Chinese junks which explored the world. It is fitting that our latest fleet of destroyers will be named after the admirals and captains of that historic exploration fleet. We can say 'thank you' to our fellow nations around the world, whose scientists and technicians have in their many different ways have helped contribute to the ship we are launching today. For humanity must move forward as one body with one mind and one set of skills.

As a British poet once wrote 'No man is an island.' Today we applaud his wisdom. For in our own times no country is an island either. We are all just part of humanity's greater whole." Coming from a leading light in the Beijing Patriotic Association it was perhaps all a bit rich, but such philosophical profligacy never troubled Liu Fun.

The article had been written for the Chinese People's Daily over a period of several weeks, its sentiments calculated to a level of precision peculiar to the Forbidden City. Its real audience, as the vice-premier knew only too well, was in countries around the world which had once been under the yoke of European colonialism. Beijing wanted to send a message of peace, hope and prosperity to them all. Beijing also wanted them to understand which country was becoming the world's new technology powerhouse. Looking forward to her naval ambitions Liu Fun also wanted their cooperation. That was something for the future, when China would once again walk softly and carry a big stick. As the latest Chinese warship took to the water, today was an opportunity to congratulate the thousands of workers whose efforts alone had built her.

The vice-premier was unstinting in her praise. A ship for the People's Liberation Army (Navy) was the handiwork of the liberated people of China. Standing beside vice-premier Liu Fun's and applauding these patriotic sentiments was another, much more recent Admiral Zhou Man, the naval officer who had steered construction of the Advance class for over ten years. He watched his latest military baby slide into Dalian Wan with more pride than most.

Also watching with pride from a distance were Craig Holliday and Kevin Wilson, freelance shipping correspondents in China for trade newspapers of distant lands. Only part of the time did they spend writing innocent stories about shipping for trade magazines around he world. They hnad othe busines too. Their coded reports on construction of the ship now revealed as the Advance class had been fed back to Canberra for almost three years. A generous budget in American dollars had enabled them to buy secret technical information with some ease. Nevertheless the two trade journalists were relieved to know their broad predictions had now been proved correct.

In the Russell Building offices in Canberra, the intelligence reports from the spies in Dalian had been much valued if not greatly welcome. They had been marked Top Secret. Now a translation of Vice-premier Liu's public triumphalism put the news in the public domain, and it could be circulated widely among the Australian military. It promptly split strategic calculations in the commonwelth's capital down the middle. Many in Canberra's military still preferred to look in the other direction. But there were some, just a few, who noted with considerable anxiety the Chinese vice-premier's predictions.

A further nineteen Advance class destroyers would follow the pioneering Zhou Man. China clearly intended to become the dominant naval power in Australia's part of the world. Maybe the Royal Australian Navy would at long last be restored to its former importance. Just twelve months previously Bill Boyce had been put to rest, a lonely naval voice marooned on a sea of political apathy. His small fan club in Canberra could now see him grinning from the heavens with a justifiable sense of triumph. Or waving to them enthusiastically from the celestial beach where old sailors like Bill Boyce finally washed ashore.

*   *   *   *   *

Ministry of Defence, Whitehall

THREE NOTES on his desk monopolised George Gould's attention. One was a tidy assessment of the thoughts of vice-premier Liu Fun, expounded at a ship-launching a couple of days earlier in Dalian. The deputy military attaché at the British embassy in Beijing, skilled in translation, had done an admirable job of work. The second was a file note from the Chinese desk at the Foreign Office about the vice-premier. It confirmed that Liu was a rarely-seen intellectual in the Chinese hierarchy. Her public appearance in Dalian had been most unusual. Among the few foreign diplomats who had actually met her, it was generally agreed that Liu Fun was not to be under-estimated. She was a formidable strategist.

The third note was a signal from naval intelligence written by James Heaton a year earlier. It had predicted that the Chinese were building a destroyer modelled very closely on Britain's Type 45, and attached to it was a note from Australian naval intelligence supporting the analysis. George Gould was impressed. The lieutenant-commander had been right on the ball a whole year before anyone else. The latest pictures from the launch ceremony in Dalian did reveal a warship looking remarkably like a Daring class Type 45. There was a knock on his door, and in walked Christopher Cunningham. "Ah Chris, you timing is impeccable. You probably haven't seen this yet but we have confirmation of everything we anticipated. The Chinese have just launched their latest warship.

"You were right that it is a destroyer, and James Heaton was right about the class. It does remind one distinctly of a British Type 45. "We also now know the person we are up against. Name of Liu Fun, a vice-premier no less. Apparently she is the cleverest woman in China, or in its political circles anyway. Is she the same machiavelli Antonia has mentioned several times? The Chinese also appear to have named their new ship after Miss Foo's former boyfriend, one Admiral Zhou Man."

Christopher Cunningham examined closely the note from the embassy in Beijing. It confirmed the ship was using an Indian tracking and guidance system, and he smiled. All the hard work put into protecting the true identity of Sharava Corporation had paid off.

"Well done with all that work on Antonia." George added. "Not an inkling that the Chinese top brass, or even the formidable Liu Fun, suspect any links between the ship's electronics and the military of Great Britain. Either Antonia knows and has said nothing, or your Chinese walls in Park Royal are superb and she is still in the dark. Either way it is a great success. Anyway after her very nasty experience with that attempted hit and run a year ago, I would assume she is none too keen on her former Chinese connections any more. Do I gather she is spending a lot of time at your place nowadays?"

Christopher Cunningham confirmed all of that. He was impressed that the Chinese were talking of as many as twenty ships. When she first arrived in London, Antonia had made it clear they would want several sets of electronics; now it seemed they would need many more. A major order. And an extensive fleet, all equipped with the top secret Bijali encoder.

"It also explains why they needed such large engines. Antonia more or less told me they are copied from the Rolls-Royce Trent. Now we can see why." George Gould agreed. These were always going to be strategic warships, not coastal patrol boats. It looks as though China was developing a new fleet, probably for new waters. He reflected that the Middle Kingdom had once been very inward-looking and isolationist, but that was clearly no longer true.

The Captain tapped the translated note from Beijing on his desk: "I think we should take all this stuff about peace and friendship with a large pinch of salt. China is going global. This top strategist of theirs is singing from a very different hymn sheet. Underneath that charm offensive of hers you can already hear the strains of the battle hymn of the People's Republic. We can safely reckon that vice-premier Liu Fun's eyes have seen the glory of the coming of the dragon."

"As to the design of the destroyer, to be honest, in their shoes I think I would have done much the same. Once a military need has been identified, the ship more or less designs itself. What is impressive is the speed with which they can move. Not what one might expect from a bureaucratic country. The Americans should take note of that too. They have their own Arleigh Burke class of destroyers, but they are 1980s technology, designed when computer technology still had far to go."

George Gould gave Christopher Cunningham a quick summary of the fighting power of modern warships. He wondered aloud whether the Pentagon was being wrong-footed once again. Perhaps for the first time since the TSR multi-role combat aircraft was aborted in the 1960s, in its latest Daring class the United Kingdom had a piece of military hardware which was well ahead of anything on the other side of the Atlantic. The Ministry of Defence now knew a lot about the Chinese Advance class, thanks to the newspapers and Antonia Foo. Perhaps the British warship was becoming another global benchmark, rather like the Dreadnaught battleships of a century earlier.

"The Americans do have their own version of a Type 45 with comparable firepower coming along. It's called the Zumwalt class but it's not due to enter service until next year. Even then the original order for thirty-two of them has been progressively pared down to just two. Whitehall is not the only place feeling the strains on its military budget nowadays. How long, I wonder, before the Chinese navy grows to rival the United States Navy? How long will it take them to develop a fleet of nuclear aircraft carriers?

"At least we still have our insurance policy. I assume all the electronics supplied to the Chinese are fitted with the Bijali device? Well worth all that effort. Sometimes I begin to understand why other folk talk about us as Perfidious Albion. They rather pay us a compliment. We were already perfidious, according to the French, during their revolution. Did you know the Greeks coined the name Albion some time before 600BC? Do you reckon our beloved Britannia has actually notched up over two and a half millennia of perpetual perfidy? Whattagirl. Makes you think quite a bit, doesn't it?"

George Gould enjoyed his little jokes. They were carefully-crafted Whitehall Jokes, slightly drier that the Atacama desert. Now he looked at Christopher Cunningham who had something else on his mind. The managing director of the Shirava Corporation rested his elbows on the desk, steepled his hands and stroked his brow on the point of the steeple. He was wondering how to put it. With his eyes tilted down toward the desk, still half closed, Christopher Cunningham explained "I want to talk to you about Bijali and its link with Kundalini. It is proving to be very tricky. We could spend the next ten years just inventing new kinds of intelligence tests, but that's not the point. Only lately have we made any real progress."

George Gould nodded sagely and turned to the file on Kundalini marked 'Top Secret'. "I'm intrigued by this rating system you have recently devised. I like the way you simply give your subjects marks out of a hundred. I gather it is the brainchild of Antonia Foo. She can be very perceptive and very ingenious when she feels like it. But are you really telling me we are able to weigh up numerically people's fitness and mental ability to handle things like warfare decisions? What does it measure exactly?"

Christopher Cunningham explained how the ideas had originated. "You recall how a few years ago, when we were discussing Bijali, we agreed it would take a certain kind of intelligence that could absorb two different streams of information, compare and contrast them and reach decisions based on how they relate, and achieve all that in real time? Well that was our starting point."

"Yes, I remember it very well. Go on." George Gould was most attentive. "As I said we began with some of the more advanced IQ testing systems, such as the ones they use to decide whether or not to let people join Mensa. Their exams are conducted over several hours but they consist almost entirely of pattern recognition and deductive logic problems. It's all quite difficult, they are clearly trying to sort the sheep from the goats, but it only measures a narrow range of intelligence functions. Or it did last time I sat them, anyway. I do quite like to keep abreast of the latest academic ping-pong.

"In more recent years I think psychologists have broadly come to accept that there are many different kinds of intelligence - logical deduction, spacial awareness, verbal faculty, creative intuition, mathematical insight, pattern recognition, analytical prediction, what they call EQ or human empathy, all kinds of quite distinct mental ability.

"The experts nowadays seem to identify yet another new form of intelligence every time you read the literature. Well, at Sharava we have taken all that a step further by testing not only whether you can solve our questions in the first place, using all those different qualities of intelligence, but how long it takes you to do so." Behind his beard George Gould smiled, his trade mark gesture whenever he was working something over in his mind. They continued discussing the different varieties of intelligence at some length. He could see why Christopher Cunningham had found the task challenging. "I seem to remember the mental time game was Antonia Foo's speciality. I'm rather pleased we agreed to bring her on board."

"Indeed it is. She has shown herself to be both very creative and extremely methodical, and it's a rare combination." Christopher Cunningham was very enthusiastic about his Chinese colleague. Her particular contribution had been to devise some very neat electro-biological mapping techniques which observed the brain at work. The trace was transferred onto a chart which already recorded the subject's test responses. "That way we can directly compare what a brain has achieved with how it has been working. We can watch how hard a subject is thinking, how quickly he is thinking, and whether he is coming up with the right answer, all at the same time. It is proving to be most revealing. You've obviously read my analysis in the file."

George Gould had read that part of the file thoroughly. He tapped it several times, frowned, then looked up at Christopher Cunningham. "You realise this could have a much wider application than just how we promote and assign responsibilities to naval officers? It occurs to me these tests could also be applied, should be applied, to the top brass directing operations, and even to the politicians handing out strategic decisions to the top brass. God help me you could even use it to test senior Whitehall civil servants. I can think of at least a dozen denizens of the Athenaeum it should be tried on immediately."

Christopher Cunningham was already drawing up a private list of leading British politicians who should be given the Kundalini treatment. Americans too. He was not necessarily choosing the brightest of the bunch; on the contrary. "In view of recent events in Tampa, it should probably become compulsory for candidates for the White House. I wonder how this Abigail Fenceville would stand up to scrutiny, or pacifists like Alan Stanley?   I've never been keen on the idea that the commander-in-chief, the person who takes the decision where to fight the war and how hard, against whom and deploying what assets, need have no military experience or relevant expertise. They would never permit such a level of undiluted amateurism with political lawyers."

Lateral thinking was one of Christopher Cunningham's passions. George Gould's main job included keeping abreast of a wide spectrum of scientific and military research. "As we have realised in this electronic age, computers can generate huge flows of data every millisecond. But what about the humans supposed to make sensible use of all that data? It depends on the mental capacity of the man, or the woman, in the middle. And when there's a war on there's no time for messing about."

Pensively Christopher Cunningham nodded in agreement. "That had occurred to us, naturally, although Antonia has primarily been building a database to compare the Kundalini performance of different levels of education, the different sexes, different cultural backgrounds, different ages, and different career experience. They all seem to play a part. What use you choose to make of all that, George, rather takes it out of my sphere. I was primarily looking for officers who could make best effective use of things like Bijali - and Antonia Foo, even, still knows nothing about that. We operate on a strict 'need-to-know' discipline at Shirava, as you understand better than anyone."

The two friends discussed the finer points of the testing and evaluation techniques of Kundalini for a further ten minutes. When they had exhausted the key points George Gould thanked his colleague from Park Royal and explained "At this point I think you had better leave this one in my hands.

"I reckon it has a much wider application than you maybe intended, to be fair either of us intended, when we embarked on the brain mapping project. It occurs to me I really ought to bring this to the attention of my Deputy Secretary here at the Ministry, one of the brightest people in the department. And if I know Peter Storey at all, he will then want to talk it through with the Cabinet Office. His network of Whitehall contacts is second to none. Who knows? A summary of your report could be on David Cameron's desk before the end of the week."

Christopher Cunningham was impressed by the speed with which George Gould could grasp a new idea and immediately plan his next move. He was probably a very fine chess player. "So George, can I safely assume you have already decided to give our Kundalini technique a push into the political sphere, and that Peter Storey is your preferred policy pusher?

"Something like that, yes. I tell you, Chris, from what I have heard so far this should spark off quite a few fireworks. No longer are we going to choose our top politicians through the ballot box. Forget about the hustings, forget all those manifestos. In the future we could choose our political leaders by setting them a Kundalini examination and may the best man or woman win. I don't quite know how it all chimes with democracy but I'm quite sure your man Plato would have been delighted. We seem to be reinventing his dream of properly-trained guardians, but with the assistance of some very ingenious twenty-first century computers."

"Well, if it means removing some of the crasser idiots from the political decision-making process, then I for one am all for it." Christopher Cunningham observed. "My thoughts exactly." replied a smiling George Gould.

*   *   *   *   *

Charles de Gaulle airport, Paris

JAMES HEATON WATCHED the passengers enter the arrivals hall as they streamed off the long flight from Sydney. It had landed less than an hour ago, and Warwick Sydenham was among the first to appear. Many years flying around the world in the service of the Royal Australian

Navy had taught Warwick to travel lightly. Whenever possible he avoided time spent at monotonous luggage carousels wearily watching baggage emerge from the hold. The two naval officers decided a cab ride was the right way to be introduced to Paris. For Warwick it was the first visit in his life, and he was thirty-eight years old.

They had allowed for a couple of days around the city for him to acclimatise, before the big events of Friday and Saturday. First it was time for the Australian to see the most famous sights of Paris - the boulevards, the Eiffel Tower, the wedding cake basilica of Sacre-Coeur. They consumed a coffee and a sticky cake apiece in the Place du Tertre, the artists' square of central Monmartre. Finally they moved to the centre of town to see Notre Dame and watch the graceful Bateaux Mouches on the Seine. Both of them loved ships of any and every kind. James then pointed out the Île Saint-Louis, ancestral home of the Chambons, before they found their way to Warwick's hotel.

That evening they were to have dinner with Xavier de Kerguelen. It would be an opportunity for Warwick to be introduced to a fellow Lieutenant-Commander. The French Navy was held in admiration by Warwick's circle of naval friends in Sydney. It was the only navy outside America with a nuclear aircraft carrier. Warwick wondered whether this Xavier might at some stage have served on her, the Charles de Gaulle.

The dinner that evening revealed an immediate meeting of minds. Top of the agenda was to agree the exact duties of a Best Man. Were the niceties the same in France as they were in Australia? There was much comparison of navy life. They were all the same age, but with quite distinct career paths in three different navies. As stag nights go, it was all very measured and cerebral but none the less enjoyable for that.

The discussions went on without let-up until Warwick's inevitable jet lag caught up with him and it was definitely time for bed. The following day Warwick Sydenham was invited to meet James's almost- wife Violaine. He was much impressed. She was beautiful.

Warwick wasted no opportunity in finding a private moment to congratulate James on his choice. "James my friend, she is quite stunning, and a doctorate from Oxford as well? You really have done very well for yourself. And well you deserve it. Already I can imagine Captain James Heaton, retired officer of the Royal Navy, living a life of elegant luxury at his almost permanent home here on the Île Saint-Louis in quite the smartest quarter of Paris. And I do have to say her mother - Louise is it? - is really rather stunning too. You can easily see where Violaine gets her looks. And I fully agree your future wife is definitely something rather more than a sheila."

Most of Thursday was taken up with last minute-preparations. The duties of Best Man started well before the church. That evening Dr Khalifa invited James, Xavier and Warwick to dinner at Le Procope, still his favourite restaurant, even if it was becoming just a trifle touristique since appearing in so many guides about the city. Tourists or not, Warwick was impressed by a standard of cuisine practically unknown south of the Mediterranean, let alone south of the Equator.

If Warwick found the food intriguing, Malik Khalifa found Warwick Sydenham almost as much so. He wondered what view the Australian Navy took of the Indian Ocean, and was able to learn at first hand. He offered no comment as Warwick explained his sense of frustration that insufficient resources were devoted by Canberra to that important segment of the Australian Defence Force. Malik was taciturn and non-committal, but took good note of the earnest young Australian officer had to say nevertheless.

On Friday James and Violaine were officially married, but only in the Mairie of the Fourth Arrondissement. It was simple civil affair. This was necessary under French law before the big event in church the following day. James's naval padre had flown over that morning from Portsmouth to provide a protestant presence in what would be otherwise entirely Catholic proceedings. He and Warwick Sydenham acted as

James's two witnesses. Violaine's civic wedding party consisted of her parents and her two godparents Tiphaine de Kerguelen and Antoine de Thirault, who also served as witnesses. It was all rather bureaucratic, much more so than romantic.

For the occasion, Violaine took the tradition of something borrowed to extremes. She was wearing the same off-white silk suit, pill-box hat and kid gloves that her mother Louise had worn at her own wedding forty years ago in 1972. It was quite old-fashioned but extremely chic. It also proved how true to type women ran in the de Chambon family. Louise had married Malik Khalifa when she was twenty-four. Her daughter, with an almost identical figure would be twenty-nine in just two days' time.

The civil ceremony was followed by a long and enjoyable lunch at yet another Parisian restaurant. Warwick began to feel concerned about his waistline but the food was unquestionably first rate. And it was quite clear from the drift of the conversation that if Malik Khalifa had ever nursed any misgivings about his daughter marrying a British naval officer, they were clearly long gone. He seemed at least as excited as everyone else, in his studiously suave Saudi style.

It was only to be expected that one of the grandest families of the Île Saint-Louis would put on a splendid show for the wedding on Saturday. Violaine walked to Saint-Louis en l'Île on the arm of her father. Her dress was slim-fitting in ivory silk, tailored to perfection by the family seamstress. It was decorated with some tastefully-understated classical Arab motifs gently reminding people of her partly Islamic pedigree. Her Titian hair was in a perfect coiffure and she was wearing the family veil. It was held firmly in place by the renowned Chambon diamond and ruby tiara.

Two small bridesmaids held her train, the daughters of her Chambon cousins, the grandchildren of her uncles Antoine and Charles. The little bridesmaids were wearing what the French called robes a smocks with ivy motifs, white shoes and ankle socks and garlands of flowers in their hair. Violaine's senior bridesmaid, aged nine, was her half-niece, daughter of Hamad, but still young enough to wear the same rather fetching outfit.

Hamad's seven year old son had teamed up with Xavier de Kerguelen's son of almost the same age to serve as pages. The two boys led the way, marching along gamely in green culottes, white shirts and green jumpers. Even if they felt a little out of place, neither was going to let the side down, and from backward glances they could see the little bridesmaids were coping magnificently. Violaine's half sister-in-law brought up the rear to keep a motherly eye on the small children.

In the centre of her little procession, Violaine walked slowly beside her father. She had to give her bridesmaids a fair chance with the train, and anyway her ivory white high heels were not the shoes for hurrying. Her father looked very tall and splendid in a grey morning coat, striped trousers, grey waistcoat and a silver grey silk tie. His years spent working in London had left their sartorial mark and Malik Khalifa adhered to the British etiquette that only the fathers of the bride and bridegroom wore grey. His opposite number, retired naval Commander David Heaton in the church ahead of them, had by prior agreement made the same choice. The small wedding procession of eight held up the traffic as they walked down the centre of the Rue Saint-Louis en L'Île, a modest police escort ensuring they came to no harm.

This visible unity of the de Chambons, the de Kerguelens and the Khalifas was important in Parisian society. It marked many things. Forty years ago, a young Louise de Chambon had quite shocked the upper circles of Paris when she virtually eloped with some dashing young Saudi diplomat called Malik Khalifa. Today Violaine's parents were both accepted at the centre of French society, and the wedding procession brought many pleasured looks of approval from Parisian old ladies as curtains twitched along their route.

The rest of their wedding guests were already waiting in the Eglise Saint-Louis-en-L'Île. The church had one of the smallest, but still smartest, parishes in Paris, which reached across its own island and included about half the Île de a la Cité. Its central church of Saint-Louis was dedicated to Louis IX, who had reigned over France in the thirteenth century. It was in his reign the Sorbonne had first been founded, something very familiar to both Violaine and her mother. The Sorbonne was Europe's second oldest university and they were both its graduates, just as with James they were all graduates of Europe's third oldest university, Oxford, as well.

So it was with a powerful sense of history, as well as of present romance and with many exciting hopes for the future they worked their way through the wedding service. The parish priest and James's naval padre went out of their way to ensure it all made good sense to the several Moslems in the congregation. By one o'clock it was over, the final hymn had been sung, and the congregation dispersed. In France, unlike in England, only the immediate family and close friends returned to the Hotel de Chambon.

The big social event for the guests event would be a dinner and dance that evening at the Cercle Interallié in the Rue du Faubourg St Honore. The choice was deliberate, the very place where Violaine and James had first met just eight years before. For the afternoon, however, it was family champagne and canapes in the hotel particulier on the Quai Napoleon, while the mysterious black barges of the Seine chugged slowly along in the distance.

Once the formal speeches and events were over, Malik spotted his daughter deep in conversation with her new husband, and the two other naval officers Xavier and Warwick. Over dinner and lunch the quartet had quickly formed an alliance. Their conversation was analytical and factual, combining the worldly wisdom of several universities, Dartmouth naval college, the French aristocracy and the secret services of at least two countries. Malik tuned in just long enough to become aware he was listening to a penetrating collective insight into the future. He was deeply impressed by a profound view of the world with which he could readily identify. It was a far cry from some of the narrow and unworldly sentiments he often endured back in Riyadh. Perhaps that afternoon, as he tuned in to the thinking of next generation the seasoned Saudi diplomat began to realise where his deepest cultural sympathies lay.

*   *   *   *   *

Palace of Westminster, London

IT HAD BEEN ONE of the bloodiest meetings of the Parliamentary Labour Party anyone could remember. Rumours had quickly reached leading members of the Coalition government about what had transpired, and they were to be seen loping round the Palace of Westminster with cheerful smirks on their faces. After three lacklustre performances at three successive party conferences, it was generally reckoned that Ed Miliband was done for. In his eleven hundred days as party leader, he had failed to make an effective impression.

Graham Crowfield expressed everyone else's thoughts for them. "I realise he wants to be the instrument of change here in Britain, but a wind instrument is not necessarily the smartest choice for our party's leader. He won't last much longer. He's going to run out of puff."

By general consensus, the one man who had come out of it looking impressive was Alan Stanley, the member of parliament for Pennine South. The view of many party colleagues was that Alan Stanley's measured attack on the Labour leader had been masterful and deadly. Some were pleased, some were furious, other were simply aghast. Not since that far-off occasion when Geoffrey Howe had taken Margaret Thatcher apart on the floor of the House itself, and effectively ended her reign, had any leader been dealt such a ruthless blow. And that had been over twenty years ago, a full six years before Alan Stanley had even entered Parliament. Alan had been honing his oratorical style and gestures for years.

"At a time when the Labour opposition needs positive leadership more than anything else, we seem to have invented negative leadership. At a time when we need to be exposing the Achilles heel of this illegitimate coalition government, instead they show us a clean pair of heels, time and time again. At a time when we should be offering the British people a dream, we serve them a nightmare. We are told that Labour's ideas are all sound and original. The trouble is, none of the original ideas is sound, and none of the sound ideas is original. At a time when the government has imposed draconian burdens of taxation on the British people, we just seem to go along with it all. What a complete load of balls that economic policy turns out to be."

The uproar in the meeting of the PLP had been tumultuous, exactly as Alan Stanley had intended it to be. There was no point going after party consensus. His primary objective was party dissent. He told the delegates that their present leader seemed to have lost his marble. "He tells us he expects to be Prime Minister one day. I tell you all that one day will be more than enough."

In his exhortation, Alan Stanley had pointed to the need for a killer instinct. Where was Ed Miliband's killer instinct? He had pointed to the need to consign the legacy of Gordon Brown to the dustbins of history, dustbins which had long since been emptied anyway. Was Ed Miliband really the man destined to become the Labour Party's refuse disposal expert? Did he have the necessary talent for that? Did he have the right teddy-bear tied to the front of his cart?

The party leader needed to be untainted by any track record of failure as a minister. He needed to be a real politician who addressed himself to parliament and to the electorate directly, not mouthing worthy platitudes to David Dimbleby on *Question Time*, not seeking audience giggles on BBC television's *Have I Got News For You*, not courting the partisan adulation of John Humphries on BBC radio's *Today* programme.

Over three years previously, the tightly-knit group of Labour members from the northern counties - the CLYND - had promised Alan Stanley that his day would come. With consummate patience, he had waited his due opportunity and when it had arisen, he had been ready for it. He had been planning his speech of destruction for almost two years, ever since the unseemly way Ed Miliband had snatched a crown relinquished by the vanquished Gordon Brown from his own elder brother. Alan Stanley was not going to pass up on the opportunity now, not with the next general election only eighteen months away. He would need all of that time to rally the party and direct its fire power away from its political next of kin, so that in fellowship they could ruthlessly pursue the Cameron-led coalition government opposite.

After all that it was time for a recuperative drink. His friends were only too willing to oblige. "Alan, I realise about half of them hated you for that little performance, but whichever way they feel about it, there's no taking away from the fact it was a masterclass in conference politics. I loved every minute of it." enthused Graham Crowfield. "Don't worry about your detractors. Just make a powerful impression. Let them do all the loyalty shuffling afterwards. Never forget that every original opinion always begins life with a minority of one."

Over his pint of beer Graham continued where Alan had left off. "If we are going to have a leader who is in hock to the unions, at least let him admit he is in hock to the unions. If we are going to have some latterday Blair who simply charms the voters with a winning smile and a good line in patter, selling them snake oil by the tanker load, at least let him be a good spieler, and at least let it be top quality snake oil." Alan Stanley peered thoughtfully over the top of a much-needed pint at his effusive old friend. "And I'll tell you something else, Alan, I've been chatting recently with my Tory pair, Rupert Devereux. He's not half as bad as his posh name might suggest. He and I get on pretty well. He reckons, and his Tory pals all reckon, that the man they fear most in the Labour party nowadays is one Alan Stanley. You really couldn't ask for a much finer compliment than that anywhere in parliament."

There was much jostling in Annie's bar by assorted Labour MPs. Their assorted suntans, or lack of them, eloquently declared where they had spent their summer holidays before the start of the new Parliamentary term. A number were already beginning to wonder whether it was the right time to clamber aboard Alan Stanley's bandwagon, and if so which particular instrument they should seek to play. He soon realised how tiring it must be to become a celebrity, even a minor one, in Annie's bar.

For the moment, he just wanted to be among his oldest and most trusted friends. He had stuck his political neck out a very long way that morning. Most of his career in Parliament had been spent with the Labour Party in power, and he wanted to know whether his rhetorical skills of opposition and demolition were up to the job. Steve Wilson, member for Liverpool Toxteth, thought they were.

"There's no point pussy-footing around like a bunch of wishy-washy dons at some Oxbridge high table, Alan." Thoughts of elitist education were never far from Steve's mind. "You are not looking to win every single vote in the country next May. You are not even looking to win votes from any diehard Conservatives. There is no point.

"You are looking to do two things. You are looking to assure our rank and file Labour supporters that their cause is right and that the Tories are wrong. So first of all you need a credible cause. And you are looking to sow doubt in the minds of the Tory fringe. At best, at the very best, more than normal of their voters will stay at home on polling day. That's good enough. You can't expect to turn them all into Labour voters overnight, so don't even try. That is not how to win an election. Elections are always won on the difference in turn-out by the supporters of the two main parties. We want to pull our supporters through the polling stations in their millions, and dissuade as many as possible of theirs from bothering to vote. Always remember that it is never oppositions that win elections, it is always governments that lose them."

Steve Wilson was clearly riding one of his favourite political hobby-horses. "Always be reasonable. Keep away from doctrine. Exude commonsense, but commonsense with a clear purpose. Labour has always won, and only ever won, when it has won admiration from the detachable fringe from the main party opposite. That should be the limit of your ambitions, and it is good enough to put you into Ten Downing Street. Remember what Harold Wilson always used to say "politics is the battle for the middle ground.' Better yet, it is the battle to spread apathy on one side of the party line, and sow enthusiasm on the other."

Alan Stanley was powerfully aware just how anxious Labour members of parliament were to ensure they would keep their seats at the next general election. Far more than Conservative members of parliament, their family fortunes often depended on their parliamentary salary. A Labour leader who could set out a clear strategy for winning the election seat by seat was money and security in their pockets. Alan Stanley came from a poor enough background himself, never to lose sight of the fact. Champagne socialist he was most certainly not.

It was generally reckoned Steve Wilson had as devious a mind as anyone when it came to election strategy, and Alan Stanley was rapidly making up his own mind who his campaign director should be. Apart from anything else, Steve was obviously angling for the job.

First of all, however, there was the clear prospect of a leadership contest to contend with if, as was widely expected, Ed Miliband had realised his goodwill account had gone into overdraft, and it was time to step aside. His performance at the party conference just month previously had been, by common consent, about as disastrous as it could get. The CLYND group were up for that. Another leadership election had been their dream ever since the last. They cherished nothing more than their constant display of invincible political unity when all around were stabbing one another in the back. It was a collective discipline which would serve them well by Christmas, when Alan Stanley would beat all comers to become the new leader of the Parliamentary Labour Party. The winds of political good fortune had all been blowing his way.

Even the prospect of a future victory led by Alan Stanley generated press coverage which was scathing. Some serious columnists were already quavering with sarcastic fear. "This was not the Christmas present the people of this country deserve. The rebirth of the old Labour Party has brought with it a remarkable rediscovery of the questionable virtues of political naïvety.

"Should a party led by Alan Stanley contest next May's general election and actually win it, the United Kingdom then faces the unappetising prospect of an occupant of Ten Downing with no understanding whatever of events beyond his country, never having worked abroad, never having served in the armed forces, indeed someone actively opposed to their very existence, never having worked for a multinational company nor for any large organisation, someone whose political vision barely extends beyond the confines of his northern wapentake, or outside the mutual admiration society he calls CLYND."

There are times when even sentences of ninety-two words are permitted of their main leader writers by Fleet Street editors. Despite its Victorian prolixity, the criticism was clear enough. For once, the domestic arguments of politics were secondary. Great Britain could be facing international challenges which its political agenda for the first time in over half a century. Yet there was now a distinct prospect of an inexperienced Prime Minister who understood none of them and apparently cared even less.

❋   ❋   ❋   ❋   ❋

Fillmore, Cheyenne

THE LARGEST CONVENTION centre in the state capital of
Cheyenne was a bustle of activity. It had been transformed into the
headquarters of Abigail Fenceville's presidential campaign. Banks of
computers and television monitors maintained minute by minute contact
with every state capital in the Union, and many other places besides.
Cheyenne politicians always fought for every single vote they won, and
their fighting machines had been honed to a high degree of
professionalism over many generations.

The very best of that professionalism was at the disposal of
Abigail Fenceville. Once the opinion polls revealed her strengthening
prospects, campaign funds were rolling in by the million. A lot of people
hoped one day to be on the new president's payroll, and a lot more
hoped to benefit in other ways from her presidency. There was a price
to pay for everything.

So on the adjacent parking lot, a large campaign helicopter was
on stand-by to begin the thousand mile victory journey to Washington
DC. The rest of the parking lot was jammed with the control trucks of
television stations from all around the world. Electrical and signal cables
snaked everywhere. Significantly only a simple white rope cordoned off
the open space for the helicopter, a couple of floodlights illuminating the
whole area. It had taken on a quite different appearance from the way
it looked just hours earlier, when that innocent helicopter arrived in
broad daylight. The dark of the night lent the whole prospect a much
more melodramatic, even expectant air.

Appearances could be deceptive. A solitary policeman wandered
around amiably, not expecting very much to happen. No-one seriously
imagined Abigail Fenceville would be a target for anyone. She was the
darling of Fillmore, that state capital named after the lucky thirteenth
President of the United States. The chances anyone would wish to do
her any harm were virtually non-existent.

Yet in her more reflective moments Abigail Fenceville suddenly saw it all it in a slightly different light. A couple of times she strolled out into the cool night air with Ezekiel Watchman, away from the frenzy indoors, just to look at the eternal moon. Both times she looked at the waiting helicopter in some trepidation. The second time, as the pattern of the election results became apparent, she suddenly sensed that once aboard it to begin her triumphal journey to Washington, she would no longer be free. Such freedom was the privilege of aspiring politicians, not those bound by the golden chains of office.

As she stepped aboard her flight of triumph, she would in that moment become a prisoner of America's political machine. She would be taken to a city which was not familiar, to mix with clever people she had not met before. She would be taken away from the reassuring surroundings of her beloved Fillmore. She would be separated from her friends and supporters. No longer would her personal security be the easy task of a solitary policeman. She was heading into a world of which she knew virtually nothing, despite the continuing bravado of her polished appearances on nationwide television.

It would be a very different game in the District of Colombia, and she wondered exactly who would take her aside and explain its rules. Until now Abigail Fenceville had been caught up in a game which was very familiar. With her political mentors she played her vote-seeking cards precisely right for over a year, ever since the fabled lunch at the Biglia restaurant where their plans had been hatched.

Under the meticulous guidance of Ezekiel Watchman and Jack Bunkerton, she ran a text-book campaign in the Republican primaries. Her late appearance in the race was sensational, just when all the other candidates were began to look stale. Ezekiel contrived to give the appearance that Abigail was pushed into the running rather than jumped of her own volition. An element of political reluctance was a calculated old stratagem, dating as far back as the Romans.

In the good old days, Ezekiel told her, even the British traditionally appointed their speakers in London's House of Commons by dragging them to the chair. "What's good enough for the British should be good enough for us." Some of Zeke's many political nuggets missed her completely, and that was certainly one of them. But in the cool of the night air, that sense of political reluctance was coming back to haunt her, although she could not understand why an experienced politician might feel that way in the mother of parliaments.

Yet once she had plunged into the primary campaign, any such sense of foreboding was left far behind. Abigail Fenceville knew of old the game of winning elections. Exactly as Ezekiel, Jack Bunkerton and their team of keen young strategists and PR specialists had planned, her campaign for the Republican nomination was quite short, very sharp and deadly. Assiduous and costly work by a leading investigative consultancy into the backgrounds of her key opponents exhumed some interesting tales. With immaculate timing they were leaked very indirectly to the twittering press. Jack Bunkerton was a past master at ensuring none of the leaks could be traced back to the Fenceville camp. On the contrary, Abigail expressed more horror than anyone else that the primaries campaign had been dragged down to that level. "I have huge sympathy for my opponents" she declared on prime time television. "If I had known the campaign would descend to this degree of unpleasantness, I might have had second thoughts about becoming involved. That is not what my politics are about.

"I have wanted, and I know all my opponents have wanted these primaries to be fought over political wisdom. I want the primaries to be fought fair and square over the fitness of any one of us to hold the office of President of the United States. It should not be fought over who they went to bed with twenty years ago. I suppose if anyone wanted to investigate me as thoroughly as that, they could even find I too had the odd fling before I was married, or after my divorce."

Indeed Abigail had enjoyed rather more than an odd fling in those halcyon phases of her Cheyennian youth. In her day she had been the Fillmore bicycle. Just about anyone could have a ride and many of them did. By defusing the story before it was even a story she effectively killed it for good. Ezekiel Watchman was an expert at turning pre-news into no news at all, and her own career in public relations confirmed the wisdom of his technique. Abigail Fenceville came through the entire primary campaign squeaky-clean which, given her romantic track record in real life, was a quite remarkable achievement.

The campaign against Glenn Silverdale was even more calculated, even more impressive. Abigail's greatest strength was as a skilled performer on television, where she could instinctively make style rule over substance. Ezekiel Watchman and Jack Bunkerton ensured she was seen on prime time programmes almost every evening. She became a familiar figure in the households of America. Abigail Fenceville's message was consistent and it was simple. She came across as the very embodiment of American motherhood, right up there with the nation's enthusiasm for apple pie. The Biglia Three were in their element, and the simplistic message of the New Republicans could not have been clearer. It bore repeating time and again.

Although Ezekiel Watchman knew little of Germany's Third Reich, and even less of its propaganda minister Joseph Goebbels, he did inadvertently share one sentiment with Hitler's key adviser. Even if the notion "tell a lie a million times and it becomes the truth" had never been uttered by Goebbels in so many words, it encapsulated Nazi propaganda philosophy.

In exactly the same way it embodied the public relations philosophy of Ezekiel Watchman, although he was never so careless as to utter the sentiment in public, not even to his closest friends. So Abigail Fenceville's version of Glenn Silverdale's platform was a travesty of the political truth, but still a most appealing one.

Confronted with earnest political analysts from the eastern intelligentsia, Abigail Fenceville rebutted their attempted barbs with ease. "You and your Harvard professors all seem to think the American eagle should try to fly into the future with two left wings." She neatly deflected any questions about her future policies when she would become President, employing a powerful argument technique cooked up by Ezekiel.

It was the classic tactic of the wise beginner, and her Mississippi machiavelli gave her a full body-suit of intellectual armour. "Look," she would say, "I am just a simple governor from the state of Cheyenne, but I understand as well as anyone in this country how politics works. There is no greater waste of everyone's time that some newly-elected President marching into the White House hell-bent on teaching Washington how to go about its business. Why should anyone keep a superb pack of dogs and then bark themsleves?

"I am much too experienced a politician to try and do that. The minute I arrive in the White House I will be surrounded by some of the finest political and diplomatic minds this country has to offer. The job of a good politician, certainly of an effective President, is to sensibly ask the right questions, not to freshly arrive in office with a set of pre-prepared ignorant answers to all of them. I recognise and acknowledge it will be their professional duty to properly advise me. It is my professional task to weigh up that advice."

Split infinitives may have set teeth on edge in many parts of Massachusetts or on the east side in Manhattan, but among people born and raised in Fillmore, Cheyenne they were still a properly recognised means of effective communication. Abigail presented herself as a politician who took her chances, a politician who rode her luck. Control was in the hands of the American people; she left everything to chance.

Abigail Fenceville silenced discussion on the great issues of the day, by far her weakest suit, and the people of America fell in love with her disarming honesty. Her opponent Glenn Silverdale, for all his years as a senator, was left gasping. His Capitol Hill wisdom sounded shrill when he tried to take on the great press commentators on specific policy issues and lost. Abigail also set mouths watering among the nation's self-acclaimed experts on almost everything. Her declared plan was to use advisers, not to invent answers. Once Fenceville was elected, clearly there would be plenty of jobs for the boys. And for the girls as well. That generated hundreds of positive press articles from enthusiastic and hungry experts looking forward to her victory with keen anticipation.

Even so, Abigail incurred the opposition of the thinking tendency in the media. Epithets such as 'buying a pig in a poke' or 'the politics of devastating innocence are indistinguishable from the politics of disastrous ignorance' were enjoyed by everyone who read the newspapers with long sentences. They peppered the leader columns and the late night television analysts. But such intellectualising was all to no avail. It was not the message the Great American Electorate wished to hear.

And even if that was not enough, there was a sudden revelation in the newspapers in the last two weeks of the campaign. Its timing could not have been more damaging to Silverdale's cause. It explained how the supposedly squeaky-clean junior senator from Cheyenne had once indulged in some far from savoury politics as a realtor and councilman in his state capital of Fillmore. It had been many years ago, it was true, but there were those even his home town who argued he was tarnished for life.

It was now revealed he had known about certain criminal double-dealing in advance. That now explained why he had shown minimal surprise when it was exposed and scarcely lifted a finger to uncover what had really happened. Timely revelation of his apparent complicity dealt a crushing blow to the morale of his party, of his campaign workers and his activists, while the flow of funds into his campaign abruptly declined.

Although the Fenceville camp expressed dutiful shock at the sudden revelation, behind the scenes they were rubbing their snow white hands with the utmost glee. The categorical detail of his double-dealing episode proved to be the knock-out blow to any hopes of success Glenn Silverdale espoused. By eleven in the evening, Central time, on Election Day, the first results from the Eastern seaboard were starting to show on the screens. That would be a great test. For all her television prowess, Abigail was not a popular candidate among the educated middle classes of New England. She knew she would lose there - the important question was how heavily?

The results, though negative, were better than many had feared. Then the big number results from New York started to come in, and they brought huge cheers all around the convention hall. Many of her analysts already reckoned the women of America, if perhaps not the Daughters of the American Revolution, had rallied behind Abigail Fenceville and set her on course for the White House.

As the computers picked up results further and further across the nation, the picture became clearer and clearer. The state of Cheyenne gave Abigail Fenceville a massive majority, even ignoring its own senator. By the early hours of the morning, while the results were still emerging from the big states on the west coast, it was beyond dispute that she had won the day and left her Democratic opponent in the cold..

The computer-driven media analysts reckoned she had split both the Democratic and the Republican votes as never before, but ultimately in her own favour. The middle classes, the wealthy and the well-educated, no matter what their party loyalties, seemed to have deserted her. But the ordinary people, to her the real people of America, flocked to her cause. Quite apart from a solid vote from America's women, she had tailored her campaign to appeal to the minorities, to the immigrants, to the underclass, to the farm labourer and the factory worker. She held out a ray of hope, no matter how economically illiterate, to the unemployed factory workers and the jobless students trying to get a foot on the first rung of the ladder.

It had all worked exactly to plan. Her chosen groups of voters outnumbered the smart and the rich many times over and that arithmetical imbalance shone through the election results. Abigail Fenceville was about to become the forty-fifth President of the United States. Less than a mile away at Glen Silverdale's campaign headquarters, the mood was rather more sombre. By their own reckoning they had beaten Abigail Fenceville hands down in the rarified policy debate, but it was more than apparent her campaign PR machine had won the blustery battle of tactics. After the bruising primaries, they were never quite able to unite the entire Democratic Party behind them. The fact that his opponent was a woman added to the general discord.

For all that the result was a major disappointment for them personally. For the United States, as they saw it the result was not just a disappointment, but a serious danger. The very detachment and disinterest of the Obama years which Fenceville attacked so fiercely in her campaign was about to be repeated, only worse. If, as looked increasingly likely, there would be a woman in the White House for the first time in American history, she would be a woman totally unversed in the ways of Washington.

"Glenn, this is a disaster. You know your way round the nation's capital, all its funny little habits and the way it approaches the major issues of political life. Your track record is worth ten of hers." A defeated Duane Stracken was fulminating. He pointed out that Silverdale, unlike his Republican opponent, had actually been to university. Then he had worked in Fillmore with Duane, now a sore point between them. Nevertheless Duane Stracken had spotted Glenn Silverdale's talents earlier than anyone.

"Glenn my friend, you were only twenty-six when you got a job as an economist in Washington. It was worth as much as three university degrees in your political education. You and I both know you were spotted as a potential high-flyer, which is how you become a staffer at Democratic Party headquarters. When did Abigail Fenceville ever do anything like that? When indeed did she ever do anything other than wiggle her assets?"

Glenn Silverdale sipped on a much needed large bourbon, a beverage distilled in Fillmore, Cheyenne, and listened to his old political friend dissecting the result. The same disquiet continued in the following morning's newspapers. Across the United States the press was also divided. The more popular newspapers hailed Abigail Fenceville's victory as a triumph for the ordinary men and women of America. The Filly from

Fillmore had won her big race. In marked contrast the serious end of journalism was more circumspect, often quivering with sarcastic fear, but by and large scathing. The New York Times was particularly so. "The New Republicans have resuscitated the dubious art form of political naïvety. The United States faces the dreadful prospect of an occupant in the White House with no understanding whatever of events outside this great country of ours. Often enough Abigail Fenceville gives the impression she has never even visited a foreign country, not even Canada or Mexico.

"She has no understanding of the military challenge facing the United States, no understanding even of its military. She has never had the advantage of working for a international company which might have exposed her to the realities of a wider world. Her political horizons seem to extend no further than the city limits of Fillmore, Cheyenne. Rarely in the history of the American presidency can it have been occupied by anyone quite so myopic as that." As Duane Stracken read the extract from a leader column, he did not even have to tell Glenn Silverdale which newspaper he was reading. He could guess. Such backhanded support just made their defeat all the more painful.

The message was clear enough. For once the domestic arguments of American politics were secondary. The United States could be facing international challenges, global considerations to dominate its political agenda for the first time in over half a century. Yet there was now every prospect of a President in the White House who understood none of them and apparently cared even less.

Chapter Eleven

Imperatives

The United Nations, New York

IT WAS RARE occurrence for Vice-premier Liu Fun to leave China. But now she was in New York, a city she had not visited for some years. As always there were many new things to see, but meantime China had changed even more; the skyscrapers of Manhattan no longer seemed awe-inspiring. Those of Shanghai or Hong Kong or other Chinese cities looked much newer.

In recent weeks many international politicians had been arriving privately in the USA to learn more about the previous month's extraordinary presidential elections. Liu was just one of the crowd. To those who did not follow the detail of America's domestic politics too closely, victory for a total unknown called Abigail Fenceville had come as a huge surprise. Tactful reports about her abilities sent home by ambassadors had seemed so damning, world statesmen had now come to the USA to find out for themselves. They sought the truth behind the tact, for sometimes it could not be put adequately into diplomatic language intended for the permanent record. In this electronic age, who knew who could tap into what? Experienced globe-trotting politicians also knew that in a run-up to Christmas, New York was one of the finest places in the world to go shopping.

For Liu Fun, Fenceville's astonishing victory was a handy excuse on several counts. Her real reason in coming to New York was to talk to China's ambassador and his team at the United Nations. As she drove round the city, the winter festivities reminded her of Chinese New Year. They seemed to have little to with religion, of which omission she approved. The Americans had turned a once-religious festival into an orgy of brash consumerism, one which the entire Christian west indulged in the midst of their winter. The Vice-premier approved of that as well. It brought much profit to the consumer goods factories of her native China, much welcomed by the Beijing Patriotic Association.

Yet Liu Fun was in New York to talk about something very different. Neither consumer over-spending nor a bizarre new occupant of the White House held more than passing interest. Rather she was quietly constructing another step in her unceasing quest for China's global dominance. The Beijing Patriotic Association had many twists and turns in its convoluted, unpublished agenda, not just economic, and she was its agent provocateur.

A handy public starting-point for her secret military ambitions was Japan's disastrous tsunami. It had been triggered by a huge offshore earthquake less than two years previously and had caused disaster on an unprecedented scale. Even now the Japanese were still recovering from its effects. An awesome demonstration of earth's raw power had generated deep concern in China; after all its government at the highest level was highly attuned to the challenges of earthquakes.

The Chinese leadership was well educated in such things. Premier Wen Jiabao was a graduate of the University of Geosciences in Hubei. He also held a postgraduate degree in geology from its specialist institute in Beijing. Not surprisingly, earth-shaking events in the north-west Pacific in March 2011 had attracted his personal attention. That had galvanised people close to him as well. At the heart of Chinese politics, Vice-premier Liu Fun understood the basic principles of political correctness almost better than anyone. It was always good tactics to identify a leader's technical expertise and show a keen interest.

In the privacy of the UN ambassador's office, Vice-premier Liu Fun explained what she really had in mind. China was one of five permanent members of the Security Council alongside the USA, Russia, the United Kingdom and, most importantly on this occasion, France. "I take it you have a good working relationship here at the UN with your French opposite number and that is now a line of communication I wish your team to develop. I should add what I am about to say has the personal support of premier Wen, or most of it has anyway."

Liu Fun knew full well that the premier had little if any understanding or even knowledge of the Beijing Patriotic Association and least of all anything about its covert ambitions. Instinctively she always operated on a strict 'need to know' basis and there were many things even now that the Chinese ambassador did not need to know either. He was about to receive a briefing devised at one of the association's clandestine meetings, although never in a thousand years would he have guessed its true source.

China's vice-premier explained her mission as openly as she could. On the face of it she wanted the ambassador to help China strengthen its understanding of earthquakes. The premier was personally interested, the subject was topical and Liu Fun had an ulterior motive. As she explained "China is keen to build a more detailed understanding of earthquake potential worldwide. It can affect people, it can affect buildings, it can affect extraction of mineral resources.

"We want to build a much more complete picture than we have at present. Specifically that means studying the processes where the earth's huge tectonic plates are slowly driving into one another. Where they are moving apart, for example down the spine of the Atlantic or around Antarctica, is also of great interest. Obviously the two must always balance out somewhere around the globe.

"I wish you to explore this scientific interest with the French, who themselves have an honourable tradition of studying natural science. Their military leader Napoleon showed himself most interested by such phenomena two hundred years ago and even took scientific researchers with his army on his military adventures. Do remind them of that. Flatter them. Tell them Premier Wen Jiabao admires their great emperor. And if they start to show interest in any of our current scientific pursuits in China, please let me know. I am sure we could be most accommodating."

Liu Fun now alerted the ambassador to a little-known island in the middle of the Indian Ocean owned by France. It was called Amsterdam Island and she wanted the French to know the Chinese had a scientific interest in its location. Privately Liu had another reason as well, but there was no need to burden the Chinese ambassador with too much information.

For the moment, however, she explained the modest island was the only useful dry land in a huge ocean anywhere near the boundary between the Indian and Antarctic tectonic plates. In that region they were moving apart at over six centimetres a year, which was almost three times as fast as tectonic divergence which runs right down the middle of the north Atlantic.

Liu Fun had done her homework long before she left Beijing. "That divergence beneath the Indian Ocean has its balancing effect far to the north. There the Indian tectonic plate is pushing against the huge Eurasian plate, the one which stretches all the way from Japan as far as the Atlantic Ocean. That convergence on the northern boundary of the Indian plate is building the Himalayas. That brings matters to the very frontiers of China itself. It should not be too difficult to explain to the

French why we are so interested." The Vice-premier paused to sip some tea to assure herself that her scientific explanation had sunk home and that her hints had been noticed. She had chosen the ambassador as a non-specialist, deliberately, for she wanted the approach to the French to have a cosmopolitan air of genial informality, which over-enthusiastic Chinese experts would find quite impossible. Too much overt knowledge could have been overwhelming.

In her measured, impassive, Oriental way Liu Fun observed her diplomatic colleague closely. A slight nod of his head indicated clearly her drift had been grasped, so she continued, "Now for the second official reason we are interested in Amsterdam Island. As you should know, our historians at Beijing University have spent several years gathering information about Chinese treasure fleets of almost seven hundred years ago. They were sent on a global mission by the Ming emperor Zhu Di, yet almost as soon as they had departed they were forgotten again; attitudes had changed in Beijing.

"Some people even argue their heroic voyages of maritime exploration even circumnavigated the globe. Personally I'm not entirely convinced about that, but if they did so it was a whole century before Europe's Ferdinand Magellan. He's the explorer the West always claims discovered of the Pacific Ocean. I have always considered that to be most conceited. China knew all about the Pacific Ocean for thousands of years, long before Magellan sailed into it. The European view of history, like their view of society, can sometimes be very distorted and narrow-minded. Christopher Columbus, their other famous explorer, never even set eyes on the mainland of America.

"Whatever the truth of the matter about our treasure fleets, they are worthy of proper research for all kinds of reasons. Some may try to claim our investigation is just a belated attempt to show the Chinese we are the real masters of exploration and discovery. That is wholly unnecessary, but we would certainly wish to set any errors in the historical record straight. One useful theory we are supporting is that a Chinese fleet explored the Indian Ocean. I think we may say for the sake of argument that in due course our fleet found and made landfall on Amsterdam Island. They would have been searching for fresh water and supplies. There was nowhere else to look.

"With French co-operation we would now like to look for any evidence of that landfall. Again the French themselves have a long and honourable history in archaeological investigation as well. It should not be too difficult to engage their positive, scientific interest."

The ambassador looked expectantly at his senior colleague from Beijing. "That all makes eminent sense and I fully agree with you it could surely be explained to interest the French. As you indicate I know their ambassador well. It intrigues me you want to do this through my team here at the United Nations rather than direct diplomatic channels. What do you wish me to do?"

"I wish you to persuade the French it would be to our mutual interest if China could develop research facilities alongside theirs on Amsterdam Island. I would rather you led into it gently, as low a profile as you can. Hence the United Nations, where routine co-operation is discussed all the time.

"At present France has a small research base at a forlorn place called Martin de Viviès. It consists of about fifteen buildings either side of a main track, with a total population of about thirty scientists. They live in almost total isolation from the rest of humanity. Scientific bases in Antarctica are practically a metropolis by comparison. The nearest supermarket for scientists on Amsterdam Island is in Australia, about three thousand kilometres away.

I cannot believe they wouldn't welcome some company and we could always ensure our team of scientists spoke the French language at an acceptable level." The Chinese ambassador nodded in agreement. "So far, all that seems to make eminent sense. What exactly are we asking the French to permit us to do?" The ambassador was quickly reading behind the lines of her proposal. "I would estimate, combining geologists and archaeologists and their support personnel, we might want to base a minimum of a hundred of our own people on Amsterdam Island. We would actually like more than that but let's see what the French say first. We may need to bring in some large scientific equipment. Naturally we would wish to provide a better harbour facility, even an airstrip. China will of course pay for everything.

"There is plenty of land to go round. The total area is over fifty square kilometres and there is good water supply. Amsterdam Island has a mild oceanic climate. It is warm. The island is in almost exactly the equivalent southern latitude of Lanzhou, say half-way between those of Beijing and Shanghai. It is a much more pleasant part of the world than Antarctica. Who knows? We could even have our comrade scientists queuing up to go there once we develop a base with enough facilities to make life more civilised. It will never be Tahiti, and certainly not Hawaii, but it will certainly be much more congenial than the present French facilities at Martin de Viviès.

"If France shows interest in principle, tell them we will arrange a team at purely scientific level to meet in Paris and work out in detail what we have mind. And if you need to offer any diplomatic inducements - they may not be necessary - you will receive rapid clearance from Beijing to make minor concessions in a number of other areas. I shall see to that personally.

"In fact a decent-sized permanent base on Amsterdam Island is of even greater strategic value to China than anything I have said so far, but don't give the French any inkling of that. Just consider yourself to have a green light to negotiate a scientific deal and do not worry too much about the cost." Liu Fun had it all carefully planned. Once the UN ambassadors had agreed a deal in simple outline, she would send some top level experts to Paris to work out the details. On her return to

Beijing, the Vice-premier sent for Zhou Man. The admiral was in the final stages of courses in both geology and the French language. Now he was about to find out why Liu Fun had organised such an intriguing diversion in his naval career.

* * * * *

Washington DC

RYKER PARDREY had worked for the Washington Post for thirty years. A native of New York, he had risen through the paper's ranks to become one of its most respected columnists. "What Pardrey doesn't know about Washington is hardly worth knowing," they generally concluded in the drinking haunts frequented by journalists around the American capital.

He was seated at his desk, that of a senior political writer, when suddenly he exploded with indignation. "Jesus! Who on God's earth is this Ezekiel Wachman?" A couple of minutes earlier, the White House had announced its new Secretary of State. "Do they seriously imagine some hick from the Mississippi, some dime store political fixer who doesn't even know whether Frankfurt is a banking centre or a sort of sausage, can pick things up where Hillary Clinton left off?

"And who the hell is this unfunny comedian Jack Bunkerton? Does Fenceville imagine for one moment he has the expertise, the finesse, the financial and economic insight, to be her Secretary to the Treasury?   If memory serves me right, this odious man Bunkerton served his life's apprenticeship devising petty real estate scams in beautiful downtown Fillmore.

"Now call me an intellectual snob if you must, but that's about as useful to the US Treasury as a couple of peashooters would be to the US Marine Corps. Abigail Fenceville must be off her rocker. They put brighter heads than hers on matchsticks. Just look at this list." Further details of her cabinet were now coming to light. Ryker Pardrey was already hard at work thumping out a scathing column headed "A Government of Nonentities and Crooks." It was going to be skilfully drafted. Pardrey knew it was not defamatory to call someone a nonentity, while none of the alleged crooks would be named individually. That technique should ensure his column would pass muster with the Post's libel lawyers. If any members of the Fenceville Cabinet subsequently wished to volunteer for the epithet of 'crook', that of course would be entirely up to them. Meantime the Washington Post could not possibly be sued for libel by a non-person.

Pardrey broke off from his energetic writing to sound out some more ideas with his colleagues. "Correct me if I'm wrong, but surely the whole point of our system of government is that its members can persuade Congress to do their bidding. Have any of these people the vaguest notion of politics at the Washington level? They are going to get eaten alive. The American voter normally sends a complete zoo full of wild beasts to chew up Washington's regulars. This time round, book your ringside seats in the forum to watch new arrivals being eaten by Christians. The only conceivable reason Abigail Fenceville's troupe of untested chimpanzees from Cheyenne are being rewarded with a string lucrative government positions is their hefty donations to her campaign.

"I don't suppose the Court of St James is going to be over the moon exactly, when the new American ambassador to Great Britain turns out to be a used-car salesman from Fillmore, Cheyenne. According to local sources he's about as straight as a concertina. He must have made one hell of a campaign donation to La Fenceville. Why else would that particular appointment have been announced as early as this? Usually it's the domestic politicians who get announced first.

"I tell you, this parish list of political nonentities makes even Juneau, Alaska look positively cosmopolitan. Dear Abigail really has been scraping her local barrel to put together this tawdry, disreputable team. God alone knows what ours allies are going to make of it all." His colleagues nodded in bewildered assent and provided him with further pungent biographical snippets from what was now considered a putrid backwater of the Mississippi.

Leading from the front, Ryker Pardrey returned to his word processor with renewed vigour. He was thoroughly enjoying himself. The final five sentences of his article read "So the political fate of United States, the world's greatest democracy, is now in the hands of the Biglia Three. What that unsavoury trio lack in intellectual substance, it seems they make up for with political chutzpah. The government of America has set sail for the dark side, across unfamiliar oceans into unknown seas. On her poop deck they have neither reliable charts nor a workable compass. As your ship of state slips from her moorings and sails haphazardly into the way blue yonder may you, my fellow Americans, try to sleep soundly in your beds tonight."

The Pardrey column appeared the following day and it caused an uproar, around the USA but even more so in major cities in countries abroad. That morning's Washington Post quickly sold out once the word went round. And suddenly the floodgates were opened to hostile media criticism of the new Fenceville administration from all corners of the United States and in places far beyond and in all parts of the media.

Far from enjoying the usual honeymoon period granted to a new government, the Fenceville administration looked set for immediate divorce. It was hardly surprising that Fillmore, Cheyenne was soon crawling with expensive private investigators. An alarmingly high proportion of Fenceville's nominees came from the district and the investigators were looking for printable dirt. They soon found plenty.

The Senate hearings on her government promised to be a vintage treat for the more cynical observers of American politics. Not since Senator Sam Ervin led the investigation into the misdeeds of President Richard Nixon at Watergate, had there been quite so much media

excitement.   Where Bob Woodward and Carl Bernstein of the
Washington Post had marched fearlessly in 1972, if necessary Ryker
Pardrey of the Washington Post would march equally fearlessly some
forty-one years later. That said, a major clash between the White House
and Capitol Hill was not exactly what the American people needed at this
particular juncture on the world's political stage.

The melodramatic events in Washington were also studied with
particular interest, almost disbelief, in Beijing. No-one in the Forbidden
City could imagine for one moment any Chinese journalist being allowed
to criticise a Chinese government in the same way Ryker Pardrey was
apparently allowed to criticise the new government in Washington. That
the criticisms were appearing in the most respected political newspaper
in America, not just on some out of the way television station, simply
added to their weight.

On the other side of the world, vice-premier Liu Fun, recently
back from her visit to New York and Washington, was in a particularly
good position to comment. "The United States takes the notion of a
free press to extremes, but let us on our side of the Pacific be thankful
they do so. Mr Ryker Pardrey of the highly respected Washington Post
has done for free what it could have taken our embassy staff in
Washington several weeks to compile.   Now most of the media
commentators in America are agreeing with him. Mr Pardrey is clearly
not some kind of isolated maverick. Here in Beijing we therefore have
to take what is unfolding in Washington with the utmost seriousness."

Liu Fun offered a slightly different interpretation of events in
America to Admiral Zhou Man that evening. The old friends were
enjoying a quiet drink together before the admiral departed on his crucial
mission to Paris. The vice-premier raised the first of several mirthful,
grateful toasts. "If ever there was a time in history for China to exploit
a weakness in the American administration, now is that time. I would
predict President Fenceville and her absurd government will survive the

media onslaught, but will be crippled for the rest of its time in office. Such things could never happen here in China, but there again we do manage our politics somewhat differently. In Asia we have never quite shared the boundless enthusiasm for extreme democracy so beloved by the Anglo-Saxons. Sometimes they are forced to pay a high price for their romantic attachment to the political machinery of some populist paradise. Even the ancient Greeks found such things abhorrent and yet it was the Greeks who originally invented the word 'democracy.' To them it meant mob rule and I totally share their assessment."

The vice-premier mused that America's latest mistake played straight into China's hands. If in the next few years they needed to make diplomatic and military moves which in any other era would have brought a powerful response from the White House, this time the Middle Kingdom might well get off lightly. It was time to celebrate their good luck in this, the Year of the Dragon.

"And now I wish you good fortune in your endeavours in Paris. I think we will not draw attention to the fact you are a serving officer in the navy. Rather let's give the impression you have crossed into civilian life and are working for our scientific ministry. We don't want to raise unnecessary alarms.

"I am sure you will agree with the French on the size of base we require on Amsterdam Island. Our ambassador in New York has made excellent progress. I recognise with gratitude the location was your choice in the first place. Now go to the West and craft the pivot of your plan for the Indian Ocean. You have valuable experience as an embassy attaché. So you know how diplomacy should work in the West.

"In this year of the dragon, do not falter in your mission. With luck you will even find, after recent events in the United States, the French are now wondering who their future friends will be. Do not leave them in any doubt about that." Several weeks later a carefully-selected team of Chinese scientists, led by Zhou Man, was on its way to

Paris. His new-found fluency in geomorphology and archaeology would have startled many of his old friends in Beijing. For their part, the French were much impressed that some former naval officer with such evident access to the higher authorities in Beijing had been assigned to the team. Decisions over such matters as finance, which could easily have taken weeks, were being settled within a matter of hours. All in all, Zhou Man seemed the perfect choice for the task.

By springtime in 2013, the first Chinese construction teams had arrived on Amsterdam Island. Although China was willingly footing the bill, the French government was given the lead authority to decide the precise detail of how the facilities should be designed. They were a little surprised by the length of quays and size of fuel tank the Chinese proposed to incorporate in the plans. But as Zhou Man and his planning team pointed out, Amsterdam Island would be at the end of a very long supply route from mainland China.

The Chinese also now proposed two further roles for the new base. In the region they were planning remote control submarines to explore the ocean floor and these would need a mother ship and technical support. They could co-operate on that with the French. Zhou Man was keen to show his admiration for the pioneer deep sea explorer Jacques-Yves Cousteau. Further afield, China now saw Amsterdam Island as a handy staging post for supply ships servicing research bases on the Antarctic continent, some three thousand kilometres, or about four days' sailing, directly to the south.

When there was so much worldwide concern about global warming, any expansion of climate research also made eminent sense to the French. Work on the expanded harbour facilities proceeded at commendable speed, the aim being to have them fully operational by the middle of 2014, little more than three years after that fateful earthquake beneath the ocean off Japan. As the scientific importance of their small island possession in the Indian Ocean increased, the French planning team were only too happy to endorse Chinese development proposals in their reports to the French foreign ministry. The atmosphere of friendship surrounding the development of facilities on Amsterdam Island was seen as a model of scientific co-operation between the two countries. This in turn improved relations between them at diplomatic level, even in the Security Council of the United Nations and brought France benefits in bilateral trade and economic co-operation.

At the same time as the facilities were being built, an advance team of Chinese archaeologists started searching for evidence of visits by fifteenth century treasure fleets. Preliminary reports sent to Beijing indicated there were encouraging signs of just such a visit. They said exactly what everyone hoped they would say, but then the preliminary reports had been drafted before the scientists even arrived on Amsterdam Island. They had served Liu Fun's purpose. The French were intrigued, exactly as intended and none too upset when China suggested further increases in the number of personnel it wanted to base on that lonely Indian Ocean outpost.

*   *   *   *   *

Downing Street, London

PRIME MINISTER David Cameron was discussing the emerging phenomenon of Alan Stanley with his Foreign Secretary William Hague and his Minister of State for International Development, Alan Duncan. A discussion about Abigail Fenceville's victory in the American presidential election had raised the inevitable question 'Could that really happen here?' They had all read her caustic welcome by the American media, a drubbing then taken up by the British media too.

It was a brief interlude after lunch when none of them faced a ministerial question session in the House. Theirs was a meeting of political minds: two Oxford first class honours degrees in politics, philosophy and economics, two former presidents of the Oxford Union. As had been true for over a century, it was Oxonian business as usual at the top of the British government. Cameron summarised the position.

"Our northern friends in the Labour Party are embarking on a voyage into the unknown. But let us not forget that what is an unknown for them is also by definition an unknown for us. If they ever control the ship of state, the Labour Party would apparently put a loose cannon called Alan Stanley in charge. They normally keep people like that below decks." Ryker Pardrey's widely-read column in the Washington Post of two days earlier, and the expansive maritime metaphor with which it concluded, had lodged firmly in everyone's minds.

William Hague, a full-blooded northerner himself, nodded with grim approval, his bald head catching the sunlight as he added, "For a moment let's just follow that thought through. In particular, do not lose sight of the fact that whatever her limitations, and they are almost beyond reckoning, Abigail Fenceville has just taken charge of the US economy and also has her finger on the nuclear button. She is Commander-in-Chief of the largest military forces in the world. Now imagine a British administration trailing in her wake, towing this country into those same unknown waters. It's a prospect that could keep you awake at night, worse even than that. I hope both of you are well stocked up on valium."

Alan Duncan continued the theme. "I don't know exactly what the so-called Special Relationship between London and Washington has been built on in the past, but the lack of common ground means it would be very difficult to build one now. Where exactly that leaves us on a shared understanding of international development I'm not quite sure. It would appear as if President Fenceville has never travelled anywhere outside the borders of the United States in her entire life." He tapped the clipping from the Washington Post, its damning headline highlighted in orange. 'A Government of Nonentities and Crooks' and asked his two colleagues "do we genuinely want a Special Relationship with people like that?" Duncan explained what he had in mind. "Just reflecting on my own department, I find that a chilling prospect for American understanding of international development, a subject which I suspect is far beyond her grasp. And if you extend that across all the main functions of government, including even largely domestic issues such as managing the economy, it does make me distinctly uncomfortable. I don't imagine you are exactly ecstatic about it either. William had better put in a bulk order for that valium."

David Cameron nodded. He was thinking about the prospect of Alan Stanley ever taking his job. "The really chilling thing is this. God forbid, but if a reborn Old Labour administration under Alan Stanley were to beat us at the next general election, once again there could be a matched pair on either side of the Atlantic. They might not even know where to find each other's capital cities, but when they do eventually encounter one another they could discover a meeting of the minds. I know they always say that great minds think alike, but utterly stupid minds probably do the same."

The three men sat in silence at as they contemplated the prospect of a special relationship between London and Washington built on mutual ignorance of the world at large. "If that were the case, where would that leave Russia? Where would that leave China? Can you just imagine what the briefings might be from the White House, or from here in Ten Downing Street, to our ambassadors at the United Nations? If they did as they were told they could have the rest of the Security Council reduced to a blend of utter disbelief and total hysterics.

"Where would the leadership of the world come to roost then? It could hardly remain in Washington DC. Just think through the implications of that for a moment. And who could our own friends be, as we look a little beyond Alan Stanley's prospective Commedia del' Accrington? Would we in opposition prefer a revival of the Entente

Cordiale with France, perhaps? Would they snuggle up with us or would they prefer to snuggle up with someone else? You can never quite tell with the French." The three government colleagues agreed the developments in Washington raised far more self-evident questions than self-evident answers. So they moved on to the more routine government business items which had been the primary reason for the meeting. Then the two ministers returned to their departments.

The prime minister's next meeting was with the Cabinet Secretary. "Prime Minister, before we begin today's scheduled topics, there is something else I should explain to you. It arises because of events over the last few days in Washington. I am sure you share your concern over those with many of your colleagues in the government, just as I share them with many of my colleagues here in Whitehall.

"Just imagine a Fenceville-led administration, especially with that gentleman Ezekiel Wachman as her Secretary of State, threading its way through some sensitive international diplomatic negotiations. It scarcely bears thinking about. My first sympathies lie with the American ambassador to the United Nations, but one does begin to wonder just how many more months, weeks even, he will keep his job before another used-car salesman from Cheyenne takes his place. I have to confess that is a prospect which could very easily keep me awake at night. In my professional opinion she needs to be put to the test."

"Yes, yes, Anthony, I've just been having exactly the same conversation with William and Alan Duncan. We can all see the problem, but can any of us identify a solution? There's little point beating ourselves to a pulp over it. Let's just put Fenceville out of our minds for a moment and look at our own patch. Suppose it happened here. Suppose I am succeeded by Alan Stanley. Is there anything we can do about that?" The Cabinet Secretary was now on more sensitive ground. His loyalties were to the Crown, not to any single British political party. Silently he leaned forward and placed a file labelled Top

Secret on the Prime Minister's desk. It was called Kundalini. David
Cameron asked him to explain. "Kundalini is a remarkable aptitude
evaluation system developed originally for the Ministry of Defence.
They were looking for ways to identify those naval officers with the
necessary, and I might add scarce, mental ability to cope with modern
weapons systems in real-time battle situations.

"These days those warfare officers would be called upon to digest
information from a whole array of electronic tracking, evaluation and
guidance systems of the kind you find in the operations room of a
modern warship. They must match that with other intelligence and with
their primary orders. They would have to do all that within a matter of
seconds, even, rather than minutes and then take serious warfare
decisions based on the information.

"You've seen for yourself those warship operations rooms. They
could look, indeed be, quite terrifying to anyone not fully trained to work
in them. MoD realises better than anyone else that they are not
situations where you would put anyone less than supremely competent
in charge. It is not just a matter of training but of aptitude as well."

David Cameron was intrigued, he vaguely guessed where
Anthony Pilkington might be leading. "When did you first become
aware of this Kundalini and what has it to do with Abigail Fenceville?"
he asked. "Let me explain, Prime Minister. I was talking in September
last to Peter Storey, a senior colleague at the Ministry of Defence. His
responsibilities include some of the less apparent things we get up to.
He is also a very sound analyst and his policy proposals over the years
have always been sensible and watertight. I have come to place great
confidence in his judgement. It was he who pointed out that the tests we
are starting to apply to naval officers in the front line could also be
applied to the senior figures in naval command directing them. And
here's my main point, they should perhaps be applied to those political
figures ultimately directing the military."

"In fact you mean people like me or the Defence Secretary? In fact any of us holding office who might suddenly find ourselves in a fast-developing COBRA emergency or something even more serious?"

"Certainly, Prime Minister, that is precisely what I had in mind. But if I am honest I was also contemplating the possibility that, should events next year unfold in a direction you would not personally welcome, we could even be talking about someone like Alan Stanley and whoever he chose to be his Defence Secretary."

"The prospect hardly bears thinking about, Tony, given Stanley's declared pacifist attitudes, but I do take your point. Why are you telling me this in January when you have known about it since September?"

His civil servant extended a forefinger vertically across his forehead and slowly rubbed it up and down, slowly nodding his head as he did so. "At the time it all seemed rather academic and, to put matters in perspective, we have in the meantime had some educative fun here in the Cabinet Office. One or two of us volunteered to be informal Kundalini guinea pigs ourselves before we judged it worth bringing to more formal government attention.

"May I now take it you yourself have been Kundalinied? How did you get on? And what was it like?" The Cabinet secretary smiled. "Let me put it this way, prime minister. There are some colleagues in the department who have dabbled with advanced intelligence tests for places like Mensa in their time. They tell us that Kundalini is many times more difficult than Mensa and far more revealing. On a day when there was no-one better around, I would just about allow myself to try guiding the Royal Navy, provided no-one on the other side was making life too difficult for us. However I would not rate myself all that highly even then, having seen some of the scores attained by the best warfare officers in the armed forces. Let me just say there are some very definite limits, I rapidly discovered, even to the talents of a Cabinet Secretary. It was all really most enlightening and to be honest, I rather enjoyed it."

"And I assume the talents of a Prime Minister as well. How do you think I would cope, for example?" The Cabinet Secretary smiled again. "Well I would personally put a few bob on anyone with a First from Oxford, but to be candid even that does not tell the whole story."

"Are you suggesting we allow one or two members of the government, people whose responsibilities might one day put them in that daunting military position be - what's the term - David Cameron peered at the file on his desk, be Kundalined too? I imagine it would be a bit like going back to university."

"It did occur to me, Prime Minister, that if you went that far you could then write a new set of rules into confidential Whitehall procedures. Future cabinet ministers who might one day find themselves called upon to oversee a military situation, or as you mentioned in an executive rôle within COBRA, should all be Kundalinied too."

"You mean a kind of intellectual time bomb waiting for Alan Stanley and his merry band of ministers should they ever come into government? I might predict even now it could lead to some extremely interesting parliamentary questions."

"Well, yes, Prime Minister."

*   *   *   *   *

Île St Louis, Paris

LOUISE KHALIFA WAS in her element. Over the past six months or so she had turned into the matriarch, busily organising her far-flung family from supreme headquarters at the Hotel de Chambon on the Île St Louis. A few days ago her husband had telephoned from Riyadh with a very unusual request. "Darling, I am planning a brief trip to Paris, it's been a hectic few months at work and I need to break away for some rest. It would also be nice to see my daughter and son-in law as well.

It's been a long time since their wedding and I am missing them. Perhaps we could arrange dinner for the four of us at the Rocca?" There was no restaurant in Paris called Rocca known to either Louise or Malik, though there were some in other major cities. Dr Malik Khalifa was using a simple code. Husband and wife had devised it in the early years of their marriage when they did not wish to be specific over untrustworthy telephone lines. He was actually saying he wanted to see James. Louise wondered why. And the code meant that the request was an important one and that Malik did not want anyone else to know.

Louise promptly telephoned her daughter in England. Since their marriage, she and her new husband had settled in the naval city of Portsmouth. James's present ship HMS Daedalus was part of the destroyer fleet based there and they were buying a house in the old town right by the harbour. While James was away at sea, the trilingual Violaine had revived her contacts with Oxford University. It was not a difficult drive from Portsmouth. She was researching beyond her doctorate into even more rarified strata of the Islamic manuscripts owned exclusively by Oxford's Bodleian Library.

"Darling, is there any chance James and you could visit us here in Paris for a few days? Your father has asked me to arrange a family reunion. He seems to think it is rather important." Louise was not to know it, but the timing was good. HMS Daedalus was alongside in Portsmouth dockyard for a minor refit and for once in his life James was keeping normal working hours and living at home. His seniority on the ship meant he could probably arrange an extra couple of days leave. A further phone call to his mobile by Violaine and it was quickly agreed.

They would drive across at the weekend. The ferry from Newhaven to Dieppe would be the fastest. Louise's next phone call was to her husband in Riyadh to tell him the good news. As she heard herself making the arrangements over the telephone, Louise Khalifa, née de Chambon and aged 65, realised she now sounded exactly like her own mother. Today's social arrangements were however international, reaching far beyond the inward-looking haut monde of Paris in her youth. By noon on Saturday the family was assembled in the Hotel de Chambon. Its chatelaine had spent all morning organising the lunch. In France, unlike England, it was normally rated the most important meal of the day. A home-made pâté was followed by confit of duck, accompanied by a 2005 burgundy supplied privately by a friend in the trade. If you could still find them, French wines of that particular year were rated some of the finest - it had been a "deckchair" vintage. That was when the weather was so perfect throughout the growing season the vignerons hardly had to lift a finger until their grapes were ripe.

Malik Khalifa congratulated his wife on her stylish cuisine; for the thousandth time he rejoiced he had married a Parisienne. The wine was extremely good. His moderate Islamic convictions had never yet interfered with his enjoyment of fine alcohol. Too many years spent on the international diplomatic circuit had seen to that.

By contrast Violaine was very circumspect in her drinking. Normally she enjoyed a glass or two of fine wine as much as any Oxford don, an enthusiasm developed in her three years studying at the university. It was generally quite difficult to find many teetotallers among the dreaming spires. Noting her reticence, her mother asked whether she was well and Violaine could hold back her news no longer. "Maman. James and I have decided it is the right time to tell you; I am expecting our first baby".

So that was it. In her pregnancy, especially its nauseous early months, Violaine Heaton had lost all taste for alcohol. But her father was already wreathed in smiles and within moments her mother was almost crying with delight.

"And when is the baby due?" enquired an ecstatic Louise. Apparently some time in October, or late September, the usual family season for birthdays. As mother and daughter discussed the finer details,

Malik had already reappeared with his customary bottle of champagne. It was congratulations all round, but when the immediate celebrations were completed Dr Khalifa signalled to his son-in-law to come into the study and leave the ladies to absorb themselves in the more technical aspects of maternity. As the two men left the dining room, Louise was already extolling the particular virtues of a family larger than one, especially to her only daughter.

Once the study door was closed behind them, Malik put on a pair of thin gloves and opened a briefcase. He removed a slim folder with a title in Arabic. "James, I want you to treat this as top secret. It did not come from me. It has no fingerprints on it. If anyone ever found out it was me who had leaked it to the British navy, it would be more than my career that was in tatters. He then handed James a pair of polythene gloves as well.

"Perhaps I am even entrusting you with my life. You are the only person I know well enough to do what I am about to do. You have worked in naval intelligence in London and you will know the right people to receive this file." James noted the extreme caution his father-in-law adopted for handling the document. They were unlikely to check it for fingerprints in London and anyway Malik Khalifa's fingerprints would not be on file. Working closely together, father and son-in-law made a very effective team of conspirators.

James had always known his father-in-law to be a senior Saudi diplomat, but had judged it prudent never to delve too deeply into what Dr Khalifa actually did. His next question was carefully judged. "Am I to take it there are certain developments in Riyadh of which you do not fully approve? Is that the gist of the message I am to carry to London? Some senior, but disaffected Saudi who has trusted me to protect his anonymity ?" Malik Khalifa nodded.

Lieutenant-Commander James Heaton RN took the slender document upstairs and buried it in his case. There was no point involving even his wife in what he saw, rightly, as a tightly confidential arrangement between son-in-law and father-in-law. The fewer people who knew about it the better. He wondered what the file contained but was much too sensible to ask. On this occasion he was the messenger boy. The intended recipient was the Ministry of Defence.

*   *   *   *   *

Ministry of Defence, London

THE ARABIC DEPARTMENT of the Secret Intelligence Service had produced a translation of the document brought by James Heaton, now codenamed Solent, within 24 hours. The department had also made further enquiries with Britain's military attachés in the four Islamic countries which James Heaton's document had identified. The document now had the legend Top Secret emblazoned across its cover in large red letters. Each copy was individually numbered and one of them had now reached the desk of George Gould.

It had been a clear understanding between George Gould and James Heaton, even before the original was handed over, that the material had to be taken entirely on its merits. James could not name its source. He could only confirm that it came at first hand from a senior Saudi official, one who was becoming disenchanted with the policies of his country. The SIS arabists had further added a note explaining that in their opinion, despite its anonymity the document bore all the hallmarks of a genuine file from the Saudi Ministry of Defence.

To anyone who understood the background, Solent was explosive. It minuted secret meetings between the Saudi diplomat, whose name had been redacted so thoroughly it was beyond any electronic means of recovery and named high-ranking military representatives from Indonesia, Malaysia and Pakistan. In each case, the SIS had confirmed with Britain's embassies that the officials named were all genuine, although the highest-ranking were already known to the security services in the UK. It was also apparent the document chronicled the outcome of several years' work. It clearly concerned some grand ambitions for the Royal Saudi Navy, the RSNF, taking it far beyond its known spheres of interest. The earliest notes referred to meetings in the Indonesian capital of Jakarta held in March 2008, over five years previously.

The Solent document now provided chapter and verse on the entire Saudi naval strategy. It had totally escaped the attention of any British sources in Riyadh. Saudi Arabia was known to have provided generous foreign aid to at least one former member of OPEC, Indonesia, whose declining oil production had obliged it to withdraw from the organisation in 2008. Significantly this was not long after the visit to Jakarta by the unidentified Saudi official.

In all probability the two events were connected. The Saudis had offered financial reassurance in exchange for some maritime favours. The document made clear that the Saudis had requested specifically that Indonesia's existing base at Kupang in western Timor should be considerably expanded. The construction work had been fully monitored by Western observation satellites, but its wider international significance had not been properly understood until now.

Much further west, military facilities had also been added to the civilian port of Belawan on the north coast of Sumatra. This naval base effectively gave military control over the Straits of Malacca, a notorious region for piracy. That was a potential solution to the pirate problem and an argument on which the Solent document supplied by James Heaton laid particularly heavy emphasis.

The military strategy was becoming clear. Kupang provided a base from which to control the southern route from the Indian Ocean into the Western Pacific. With sufficient naval resources and determination, the two bases working together could provide a vice-like grip over a strategic international sea route between the Indian and Pacific oceans. They could force any unwelcome commercial shipping to go far into the turbulent Southern Ocean to seek a passage right round Australia. This was far beyond the geographical or strategic needs of Saudi Arabia. What lay behind such far-reaching interest?

George Gould asked his assistant for a large map of the Indian Ocean. As he examined it and marked on it the ports identified for development, the thinking behind Saudi naval ambitions soon became clear. The third Indonesian port was clearly intended to cover the exposed eastern coastline of the Indian Ocean. It proposed a major development at a place called Singkil on the west coast of Sumatra. The location chosen had good deep water and was protected by a natural headland. Offshore a small island called Pulau Tuangku offered further shelter, in much the same way that the British naval base at Portsmouth was sheltered by the Isle of Wight. With suitable naval assets, Singkil could clearly police a large area of open seas in the eastern Indian Ocean.

Until the SIS had seen the Solent document, the expansion at Singkil had been taken as an exercise in economic reconstruction by the Indonesian government. It had explained to anyone interested that commercial development in that poor region was a way to recover from the disastrous damage inflicted by the tsunami of October 2010. Any hint of Saudi money supporting the project could be considered humanitarian. The fact that work on the port had actually begun almost a year before the tsunami was not over-emphasised.

Now a totally different reason for developing the Sumatran port emerged. Together with Pelabuhan Belawan in the Malacca Straits and Kupang in western Timor, the three bases extended the naval sphere of influence of Saudis from the Red Sea and the Arabian Gulf to the furthest shores of the world's third largest ocean.

George Gould moved on. In its supplementary notes the SIS confirmed satellite reconnaissance had shown the three requested port expansions were virtually complete and construction equipment had already been taken away. There had clearly been no shortage of money. All these Indonesian developments related to agreements drawn up in secret five years ago. The next section of the Solent document went on to list Saudi demands for naval bases on their own western flank of the Indian Ocean in the west and those discussions were much more recent. The first concerned the Yemeni port of Aden. The SIS had added some useful political background. Its harbour dated right back to around 600BC when it had been part of the ancient kingdom of Awsan.

Aden's excellent topographical advantages at the southern tip of the Arabian peninsula had long been a natural base for commerce. With the advent of regular shipping services between Britain and its Indian empire, it had escalated in importance simply because of geography. The territory had little else to recommend it. It was used as a base for exchanging British international mail from about 1837 and a full-time postmaster was appointed in 1839. It had become a British protectorate in the 1880s. After about a hundred years under Anglo-Indian rule, in 1937 Aden had become a Crown Colony in its own right and was chosen after the war for construction of a British-owned oil refinery.

Yet direct British rule did not last for long. Local tribal rulers were never happy about the Europeans. The sultans in Hadhramaut, in the state of Seiyun, in Shihr and Mukalla all objected even to the portrait of Britain's King George VI on the stamps produced for Aden and demanded special issues showing themselves instead.

Within twenty years the British had yielded control of Aden to the Yemenis. The military presence had not been popular, but internal strife soon followed independence. Then in 1968 Great Britain made fundamental changes to its worldwide military strategy. Prime Minister Harold Wilson and defence secretary Denis Healey abandoned all British military activities east of Suez. The Indian Ocean had become a power vacuum and power vacuums do not last. International events moved quickly in those few years. The Organisation of Petroleum Exporting Countries, OPEC, soon flexed its global muscles and imposed massive rises in oil world prices in 1971. The greatest beneficiary had been Saudi Arabia. It was the world's greatest oil producer and gradually became one of the richest countries on the planet. The Saudis were in a position to offer huge assistance to an impoverished and war-torn country like the Yemen. In exchange for economic favours, it had not been difficult to secure free use of the port in Aden.

Solent explained it all. The specific military negotiations were as recent as 2013. In Yemeni eyes, Saudi Arabia could be a friendly Islamic neighbour in ways which the British colonialists had never been. Saudi's military expansionism was not confined to the Arabian peninsula.

At the same time, Solent revealed that Pakistan had been asked to provide free access to its naval base at Jinnah, to the West of Karachi. This was an entirely new development dating from as recently as 1990, with an eye turned primarily on Pakistan's traditional enemy, India. It had been named after Quaid-el-Azam Mohammad Ali Jinnah, the man who had founded Pakistan. He had done so amid the bloodbath which had seen the country break away from India on independence in 1947.

The harbour had been built by a Turkish company in a noted demonstration of Islamic solidarity. In Saudi eyes Pakistan had scored more brownie points when its navy went to assist Sri Lanka and Indonesia in the aftermath to the appalling tsunami of 2004. Now, over eight years later, it was not hard to argue such naval mobility would stand Islamic neighbours around the Indian Ocean in good stead. Many faced the risk of earthquakes, hurricanes and tornadoes. As George Gould worked his way through the Solent document, he was looking much further than that. This was not just about natural disasters.

The document revealed a very new perspective of developing naval power in the Indian Ocean. The days when Britannia ruled the waves might be drawing to an end, to be succeeded by an era when the waves were ruled by Islam. Nature abhors a vacuum and so, it seems, do the seven seas. No-one in the Ministry of Defence rejoiced at that. A final summary spelt it all out. The secret strategy revealed by Solent brought together three naval bases in Indonesia, one in Yemen and another in Pakistan.

Together with Saudi Arabia's three naval bases on the Red Sea for its Western Fleet and its four naval bases for its Eastern Fleet in the Arabian Gulf, it all added up to a naval resource which rivalled the British Empire at the height of its maritime authority. The document also went on to explain the new naval treaties were to be formalised as INA, the Islamic Naval Alliance. It probably would not amount to very much, but naval vessels from all five member countries would be free to use the naval facilities of any other.

The big player would be Saudi Arabia especially if, as the Chinese were doing, the country then embarked on a programme of major naval expansion. It could certainly afford it. Finally there was a draft of a speech which explained how INA was intended to be a practical demonstration of Islamic unity in a new era to succeed Islamic discord. Clearly there was a subtext seeking to undermine the ambitions of Iran.

George Gould wondered about that, but he also wondered about the short typed note on the very end. It seemed the same anonymous Saudi diplomat who had built the Islamic Naval Alliance was now worried about its intended purpose. Perhaps it was not quite so peaceful after all. The American Fifth Fleet had already been encouraged to leave its base in the Gulf and go somewhere else. The major states of the Indian Ocean which were not in the Islamic brotherhood; India, Sri Lanka, south east Asia and Australia, had better be warned. Whether they would pay any attention would be another matter. George Gould thought for a moment, then picked up a secure telephone.

Chapter Twelve

Advances

Hong Kong

THE DIRECT FLIGHT from Riyadh made its approach to Chek Lap Kok airport through opaque cloud. It was that time of year. Only as the aircraft came within feet of the runway could the small team of Saudi diplomats see anything at all. They found it slightly unnerving. Over Arabia, their home skies were clear most of the time and you could see straight down to the ground from ten thousand metres. They put their trust in Allah and waited anxiously until the wheels touched the ground.

The delegation was even more apprehensive about its meeting with the Chinese vice-premier Liu Fun. Her once meagre reputation now extended far beyond Beijing, far beyond China. She was nowadays rated among the most daunting of the world's political thinkers. But just like the clouds enveloping Hong Kong airport, she too was opaque. Her global reputation had been earned on merit alone, for the one thing Liu Fun never sought was personal publicity. The Saudi intelligence file on her was only as detailed as her calculated obscurity permitted. For all that, she was clearly not a woman to be taken lightly. The protocol for their meeting had been drawn up over several weeks through strained diplomatic channels and the stakes were high.

Relations between the two sides were frosty from the outset. It was hardly a meeting of close allies. China's implacably intolerant attitude toward religion did not chime easily in Saudi Arabia, whose Wahhabi-driven Islamic faith was invincible. For that reason it had been agreed to hold the meeting somewhere other than Beijing.

A group of Saudis arriving in China dressed in the distinctive style of their country could have attracted both the attention of photographers and some penetrating questions. Hong Kong was much preferred, a more cosmopolitan, far less controversial rendezvous. In Hong Kong people from all over world, dressed in all kinds of national costume came and went all the time.

The Saudi delegation was led by a seasoned diplomat, Dr Malik Khalifa, now seventy-five years old. He was already planning this to be his finale in the tough world of international affairs. He would rather not have been taking part at all, but since the British security services now knew about his doubts and his shifting loyalties, the best way to preserve his reputation in Riyadh was to carry on as normal. Backing out at this stage would have raised eyebrows and probably suspicions.

So the stakes were doubly high for Malik Khalifa. If it all went wrong, retribution could be harsh. He was not yet under direct suspicion, he hoped. Even so the Saudi foreign ministry had included a fanatically patriotic princeling as part of the delegation just to ensure Malik Khalifa kept strictly to the script.

In the Saudi view of China, they were merely attempting to arrange a marriage of convenience. Both countries were working on the broad principle that your enemy's enemy is probably your friend and their mutual enemy was the United States of America. For many years it had been a widely-held view in both Riyadh and Beijing that America had become a self-righteous bully and needed some discipline. If even the two richest countries in the world, outside the USA itself, could not do anything about it, then whoever could?

This was not a viewpoint which Malik Khalifa shared. Some of his colleagues in Riyadh suspected he was becoming conspicuously westernised in his cultural preferences. His vituperation over the antics of Osama bin Laden years ago had been noted and had not been forgotten. He and his outspoken academic daughter advocated a return to the Islam of a thousand years earlier, citing some golden era when they reckoned Islamic scholars had led the world. They even wanted Islam to undergo a repetition of the Christian reformation.

None of that made much sense to the Wahhabis, whose distinctive vision of a militant Islam dominated political thinking in Riyadh. Malik Khalifa would not subscribe to that simple xenophobia and was therefore considered a risk factor. There were probably many more Saudis who privately shared his outlook, but lacked his prominence and authority. Every country has its own lexicon of political correctness; the main difference is that some enforce it more ruthlessly than others.

Rather like the urbane oil minister Sheikh Yamani before him, the diplomatic Dr Malik Khalifa seemed over-attuned to the Western view. Among Islamic fanatics the question was increasingly asked whether he was still 'one of us'. However such questions about loyalty had of necessity been brushed aside for this delicate military mission. Malik Khalifa was possibly being re-assessed for the depth of his patriotism, but his grasp of the Islamic Naval Alliance was still second to none and his involvement in the talks was an imperative.

The Saudi delegation was met by the country's own commercial representative in Hong Kong. Any Chinese diplomat doing so would have attracted too much attention and made the event official. Two Rolls-Royce limousines took them speedily and without apparent ceremony to their hotel, the Dragon of the Fragrant Harbour. This architecturally eye-stopping edifice had opened just a year previously. It offered a level of individual service which only the richest could afford and the local Saudi representative considered it the most luxurious in the territory. That was quite something; Hong Kong had about forty hotels of five star status all vying for that highly rewarding accolade.

The Saudis agreed among themselves to meet in Malik Khalifa's extensive suite once they had settled in and while he waited for them to put in an appearance he admired the panorama from his verandah. Without any bidding, his personal butler appeared with a much-needed kir royale and discreetly unpacked Malik's belongings. The hotel prided itself on discovering its clients' personal tastes even before they arrived.

With his welcoming drink to hand, the distinguished diplomat contemplated one of the most famous views in the world. Beneath the low clouds he looked out to Hong Kong Island across the busy waters. Their original name in Chinese, fragrant harbour, had been a reference to the small incense factories which once lined this Kowloon waterfront. In British eyes he was looking straight across the harbour to Victoria Island, as they had originally named it when they first arrived to take control back in 1842.

The rocky island had provided a safe haven where they could build a small colony of warehouses. These profitable establishments were run by compradores, bilingual wheeler-dealers who facilitated trade. To begin with the place had been a 'worthless barren rock' according to their own Queen Victoria, but it was anything but worthless today. The central district of Hong Kong was a mesmerising forest of skyscrapers, occupying some of the most valuable real estate in the world.

Crowning it all was the Peak, which appeared fleetingly through sudden gaps in the cloud. These days it displayed a line of expensive apartment blocks separated from the rest of Hong Kong Island by a steep slope of trees and shrubs. The British had built their most desirable homes high up, five hundred metres above the sea, well above the oppressive humidity of the harbour, above the constant noise, the smells and the local inhabitants. In the centre of the Peak was the apartment where the Saudi team were due to meet Vice-premier Liu Fun the following afternoon. It had become her second home, well away from the political tumult of Beijing, her private haven where she preferred to think, to plot and to pursue her often convoluted, invariably unpublicised political business.

That was for tomorrow. Today was the occasion for a team talk. Once his Saudi colleagues had arrived in his suite, Malik Khalifa reviewed their position as he saw it. "We are here simply to agree a naval treaty. Even if we do not particularly like China for other reasons, so far as naval power is concerned, we do have a community of interest. The Chinese are keen to secure their vital trade routes across the Indian Ocean to Africa. They have the wealth and resources for a substantial military, but they still lack the bases in our sphere of the world from which to operate a navy.

"That is our bargaining counter. Thanks to the Islamic Naval Alliance, we now have a network of bases they would greatly like to be free to use. For our part, we would of course welcome a Chinese reassurance of our maritime security and non-aggression. They have announced and are building a large fleet of state-of-the-art warships and the obvious location for them is the Indian Ocean.

"We are not here on a trade mission. Even though we know China has a virtually insatiable appetite for oil and we have almost unlimited supplies, we have been instructed that oil is not for discussion in these negotiations. We are not committing ourselves to supply China with the oil it needs on favourable terms. We are only prepared to negotiate as far as a mutual defence agreement, nothing more nor less."

His colleagues agreed. The enthusiastic princeling from the foreign ministry underlined his point. "Saudi Arabia is a rich and powerful country. We need to make no generous concessions to anyone.

This is a strictly political and strategic arrangement, not a commercial one. We do not have to like the Chinese culturally to do political business with them. In any case they do have a permanent seat on the United Nations Security Council and in my view rather them than the Americans, the British, the French or the Russians." It was a pile of worthiness straight from the official Riyadh diplomatic song book and the delegates all nodded in dutiful if somewhat wearisome agreement.

The following day the Saudi delegation was taken to meet the vice-premier in her apartment on the Peak. The sinuous road swept through hairpin bends as their cars climbed through the mist. The apartment was surprisingly spartan by Saudi standards. Liu Fun was more ascetic than sybaritic. She was a woman far more interested in ideas than in personal luxury, a Confucian through and through.

They had been well-advised by the Chinese specialists at their foreign ministry about her intellectual capabilities and her global outlook was readily confirmed by her choice of furnishing. A large bookcase full of both English and Chinese volumes proclaimed a wide range of personal interests. Her walls displayed thoughtfully-chosen art from all over the world, from Oriental to Rembrandt. Quite clearly she did not confine her tastes to the traditional cultures of China alone.

But Chinese intellectuals also have their practical virtues. It was soon apparent that everyone present spoke good English. Perhaps they were all compradores now. Negotiations would not need to be conducted slowly through interpreters, although one of the Saudi team did speak excellent Mandarin, just in case.

Once the formal courtesies of greeting were completed, the Saudi position was set out exactly as it had been agreed in Malik's hotel suite the previous afternoon. Vice-premier Liu Fun smiled as she listened to his well-rehearsed opening salvo. This was going to be somewhat easier than she had previously thought. In turn she explained that the Chinese People's Republic was also a rich country. "We can buy all the raw materials we possibly need and please be assured that does include oil. We are fully prepared to pay the going price on world markets and have no desire today to seek what the West likes to call a 'sweetheart' deal with your country.

"And so to our main business. I am instructed by the Central Military Commission in Beijing to propose informally a naval treaty with the Kingdom of Saudi Arabia, acting as we understand it on behalf of the Islamic Naval Alliance. Nothing more, nothing less. The shape of our new relationship, I might add, will owe something to that powerful treaty which has steered Western military strategy since the Second World War. I refer of course to the North Atlantic Treaty Organisation, which will be sixty-five years old in just a few months' time. Under the circumstances it has lasted remarkably well.

"Their NATO has proved more durable than most international treaties of its kind, more so even than the competing Warsaw Pact with which the former Soviet Union once sought to bind its neighbours." Liu Fun permitted herself a brief smile at the ephemeral nature of Russian politics, privately contrasting them with the unwavering consistency of China's own. Her fleeting expression was not lost on Malik Khalifa, whose diplomatic understanding of old international rivalries was second to none. The clear hint was there. Today China was seeking a relationship that would last and possibly it would be willing to make some concessions to enable it to do so.

The Chinese vice-premier returned to her theme. "This NATO has always been dominated by the Americans, who provide most of its military strength. They do not use it wisely. It has been interesting to see how their treaty has been flexible when its members disagreed over political and military strategy, yet without the agreement itself breaking apart. I need only mention British and French adventures with the Suez Canal in the 1950s, American adventures in South East Asia, the wide variety of NATO attitudes toward the Jewish state of Israel, even British adventures in the Falkland Islands. Despite all those internal pressures and conflicting military priorities, NATO has survived.

"We in China recognise that, in a community of interest with the world of Islam, there will be times when we might wish to pursue different objectives. But our compact should be strong enough to contain that diversity. In that regard NATO teaches us all a lesson." There were relieved nods of widespread agreement from the Saudi delegation. Without any bidding on their part, Liu Fun had swept away what they had anticipated might be a barrier to progress. Her following remarks did however divide Malik Khalifa from his colleagues, but the veteran diplomat studiously offered neither comment nor visible reaction, which would have been extremely foolish.

"We have no enmity with, no designs on, no strategic disagreements with the nations of the so-called Indian Ocean. If we perceive any military threat at all, it is that of the United States. The Chinese People's Republic has long been tolerant of America's excesses, a tolerance overlooking our profound lack of trust in the warmongering American psyche. The naval treaty we are proposing today will help to redress the balance. As we understand it, the Islamic countries who are members of your naval alliance all feel much the same way."

So that was it, Malik Khalifa thought. This was not so much a peaceful alliance to protect security in the Indian Ocean as a deliberate military challenge to the United States. While his fellow members of the Saudi delegation made their enthusiasm for that wholly apparent, he just smiled sweetly and hoped it would be taken as tacit agreement. Maybe alone among them Malik Khalifa realised he had just been listening to a diplomatic formula which could even lead to another world war.

In over fifty years travelling round the world, he had come to prefer the Western view of civilisation by a very substantial margin. Malik Khalifa did not relish the prospect of a calculated challenge from a China seeking to impose it culture, its economic imperialism, its moral standards, its environmental hygiene, its penal code and its idiosyncratic ideas about civilisation on the rest of the world. Nor did he relish the extremes of Wahhabism and Sharia law being imposed either, even if Saudi Arabia had the money and influence to try and make that happen. If the cultural choice really lay between the West, the Middle East and the Orient, then Dr Malik Khalifa chose the West.

In that moment he decided his work and his life in Saudi Arabia were over. This would definitely be his final diplomatic mission for Riyadh. He was wealthy, so working at this demanding tempo was no longer essential to his finances. His personal destiny now lay with his family on the civilised and sophisticated Île St Louis in the centre of Paris. Where better?

After travelling the five continents, that was his ultimate ideal of a civilised existence. To that end Malik recognised that thanks to today's meeting, he would also have some vital information to pass through his excellent son-in-law to the British security services. The Saudi prince spotted that Malik Khalifa's thoughts were somewhere else and noted it. He had been privately warned before they left Riyadh that the eminent doctor and diplomat was under some suspicion.

He would have been shocked if he had been able to read minds. Malik wanted to communicate with his son-in-law. He happened to know that James was currently in Great Britain, on a long course at the Joint Services Command and Staff College. His daughter always kept her mother well informed, while Louise Khalifa had become both the matriarch and the switchboard for family information.

It was clear both to her and her husband that their son-in-law was destined for a high position in the Royal Navy. Knowing all that, it should be easy enough for Malik to arrange a quick visit at Heathrow airport on his way home from the Middle East. Those were just momentary thoughts, as discussions with Liu Fun were turning to the geography of the proposed alliance. It emerged that the Chinese had reached agreement with Tanzania for naval use of their main port on the African mainland. They were about to secure another agreement further south in Africa, the Vice-premier hinted, but she was not yet prepared to say exactly where.

She also indicated that agreement had been reached to expand a small scientific base on an island in the middle of the Indian Ocean, again its location not explained in detail. The vice-premier indicated that the European country involved was not yet fully aware of China's military plans, which was why she was unwilling to provide further details.

For their part the Islamic Naval Alliance could offer three bases in Indonesia, several in Saudi Arabia, one in Pakistan and the large port of Aden in the Yemen. Everything was on the table and with that Liu Fun realised that the network of bases, sought by her Admiral Zhou Man in this very apartment just over eight years previously, was about to become a reality.

The admiral would be able to sail his Advance class destroyers from a friendly base to any location in the Indian Ocean within less than two days. Not only was China about to become a major naval force on the world's oceans, but one of the speediest too. The Americans might share the North Atlantic with their NATO partners, they might have a powerful presence in the Pacific, but thanks to today's agreement, the world's third greatest ocean was about to become a Chinese lake.

Further discussion concerned freedom of access for all naval ships belonging to alliance members to use all its naval bases. Part of this was a mutual non-aggression pact. The question of mutual military aid was put to one side for the moment: internationally that would be seen as a step too far. China's vice-premier was not wholly convinced that Riyadh would be able to deliver such assurances in entirety anyway. The Islamic nations could be very independent-minded, eccentric even. Malik Khalifa was considered in Beijing to have pulled off a major coup to have succeeded even as far as he had done with creating the INA. China could live with Islamic squabbles, so Liu Fun said nothing. Her country would now have the naval strength and presence to keep them in order, a prospect which was not part of the agreed agenda..

Sooner than expected, the heads of agreement were in place. It had not been a long meeting and it would be a relatively simple task to fill in all the details at ambassadorial level and draw up an appropriate document. As a parting shot, the vice-premier mentioned the new treaty would need a new name. "I think we might call our new child the Central Ocean Treaty Organisation, COTO, just to remind the West we are equally as capable as they are to mastermind a wide-reaching and long-lasting military alliance."

The Saudi delegation envisaged no great problems with that. The name was neutral enough, geographically tidy and unlikely to upset anyone in Riyadh. Better yet, the notion that the centre of global power was being moved to a new ocean was one they all found most appealing. Why should the spiritual bond between Washington, New York and London, the so-called 'Special Relationship', continue to be so influential in world affairs? \Was it not someone else's turn to be top dog?

With the formal part of their meeting concluded, Liu Fun invited her guests to admire the view across the harbour from her verandah. From the Peak they were looking above the clouds across to Tai Mo Shan, the highest mountain in Hong Kong. On a clear day, the vice-premier explained, she could see even beyond the border of Hong Kong as far as the true China.

The Saudi delegation now realised what 'true China' meant. It seemed destined to become the most powerful nation on earth. No longer, when they were choosing a global military umbrella, would countries be faced with an unrewarding short-list of one. From then on they would be able to choose which umbrella to adopt and so indulge in diplomatic horse-trading from an unfamiliar position of strength, while the invisible Beijing Patriotic Association would at last have achieved its ultimate goal. It was an intriguing prospect. Once its meeting with the Chinese vice-premier had been successfully concluded, the Saudi delegation was keen to leave Hong Kong as quickly as possible. It was not a place much to their liking, nor had it been from the moment their aircraft had approached Chek Lap Kok airport.

With the minimum of ceremony they went their separate ways. Most of the delegation were returning directly to Saudi Arabia, but not all. Malik Khalifa mentioned in passing that at his age, he now wanted to spend some time with his own family in Paris. It had been an arduous few days. At the airport it emerged the quickest way to do so was to take the next British Airways flight direct to London and then the short hop home across the English Channel. Such travelling around the world was second nature to Malik Khalifa.

As other members of the Saudi delegation recognised somewhat enviously, even suspiciously, he was by their standards a long-standing international diplomat, a philosophical Olympian who spent his time globetrotting. Not to their liking, Dr Khalifa was anything but a stick-in-the mud, flag-waving permanent resident of Riyadh.

*   *   *   *   *

Ministry of Defence, London

GEORGE GOULD WAS reading once again the brief, succinct memorandum written by James Heaton. This one needed no translation, unlike the 'Solent' document about INA which the Commander had provided ten months previously. This time the text had been dictated directly to the naval officer in English by his unnamed source. Apparently the two had met inconspicuously at a hotel near Heathrow airport while the source was passing though London. James had posted a copy of his hand-written note to a known safe address, one used by the security services, before returning to his staff course in Shrivenham. He had addressed it, simply, to 'George Gould' and equally simply signed it just 'James Heaton.' Few if any knew who those people could possibly be. In the absence of a secure code it was not a document to be entrusted to the penetrable internet.

George Gould could see that James Heaton's brief memorandum would be politically devastating. It was factual, terse and methodical. It described how 'An undeclared diplomatic meeting took place in Hong Kong on Wednesday 15th January 2014. The venue was on the Peak, in the private apartment in Plantation Road of China's vice-premier Liu Fun. Her visitors were a delegation from Saudi Arabia which had arrived the previous day without the usual formalities and without diplomatic protocol. My source was one of the delegation's leading members.' It did not take George Gould very long to realise James Heaton was talking about his own father-in-law.

'The immediate purpose of the meeting was to agree the structure of a new naval alliance between the Chinese People's Republic and the Kingdom of Saudi Arabia, with the Saudis mandated also to act on behalf of the Islamic Naval Alliance, formed just last year. The model for the new naval and military alliance was stated by the Chinese to be that of NATO. The underlying strategic purpose was to pose a major and united military challenge to the West.

'The principal achievement of the Hong Kong meeting was to agree that member countries of the alliance now had free use of all the naval bases included all those in INA, three in Indonesia, one in Pakistan one in the Yemen (Aden) together with the several in Saudi Arabia. These would be linked with the naval base agreement China had at Dar-es-Salaam and with several others China was currently negotiating with friendly regimes around other parts of the ocean. The Chinese made it clear their ambition was to have sufficient bases to be able to place ships from their navy anywhere in the ocean quickly. The bases would all be willing to provide fuel and other supplies to visiting warships of the Alliance. There would be no question of exclusion because of their military rôle.' Heaton's economical prose style continued to set out the new military realities. 'The purpose of China's fleet of Type 45 destroyers currently being built in Dalian now becomes clear. They aim to become the masters of the Indian Ocean; it is to become their private lake.

'The detail of the new alliance, with an associated non-aggression pact, is currently being worked out at diplomatic level between the two countries. In the near future I anticipate a formal announcement from China and Saudi Arabia explaining the creation of COTO, the Central Ocean Treaty Organisation. My diplomatic source for the information has left Saudi Arabia for good and is already here in Europe where he intends to remain. He has a well-established wife and family in Paris, so his seemingly routine visit there will not arouse particular interest.

'He is however requesting that the British authorities now assist him with protecting his personal safety, liaising where appropriate with the French authorities and in return he would like face-to-face discussions on all these matters with the Ministry of Defence.'

The spy had finally come in from the cold, if the climate in Saudi Arabia could ever be described that way. With the COTO document to hand George Gould wanted to talk to James in person and on his way back to his office of obscurity in the Ministry of Defence, George Gould took the opportunity to discuss this latest information with the Chinese and Saudi desks in the Secret Intelligence Service. Everything checked out. They even knew about vice-premier Liu's personal hideaway on Plantation Road on the Peak in Hong Kong.

From the information provided, the security services had examined flight records and listed the identities of the unofficial Saudi Arabian delegation. It was led by Malik Khalifa. James Heaton had remarkably useful family contacts and it was now patently obvious the Saudi diplomat was the source of Solent. No wonder the latest memorandum was so authoritative. Enough of its detail had been corroborated to show it was 100% authentic. And that in itself was a most chilling thought.

With impeccable timing, George Gould sat down at his desk after his tour round some less publicised corners of Whitehall just as his telephone rang. Lieutenant-Commander James Heaton was already waiting in reception. Minutes later as the naval officer walked through the door, the unorthodox civil servant had thoughtfully poured two recently- brewed cups of tea. "Well, James, you have certainly excelled yourself this time. A one-man naval intelligence service. What do you want us to call you? 008? This Memorandum of yours: you obviously understand its daunting implications. Have you also had time to think what we should do about it? What do you suggest? I'd like to hear your thoughts first; you've had more time than me to think about it."

James Heaton had anticipated the question and had worked out his answer in advance. "The very first people we need to tell are the Australians and do so immediately. The news of COTO, even before the Chinese make it official, will be devastating in Canberra. The longer notice period we can give them the better. I know from my own sources, as I am sure you do, that until now they have taken a very laid-back approach in deciding their naval strength and requirements.

"We can both safely anticipate that they need now to change things around very quickly. Even if they all sing Waltzing Matilda in perfect unison, they still cannot turn their entire naval strategy round in ten minutes." James Heaton had a distinctive perspective of the Australian military which owed much to his close relationship down the years with Warwick Sydenham.

"Exactly so. I fully agree with all that." responded the enigmatic captain. "I think we should suggest immediately that the Foreign and Commonwealth Office calls in the High Commissioner, not only of Australia, but those of India and probably Sri Lanka as well. The sooner they know, the better. They face many unfriendly neighbouring states round the perimeter of the Indian Ocean. And it now appears the opposition will be able to act in concert. Very disconcerting." It was another desiccated offering from the distinctive George Gould school of Whitehall witticisms.

"Then there's the Pentagon. I think I should talk to the military attaché at their embassy here toot sweet; I know him quite well. Washington ought to be rocking on its heels. Whether Abigail Fenceville will show the slightest interest is quite another matter, of course. I'm not so sure about Malaysia or the South Africans, or indeed any of the black African states along the ocean's western coastline. I'm far from convinced they could do much about it anyway."

Then James Heaton made a personal request. "When you do talk to the Australians, there is one officer in particular in the Royal Australian Navy I would like informed about this COTO. He will make at least as much sense of it as anyone else in Canberra. I could have sent it directly to him myself, but I thought it better to clear through you first, need to know, that kind of thing.

"His name is Lieutenant-Commander Warwick Sydenham. He and I met at Dartmouth almost twenty years ago and we have a firm understanding between us to share relevant information. He was the first to warn me about the Chinese in Dar-es-Salaam. It was also he who told me a lot about the Chinese Type 45s, what they call their Advance Class. I understand our mutual friend Antonia Foo knows a fair bit about that too. Now we know why she established that engine factory in what they modestly called their Yellow River Industrial Research Facility in Lanzhou and why the Chinese need a whole pile of badge-engineered Rolls-Royce Trents.

"I tell you, Sir, we have before us most of the pieces of a huge worldwide jigsaw puzzle and the military picture on the lid of the box is one I find rather disturbing. I'm sure you're right about telling your chum the military attaché in Grosvenor Square. Best to keep it at that level. Taking the formal route straight to the White House, given its present occupant, could be less productive. In the recent past this would have had the Americans whirling around like dervishes and it would still today if President Fenceville actually understood any of it. I do rather wonder about her."

Captain George Gould looked quizzically at the more junior naval officer. James clearly had the abilities and calibre of mind which qualified him for a more senior rôle than commanding Type 45 destroyers. He decided to probe James's thinking ability another step further. "Tell me, why do you think the Chinese are doing all this? No-one has declared war on them and no-one is likely to do so either. What's their rationale?"

James Heaton had been pondering that one as well and it had also cropped up more than once in his discussions with Warwick Sydenham. "I don't think it's just about Africa. I think the Chinese take a very long view of history, they see it all in terms of a gradual ebb and flow of global power and they are strongly aware that diplomacy, just like nature, abhors a vacuum.

"They take the view that the United States has just about had its day, that Europe was knocked out of the long-distance running by the Second World War and that some other power will steadily emerge to occupy the space from which the West is retreating. Military instinct will never permit a power vacuum. It could be the Islamic world with its oil wealth and its determination to recruit devout followers for the Prophet. It could be Russia, but that no longer has the strength and influence of the old Soviet empire, even if Mr Putin wishes to bring it all back. Theoretically it could be someone completely different from either of those two. We are all supposed to be prepared for the totally unanticipated as well. I would estimate that once having followed that line of logic, on balance the Chinese would prefer the new power in the land, or rather the new power on the world's oceans, to be themselves. To them it is the least worst option. They have the money, the manpower and the technology to create any military presence they want. Along with America and Russia, they are the only state capable of putting a man into space. It is an ancient Chinese curse to say 'may you live in interesting times.' But you can at least minimise the uncertainty, if not the interest, if you are running most of the show yourself."

For a moment George Gould looked silently at the Lieutenant-Commander, only in his forties with a good naval career still ahead of him. He had strategic vision, he had many facts at his fingertips and he saw the world through both diplomatic and military eyes. These were not talents to be squandered. Once James had completed his senior staff course at Shrivenham, George decided he should go to the headquarters of naval intelligence at Northwood, where he would be the right man to take charge, a post that involved comprehending all these significant events and more subtle situations in real time.

Northwood would be an ideal challenge. Despite a profusion of melodramatic novels and films suggesting otherwise, the actual work of Britain's naval intelligence service was decidedly down-to-earth. Its primary task was to keep constantly up-to-date on the state of opposing navies. It monitored their weapons capability, how competent were their commanding officers and crews, and how soon a ship of the Royal Navy could reach somewhere else.

The stream of information was called 'preparedness for war', valuable intelligence against the day High Command in the Navy suddenly required a ship or even a fleet to be sent on active duty somewhere in the world. It had been the task of naval intelligence since the invention of the electric telegraph in the 1870s. The way things were going, it looked as if Northwood needed to expand its Chinese-speaking section, as would GCHQ. As all this flashed though his mind, the enigmatic civil servant made a mental note to talk to the lieutenant-commander's naval appointer at an early opportunity. Although James Heaton could well attain high rank in the Royal Navy, George Gould was quietly hatching quite different plans.

Their discussion returned to COTO, to China's latest move in its finely-calculated game of intercontinental chess. George looked straight across at his companion and explained something else. "Our greater problem, James, is the likely political response. Or lack of it. You've already mentioned what we can expect, or not expect, from the United States. After all, nothing has actually happened other than the Chinese and the Saudis have agreed to sign a piece of paper. Even waving it from the steps of an aircraft at Riyadh airport and declaring peace in their time would still not constitute a serious military threat to the West, in the eyes of many.

"Why invent problems when there apparently are none? Why not take the line of least resistance instead? There are many people in both London and Washington who even when told about COTO will prefer to do nothing. They'd rather let sleeping dogs, sleeping dragons, even sleeping camels just lie."

In Britain a general election was gradually looming and the opinion polls suggested the Whitehall-tractable David Cameron would be replaced by a militant pacifist called Alan Stanley. James Heaton was right. The White House was already occupied by a bird-brained woman from the state of Cheyenne whose notion of foreign policy was anything on the other bank of the Potomac. There was no time to lose.

*   *   *   *   *

Russell Building, Canberra

The note about an imminent Sino-Islamic naval treaty to be called COTO, received overnight from Australia's High Commission in London, was causing the Australian version of pandemonium.

Confidential messages to return to headquarters immediately reached senior military and civilian officers. Despite it being the middle of summer, plans for weekend barbeques were being extensively scrapped. Rarely in Canberra was the turn of events as deadly serious as that.

By late morning the news about COTO had divided Australia's most senior military officers into three factions. There were those who now wanted everything done differently and preferably done yesterday; there were those who steadfastly maintained there was really nothing new to worry about; and then there was a small minority, rather unpopular with everyone else, generally referred to by everyone else as the 'I told you so brigade'.

The Prime Minister had asked for a full briefing and promptly at noon a dozen people were gathered round the cabinet table. She was accompanied by her ministers for defence and foreign affairs, by the government's director of information and by the federal treasurer. Someone was going to need to spend public money, in potentially large amounts and to spend it quickly.

The chief of the defence force brought an intelligence specialist, while a very senior civil servant from the ministry of defence brought along a specialist on naval procurement. The governor-general's office had asked to be represented and the military attaché from the British High Commission had been invited to attend. It was a large, fairly animated and tense meeting.

The prime minster began by thanking the British attaché for the way London brought Canberra into the picture so speedily. An official announcement from Beijing and probably Riyadh could be expected before long. For now, every extra day gained in such a tricky situation was a day to be valued. Next she wanted to hear the view of the armed forces. Much depended on the attitude taken by the Chief of Defence. After the heated discussions around the Russell Building throughout the morning, he had elected to side with the 'do something quickly' faction.

This was welcomed by the senior politicians present, who feared an eventual backlash from the Australian electorate should they complacently decide to do nothing. The spectre of a political and military threat from the north had hung over the people of Australia far too long for its government to continue wallowing in benign neglect. Some unfriendly press commentators had even likened the Australian government to an ostrich which carried its own bucket of sand around wherever it went. That would no longer be the case.

The intelligence from London demanded some ingenuity, to minimise the impression the Australian government was not in the game. The meeting rapidly decided an early announcement from the Australian government was needed to pre-empt any official revelation of COTO from Beijing and Riyadh. Australia needed to look as if it was master of its own house. How could they steal China's thunder?

The Director of Information had brought along a file of press clippings showing what facts were already in the public domain. There had been items in the press about the Chinese destroyers being built in Dalian. They were on the record, fortunately. The broad outline of the Islamic Naval Alliance had also been noted the previous year. China's proprietorial attitude towards the continent of Africa was generally known, but until now it had been assumed to be economic and diplomatic rather than military.

The Director of Information continued: "I suggest we make a prompt announcement saying that after a broad-ranging strategic review over recent months by the Ministry of Defence it has been decided we need to strengthen our defence capability. Our announcement will not then look like some panic response, more like something with a long pedigree. Let us remember, London has put us right on the inside track about COTO, it's not even public knowledge yet. That gives us the initiative. If we move quickly we can beat the opposition into the media. I also suggest we say that at the urging of the Prime Minister and her team, who have been simultaneously reviewing the wider global political perspective, Australia has decided the time is ripe to develop a new fleet of surface vessels capable of countering any threats to our shipping and security. We go on to explain that for some time we have been in discussion with the British about adapting their excellent Type 45 destroyer for our own needs.

"I'm pretty sure London would not object to our inventing afresh that convenient chunk of recent of history. They, after all, will be able to read straight between the lines of our announcement since it was they told us about COTO in the first place. I rather imagine Whitehall would appreciate some such creative public relations. They do it themselves all the time. It's been a British speciality for years."

The British military attaché smiled quietly and nodded gently in assent. The Aussies were learning the diplomatic tricks of perfidious Albion with commendable speed. He greatly approved. "We must assume that any such announcement by Australia is bound to provoke some reaction from other countries in our region, but that is always the price to be paid by those who are vigilant and prepared. Let's show that any forthcoming announcement of this unwelcome COTO concoction is merely something the Chinese have cooked up at short notice in response to our own military initiative. Then they, not us, are the ones who are panicking. That would defuse it all as best we can.

"We must also play to our regional audience here in neighbouring Asia. Not They need to know it is Australia that still calls the shots. Meantime, here at home, the announcement should assure our Australian public that this government is fully in charge of Australia's destiny and other countries are merely following in our wake. Let's make it look as if we have known all this stuff for years without actually saying as much.

"That should undermine the impact of any COTO announcement from Beijing. Old news is no news. Meanwhile our steadied and measured decision assures the rest of the world that

Australia would still prefer harmonious peace to regional belligerence. We want the United Nations to recognise that Australia is a stabilising force here in the Southern Hemisphere, not a provocative one."

Under the circumstances, it was generally agreed by those present that the Director of Information had acquitted himself really rather well. The Prime Minister asked whether anyone disagreed with the suggested announcement. No-one could think of anything better, so the Director was invited to go and draft a suitable text along those lines which the government could issue as quickly as possible. The Minister for Defence further suggested he should go to work with his media staff to prepare succinct answers for the inevitable television interviews. Professional calmness and preparation were everything. Even if they were re-defining Australian defence strategy on the hoof that morning, at least it should not look like they were doing so. No matter that it was government by media release. Everyone was doing that nowadays.

"I think we now need to delve a little more deeply," said the prime minister as they departed. "Just how much of this stuff did we really know in advance? Put it another way, do we have any defence experts who can hit the ground running? I'm beginning to think that old warhorse Bill Boyce - I probably remember him better than most of you - could have been dead right after all. Perhaps not enough of us recognised it at the time. I bet he's up there peering through binoculars and grinning at all of us now with a very satisfied look on his face."

The mention of Bill Boyce jolted something in the memory of deputy chief of defence. Suddenly he recalled a funeral three years previously and a remarkable eulogy given by a young naval officer. He had crossed that same officer's path once or twice since. Over the occasional conversation at a mess bar, he had some very sensible things to say for himself. Taking his cue from the suddenly creative Director of Information, the admiral also decided it was the psychological moment to invent a trump card.

"It's not too much of a surprise, Prime Minister. In the navy, we have been taking the prospect of China's increasing militarism seriously for some time. I've had a very bright naval officer keeping a particular eye on the situation for several years. I might add we have such officers keeping eyes on all kinds of other situations too; given our present level of manpower resources we have to encourage our people to double up such watching briefs with their regular duties."

The admiral shot a steely glance across the table at Australia's treasurer. "His name is Lieutenant-Commander Warwick Sydenham and Warwick has been keeping us informed on a number of things. Back in 2010 he wrote one of the best papers I've ever read analysing the inherent weaknesses in the Australian fleet. Not everyone in the Navy agreed with him at the time and I have to admit he ruffled quite a few feathers. It was not the kind of move to advance one's career, exactly, but as these latest events have shown, he seems to have been absolutely right. Personally I always hold independent-minded officers like that in the highest regard. Not everyone can think right out of the box.

"This officer was one of the first people to draw our attention to China's construction of Type 45s, which we have since monitored covertly. He mentioned about three years ago the link the Chinese have established with Dar-es-Salaam. So none of this latest stuff about COTO comes as a complete surprise to the Royal Australian Navy. As we often say to people, a true military officer is expected to plan for the unanticipated. That's part of our job."

The chief of the defence staff gave his deputy a surprised look, but then rustled his papers to make it look as if all this had been fully discussed in advance. His deputy had just scored a beautiful clean goal for the navy. The prime minister and the defence secretary both looked relieved, perhaps even impressed. Maybe they even believed Australia was on the ball after all. The Prime Minister next turned to her senior military officers and asked "So is that also your answer to my question earlier, whether we have any defence experts who can hit the ground running on this one? This Warwick Sydenham, how good is he? Could he do the job?"

The deputy chief of the defence staff had his answer prepared for that one too. "I suspect he could be our ideal man for the rôle. He was a favourite of old Bill Boyce's, now that we are allowed to mention that name in polite company. Warwick Sydenham is clever, well-educated, a university graduate, he has done all the right things in his naval career so far. I like to think the Australian navy is as good as anyone, and better than most, at talent-spotting. We sent him to train at Britain's Dartmouth Naval College at the beginning of his career. That investment is starting to come good. I think we should reasonably assume he still has some close personal contacts in Britain's Ministry of Defence. That could all come in very useful as well, given the constructive way forward I am about to propose."

The chief of the defence force shot another quizzical look at his deputy; he could not help wondering who was now running the show. So far, however, everything he had heard made eminent sense and the Prime Minister was showing evident signs of enthusiastic agreement. So perhaps it was just one of those benign occasions when it was appropriate to sit back and enjoy the performance.

"Tell me, exactly what do you have in mind?" asked the prime minister. The response was straightforward and logical. "If everyone around this table is agreed we need to expand and update our navy to meet this Chinese expansionism, it then come down to a straightforward question of hardware and money. I think we should try to do as much of the work as we can here in Australia. Our shipbuilding industry could do with a shot in the arm. As for the advanced military technology beyond that, we have excellent working relationships with our opposite numbers in London. Let's just buy it all from the Brits, straight off the shelf. If the British will share the plans for their Type 45 destroyers with us, and I imagine they will, we have ample shipbuilding capacity here in Australia to build the hulls. I'm sure the Treasurer would agree, even if we have to borrow the money, that could only improve the Australian economy. And it seems to me a fair old proportion of what we spent that way would find its way back to the Treasury in various sorts of taxation anyway. It would not do so if we bought abroad."

It was the treasurer's turn to smile, at last. "Beyond the basics, we do then have to start thinking about the overseas procurement. That is where I would like to establish a specialist unit under this Warwick Sydenham. As I mentioned he's been thinking for years about the sort of Australian navy he would really like to see and his thinking is good. He is the right age, he is looking sensibly to the future and this is his chance to put his ideas into practice.

"For a start, Britain's ships are powered by Rolls-Royce jet engines. We would have to buy those. Beyond that, they use advanced technical gear, electronics and computer software that would take us years to develop here in Australia. I think they might be willing to let us buy those as well. It would save us a lot of time, which is the one thing we don't have in abundance." The Admiral looked across at the civilian procurement expert from the ministry, whose sense of relief was evident. If the navy bought all the difficult bits from the British, his work would not be nearly so frantic. Maybe he would only have to sacrifice a few of his weekend barbies.

In the space of a few hours, Australia's creaking defence policy had undertaken a tight $180°$ turn at full speed ahead. The naval officers present were quietly relieved the vulnerable ship of state had not turned turtle in the process. Instead the Royal Australian Navy was about to become, if not its senior service, at least its most significant. A new unit to mastermind its expansion with a new fleet of ships had just been agreed. And Warwick Sydenham, among the navy's brightest, an officer about to be promoted to full Commander, was in pole position.

Ministry of Defence, Whitehall

THERE WAS A definite spring in James Heaton's step as he walked swiftly along Whitehall. Although little had been revealed about his meeting at noon, it was not every day that a middle-ranking naval officer was summoned to a confidential briefing with the Permanent Under-Secretary for Defence. Fortunately it was a pleasantly warm day in London for January and the stroll down Whitehall gave the naval officer time to marshal his thoughts. What else could the news be but good?

As he arrived in the lobby of the Ministry of Defence and produced his security pass, he was joined by a rear-admiral. He immediately recognised Sir Walter Boothroyd, the man ultimately responsible for naval procurement. The very senior officer scarcely needed to introduce himself, but he did so anyway. And his tone was noticeably friendly. "James, congratulations, you are the man of the moment. Not only does your own country need you, but it appears Australia needs you too. Let's pinch that conference room and I'll fill you in as best I can. We've got about ten minutes before the PUS can see the two of us."

They settled down at a typically austere civil service desk while a secretary brought in some welcome coffee and biscuits. A staff car from Shrivenham, a train from Swindon, the Circle Line on the underground from Paddington and the stroll down Whitehall had left few opportunities for food and James Heaton was hungry. The modest bacon, lettuce and tomato sandwich consumed in the buffet car as his train sped through Didcot seemed a very long time ago.

As James munched his way through a pile of official civil service biscuits, the Rear-Admiral sketched a flattering and very interesting picture. "Let's start with your one-man naval intelligence service. Your confidential notes to our mutual friend George Gould about INA and then about COTO, could not have been more timely or better written. You have won yourself a whole pile of brownie points and not only in the Royal Navy, but here at MoD as well. And, as I gather you anticipated, your memorandum about this COTO duly relayed through their High Commissioner, has had all the top brass in the Australian military jumping up and down in their cages.

"To cut a long story short, in the space of four hours the Aussies have just reversed their previous naval procurement policy, if that is not too strong a word. About time too. They urgently want Britain's help. We have been on the receiving end of a flurry of signals from Canberra. The UK's military attaché has been sending a steady stream of them right through the night. Keeps him out of mischief.

"Since it directly concerns you, there is some further news. Because he seems to be the one officer in the entire Royal Australian Navy who understood beforehand what all this is about, your old Dartmouth chum Warwick Sydenham has been bumped up to full Commander and put in charge of their procurement programme.

"Straight away the newly-promoted Commander Sydenham has personally requested that you become his front-line liaison officer here in London. We've run that past the Second Sea Lord, he's read your files and talked to George Gould and it's green lights all the way. Oh and by the way, we've advanced the promotion you would probably have received in June anyway and you are now an Acting Commander too. Congratulations."

"Does that mean I shall be leaving the Joint Command and Staff Course at Shrivenham?" The Rear-Admiral was ready for that. "Yes it does and with immediate effect. But don't worry about that too much. Here you will probably be working your balls off anyway. What Shrivenham would teach about military management in theory, you are going to work out in practice here at MoD. I believe it's called learning on the job, best education of the lot. And as far as this job in MoD is concerned, welcome aboard but beware. You are now moving up in the Navy to the level where you will begin to sprout grey hairs.

"I gather you also know Christopher Cunningham and his team at the Sharava Corporation. Dammit man; I must say, your contacts book appears to be at least as good as mine. You are one of the very few officers in the Navy who knows about Bijali and Kundalini, let alone about Sharava. I understand you have also had a go on the Kundalini simulator at Park Royal. I don't mind admitting that scared the hell out of me and that's not because I haven't spent any time at sea as a warfare officer, because I have. Your generation has grown up with electronic warfare. I came into it the hard way."

The Rear-Admiral went on to explain that, officially, James would be director of naval intelligence at Northwood, but temporarily seconded to the Ministry of Defence while the Australian naval procurement order was put in train. Obviously George Gould had been granted his wish; James was going back to his favourite stamping ground of naval intelligence, much that he enjoyed commanding ships at sea.

Shortly after that, the Permanent Under-Secretary welcomed the two naval officers and asked for yet more cups of coffee. It was rapidly becoming apparent to James Heaton that British defence policy floated on a boundless ocean of caffeine. "Commander Heaton, as I understand you now are, I trust the Rear-Admiral has been putting you in the picture, so I don't need to repeat any of that. In strict confidence, I can tell you we have had an urgent request from the Australians to help them to modernise their navy. It is all very sudden, but thanks primarily to your intelligence reports I think the three of us and certain members of the government, fully understand why.

I can further tell you, it's hardly surprising that Britain is one hundred per cent sympathetic to the Australian request. Exporting arms to friendly nations is something we do rather well and we could never ask for a more trustworthy customer than the Aussies. Already in the course of the morning, I have secured full Cabinet approval to let them have whatever they want. Sir Walter and I now need to get down to the nitty-gritty, while you are to become our primary liaison with Canberra. I also gather an old friend of yours is doing the same job at the Australian end, rapidly promoted yesterday by their department of defence. The two of you originally met one another at Dartmouth, I believe. That's a relief; there's hope for us all yet.

"George Gould has also told me who your father-in-law is and that may well be something we wish to revisit in due course, but right now this Australian shopping list is our primary concern." The under-secretary and the rear-admiral then took James through an impressive list of naval requirements. The Australians had made the wise decision to buy British hardware off the shelf, as it were, rather than try to re-invent the wheel. Time was of the essence. They were looking to build a fleet of destroyers cloned directly from the British Type 45, adopting much the same weapons systems and operations technology.

"All we need to do is hang some photographs of kangaroos in the ward room and our Australian friends should feel completely at home." Rear-Admiral Sir Walter Boothroyd was clearly enjoying every minute of it. For once he was not fighting for more defence budget from Britain's parsimonious Treasury, nor was he weighing up whether the end customer for armaments sold overseas was actually to be trusted.

"The Australians are being very sensible," explained the under-secretary "and this is where you and your Australian opposite number will be in control. They want to do as much of the work as they can themselves down under and only look to us for the difficult bits like engines and weapon systems.

With the best will in the world and even using our designs unaltered, they are unlikely to get a completed Type 45 hull into the water in much less than a couple of years and you've seen at Portsmouth how the fit-out stage can then take at least as long again. For our part we want to ensure nothing to be supplied from the British end will hold them up. That will be your job.

"However I think I ought to mention something else. As you know, next year this country will hold a general election. Obviously the present government is supporting the Australians one hundred per cent. But let me be perfectly candid; after all it's not exactly as if we are talking in front of the press. If through some mix-up we do not get a clear majority, or if God forbid that pacifist Alan Stanley takes over, he might start to make things rather difficult for Britain's arms exporters.

"Stanley's the kind of politician who regards every military alliance as an excuse for war rather than as a means to preserve the peace. We don't think he is to be trusted and the Australians seem to have got that idea as well. Even more reasons to get on with it quickly. I have clear instructions from the highest level to push this Australian armaments order to the point where it could not be reversed after the next election, whatever happens, so you'd better get cracking."

The meeting had lasted all of thirty minutes. The civil servant was anxious to keep an important lunchtime appointment, so the Rear-Admiral decided to buy James some food as well. They strolled across the river to a very acceptable gastro-pub at Waterloo Station called, appropriately under the circumstances, the Fire Station. "We can talk here a little more easily, not quite as many wagging ears as there are around the restaurants of Whitehall and Victoria Street, but just remember the Official Secrets Act applies to everything we've talked about this morning, so do watch what you say."

In fact to anyone eavesdropping, their conversation would not have seemed all that unusual. The Rear-Admiral was anxious to discuss how they would set up this 'Anglo-Australian Liaison Group' as he now called it and what its staff requirements might be. "You will find the Second Sea Lord has moved mountains this morning to clear the way. By the time we get back to MoD after lunch, you will already have been allocated office space and you need to find yourself a deputy, a couple of technical assistants and a small secretarial staff.

And I have further good news. Our mutual friend Christopher Cunningham is fully in the picture, naturally. He has decided to help speed things along, so he is going to second his deputy to work closely alongside you. The Aussies will have a lot to learn very quickly about their exotic range of products. Did you ever meet Martin Barraclough when you went to Park Royal? Clever chap. He and Chris Cunningham go way back. He is in his early 50s, knows all this electronics stuff back to front. He helped design large chunks of it. He will be a big asset.

"And there's something else. Chris Cunningham has given us a list of a number of naval personnel who have scored particularly highly when they have been Kundalinied. We both of us know exactly what that involves. It's tough, but up there at Park Royal as they refine their testing, they reckon they have come up with a very accurate method for sorting the sheep from the goats. Chris recommends you only have agile goats on this programme, people able to think quickly and adjust to new and unexpected priorities as they emerge by the hour. That's exactly what Kundalini can spot."

Over the next few days James Heaton worked from early morning until well into the evening combing on-line personnel reports and summoning potential candidates to Whitehall. Part of his being tested was to demonstrate just how quickly he could assemble a team. Part of their test would be to see how quickly they could handle a surprise situation coming out of the blue. Fortunately, quite a lot of ships in the navy were alongside at their home ports, so day trips to London for individual crew members were not hard to organise.

James was impressed by the authority he could suddenly wield. Between them when they needed, the Second Sea Lord, Sir Walter Boothroyd and George Gould could excavate mountains and they were happy to let the newly-promoted Commander James Heaton sit in the JCB's driving seat. Already by the end of the week the Royal Navy's modestly titled "Anglo-Australian Liaison Group" had taken shape.

Fleet Headquarters, Northwood

THE TELEPHONE on James Heaton's desk rang and the Second Sea Lord's secretary asked him to present himself in an hour. Northwood was expecting an unusual visitor and the Director of Naval Intelligence was required at the meeting. He was now back in his regular job after the liaison job with Warwick in Canberra had run its course, with great success. Thanks to their combined efforts the Australian Navy was now steaming with full despatch into the twenty-first century.

The morning's visitor turned out to be George Gould, on one of his rare trips away from the Ministry of Defence in Westminster. Rather than make a fuss with a departmental car, he had anonymously taken the London Underground Jubilee Line from Westminster to Finchley Road, where he had changed onto the Metropolitan Line to Northwood. There changing trains is a much easier cross-platform manoeuvre than doing so in the labyrinths of Baker Street. At Northwood he was met by a car. George Gould instinctively covered his tracks around London even when it was not strictly necessary.

The purpose of the meeting was to fill in the small print of a secret deal which was being hatched with the Pentagon in Washington. The Second Sea Lord explained. "The thing is, the Yanks are only about a year off completing their first Zumwalt class destroyer. They are only building two at the moment, compared with our six D45s, but as we all know Zumwalts are what they consider to be a state-of-the-art stealth warships. In shape they hark back to our Dreadnought battleships of a century ago, but the cousins now reckon something along those lines makes itself pretty well invisible to modern radar.

"They've reached the point where some very clever electronic kit is being installed and our guys in Washington have been chatting with their guys about it. That's where we come in and that is why you are here, James. To be specific, it concerns the ability to recognise individual ships by the variety of signature signals they give out. Nowadays those signals can be picked up even thousands of miles away. We think we know how Uncle Sam is doing it. It's something we've been working on here in the UK for a number of years, but now we want to take our understanding of their technology a bit further.

"To be blunt and this is strictly among ourselves, it is not so much a matter of wanting to crib their system as wanting to know how to immunise our ships against it. Of course for these purposes the Yanks count as the good guys, but just suppose the bad guys have latched onto the American system?" George Gould nodded in tacit agreement. In his jaundiced view, any military secret developed by the Americans would be fully explained in an exclusive and accurate article in the Washington Post within the week.

The Second Sea Lord continued: "From sources which it is not necessary for me to disclose even at this meeting, we reckon the bad guys may have already done so. If they want to start recognising our ships from thousands of miles away, we now want to know how to screw up that kind of high technology snooping. But to do that, we want to know more about the American system we think the bad guys have copied. Have I made myself clear so far?"

George Gould smiled. This sort of under the counter-trade dealing in military secrecy was right up his street. It was the very warp and weft of the imperceptible mischief he had been up to for years. Of course he fully shared the Second Sea Lord's assessment of the leakiness of the American system for keeping such secrets secret. He now took the logic one step further. "Let me guess. Our chaps reckon that for the Yanks to reveal their long distance maritime recognition technology to us, they will want something technological from us in exchange. Have I guessed right so far?"

George Gould had guessed right. He usually did and continued "Let me guess some more. The bit of technology we are proposing to give them is Bijali." The Second Sea Lord nodded. This was promising to be a short meeting. But neither senior officer had reckoned on the contribution about to be made by James Heaton. "If I may, sir, I'd like to refine the plan a bit. First of all the Americans do not need to know our system is actually called Bijali, nor do they need to know it is the work of the Sharava Corporation. In fact so far as I am aware, they are totally unaware of any kind of British link to the self-effacing Sharava Corporation. Like everyone else, to the extent they have heard of it at all they probably believe it is, if anything, Indian. After all, for Sharava to sell its kit anywhere in the world, a wide chasm separating it from any active military power such as the United Kingdom would be an absolutely essential pre-requisite.

"I would prefer us to take the slightly different line with the Americans that although our Type 45s make use of a bog standard tracking and fire control system which is commercially available anywhere in the world, we Brits have simply added one or two gizmos that no-one else has thought about.

The last thing the cousins need to know is that we have actually persuaded the Chinese to install it in their Advance class destroyers. That would be giving far too much away. The Chinese have announced publicly that they have bought a bog standard Indian system for their ships. Let's just leave it at that, undiscussed. We then leave the Pentagon with the clear impression there is nothing special about the system the Chinese are using. Let us just agree among ourselves that it is one of those occasions where ignorance is bliss, even if the bliss is entirely Uncle Sam's."

George Gould was enjoying every minute of this and smiled. His protégé had obviously taken to the black art of military disinformation like a duck to water. Never give anything away you didn't need to give away. Better yet, lay thick smokescreens round sensitive truths as a matter of routine, even before you know who might be looking, if indeed anyone was.

The Second Sea Lord agreed. "James, thank you very much for that. You have put very clearly some vague thoughts that were already germinating at the back of my own mind. But now I've heard it from your mouth as well they sound even cleverer. Very articulate. So let's play it your way. Well done."

The discussion then moved onto the practicalities of impressing the Americans that the British had something worthwhile to swap for the secrets of Zumwalt. It was quickly decided the right thing to do was to stage a demonstration at sea and the Second Sea Lord appointed James Heaton as his personal representative to ensure it all went to plan. He would be the only person involved in the sea trials who actually knew the whole truth about Bijali and Sharava. That put him in an ideal position to lay a logical smokescreen to conceal what was actually happening, without any risk someone else in the know might lay a dangerous smokescreen in parallel which would turn out to be contradictory. If there was to be a battle hymn sheet at all, best there was only one copy.

George Gould agreed with all that strongly. James Heaton was now his man too. A carefully-crafted file note composed by George would in due course find its way into the official machinery of the Ministry of Defence. The note would be one which gave a perfectly satisfactory explanation of everything that was about happen at sea, yet a note which was about a million miles from the truth. In George Gould's very personal view naval disinformation, rather like charity, should always begin at home.

*   *   *   *   *

Portsmouth, Hampshire

TWO CLASS 45 destroyers were moored side by side along the quay in Portsmouth naval dockyard. HMS Daedelaus and HMS Dichotomy were about to take part in top secret warfare experiments in the North Atlantic. In the wardroom of HMS Daedelaus, Commander James

Heaton, director of naval intelligence, was giving the ship's Commanding Officer, her Executive and Warfare Officers and an American visitor an introductory briefing.

"First may I on behalf of the Royal Navy welcome Commander Chuck Wellie of the United State Navy. Except that we prefer to drive on the left around here, I'm sure you are going to find all this stuff pretty familiar, Chuck. Despite the odd altercation about two hundred and forty years ago we have generally been on the same side. And whether you are based in Norfolk Virginia or Portsmouth, Hampshire, ultimately we agree both our navies owe a lot to King Alfred.

"Before I came to this briefing, I did my sums and it is currently about one thousand, one hundred and twenty years since Alfred took on the Danes in the Thames estuary and beat them off. It's the first English naval engagement of which we are aware and whether you are the Royal Navy or the US Navy, we both reckon that was when it all began. It is the beginning of all our naval history.

"Earlier this year, archaeologists found a cardboard box containing human bones in Winchester Museum and they believe those could be the mortal remains of Alfred the Great. That's how we seem to treat out naval heroes. Nelson's remains were brought back from Trafalgar in a barrel of brandy. Winchester is only about twenty miles up the road from here and if you've not seen the cathedral it is well worth a visit. We Brits will treat you and your fellow American on Dichotomy for a look-see when we get back.

"We ought to do a private tour of Victory as well, but mind your heads. Sailors were little chaps in those days. We have it easy in the modern navy: the men who sailed those ships must have been astonishing. After all we are all serving naval officers and Victory is still commissioned in the Royal Navy, somehow the Ministry has forgotten to strike her off the list. So now let's come up to date. If anyone doesn't know all about these Type 45s already they shouldn't be here in the first place. I don't intend to say too much about the ships themselves, other than we are very interested to see how you guys across the herring pond are coming along with your Zumwalts and how the two classes of stealth destroyers compare.

"Both are fitted with all kinds of clever electronic gizmos to keep our opponents in a state of permanent anxiety and that is what we are about to test out in the Atlantic. I don't need to remind everyone that everything I say from now on is covered with as many layers of military secrecy as we can possibly apply. If the other guys know what we are capable of, there will be little point being capable of it in the first place.

"Next, let me explain a little about the tactics of our Operation Reflection, which begins right here with this briefing. Here on Daedelaus we will be the command ship, the good guys, the blues. Dichotomy over there is going to be at a fighting distance and for the purposes of this demonstration they will be the bad guys, the reds, but also the guys who do not have the foggiest idea what is happening.

"I've known her commanding officer Barry Jones for years, we're old shipmates and as you will see for yourselves shortly Barry looks about as evil a commanding officer as we can muster in the Royal Navy of today. I had him chosen specially for this exercise. For despite this briefing, once we put to sea, Barry will not have a clue what happening. He is to be given no advance briefing. The same goes for your colleague Commander Brown on board Dichotomy, Chuck. He cannot know what is going on either. Their ignorance is our bliss.

"Barry and Graham will be joining us later on and they will be given a slightly different explanation before we set sail. Just look upon me as the living embodiment of dear old perfidious Albion and you won't go far wrong. Until we get the new aircraft carriers, Albion and Bulwark are the two largest ships in the fleet. I need hardly say more." Over the next fifteen minutes James Heaton explained in detail how Bijali worked. Unknown to its senior officers, the Ops room of HMS

Dichotomy had been fitted with an all-British gizmo which enabled the Ops Room on Daedelaus to watch exactly what was happening across the water and to do so in real time. Chuck Wellie whistled in surprise at that. "Jeez James, that must be any military officer's dream. To know what the other guy is thinking and doing second by second. Sheesh. The ultimate military advantage."

"Chuck, it can get even better than that. Provided they are talking anywhere near a microphone for the on-board record, or on standard headsets to communicate with one another, we can actually hear what they are saying as well. You'll be able to test that by calling up your chum Graham Brown on Dichotomy on a special mobile phone - sorry, cell phone - we are going to give you. Get him to say something completely off the wall which could never have been scripted beforehand and then listen to him saying it in their Ops Room a few moments later. You'd better agree with him he is likely to get an offbeat request or two from you before we set sail."

"Obviously today we are conducting this trial with two identical ships of the Royal Navy, but that's hardly the point. For reasons I need not go into, we happen to have the same capability listening in to the Ops rooms on ships of other navies as well. If push ever comes to shove and it is appropriate, we Brits will be in a position tell Uncle Sam exactly which those ships are."

James Heaton then led his small party down to the Ops room on Daedalus. Chuck was impressed to see she had been temporarily fitted with what looked for all the world like a duplicate tracking and fire control system. James Heaton explained. "That is actually a clone showing us what is happening real time in the Ops Room on Dichotomy. I'm sure we'll all find it very entertaining as they eventually realise they haven't a bloody clue what is going on." The senior men aboard Dichotomy joined them later. While the men of Daedalus smiled quietly in the background, James Heaton explained that Operation

Reflection was essentially to compare the warfare abilities of the two Class 45s. They both had exactly the same kit, so it was all down to military guile. James Heaton did not even smile as he explained the two ships therefore had exactly the same military capabilities and it was then a matter that he who dreamt up the cleverest tactics would win.

Chuck Wellie had to cover his face at that point in case he caught the eye of Graham Brown. A day or so later and in a rarely visited corner of the North Atlantic HMS Daedelaus took on HMS Dichotomy in what turned out to be an entirely one-sided contest. Not only was the command ship second-guessing everything Dichotomy tried to do, sometimes she was there even before them. It did not take long before Commander Barry Jones decided to throw in the towel. His American shipmate, Graham Brown, called Chuck Wellie on Daedelaus and asked what hell was going on.

"I'll explain it all later when we get back to Portsmouth. You might be a tad mystified now, Graham, but you'll just love it when you learn the underlying truth. The golden rule, you'll find, Graham, is never to piss around with the Royal Navy. They can be a right bunch of bastards when they feel like it." Commander Chuck Wellie of the United States Navy was already becoming quite adept at English slang.

Chapter Thirteen

Reversals

The 18th Arrondissement, Paris

The 18th Arrondissement, Paris

HASHIM BIN KHAZMI lived in Paris, just off the Rue Myrha. It was one of the poorer parts of the inner city, a district virtually unknown to tourists. That section of the 18th arrondissement was known as the Goute d'Or, but if there was a single drop of gold in it anywhere, Hashim had still to find it. Located midway between the Gare du Nord and Montmartre, about three kilometres north of the river, it was a neighbourhood of dirty narrow streets, tawdry bars, boarded-up shops and derelict building plots with scant evidence of any builders.

These days it suited Hashim to keep a low profile and live as quietly as possible, running his one-man motor business. It had been that way for over ten nerve-wracking years. Although none of his neighbours in the Goute d'Or knew it, Hashim had a criminal past which always threatened to catch up with him.

It had all started thirteen years ago when he was young Algerian chemistry student in Paris. He had not taken kindly to the racial prejudice he often encountered. To buttress pride in his racial and religious identity he had become a devout Moslem. Gradually he was drawn into a Paris mosque which was a favoured recruiting ground for idealistic extremists. The young men there regularly encouraged one another to join the jihad.

Unknown to them, like many radical mosques it was monitored by the Saudis, to check on both its propaganda and its adherents. A popular member of the congregation, a man who had adopted the name of Lubayd, led a further covert existence working for an esoteric branch of Saudi security. Because Hashim the Algerian was clever, rather better educated than many, he was befriended by the Saudi gatekeeper. There was far greater potential in the young man than his merely becoming another disposable suicide bomber.

Lubayd was privately intrigued by Hashim's evident familiarity with chemistry and more publicly by his fanatical, if not particularly well-informed, Islamic beliefs. However, he showed little hint of any of that when, as their friendship was sufficiently cultivated, he offered to take Hashim on the Hajj. Lubayd seemed to have plenty of money and he told the young man that "the Hajj is not only a great privilege and honour, but there are people in Mecca I would like you to meet."

In his innocence Hashim was taken on the Hajj, the dream of any devout Moslem, only to discover that once in Saudi Arabia he was offered a stark choice by the men Lubayd knew. Either he could be exposed and charged as a dangerous militant and finish up in prison, or he could become a spy for the Saudis. On their behalf he would be expected to keep his controllers secretly informed on the goings-on in the tough world of freedom fighter training camps.

He had only been given a one-way air ticket from Paris; it was not a difficult choice. He was first equipped with a new Libyan identity with the nickname Fateen and warned never to reveal his real identity involving his life in Paris. And that is how the former Hashim bin Khazmi found himself in an Algerian training camp for freedom fighters, as their admirers usually called them. It was tucked into a valley beyond El Golea, that isolated oasis town on the Trans-Saharan Highway, a grandly-named dirt track heading south into Mali.

The training camp was a desolate place, hidden away in the foothills of the Atlas mountains. The newly-named Fateen received some modest remuneration for his sporadic reports to his Saudi controller, whom he always arranged to meet on occasional recreational visits to the town. He was careful not to show any signs of excessive prosperity which might arouse suspicions. Far better to save his income, which at his request was in Euros, for some future rainy day. Not that there were many of those in a desert training camp.

To allay any suspicions of his double life as a spy, Fateen was determined to be seen as one of the most enthusiastic and determined trainees. This, plus his evident cleverness, attracted a small group of admirers. Among them were fellow French-speakers from the Basque country, planning to work for their freedom movement ETA.

Hashim's education in France had given him a well-grounded insight into inorganic chemistry and as the recently invented Fateen he grasped the principles and practice of explosives much more readily than most. This expertise also made a powerful and lasting impression on his new-found friends from ETA, among quite a few others.

The aptitude was duly reported by the training camp's deputy commander to a scout for Al-Qaeda. After just a few months Fateen was sent to join an advanced group of bomb-making specialists at a camp in distant Afghanistan. There he worked alongside experts from the Taliban, old Mujahideen who had acquired their bomb expertise the hard way, fighting the Russians. He made it apparent he wanted to become a specialist in delayed-action timing devices.

After several months in Afghanistan he was far too valuable ever to be considered as a single mission suicide bomber.   Instead he was sent back to the camp in Algeria as a bomb-making instructor, still

operating under his invented Libyan legend. His growing expertise once
again attracted the attention of trainees from ETA. They were impressed
by his seemingly easy European manner, a man at home in the capital
cities of Europe, quite unlike the Mujahideen. He was invited to move
to Spain and provided with a free apartment on the outskirts of Madrid.

After the desolation of the Algerian desert and the inhospitable
mountains of Afghanistan, living in a sophisticated European city once
again was a welcome return to normality, but the enjoyment did not last
long. He discovered soon enough why he had really been invited to
Madrid. He was to become the bomb-maker for a terrorist gang
planning a major attack. For him, the justification of so doing was the
appalling way Spain had treated its Islamic population in the distant past.
The group of which he was a leading member was soon joined by other
militant Moslems with similar thoughts.

For his Spanish colleagues from the Basque country, their pretext
was a much more recent enmity with Madrid. Everyone in the group
considered they had deep Spanish-inflicted wounds which needed to be
redressed. Some had lost brothers, fathers, uncles or cousins in the
long-running war on terrorism. None of them had the slightest qualms
about what they were planning. As their specialist bomb-maker Fateen
was provided with mining explosives he had not used before and told
precisely what would be required of him.

On Thursday 11 March 2004, ten bombs exploded in four
different commuter trains in the centre of the Spanish capital. Such was
Fateen's expertise and the way he had trained his team, they all exploded
within three minutes of each other. The death toll was a massive 191,
mainly Spaniards but from sixteen other countries as well. A further
1,800 people were wounded.

Fateen was astonished by the scale of the slaughter. Not
surprisingly the Spanish police and security authorities went into
overdrive, promptly rounding up twenty-nine suspects. Well before they

had done so, Fateen had destroyed his invented Libyan identity and burnt all the papers ensuring there was no surviving evidence that the Libyan Fateen had ever existed. Within an hour he reverted to being Hashim bin Khazmi, an earnest Algerian chemist living in Paris.

This reborn civilian crossed speedily into France, giving a wide berth to the constantly monitored Franco-Spanish crossing in the heart of the Basque country, the border between Irun and Hendaye. Instead Hashim routed himself round the eastern end of the Pyrenees north of Barcelona. He used the less conspicuous crossing point into Cerbère on France's Mediterranean coast. Well clear of the Basque country, his clearly Parisian accent and manner aroused little suspicion. From the Spanish border it was a simple train ride back home to Paris, his wallet still stuffed with his supply of very useful terrorist Euros.

This was the criminal past which Hashim bin Khazmi now lived under in the 18th Arrondissement, rebuilding an ordinary life once again in the very ordinary Goute d'Or. He hoped with the passing of time his history would dissolve. After all, none of his Madrid, nor training camp, contacts knew where he was nor even who he was. For them, Fateen the Libyan bomb-maker had simply vanished from the face of the earth.

Although his own speciality was now car alarm systems, he had preserved the identity of the previous business on the premises. To the casual observer the shop sign saying Auto Repairs all seemed obvious enough. There was a pile of worn-out tyres by the entrance which easily satisfied any passing curiosity. The unchanging pile gathered dust from one month to the next. Concealing his true activities had become second nature, for Hashim's work with cars never included supplying new tyres nor even repairing punctures.

In a back corner of the premises his new girlfriend Lubabah and her sister ran an Arabic-speaking minicab service. Hashim had made good use of his specialist skills by installing car radios in the taxis owned by his small team of freelance drivers. They would hang around the run-down café next door chattering, smoking good Gauloises and drinking cheap coffee while waiting for their next turn of duty. Hashim dreamed that one day he would be rich enough to own a stylish business in smart premises selling high-tech audio systems, but definitely not in the Goute d'Or.

In the meantime he built a travelling repair business for car audio systems, which he publicised by posters displayed in the district's petrol stations and workshops. Most of his business came from repair mechanics who welcomed his expertise. Hashim was always careful to pay them ten euros for sending him the business. His battered Renault van was a familiar sight around those mean streets of Paris, although sometimes he found work further afield.

Over the years since he had fled Madrid, Hashim's life had returned to a reassuring, insignificant routine until one day he had a surprise visitor. It was his old mentor Lubayd, for the Saudi was probably the one person left alive able to connect Hashim's present humdrum life with that of the former Fateen the bomb-maker. The Saudi informant and fixer did not bring welcome news, on the contrary. With few courtesies he came straight to the point.

"Hashim. I now have an important job for you. You realise of course you owe us a great deal of gratitude and much more than that. For years we have protected your identity while your comrades who also took part in the Madrid bombings have all paid a very high price. So now is the time for you to return the favour. There is a traitor to the Saudi cause who lives here in Paris and I have promised my own people that he will be dealt with. That obligation now becomes your task."

Hashim was given a car description, a registration number and a smart address in Paris. He was told to observe the situation until he was familiar with the target's routine and choose his own moment to make his move. Lubayd handed over a sealed package containing specialist explosives and various devices for making a magnetic bomb. Lubayd was even wearing gloves. Two weeks later there was a huge street explosion in a very exclusive district of central Paris, close to the river Seine. The bomber remained a mystery: he was never caught. The owner of a very expensive car did not however stand a chance of survival. His name was Malik Khalifa.

*   *   *   *   *

Pretoria, South Africa

VICE-PREMIER Liu Fun arrived in the dark continent with a renewed sense of urgency. The Australians had announced a much-strengthened defence policy which sounded like a direct challenge to her embryo COTO. The timing of the irritating announcement was much too close to be just a coincidence. It aroused strong suspicions in her mind and she had asked the Saudis whether perhaps the Australians somehow knew about COTO before it became news and if so how.

Even as she arrived the dark continent promptly gave birth to another mystery. Liu Fun prided herself on knowing the faces and names of the world's leading politicians and dignitaries, her memory for them was legendary. Yet even she had never even heard of O R Tambo. Whoever this mystery celebrity was, the South Africans clearly considered him or her of sufficient importance to provide the name for their principal international airport. Fun speculated what he or she must have done to deserve such honour.

To be fair African potentates came and went with mind-boggling frequency, and only the names of the craziest such as Idi Amin or Muammar Gaddafi seemed to linger in the global memory. The rest were generally forgotten, preserved only on banknotes or in the names of tree-lined avenues and new airports. Liu Fun was here in South Africa on a mission to make quite certain she would be remembered too. On the rare occasions the vice-premier made an official visit from China or from her hideaway in Hong Kong, she nevertheless expected the host country to recognise it as a noteworthy event. It would suit her purpose if the South Africans not only treated her as someone at least as important as this O R Tambo, but also held her in awe.

China's ambassador to South Africa greeted the vice-premier on the tarmac shortly after the aircraft came to a stand. Direct flights between China and Africa were becoming more commonplace, as more and more African nations embraced the protective benevolence of the Middle Kingdom. It suited Air China to monopolise them, for they were no longer the legitimate business of Europeans or Americans. Or so the Beijing Patriotic Association maintained. Even so the flight from Beijing had taken over ten hours and First Class was still an exception on the airline. Special arrangements had been made for vice-premier Liu and she had managed to get a fairly good night's sleep.

Large Chinese limousines were still an infrequent sight on the roads around Pretoria, almost as rare as Rolls-Royces. This was no longer a prosperous country and Liu Fun was prepared to see the worst. Yet as her embassy car swept majestically northwards along a modern dual carriageway, she looked out at well-maintained industrial estates, parklands and then the extended comfortable-looking middle class suburbs to the south of the capital.

"South Africa's not all like this," explained the unctuous ambassador. "Less than fifty kilometres over there is the place they call Soweto, where they keep all the displaced natives who work in their gold mines. There's another place like that even closer to where we are they call Alexandra. Believe me, vice-premier, you would not wish to see that side of Africa. It is quite appalling."

Quite clearly the ambassador's gentile upbringing in his homeland had shielded him from the less salubrious regions of China itself. Liu Fun wondered to herself what Alexandra, that most gracious English queen of a century earlier, might have made of a filthy slum being named after her. What strange legacies the departing European colonialists left in their wake. The car sped on. It took less than forty minutes to reach the Chinese Embassy on Pretorius Street, where arrangements had been made for the vice-premier to stay during her visit to the South African capital. The hotel facilities here were not comparable with those of Hong Kong.

"Exactly which of their motley assortment of politicians shall I be meeting?" she asked the Chinese ambassador over a cup of diplomatic tea. "I need to talk to someone who can take major decisions without constantly referring to higher authority. The fewer people we have to deal with on this mission, the better." China's vast wealth spoke more eloquently than any words of persuasion. In the considered view of Beijing, potentates in the liberated nations of Africa were there to be purchased. Preferably one at a time. Most of them chose to be well-disposed towards Chinese persuasion, especially when each revealed a personal numbered bank account in Switzerland.

The next day Liu Fun was collected by a very tall and slender junior official and taken to meet her South African host. Like her, he too proved to be a vice-premier, one called Bongo Mathanzima, a name which doubtless meant something significant in Xhosa. The diplomatic balancing act to maintain protocol had either been organised adroitly, or maybe almost anyone could be relabelled a vice-premier nowadays.

Mr Mathanzima had already been on a short list prepared by the commercial attaché at the Chinese embassy. Beijing had confirmed he did indeed have a numbered bank account in Geneva. Once the Chinese ambassador to South Africa had been greeted by this Bongo Mathanzima like an old friend and all diplomatic courtesies scrupulously observed, Liu Fun immediately got down to business.

"Mr Mathanzima, I understand our people have already given you some inkling of the purpose of my visit. It is perfectly straightforward and natural and will not take me long to explain. In recent years the People's Republic of China has concluded that the Americans can no longer be trusted to maintain global security. Far from being the international policeman, the United States of America is nowadays the international criminal. Rôles have been reversed.

"As you are no doubt aware, we are arranging a treaty with the Islamic countries around the Indian Ocean, as they choose in the past to call it, so that they may be brought under an umbrella of military security guaranteed by the Chinese People's Republic.

"Specifically, we are building a state-of-the-art navy which can provide protection all around this ocean. Already countries as far apart as Indonesia and Tanzania are availing themselves of our services. China is now a very wealthy country and we consider it our duty to bring the twin benefits of universal peace and individual prosperity to others."

Liu Fun caught the eye of the South African as she pointedly mentioned the benefit of individual prosperity and was pleased to note an instant flicker of understanding. Enthusiastic personal understanding. This would all prove to be much easier than she had originally thought.

"I can well understand and sympathize perfectly with all that you say." came the formal response from vice-premier Bongo Mathanzima. "However I must point out that our Republic of South Africa has, since the end of the revolting and loathsome apartheid regime, become a peace-loving country. Our rainbow coalition of all creeds and races has no reason to fear or antagonize anyone. This is beyond all doubt the friendliest country in the whole world. All our loyal peoples live together in happiness and beyond our borders we seek to be the driving force for greater harmony among other, less fortunate, countries throughout this beautiful continent of ours."

Liu Fun had arrived suitably prepared for all this boloney and rose to the occasion in style. "I am sure we both recognise that the peoples of Africa and the peoples of China share the same aim. All of us want peace and harmony, now that the warmongers of Europe and

North America have had their day. But there are still military risks. Even now the diabolical Americans cannot resist sending their soldiers and bombers to interfere, causing bloodshed in other people's local difficulties. For our part we wish to extend the privilege of lasting peace to this southern part of Africa. That is why I am here today."

"And how, may I ask, can the people of South Africa assist you in that praiseworthy endeavor?" asked the South African. At last vice-premier Liu Fun had opened her opportunity. "In its modern peace-keeping Rôles, the Chinese People's Navy needs freedom of access to friendly harbors to replenish its supplies. Although our greater purposes are entirely different from the British colonialists of the last century, our practical needs are not dissimilar. Just like they did, we now need a network of naval bases. And the finest to be found anywhere in Africa is right here in your country. Mr Mathanzima, I have come to talk to you about Simon's Town."

So that was it. The South African minister was being asked to provide China with freedom of access to his country's premier naval base. There was irony in that, as one new colonial power sought to replace its departed predecessors. The naval base owed its name to one Simon van der Step, governor of the Dutch East India Company who surveyed False Bay, near the Cape of Good Hope, in 1687.

Vice-premier Bongo Mathanzima blinked impassively as he listened and pondered. He knew his history every bit as well as this Chinese vice-premier Liu Fun. Simon's Town dated from an era when the powerful nations of Europe - Britain, France and the Netherlands - were locked in rivalry to win colonial supremacy. It was under the British after their second invasion that Simon's Town naval base had grown rapidly in the Napoleonic Wars. Its Admiralty House dating from those times was currently celebrating a 200th birthday. Liu Fun knew all this before she left Beijing. Her ability to absorb a brief was legendary. The naval base had been developed by the British to combat the African slave trade, it had been responsible for the imprisoned Napoleon on the remote South Atlantic island of St Helena until he died there in 1821. With the coming of the twentieth century, Simon's Town and its South African sailors had played an important part in both world wars.

Then in 1957 the British handed the naval base back to South Africa and four years later the country had become an independent republic. A colonial history tracing right back to the sixteenth century had been brought to an end. Yet the Chinese were in town suggesting an arrangement which might bring it all back again. Now as in times past the naval base was seen as a strategic asset of global significance.

Less than thirty kilometres south of Cape Town, Simon's Town sheltered beneath the eastern flank of Table Mountain. In their diplomatic gavotte that morning, the Chinese and the South African both knew exactly what was at stake. The naval base commanded a strategic position where three of the world's five oceans all came together. It was in a perfect location to police the world's vital sea route round the Cape of Good Hope.

There are few seagoing routes to choose between Europe and Asia. Ships must either go round the Cape or through the Suez Canal. The Russians offered a further two choices, of a sort. It was in principle possible, at the right time of year, to find an open sea route through the Arctic Ocean and sail round the north coast of Russia between East and West. A less fraught if more dependable alternative could be to load intercontinental freight onto the trans-Siberian railway. Yet the costs of putting cargo on long-distance Russian trains would be very high when compared with the economies of a very large ship.

Although the Egyptians kept deepening their famous canal to take larger and larger ships, the ships grew even larger still. The most economical of all the routes between East and West still had to be sailing round the open oceans of the Cape of Good Hope. The precise position of Simon's Town was ideal for its military purpose. The Table Mountain

National Park and the Kogelberg Nature Reserve on the opposite shore sheltered a fine natural harbour. This topography fended off the constant storms of the Atlantic, Indian and Southern oceans where they all met at Cape Agulhas, just about a hundred kilometres out of the naval base. The seafaring British had never been slow to recognise the benefits of a calm water harbour to support their maritime adventures.

Liu Fun could see that the South African minister was now in a post-colonial quandary. It was time to apply a little pressure. "Vice-premier Mathanzima, perhaps it would help clarify the situation if I explained what was at stake. Within these four walls we can surely agree that your country is no longer as prosperous as it once was. Not only that, you are still highly dependent on producing and exporting exotic commodities such as diamonds and gold. Without those exports you cannot afford to buy enough oil.

"Our Chinese scientists are now in a position to challenge the world's traditional diamond industry. In recent decades our laboratories have found ways to manufacture gemstones out of elements very similar to carbon which are then indistinguishable from the diamonds you win from your mines. And we can manufacture them at a vastly lower cost.

"Again, the world economy is changing after the turmoil of almost seven years ago. Our bankers and economists predict that the importance of gold on the world's financial markets is in serious decline, while my country has become one of the most powerful players in the global economy.

"It is already some fifteen years since Britain's Treasury decided it no longer needed its gold reserves. The powerful Bank of England sold its gold reserves into the world market. We anticipate other countries will steadily follow in their wake. None of us can stem the forward march of economic wisdom and financial expertise." More followed in the same vein and Liu Fun could soon see her threatening message was getting through. Despite his determined efforts to look quietly confident, Bongo Mathanzima was on the back foot. Behind the courteous phraseology he could recognise old-fashioned economic blackmail just as speedily as anyone.   The Chinese woman was deliberately underlining South Africa's greatest fears. Neither vice-premier needed to spell out the wider implications. China, perhaps the richest country in the world, held the economic destiny of South Africa in the palm of its hand and they both knew it. Once again Liu Fun's machiavellian instincts, a veiled threat and her Oriental inscrutability had won the day. They always had that result.

A crestfallen Bongo Mathanzima was soon starting to negotiate. "Would it perhaps be possible to draw up a modest agreement giving Chinese access which my government colleagues would not find too onerous?" The South African was weakening by the minute and the Chinese vice-premier could afford to be considerate: "That is exactly what we in China have in mind anyway.

"Please assure your colleagues, should they ever ask, that China does not have any colonialist designs on your great country. We wish our ships to come in peace, typically to refuel, to help protect the peace and harmony of South Africa and then sail away again in peace. You are no longer dealing with the warmongering United States of America."

Bongo Mathanzima rang for his secretary and ordered some tea. The interlude gave him time to think how to phrase his next request. After tea had been served he turned to his guest and said "We know of course that our friends in Tanzania have already agreed to your request and had heard other countries such as Indonesia and Saudi Arabia are involved as well. These are good countries and we admire them. They can help set us a pattern. Perhaps what you are asking is not so very exceptional, but I will need your help.

"Vice-premier Liu, I think I can see a way to persuade my government colleagues to agree to your proposal. However the effort required of me personally would be considerable and I am a very busy man. My time is valuable. I can see the great benefit of what you propose to China, but what would be the benefit to me?" Liu Fun was already on the home straight. With no-one listening and no-one watching, Bongo Mathanzima handed over a note showing the number of his private bank account in Geneva. Although the Chinese knew it already, it seemed diplomatic not to reveal such intimate prior knowledge. Much better to be told of the bank account afresh. Within a few moments a sum of twenty million US dollars had been agreed and the South African vice-premier was already looking forward expectantly to a life of luxury around the warmer and more sophisticated watering holes of southern Europe.

China's vice-premier had no desire to linger in South Africa any longer than was necessary. In her Mandarin opinion it was an appalling country. While she waited for her embassy staff to confirm that the South Africans were moving forward to formalise her proposals, she was taken to inspect the Simon's Town naval base for herself. For the thirteen hundred kilometre journey southward from Pretoria to Cape Town she decided to travel on the Blue Train.

It was said to be the most luxurious train in the world, a prospect which intrigued even the normally abstemious Liu Fun. She saw it as her personal responsibility to investigate such sumptuous living at first hand. After all, China's planners and industrialists needed to understand the burgeoning international market for railway rolling stock and how to approach it. Despite a serious and embarrassing crash in 2011 with its own high speed railway, which had tragically killed forty people, her country was fully aware of the global potential for providing suitable trains as well as for building the railways themselves.

No doubt her comrades in the Beijing Patriotic Association would have acknowledged her purely commercial train of thought all the way to its last Yuan. If China wished to sell high speed railways and railway equipment successfully, its vice-premier had a clear duty to assess the degree of luxury which future customers might seek. One day those international customers might even include Russia itself. There had to be potential to speed up passenger train services along the trans-Siberian. Trains travelling at the speed of those crossing China, Japan or Europe could cut the time required to cross that huge and tedious country by half, at the least. They would need to be as luxurious as possible.

`Or so Liu Fun reminded herself on numerous occasions as she sampled the sumptuous Blue Train. Chinese exporters did need to keep abreast of the latest fashions in express trains, just as much as they did in kitchen gadgets, computer equipment or expensive women's clothes.

The Blue Train lived up to its global reputation. After the unrewarding rigours of her visit so far, Liu Fun was pleasantly surprised. Her luxury compartment featured a double bed and a bathroom complete with its own full-sized bath. The train had a welcoming dining car. Its excellent meals, fine South African wines and even Montecristo Havana cigars for those who wanted them were all included in the basic fare. For exercise she strolled to the observation car at the rear of the train, enjoying its splendidly primitive panoramas as they swished effortlessly across the high African veldt.

The price of the ticket was over $2,000, exorbitant when compared with rail fares at home. It was considerably more than the annual income of the average African living south of the Sahara. It was over five times the annual income of a citizen of the Democratic Republic of the Congo. Chinese diplomats could afford such gentle indulgences with ease; so who cared about peasants? Given its world-beating economy, China could afford everything nowadays.

Liu Fun was repeatedly impressed by the degree of luxury. Trains currently being built and sold by China could not even begin to match it. She began to wonder whether, like her recent South African counterpart, she should perhaps have a few words with some influential colleagues back home. Yet for all its luxury, the Blue Train deposited its affluent passengers at a humdrum railway terminus in downtown Cape Town. An over-anxious Chinese assistant chargé d'affaires apologised for the long walk to a waiting car in Adderley Street. The vice-premier contrasted Cape Town's workaday terminus with the splendour of the grand railway station in Beijing. As she drove through its streets she saw that even Cape Town, considered the most advanced city in Africa, was easily overshadowed by several in modern China.

By the standards of other parts of Africa, however, the port facilities of Simon's Town were most impressive. Decades earlier the British had developed them to their own usual standards, but now things were starting to look dated. Liu Fun was confident that Chinese engineers and technologists could bring things up to date and decided that generous modernisation clauses should be written into the Sino-South African agreement.

It did not take her long to see everything she needed to see in the naval base. She spent a day or two taking in the region's tourist attractions like the cable car ride up Table Mountain. Her hotel suggested a visit to Stellenbosch, the old town of the Boers, founded by the same Simon van der Stel who had given his name to the naval base. It was in the heart of the wine-growing district.

The highlight of the town was a collection of preserved Cape Dutch architecture, displayed as some of the oldest in southern Africa. It struck Liu Fun as rather odd just how much attention the modern South Africans sought to focus on their European colonial past. Obviously they were conscious of rather more in their heritage than just the appalling memory of relatively modern Apartheid.

Then news came that the basic treaty which Bongo Mathanzima's officials had drafted posed no significant problems. They required no further negotiations at Liu Fun's level of seniority and she was free to go home. Her homebound flight provided an ideal opportunity for reflection. The deal for Simon's Town was the final link in her master

strategy for the ocean, devised with Admiral Zhou in Hong Kong almost
nine years previously. She had secured the naval facilities in Africa he
needed; Simon's Town would be the jewel in her crown. In addition to
that, a malleable team of diplomats from Saudi Arabia had provided
China with all the bases of the Islamic Naval Alliance. Together they
had given substance to her grand design for the Central Ocean Treaty
Organisation. With satisfactory agreement over Simon's Town, the
world's third largest ocean was now surrounded by a ring of military steel
under China's command. The global rôles had been reversed.

In the space of eighteen months, the game of military visibility
had swung heavily China's way. Much of that was Liu Fun's own doing,
but she had been helped immeasurably by the intrinsic fault lines of
popular democracy in the West. First, that foolish woman Abigail
Fenceville had been elected President of the United States. Reports
through diplomatic sources, supported by articles in the American press,
confirmed she had all the key ingredients for becoming a political
disaster for her country. It was increasingly unlikely an America under
her leadership would have any effective answer to a military challenge
from China. In previous eras the United States of America would have
invariably resisted, almost certainly responded with vigour. But not now.

At the other end of the north Atlantic axis, China's diplomatic
analysts sensed a parallel shift in Great Britain's attitude to the wider
world. Through history the British had naturally been an aggressor in
international affairs. But it was a difficult rôle to maintain indefinitely
and every now and then the British electorate decided they had had
enough. In the peculiarly British version of democracy, more than in any
other, the wishes of the electorate reigned supreme. How generous of
them to support the Chinese cause.

Latest diplomatic intelligence from London suggested the mother
of parliaments was about to give birth to a paraplegic government.
China's team of political analysts were making the powerful point that

governments drawn from Britain's Labour Party could usually be relied upon to take a softer line on communist regimes than their Conservative opponents, while the British electorate seemed instinctively to believe in giving both sides an equal chance.

It was just the kind of weakening in her political opponents which Liu Fun relished. Had the founding fathers of Western democracy ever considered for one moment just how generously their cherished political institutions would one day play straight into China's hands? All the Middle Kingdom had to do now was sit and wait.

Lenin had reputedly referred to their communist sympathisers as 'the useful idiots' of the West. Yet as Liu Fun saw it the biggest idiot of the lot was probably the omnipotent deity of democracy which stood at the very heart of the Western psyche. Their politicians worshipped it daily in a hypocritical performance solely designed to dazzle their own version of peasantry; what an antiquated idea. Not since the pharaohs of Egypt had there been anything quite so cynical.

Liu Fun was not remotely religious and smiled more than once at the delicious irony. Liu Fun forgot nothing, recalling events of seven years ago when a Russian aircraft carrier group had steamed straight into the inner sea of the British Isles without eliciting a murmur of protest from its leftist government. London had simply ignored it. If that was the British reaction to a Russian naval presence in their home waters, would they even be remotely interested by a Chinese naval presence in waters ten thousand kilometres from their island shores? Somehow Liu Fun doubted they ever would.

China would have to tread carefully for fear of alerting the NATO high command. The western military mind, quite unlike the western political mind and not owing its position to the democratic process, was somewhat more vigilant. Politically China's progress to becoming the world's leading power was being given a free hand by even the most powerful countries of the west. The Chinese vice-premier lay back in her specially arranged aircraft seat and smiled yet again as she realised her ambitious plans for the Middle Kingdom, now the greatest nation on earth, were speedily coming to fruition. All she needed now was her fleet of Advance class destroyers. Everything else she required was cemented in place. Once more she reflected how the former Indian Ocean was about to be transformed into a Chinese lake.

*   *   *   *   *

Royal Navy Fleet Headquarters, Northwood

IT HAD BEEN almost seven years since James Heaton first arrived at Northwood as a newly-promoted officer. He was back again. After several months sorting out the Australian order for defence equipment, it was now time to resume his formal job with the navy. He had been promoted and was to have his own command, as the staff officer in charge of naval intelligence. His personal job description also involved a direct link with the Ministry of Defence in Whitehall, sidestepping the navy's usual chain of command. This was exceptional for the commanding officer of N2 but the secretive George Gould wished to retain close contact. It was a sign of the times.

Fortunately fleet headquarters at Northwood was all rather familiar territory, James he knew his way around. Among the most senior officers in fleet command, his formidable reputation had arrived ahead of him. Some of the civilian staff were still there from his previous posting. Most of the first day was spent saying "hello again" to old friends and sorting out his office.

The following morning he was summoned to a meeting with the commander of naval operations. Although they had met several times at social functions and navy briefings, this was the first time they were in the same line of command. "Welcome aboard, James. I think we can skip the usual chit-chat about the rôle of naval intelligence here at Fleet

Headquarters. You know N2 as well as I do, probably better. I've been taking a look at your record. Last time you were here you reported on a Russian carrier group playing hide and seek with us, all the way into the Irish Sea. I must say I'm a little surprised by the unwillingness of your senior officers to respond, or just how few people in the Navy or the Ministry were told about it at the time.

"You were absolutely right to file a formal report saying what positive actions you had proposed and what happened to your recommendations. It appears they were summarily rejected. That particular officer has now retired. I'm sure it is all very well to champion the freedom of the seas, but such laissez faire can leave the distinct impression we don't really care. I imagine our total lack of response had them whooping with delight in Moscow and maybe even Beijing. If the Chinese ever whoop at anything, that is. I rather imagine they invariably restrain such enthusiasm to an quietly inscrutable smile.

"I've also been reading some very complimentary stuff by our mutual friend George Gould. One way and another he seems to regard you as his personal protégé. He is one of those clever naval officers who never went after the top jobs, preferring his quietly inconspicuous backroom in Whitehall. He has become the country's leading expert on all kinds of things we very rarely talk about. George is retiring in a few years' time and reading between the lines, he would like you to be the one who succeeds him. You can take that as a singular compliment.

"Reading this file I am also reminded it was you who gave us that memorandum a little over a year ago about the Islamic Naval Alliance. It was read by a large number of top people in Whitehall. Even so, we rated it Top Secret to protect your source. The chapter and verse it contained had several people jumping up and down, including me. All kinds of diplomatic and military links started to look different. Pakistan's involvement in a pan-Islamic deal raised lots of eyebrows. Generally they had been seen as reluctant allies of the United States.

With your memorandum all that suddenly changed. Then I happened to bump into an old friend in the upper echelons of the Indian Navy. As you know yourself, Dartmouth friendships can last a lifetime. I felt it right to bring him up to date. He said the perspective from New Delhi, if there was now to be a ring of Islamic nations acting in unison, was quite terrifying. Until I told him about the INA it had been assumed by the military and politicians that India's external security in the region could rely on the principle of divide and rule. No longer.

"Then earlier this year you followed up with your report on the imminent formation of a further link with the Chinese. China Magna no less. This time around I think we were all reaching for the medicinal brandy. Put it this way, Commander Heaton: you have earned yourself a first-class reputation for making waves. Good. Not all of my naval colleagues agree with me by any means, but in my view that is the prime duty of a staff officer in the Royal Navy. You make the waves, then we rule them. That's what the famous song is really about. Everyone joins in singing it at the Last Night of the Proms, but do any of them realise it actually refers to our mutual *alma mater*, Britannia Royal Naval College in Dartmouth? By rights they should all be brandishing the Blue Ensign. You can forget the mythological lady in the tin helmet sitting comfortably with her spear and shield and draped in a flag.

"The first task of any military officer is to know what the opposition think they are playing at. His second task is to make them wish they hadn't." James Heaton smiled. That was proper fighting talk. I gather your unnamed source for the 'Solent' memorandum on INA then came in from the cold. He gave a most forthright briefing to the Prime Minister, the Secretary of State for Defence and some others. David Cameron and his colleagues hauled it all on board with alacrity. Forewarned is forearmed and all that. Dr Khalifa paid a very high price for his benevolent co-operation. Blown to pieces in Paris by a terrorist bomb. I gather he was also your father-in-law; I don't really know what to say to you about that. My deepest sympathy and condolences of course, but they deserve to go much deeper." James Heaton nodded in quiet gratitude for the supportive remarks. The matter did indeed go much deeper. He alone knew just how close he had grown to Violaine's remarkable father, a genuine meeting of minds. For his wife and her mother and half-brother it had been an appalling family tragedy. For James Heaton it had also been a deeply personal philosophical and diplomatic tragedy as well.

His commanding officer stayed quiet for a moment to allow James a chance to gather his thoughts, then continued "To be honest I hadn't really made the family connection. How many more surprise connections do you have up your sleeve? No wonder George Gould keeps referring to you as 008. "Now let's move on to your immediate tasks; look upon it as something done to honour your late father-in-law. I would like a full assessment of what the Chinese are up to, combining what you already know with any fresh information you can bring to light. The usual SWOT stuff: Strengths, Weaknesses, Opportunities, Threats.

"You deserve to know you this time around you have the total backing of everyone senior here at Northwood and down at Whale Island, no matter what you uncover, no matter how disconcerting. I think it was Sir Walter Boothroyd who said you are the man of the moment. Okay, James, now's your chance to live up to that."

As he left James respectfully saluted, the preferred way in the Navy to indicate assent. He had soon settled in with his new department and the first task he chose was to track the latest progress with China's fleet of Advance class destroyers. The first in the class, the Admiral Zhou Man, has been launched less than two years previously. Already she was said to have done sea trials and showed a fair turn of speed. The data made available to James showed her to be closely comparable to a British Type 45 destroyer, a very handy piece of kit. The technical fit-out must have been completed at the Chinese shipyards with quite remarkable efficiency. Britain's military attaché in Beijing had organised himself some efficient lines of observation and communication and so had the Australians. The upper floors of the Shangri-La Hotel in Dalian commanded a splendid view of the Dalian shipyards. These days every worthwhile representative office could manage with an hotel to provide a virtual office, rather than spending huge sums of money on extensive staff accommodation.

The Chinese were clearly taking their naval expansion very seriously. A further Advance class hull had been launched in late 2012 and a further four in 2013. Their fleet was already as large as the entire British fleet of Daring Type 45s and so far two more Advance class completed hulls had entered the waters of Dalian in 2014.

James Heaton and Warwick Sydenham, on opposite sides of the globe, were keeping one another clearly in the picture. The Australian naval command was also doing its naval arithmetic. So were the Indians. It all began to look ominous.

Christopher Cunningham was interested in the Advance class as well. He confirmed that Chinese orders from Sharava for tracking and fire control systems matched the rate of hull construction and his best estimate was the final fleet could even be as large as twenty. He was convinced all the sets of equipment ordered by China were being used on their Advance destroyers, although the original specification from Beijing had been somewhat vague about the class of warships involved.

Now, in his view, it was all perfectly obvious. After her sea trials round Korea Bay and the Yellow Sea, duly observed by satellite, the Admiral Zhou Man had been noted passing through the Straits of Malacca. Not many shipping movements there missed a team of diligent observers. Almost at the southernmost point of Singapore, their most congenial vantage point was near the golf course on Sentosa Island. Like the English Channel, the Bosphorus or the straits of Gibraltar and of Hormuz, the narrow sea passage between Malaysia and Indonesia was one of the pinch points of global shipping. The Chinese destroyer had then paid a brief call at the Indonesian port of Belawan, as London now knew one of the treaty ports of the Islamic Naval Alliance. Much more intriguingly, she had then set course for the little-known Amsterdam Island, a French possession in the central Indian Ocean. After a short stay at France's scientific base on the island the destroyer had steamed straight for Dar-es-Salaam.

Diplomatic reports from Tanzania confirmed the Admiral Zhou Man had remained in port for two or three days. There had been some well-attended festivities on board to which the British had not been invited. She then sailed south again and some four days later arrived at South Africa's naval base in Simon's Town. More on-board jollifications were duly noted by the British consulate staff in Cape Town and reported to the Ministry in Whitehall, which promptly alerted Northwood. The Chinese were apparently hooked on diplomatic parties.

To Commander James Heaton, the pattern was all too obvious. The Chinese military were making themselves visible around their new treaty ports in COTO. Simon's Town was a revelation. If the Chinese had permission to base some of its Advance class destroyers in South Africa, it gave them effective control of the strategic sea route round the Cape of Good Hope. British diplomatic staff in Pretoria were asked to make the usual discreet enquiries and it soon became clear there had been some sort of unpublicised deal with the Chinese.

Recent satellite photographs of activity on Amsterdam Island were another revelation. On the face of it, the French had decided to transform a very modest scientific station into a significant maritime base, its facilities roughly comparable with those on the Falkland Islands. There was now a lengthy airstrip and a much larger jetty.

If anything the fuel tank was somewhat larger than the one at Port Stanley. Such generous facilities were hardly necessary for an occasional marine research vessel or French supply ship. The arrival of a Chinese warship now reversed the picture. It was time to ask Violaine how good her contacts still were in the Renseignements Generaux, the arm of the French secret service where she had worked for five years. Almost two years had passed since handing in her resignation, but she had been a forthright member of staff and made her mark. James called his wife at their home in Portsmouth and filled in that part of the intelligence picture. Could she find out if the Chinese had anything to do with the current developments on Amsterdam Island?

Violaine understood her husband's job much too well to ask for further explanation. "James, I think I might, with your permission, also contact Xavier de Kerguelen. Did you know he is now on secondment to the DGSE?" This was excellent news. James was familiar the General Directorate for External Security, the French secret service. He told his wife "Darling, you and Xavier have known one another long enough. Ask him informally and let's see what he can find out. He ought to have some personal interest. After all it was his own ancestor who discovered that island group in the southern Indian Ocean which bears the family name."

Professionally Violaine enjoyed being back in the intelligence hunt alongside her husband. It was a welcome mental distraction from brooding about her late and beloved father. Far better to do something positive to help avenge his death. While she helped James, Violaine was still pursuing her Islamic research at Oxford with greatly renewed energy. Unusually she was permitted to take home some very old manuscripts from the Bodleian Library's superb collection.

Few other people ever looked at them anyway, for not many could read the old Arabic script on which unfamiliar calligraphy Violaine was now an expert. She was not however to know that a Saudi student on a scholarship at the university had been briefed to report through London on her activities. The warning of her childhood that her father's work could put his family in danger was always there in the

background, even after his assassination. Within a day or so, her specific
enquiries to Paris had brought more revelations. The Chinese were not
only involved with the development of Amsterdam Island, they were
funding it. A deal had been hatched by their ambassador at the United
Nations in December 2012 and a team of Chinese negotiators had
arrived in Paris just a few weeks later. It was the first time James
Heaton heard the name of Zhou Man. Evidently he was a naval officer
who had been seconded to this civilian mission in Paris. Construction
work on Amsterdam Island had begun that spring and the base was to
be fully operational by mid-2014.

So far as the French authorities could tell, China's interest in
Amsterdam Island was purely scientific. The two countries shared an
interest in the problems of earthquakes and the movement of tectonic
plates, for which research the island was ideally located. The Chinese
were also pursuing some archaeological enquiries of their own. On that
basis France had been willing to comply with their request for co-
operation, especially when Beijing had offered to foot the bill to expand
harbour facilities on the island.

Xavier de Kerguelen reported on something else. Much to
French surprise, a brand new Chinese destroyer, the Admiral Zhou Man,
had stopped briefly at Amsterdam Island just a couple of weeks
previously. It was explained that her main task had been to drop off a
team of Chinese geologists and archaeologists, then to continue on her
way. It had taken the French military by surprise, but the Chinese had
gone out of their way to emphasise the call had a purely civilian purpose.

Paris was therefore willing, a little reluctantly, to let it go at that.
But seeing the wider picture, James Heaton was not at all convinced that
Beijing was simply using the Admiral Zhou Man as a taxi service for its
laudable scientists. It was a ranging shot. The next call by a Chinese
warship at Amsterdam Island might, he surmised, stretch French
credulity just a little too far.

James summarised his wife's discoveries, without directly attributing their source, to his superior officers at Fleet headquarters. Again it came as a revelation; in rarified MoD circles the redoubted reputation of 008 continued to grow. It confirmed and amplified what British naval intelligence already knew. Commander Heaton's initial report was on the desk of the commander operations and the commander in chief the following Monday.

He was sent for immediately. It led to an animated discussion. "You are telling us that the Chinese now have agreements to use three key locations in the Indian Ocean, as well as the half a dozen or so bases of the Islamic Naval Alliance permitted under their COTO treaty? And now they've wrapped up a deal with the French, of all people, our principal NATO ally in Europe, to equip themselves with a naval base, slap bang in the middle of the Indian Ocean? Hmm. Exactly which side does Monsieur Bonjour Matelot think he is on?

"God help us, it adds up to a ring of steel, with its axlebox located on Amsterdam Island. It all makes the Russian naval base in Syria look very small beer." The two senior naval officers pulled out a map and quickly calculated that a Type 45 destroyer, or rather its Chinese variant, could be placed anywhere in the ocean in less than two days, once all those bases were fully operational. In effect the West would have lost control of the Indian Ocean. They both sucked in their breath at considerable length and one of them even said "ouch". Even by the standards of the Royal Navy It was as serious as that.

The Admiral looked up at the Commander with a pained expression. "James. I must thank you for the speed with which you have brought all this unwelcome news to our attention. I knew it was right all along to put you into naval intelligence, even if some diehards voiced their doubts. Well done. Round this part of the world we never shoot the messenger. On the contrary. I'm sure you don't need to be told your particular message is far, far worse than we expected. It now becomes a political matter, not just military and I can tell you no-one's going to be at all happy about it. Better leave it to me from now on. For a start, we certainly need to alert our opposite numbers in New Delhi and Canberra. They are not going to be happy bunnies either."

*   *   *   *   *

The train from Euston to Glasgow

ANTONIA SNUGGLED against her new husband's shoulder. She had married Christopher Cunningham at Marylebone Registry Office that morning, then they had celebrated with a lengthy lunch in Baker Street. The stylish French restaurant had been closed to all normal customers for their special occasion. For her long-awaited wedding Antonia had decided to forego the conventional large white frock. Instead she was wearing a closely-tailored suit of maroon silk made especially for her by an expensive fashion house in Knightsbridge. Christopher's tie had been made to match. Her suit was worn over a simple shirt of thick cream silk. Antonia Foo scrubbed up nice.

Now in her fifties, Mrs Cunningham was blessed with an hour-glass figure which was more comely than ever. Her make-up was subtle and classic. With the cheekbones of an aristocratic Shanghainese, her thick black hair now tumbling in gentle waves, the faintest tinge of ochre to her almost translucent skin and her deep brown eyes, she was truly beautiful. When Antonia Cunningham really wanted to turn heads she could practically make them spin off their shoulders.

The couple had known one another almost seven years, ever since that memorable first meeting at Champagne Charlie's wine bar deep beneath Charing Cross Station. For their first meeting they had shared a bottle of South American pinot noir, she always remembered; the colour of her suit today was a deliberate reflection of that. Back in those days such exotic wines were still scarce in her native China, except in Shanghai of course. Or in Hong Kong. Perhaps South African wines would soon be available all over China. For the moment their work at Park Royal on computer systems could be put to one side. They now had more enjoyable things to think about. At their wedding Antonia had been particularly pleased to meet James Heaton's wife, having heard so much about her. She knew that Violaine was still suffering badly from the assassination of her father and from a miscarriage of her first child the previous year.

It was difficult to know what to say, especially when the French authorities had no idea who the bomber was who killed her father. With her mainly French, slightly Arabian looks, Antonia could see that beneath the sadness she was a lovely woman in her late thirties. As they sought to discuss other things Violaine very quickly emerged as an accomplished expert on Islamic history, something Antonia would greatly like to discuss at much greater length, but on another occasion.

It struck Antonia how Violaine made the perfect wife for a rising officer in the Royal Navy. She was clever and needed to be. James had been one of her all-time stars on the Kundalini tests and she gathered he was now in charge of naval intelligence. Antonia was pleased about that, definitely a round peg in a round hole. The two were some of the beautiful people of modern cosmopolitan Europe and Antonia Cunningham cheerfully decided she was now another herself.

Not many people had been at the wedding lunch. It had been confined to those who knew about Sharava and that kept the numbers down considerably. Antonia and her husband and his best man Martin Barraclough had agreed it was going to be just one day in their lives when they did not need to keep up a security-driven pretence about what they all did for a living. The day before her wedding, Antonia had met long-standing girlfriends she had tracked down from the old days at Imperial College. Even that was almost thirty-five years ago now and they were all into their fifties. As hen parties went, it was subdued. A pair of bunny ears had been produced with a flourish as they drank the champagne. Amid quiet cheering she wore them with pride, for almost ten whole minutes.

There had been much gossip about university contemporaries, about who was married to whom, how many babies they had produced and the inevitable later divorces. It reminded her of what she had missed about London during all those years spent working in China and was all rather nostalgic. And rather comforting too. It reminded her she totally belonged somewhere else among the British, among other old friends and somewhere most enjoyable and civilised at that.

The romantic rail journey to Scotland, for it turned out Christopher had some old family roots there, was rather exciting. The premium first class seats were spacious and deeply comfortable. These latest trains were faster than ever, the journey would be less than four hours. From city centre to city centre would have taken longer if they flown from Heathrow. In any case they had both spent too much of their lives in aeroplanes to fly for pleasure, while Antonia wanted a panorama of the English countryside to enjoy from her first class seat.

Once beyond the sprawling suburbs of London it was all tidy farms, quaint old canals, hilly woodlands and well-kept villages. Not a paddy field in sight, she found it far more picturesque than her native China. The English countryside was beautiful and prosperous. A land of educated gentlemen farmers rather than peasants, a breed almost unknown anywhere in the Orient.

Then their train swept through England's industrial heartland, a region of large factories and some empty, desolate mills. They didn't look either dark or satanic, as the traditional anthem claimed they did. They just looked rather sad. Beyond Lancaster, a historic city which Christopher pointed out as they passed through quickly, the view through the carriage window transformed into moorland. Now it was land fit for sheep farming and little else. The train swept majestically round a succession of sinuous curves as the railway twisted and turned and climbed up into the treeless hills. Christopher told her they were riding over a famous summit called Shap, a bridge of high land joining the rolling Pennine hills of Yorkshire on their right to the Lake District on their left. These were beautiful both parts of England Antonia had heard about many times and wanted to visit one day.

Beyond the historic border city of Carlisle they were suddenly into Scotland, climbing and climbing again. The Scots possessed a natural rampart to separate them from the English. Although they were now well into the north, Christopher told her the hills were called the Southern Uplands. The geographical logic must have been somewhat clearer to the Scots than the English.

There were now only two ways into Scotland: either this route through Carlisle or round the far coast through Newcastle. After climbing over another high summit the railway swooped and curled down the valley of the Clyde and they were soon in central Glasgow. It was far more fun than flying.

Antonia and Christopher planned an early night. They had booked the most expensive Corner Suite in the Radisson Blu hotel, a modern establishment on Argyle Street, conveniently close to the main railway station. Much that she loved good food, tonight a brace of bottles of champagne and not much to eat would suffice.

Tomorrow they were away again, flying to the Western Isles. Of necessity their honeymoon would be short, yet a complete break from the hurly-burly of cosmopolitan life. The June days were at their longest, with the Gulf Stream bringing warmth from the west. The Scottish isles, far to the north, would not see sunset until long after ten. Antonia and her husband would retire in the sunshine and rise in broad daylight.

* * * * *

The train from Waterloo to Portsmouth

VIOLAINE HEATON settled back in her seat as the train swept speedily through the endless suburbs of south west London. Through famous places like Wimbledon her journey eventually led into the open heath lands of Surrey, then the hills and farmlands of Hampshire as the red, white and blue train hurried to its destination. Duty done, she had changed out of her stylish wedding outfit and was now wearing a comfortable yet smart outfit of simple skirt and top. She had even redesigned her make-up in the toilet. Parisian women should always strive to look à la mode.

Violaine and her husband had discussed the wedding at some length before they decided to attend, but it had been her mother Louise who insisted. Immediately upon the appalling events in Paris with the death of her father, she had rushed to be at her mother's side.

She was never to forget the aristocratic sang froid which greeted her. "Violaine, you are a de Chambon and never forget it. Many of your ancestors went to the guillotine in the French Revolution. Violent death is not unknown in our family; many more of us died in the First World War. Your father was a very brave man and I consider it our duty to honour his memory by being brave too. It is at times like these you can show the world what and who you really are."

Louise's family and neighbours on the Île St Louis had rushed to her support. She was surrounded by kindness as people did everything they could to keep her occupied. Once the initial police investigation had run its course, a huge manhunt followed but the detectives admitted the bomber had covered his traces and would be difficult to find. His widow's initial reaction of disbelief, that it was all a melodrama which would go away, soon dispersed.

Louise had lived many years with Malik in different parts of the world and life at the Hotel de Chambon continued much the same. With a courage which Violaine admired greatly, her mother insisted that they

must look to the future, not dwell morbidly on the past. Violaine had
known since she was twelve that her father moved in dangerous circles,
as her mother reminded her. "The best thing you can do, the thing he
would greatly approve, is to try and continue to fight for the better world
he sought all his life and you must try and force yourself to think always
about the future." The dignified funeral for her father in the church of
Saint Louis en l'Île, where James and Violaine had once married, helped
set a seal on the terrible events. The church had been full of important
diplomats and dignitaries whom Violaine had never seen before.

James had already told her about the groom, the scientist
Christopher Cunningham, but his bride had been quite a surprise. A
beautiful Chinese lady of uncertain age, an electronics specialist so they
said, with the lovely name of Antonia. She had looked stunning in an
elegant tailored suit of dark red silk, hair coiffured to perfection, antique
jade dragon adorning her embonpoint, her stunning diamond wedding
ring flashing brilliantly for everyone to see.

The wedding had been a fairly modest affair, at least by the
standards of cosmopolitan Paris. But it had been stylish. Everyone had
eaten a very long lunch at a French restaurant in Baker Street, a private
occasion when there were no other patrons. Even the Parisian gourmet
Violaine Heaton was pleasurably impressed by the food. London was
becoming one of the best cities in which to eat in the world. The British
would never quite catch up with the French, of course, but they were no
longer all that far behind. Much that she loved wine, the excellent
choice on offer had not interested her. With her baby due in a few of
months' time all interest had gone, but with two now to feed Violaine
had eaten like a trooper.

Even if the event had been small, the guests had been interesting.
The bride and groom both had a chance to chat to everyone at some
length which was a compliment. Antonia had shown much interest in
Violaine's own passion, the true cultural history of Islam; perhaps they

would meet up and talk about it on another occasion. At long last Violaine had met James's mystery man, Captain George Gould from the Ministry of Defence. He turned out to be medium height, medium build, medium hair, medium everything, even adorned with a regulation civil service beard. George Gould always sought to melt into the background and he succeeded triumphantly. Apart from recalling the beard, anyone sent to observe him would find it quite difficult afterwards to provide a distinctive description.

As the train passed through the hills beyond Guildford, Violaine took the email out of her handbag and read it again. It was from her old section at the Renseignements Generaux, the French Secret Service. Someone had dug out the paper she had written in back in 2010, the one which led to such a huge row with the stick-in-the-mud Arabists who worked in the service. Now someone different had read it and, at last, had seen her point. Not before time their position had been reversed.

James had told her what he knew had happened as he saw her onto her train at Waterloo. Apparently he had mentioned to Xavier de Kerguelen that Violaine's father, Malik Khalifa, had before he died given a very impressive confidential briefing. The audience had been the British prime minister and his senior government colleagues; the subject had been the Islamic Naval Alliance and its consequence; the Central Ocean Treaty Organisation. Xavier had passed this nugget of information to the French defence ministry and they had passed it to the President's office. The French were now very interested.

People at the Renseignements Generaux wondered whether Violaine could perhaps spend a day back at her old department to help them with an international jigsaw puzzle which was quickly emerging. Obviously people in the more discreet circles of Paris had suddenly decided that now was the right time to start paying attention. Although no names were mentioned, reading between lines of the email it looked as if the President of France himself, together with some senior government colleagues, now wanted to piece together the same jigsaw with the help anyone could give, following the death of Malik Khalifa. What a remarkable reversal in attitudes. Violaine suddenly felt her baby move inside her and her professional pride simultaneously took a leap forward too. Perhaps the Heatons and the Khalifas, and she was both, were starting to change the world after all.

*   *   *   *   *

The flight from Washington to Fillmore

ABIGAIL FENCEVILLE was escaping from Washington to her home town, to wallow in the reassuring company of her old friends. Her first seventeen months, her first five hundred days in the White House had been a disaster. She was beginning to wish she had never let them talk her into running for President in the first place. Planning to win millions of votes on one pre-arranged election day was one thing. Retaining that level of popular support in the face of one unexpected political calamity after another was a totally different matter.

Within just a few months of starting her term at the White House, Abigail's standing in the opinion polls had slumped to hopeless levels from which there could be no recovery. Almost certainly she would only ever be a one-term president, if she even lasted as long as that. Was her thirty-year marriage to politics destined to end in a gruelling and messy divorce?

In her election campaign two years ago, Abigail Fenceville had repeatedly promised not to arrive in Washington with a set of ignorant pre-prepared answers to big political questions. In the months since taking office, she had still not progressed beyond a set of spontaneously ignorant questions about the big political issues. Fillmore, Cheyenne and Washington DC were two worlds apart. She could get the point of a newspaper article in the Fillmore Clarion, but now she was expected by the hour to get her head round problems she had never known existed. Her ability to miss the salient point in such matters was her one unfailing characteristic.

All she could see through the window of the aircraft between Washington and Cheyenne was clouds. That felt appropriate. Abigail was now wearing jeans and a cowboy shirt. She had changed out of her presidential suit in the rest room. It was a relief not to wear make-up either. She started to read a profile about herself in Newsweek. "The nutritionists tell us we are what we eat. They must eat vast quantities of nuts in Fillmore, Cheyenne."

It was not nice. She threw down the magazine in disgust and quickly pushed away the bowl of peanuts she was nibbling. She pulled her private bottle of bourbon from her bag. President Abigail Fenceville had been drinking a lot of good Fillmore bourbon in recent months. It blanked out the horrors. Much that she loved wine, in the past year bourbon had become her closest and least questioning friend in the whole of Washington DC.

Once home in Fillmore she sought out some old friends from her days on the local newspaper, now portly men and women living in large houses. They were surprised that the President of the United States wished to revisit old haunts, but the friends she had chosen had all agreed to treat her just like they used to do. After three or four large glasses of bourbon it seemed just like old times again. Abigail was in her favourite bar in the best hotel in town and she was buying the drinks on her capacious, virtually limitless tab.

Here she could forget about budget deficits, about her scathing opponents on Capitol Hill, ignore the constant queue of persuasive people asking for favours, forget about Iran and Israel and Venezuela and China and Europe, tell herself the United Nations did not even exist.

Abby was back to being a nosy journalist and an even nosier local politician among people she trusted. After several more bourbons she was delving into the minutiae of school scandals and hospital mistakes and petty criminals and the corruption which was driving new property developments. That was the small town stuff she loved. It was the big town stuff in Washington she hated. Eventually her old journalistic friends had to carry her bodily up to her suite and put her to bed. It had been a wonderful evening.

Back in the federal capital, Jack Bunkerton and Ezekiel Watchman surveyed the bleak political landscape. Abigail was their meal ticket, their suit of armour in the snake pit of Washington and they needed to keep her in office. "Okay, Zeke, perhaps she isn't the brightest person ever to occupy the White House. No-one has been since Benjamin Franklin. I think even Jack Kennedy owned up to that. But I think she has reached the point where she will listen to almost everything we tell her, if only because she can't understand the stuff she is being told by anyone else."

Much to the distrust of her government colleagues and even more to the dislike of senior staff in the White House, Abigail had developed the habit of twice-weekly plotting sessions, in private, with Bunkerton and Watchman. It was generally known around Washington disparagingly as the Biglia Closet. Out of these private unrecorded sessions came most of the President's answers and bright ideas and it was not very difficult to work out who was running the show. In turn, Ezekiel Wachman and Jack Bunkerton had now become the two most feared men in Washington and probably the most corrupt. They were enjoying their power and most reluctant to give it up. In any case there was always a possibility of impeachment which could best be avoided by staying in office.

"Abby has to stay in office, Jack. Apart from anything else, Dan Weisstein could never take over. We'd then have to do a Spiro Agnew and get rid of him first." Vice-president Dan Weisstein was the incurably ordinary running-mate they had chosen for Abigail, a colourless Republican from Pennsylvania who could be relied upon never steal her thunder. In the election campaign Weisstein had been given some worthy if vacuous speech material and told to go away and support candidates in parts of the country where they never stood much chance. As Speaker of the Senate he had proved himself to be unoriginal, uncomprehending and unconvincing. Ryker Pardrey had been unstinting in his criticism.

Dan's appearances on television had been completely embarrassing. His heartfelt pronouncements on America's best interests had been the source of endless merriment around the journalistic drinking haunts of Washington. The pastime of devising brand new Weissaphorisms was even more widespread than that of devising quotes attributable to Sam Goldwyn. Vice-president Dan Quayle had been a monument to unsurpassable American intellect when compared with the inimitable Daniel Weisstein.

By general consensus the ludicrous vice-president was the hapless president's most effective insurance policy for remaining in office. The double act of Mississippi machiavellis had it all worked out. Abigail Fenceville was their lifetime meal ticket, all the way from their insignificant lowly-paid jobs in Fillmore Cheyenne in the early years. She had reversed their fortunes to those of prosperous and celebrated retirement travelling around the world in the lap of luxury and seeing out their time in expensive, exclusive, enclosed estates on Cape Cod.

* * * * *

Westminster, London

THE MOOD AT Conservative Party headquarters was sombre. The opposition Labour Party under its young leader Alan Stanley had fought a masterly campaign in the General Election. Early exit poll results from key marginal constituencies were indicating a poor turnout, especially for the Conservatives. It seemed the Liberal Democratic vote had totally collapsed. There was not much to cheer about that evening for either party in the Coalition which had governed Britain with difficulty for the previous five years.

Prime Minister David Cameron was being philosophical. "I always said I would prefer to serve one effective term as Prime Minister, even if the British people did not particularly like what I had to do, than to spin it out like Tony Blair with one political gimmick after another while the country went to hell in a basket." He turned to his Chancellor of the Exchequer, George Osborne. "I do feel particularly strongly for you, George. You were pitched into the worst economic crisis this country had seen for decades and if Stanley and his populist rabble of opportunists win tonight, you will be handing them once again the strongest economy in the civilised west."

The title Chancellor of the Exchequer, as the United Kingdom quaintly labelled its finance minister, was an ancient title. The earliest known was Hervey de Stanton, who took the office in 1316 and held it for eleven years. Few modern politicians could survive it as long as that. For the previous five years George Osborne had done so, resisting demands on all sides to scrap his debt-reduction policies and take the easy spendthrift option instead.

The Chancellor had stood his ground, the economy had gradually recovered and in the eyes of agencies which rated the strength of a country's finance and its economy, the United Kingdom was once again robust. The political backwash of that in the chancelleries of Europe was not to be overlooked. The key to diplomatic influence was to be riding on the back of a powerful economic steed. In the eyes of continental Europe the British coalition government seemed to be riding Bucephalus. For all that, it still looked as if Osborne's reward for all his persistence would be removal from office over the weekend, handing his venerable post to one of Alan Stanley's northern cronies. No doubt the wave of populist sentiments which the Labour Party had been riding throughout the campaign would wash into the Treasury. Osborne's senior government colleagues knew his worst fears: government extravagance on vote-catching projects would return with a vengeance. Taxes and yet more piles of borrowing would be spent once again as if money grew on trees. The electorate would be bribed with the proceeds of borrowing, creating debts to be bequeathed to their children.

The two leading Conservatives were joined by William Hague. The Foreign Secretary returned from the television suite in the corner where he had been putting the best gloss he could on the evening's events. His modulated South Yorkshire accent - he still pronounced 'look' the same way as 'luck' - was a way of showing the electorate that the Conservatives could supply cuddly northerners too. And bald ones at that. Provocatively he was wearing a lapel badge saying 'DECLYND' only his was coloured blue rather than red.

Yet despite the show of political bravado his party had been massacred in Cheshire, Lancashire, Yorkshire, Nottingham and Derbyshire. Just as Alan Stanley had intended, Labour had reclaimed those northern fastnesses as its own. William Hague had been unable to say on television what he really wanted to say. Together with the Prime Minister and the Minister of Defence he had been given a confidential briefing over a year earlier on a new global balance of power.

It had been organised by a senior civil servant, Peter Storey, who had introduced a shadowy figure from the Ministry of Defence called George Gould and a remarkable Saudi Arabian diplomat called Malik Khalifa, who had apparently been murdered for his efforts. It had quickly emerged that the late Dr Khalifa had been the invisible source of two thought-provoking memoranda which had done the rounds of Whitehall at Top Secret level. In the briefing the former Saudi diplomat confirmed everyone's worst fears. The Sino-Islamic alliance called the Central Ocean Treaty Organisation, COTO, announced by Beijing and

Riyadh was not as peace-loving as had been proclaimed. Malik Khalifa had himself been involved in some of the negotiations and had done so in the hope the alliance would draw the international Islamic community away from the militancy fostered by his countryman Osama bin Laden. Instead COTO was to be a rallying point to pose a military challenge to the Western alliance and at that point Dr Khalifa had decided to pull out.

William Hague had articulated everyone's fears at the meeting when he summarised the position. "One has to agree their timing is masterly. In Washington we have a President whose grasp of international affairs is almost non-existent. I doubt Abigail Fenceville can tell the difference between politicians who move mountains and those who just throw dirt. It begins to look as if this weekend the British people will elect a prime minister who shares her outlook.

"In other words, the binding force of the western alliance will now be a rope of sand and we have been unable to say anything about it in public. The last thing we need is foreign policy being shaped by a couple of doctrinaire pacifists and their ill-informed henchmen. The Chinese must be beside themselves with delight. Once they read these British election results they will be popping the champagne corks in the Forbidden City. The western democracies have played straight into their hands. Everything they said about the fatal flaws of a system which buys people's votes with their own money has, in their eyes, been totally vindicated." William Hague could not be bettered on political theory.

Over at Labour Party headquarters the mood was jubilant. Both main parties used the same tried and tested computer programmes and their projections for the night's result were closely matched. Alan Stanley was convinced he had carried the country; even if it did not look like a political landslide, the indicators showed he would have an overall working majority when parliament re-assembled. During the election campaign the Labour leader had kept rigorously to the script drafted by his closest advisers, Steve Wilson and Graham Crowfield, eighteen months previously when they had masterminded the coup that won him leadership of his party. "Just remember, Alan, you are not trying to win every single vote in the country. You are not even trying to win votes from diehard Conservatives. You are trying to do two things. You are looking to assure our rank and file Labour supporters that our cause is right and that the Tories are wrong; or rather that our cause is somewhat more convincing than theirs. Just that. Keep it simple. You are then looking to sow doubts in the minds of the Tory fringe. That's all you need to win. We want their people to stay at home on election day and we want our people to turn out in droves."

Steve Wilson had devoted many years to the study of political behaviour, ever since his days at university. "Elections are always won on the difference in turn-out by the supporters of the two main parties. Hardly anyone changes their political mind on the doorstep, no matter how hard our canvassers try to convince them of our superior wisdom. That's not how it works. People whose political thoughts are so shallow they flap around like washing on a windy day are unlikely to vote anyway. Be they Tories or Labour, most voters are long-standing supporters of their parties who are unlikely to be persuaded otherwise. We are fighting for polling booth abstentions, not for votes. Your task is to make Cameron and his public school cronies lose their nerve and their supporters will then follow suit."

It only ever took a couple of pints of beer and Steve Wilson was galloping away on one of his favourite political hobby-horses, the theory and practice of winning general elections. "Always be reasonable, especially on television. Agree with the other side whenever you can. Always keep away from doctrine. Exude commonsense, but commonsense with a clear purpose.

"Remember Labour has always won and only ever won, when it has captured the detachable fringe from the main party opposite. That should be the limit of your ambitions and it is good enough to put you into Ten Downing Street. "Remember what Harold Wilson always used to say: "politics is the battle for the middle ground.' Better yet, it is the battle to spread waves of apathy on one side of the party line and waves of enthusiasm on the other."

With some misgivings, Alan Stanley had also borrowed some of the debating ploys used to such effect by Abigail Fenceville in the American elections two years previously. "Look," he told over-inquisitive television interviewers. "You keep asking me for detailed policies when I reach Downing Street.

You seem to overlook that I shall arrive in Whitehall with a clean slate. It is quite true I've never served in a government before, but I understand better than most how the political machine works. There is no greater waste of time that some incoming learner prime minister marching into Downing Street determined to teach the civil service how to go about its own business.

"I am much too experienced a politician to try anything like that. The minute I arrive in the Cabinet Room I will be surrounded by some of the finest political and diplomatic minds this country has to offer. The job of a clever politician is to be able to ask the hard questions, the tricky questions, the questions the civil servants would rather not hear. Don't ask me to arrive with a set of pre-prepared cleverdick answers to all of them. Only a fool thinks he knows the answer to everything. The professional duty of the civil service is to provide the information we need and our professional duty as politicians is to weigh up their advice."

If Alan Stanley was reassuringly open-minded on economic policies and other domestic issues, he was wholly determined when it came to defence. During the election campaign he had been asked several times about the new military alliance in the Indian Ocean and each time dismissed it. "It will be just the same as NATO. Those military clubs only exist to keep generals and admirals feeling important. They never fight any wars. "I don't think I am going to lose much sleep over COTO, NATO, SEATO any more than I will over lose sleep over polo or bingo. Military alliances are just an excuse for grown-up men to play silly games with big boys' toys. I think you will find I can save the public finances a lot of money once we begin to look at the books. My view is simple. It is a lot of men in fancy uniforms dreaming up non-existent wars just to persuade us to build lots of expensive missiles, ships and aeroplanes. I wasn't born yesterday."

By breakfast time on Friday the result of the May 2015 General Election was confirmed. David Cameron called Buckingham Palace and in a short audience with the Queen handed over his seals of office. While staff packed away the Cameron's possessions, Alan Stanley was already holding an initial meeting with the Cabinet Secretary.

The three top jobs in his Cabinet, those of Foreign Secretary, Chancellor of the Exchequer and Justice Minister were handed to his closest political friends Steve Wilson, Graham Crowfield and Brian Potter. The office of Deputy Prime Minister was scrapped. Alan Stanley thought he had it all worked out. But not quite.

Almost under his breath, the Cabinet Secretary Sir Anthony Pilkington quietly uttered a word the brand new Prime Minister had never heard before. The word was "Kundalini." The civil servant explained: "I can assure you Prime Minister, it is all perfectly standard procedure. The previous government went into the matter in great detail. Although nothing could be said in parliament, obviously, we have kept their file which sets out all the facts. It really sits in the same area of policy as the secret instructions for ministers in charge of the nuclear deterrent. In fact the two are closely linked."

Sir Anthony Pilkington, Cabinet Secretary, the most senior civil servant in the country, was returning to a matter he had raised at his original meeting with the new Prime Minister. He handed Alan Johnson a file. It was titled, simply, "Kundalini". It was also marked "Top Secret". Alan Stanley idly flipped through its pages. "I haven't time now to read all this in detail. Can you possibly tell me in a few simple words what exactly it is all about?" The Cabinet Secretary was well prepared with his answer.

"Certainly, Prime Minister. I'm sure you will fully understand that we cannot let any Tom, Dick or Harry serve on Britain's nuclear submarines. In fact the attack submarines are even more demanding than those carrying the nuclear deterrent. We now have four Astute class submarines in service, practically brand new and they are an electronic box of tricks. Three more are on the way to completion. Their crews have to pass all kinds of aptitude tests before they are even allowed on board."

"Such as what? And what has this to do with me?"

"It all depends on the level of seniority. The Chief Petty Officer grade who actually press the buttons have to work with precision and thoughtfulness under severe pressure. We can test for that. The officers in charge have to pass even more rigorous tests. They must be able to handle unexpected information at high speed, calculate its implications and give appropriate orders, all in a matter of a second or so.

"Modern warfare is as much about speed of action as sheer weight of arms. The same goes for commanding officers right up the line. That then includes ministers in a situation like COBRA, when we use the Cabinet Office Briefing Room, or even God forbid in a full-scale war Cabinet. We don't anticipate that at this moment, but sense dictates that we need to be prepared in advance, because should it ever come to that we could not do the necessary training at the drop of a hat."

"Are you saying that is the kind of test I and my senior ministers must also undergo? Is that what this? He inspected the file again, "Kundalini" is all about? Aptitude tests? Surely the very fact we have been elected by the people of this country is sufficient qualification for us to run Britain's warfare activities?" The civil servant replied "Not quite, prime minister. Your predecessors, a little unwillingly at first, did agree to undergo the Kundalini assessment. However when Prime Minister Cameron saw the results he was surprised, but quick enough to see the sense of it all. It was he who built it into the system so that all his ministers in sensitive positions and all subsequent ministers with such responsibilities should go through the same procedure. It is after all for the good of our country."

"Oh, all right then. How long does it take? And what does it involve?" The Cabinet secretary was ready for this. "I think you will find, Prime Minister, that it turns out to be rather more enjoyable than it sounds. You will go in small groups to an unmarked testing centre near the North Circular where they have all the equipment. I can assure you the tests are actually arranged by a most impressive Chinese woman called Antonia Cunningham."

"Chinese. How interesting, especially a Chinese woman with a British name. Are you sure we can trust her, to be 100% on our side, I mean?" Anthony Pilkington examined the file. "She has a doctorate from Imperial College, London and has worked on Kundalini for several years. It has become her personal baby. She is married to the managing director of the testing centre. Surely there can be no more reliable guarantee than that.

"I have no doubt she will explain exactly what they test for and how it all works. I think you will find her most engaging. I did, when they used me as a Kundalini guinea-pig a couple of years ago. I found it fascinating, learnt things about myself I never knew before. That's always useful knowledge. And she's an interesting woman. Good-looking too. I gather she is almost exactly the same age as American's President Fenceville. It would be hard to imagine two women who have so little in common."

The Cabinet Secretary was well-briefed on Antonia. Especially working with red-blooded politicians like Alan Stanley and his team, she was in a position to deliver some very useful data, rather more than any man might do. "It's worth pointing out Antonia Cunningham is British by deliberate choice, not just by birth. Originally she worked in China running an engineering centre but fell out, I understand, with the Chinese view of the world and reversed her loyalties.

"If you get into conversation with her I think you will find she regards modern China as the world's latest colonialist power. But like many Chinese the only way she can express her deep-rooted disagreement is to leave her country. " I think you will find her more pro-British than almost anyone you've ever met."

"Well that's all right then. When can we start? The sooner it's over and done with the better. Anyway I actually want to know how my own ministers score. You know, see if I chose the right ones." His mandarin agreed. "It should certainly do that, Prime Minister. With your permission I'll advise your diary secretary of what's in store, we'll find a suitable slot and take it from there."

Several days later the prime ministerial Jaguar drove Alan Stanley and his defence secretary Desmond Brightside to Park Royal. They were met at the main entrance by Dr Christopher Cunningham and his deputy Dr Martin Barraclough. Smart dark suits and silk ties were, unusually, the dress code of the day; the usual garb at the centre was jeans and tee-shirts, often with catchy slogans. Barraclough, who came originally from Doncaster, generally favoured one which read "You can always tell a Yorkshireman, but you can't tell him much."

There was little outside to identify the premises but above the Reception area there was now a legend which said Park Royal Advanced Electronics Limited complete with a PRAEL logo. It had been erected that morning. There was no need to expose politicians to the existence of the Sharava Corporation.

The two scientists led the prime minister, the defence secretary and their security officer to a small conference room where coffee was served. The door opened once more and in walked a stunning Chinese lady, her attire, make-up and hair were that of a very sophisticated woman. Alan Stanley looked up in frank admiration. "I'd like to introduce my wife, Dr Antonia Cunningham, Prime Minister. She is our in-house expert on Kundalini and will take you through the various routines this morning.

"Antonia, perhaps you should let the Prime Minister in on our secret." Antonia had been thoroughly briefed never to mention the name Sharava. With little ado, she launched straight into her usual spiel about how the programme worked. "Although the work here goes back a number of years, I myself have specialised in Kundalini since 2011. I'm sure you are familiar with the way ideas about intelligence have developed since the old days of testing schoolchildren aged eleven." Alan Stanley recoiled at that, the bête-noire of Labour Party doctrine on education for over fifty years.

"The understanding of how the brain works has come a long way since the eleven plus. We now recognise many different kinds of intelligence. Seventy years ago they only bothered to measure logical deduction. Now we can also measure spatial awareness, verbal faculty, creative intuition, mathematical insight, analytical prediction, what they now call EQ or human empathy, all kinds of quite distinct mental skills. Antonia could read her audience like a book. Christopher had told her all about the agonised attitudes to education among British politicians.

To keep them contented she went on "Every one of us has our own unique cocktail of all those different abilities. We try to measure each of them here with Kundalini so we can develop an individual profile. Let me assure you straight away there is no such thing as a pass or a fail on this assessment. Mainly we have been measuring military officers for their ability to absorb unexpected information rapidly, sort it into a coherent pattern and propose a best next step and do all that within a matter of a second or so. I'm sure you would agree that kind of knee-jerk thinking is not necessarily a skill we would be looking for in a prime minister or a defence secretary." Alan Stanley and Desmond Brightside both smiled at this generous observation. They were both men who liked to ponder a situation, sometimes for weeks on end, before deciding on a next best step. Perhaps this was not going to be intellectual torment after all.

The prime minister was warming to the really rather gorgeous Antonia Cunningham by the minute as she continued "what we shall do is this. Next door we have a comfortable suite with two computer stations, one for each of you. You will work side by side and you are free to discuss the on-screen questions at any time.

"Strictly speaking it is not a race, but we shall be looking at both the nature of your response and the timing of your response. Everyone who does this Kundalini assessment finds some bits easy and some bits quite the opposite. That is the whole point of it, as we build a profile of your natural intelligences. As I said, no two people are quite alike."

For the next hour, prime minister and defence secretary worked away at the Kundalini questionnaire. As Antonia had correctly predicted, they found some parts easier than others. The questions came in a random order and it was sometimes quite difficult to guess which particular type of intelligence they were testing. By the time it was all over both politicians felt exhausted and wanted to know whether the staff facilities included a bar. "I think we can rise to that." said Christopher Cunningham. "Gentlemen, come up to my own office. I'm pretty sure I can find you something a little stronger than coffee."

* * * * *

Ministry of Defence, Whitehall

THE SECURE TELEPHONE rang on George Gould's desk. It was the deputy permanent secretary to the Ministry of Defence, Peter Storey. To the extent that George had a reporting line at all, Peter was it. "George, you've already seen the Kundalini results for Stanley and

Brightside. Not many have, but those of us in Whitehall who have read them are extremely concerned. It appears those two political leaders of ours instinctively swing back and forth between something tantamount to gung-ho bravado and then back again to unreconstructed cowardice like some discombobulated pendulum."

"Do they ever come to rest anywhere conventional, such as half way between?" asked George Gould. "Only by accident," replied Peter Storey, "and then not for very long. Those tests they've devised at Sharava are chillingly revealing ... George, are you still there? You don't sound remotely surprised."

George Gould was forthright, as usual. "Of course I'm not surprised, Peter. They're just a couple of politicians. What did you expect? Mind you, when they tested some of the top brass in the armed forces, their scores weren't exactly scintillating either. Just be thankful we haven't been near a nuclear confrontation recently."

"It's all very well you taking the light-hearted view, George, but over at the Cabinet Office several very important people are starting to hop up and down with, well, almost with what one might *in extremis* call agitation. That means we must be agitated too. The Cabinet secretary has asked both of us to join him in a meeting at three to decide what we should do about it. The First Sea Lord will attend as well. You do have a tie with you today, don't you?"

No top-level meeting of civil servants could function without cups of tea and biscuits, it helped them think. In the navy they once served themselves pink gins for the same purpose, while in the upper echelons of the City in good years it was champagne. In Fleet Street, beer and wine were equally conducive to strenuous mental effort. In Oxford senior common rooms by tradition it was sherry.

Once the Whitehall tea ceremony was completed, the Cabinet Secretary Sir Anthony Pilkington made it clear that high levels of intellectual athleticism were expected that afternoon. He looked expectantly at George Gould, who promptly asked for another cup. George had more or less anticipated the content of the meeting and prepared his answers as he strolled along Whitehall. It was time for a brief history lesson. "The reason Christopher Cunningham and I dreamt up Kundalini seven years ago was because of the interesting gizmo they had developed at Sharava for watching the opposition's split-second military decisions simultaneously.

We decided any British naval officer analysing two operations rooms had to be able to pat his head and rub his stomach at the same time. Kundalini was originally developed to test for the mental equivalent of that ability. It is distinctive and really quite rare. We soon found we needed very similar talents in effective officers of the SAS. Nor is it dissimilar to what we require of our air traffic controllers. Or for that matter a Formula 1 driver, or even a top international tennis player with the ability to out-think his or her opponent. And the more we looked into it beyond that, the more we realised that Kundalini could test all sorts of different thinking ability.

"One must bear in mind that scientific ideas about intelligence are developing apace all the time. Nowadays it is more sensible to see each of us as a unique cocktail of all kinds of different mental abilities. It's no longer just a matter of scoring pass or fail in deductive logic like they used to do in the old eleven plus.

"The fact that Alan Stanley and Desmond Brightside would make lousy battlefield commanders or totally screw up a naval confrontation should not over-concern us. That's never going to be their job. To be charitable I'm sure Kundalini must have uncovered different positive abilities when they were tested. Typically, successful politicians score pretty highly on emotional intelligence, what some people call EQ rather than IQ. Let's all focus our attention on that instead." George looked at the Cabinet Secretary while grey and balding heads round the table nodded sagely. Perhaps they had all just been rescued by Whitehall's

intellectual equivalent of the sixth cavalry, who continued "May I
suggest you tell the Prime Minister that the Kundalini tests on him and
the Defence Secretary were in fact extremely successful? Tell him that
the technology of measurement is all rather complicated, which saves
you having to go into any embarrassing detail. Tell him the analysis
shows they are ideally qualified for the top jobs in politics, very different
from being battlefield commanders. I rather doubt they will take much
personal umbrage at that."

Sir Anthony simultaneously pursed his mouth and sucked in his
breath at this remarkable reversal of the truth. Then he looked once
again at the Top Secret report before him and slowly began to nod.
"May I take it, Captain Gould, you have an ulterior motive in this quite
unprecedented exercise in re-writing recent history?"

Whitehall's reclusive schemer smiled, as was his involuntary habit
when about to triumph in an argument. "I have been wondering about
our friends on the other side of the Atlantic." Almost everyone else
winced. "You mean that appalling woman Abigail Fenceville? What on
earth has this to do with her, for heaven's sake?" asked the First Sea
Lord somewhat intemperately.

"It's very simple" George Gould responded. "As matters stand,
whether we like it or not, that appalling woman - as you put it - still has
her finger on the nuclear button. The incumbent President is always
Uncle Sam's Commander-in-Chief. I would sleep the happier at night,
as I am sure would all of you, the greater the distance we can put
between her finger and that button."

"Exactly what do you have in mind, George?" asked Peter Storey.
George Gould felt he was now on the home straight. "I think if your
chaps in the Cabinet Office all finesse it properly, you could turn our Mr
Stanley into a splendid ambassador for Kundalini. I understand he is
planning an early trip to Washington, to dance yet another variation of
that diplomatic pasadoble, the splendid Special Relationship." Now it

was the First Sea Lord's turn to wince at mention of the Special Relationship. The military memory had far too many scars. So far as he was concerned personally the Special Relationship was the unedifying offspring of a brief romantic encounter between the Statue of Liberty and some Will o' the Wisp. The Americans needed to be kept firmly under control, not generously fed grapes peeled one at a time.

Meantime the Cabinet Secretary was more concerned that George Gould seemed to know everything before it was general knowledge in Whitehall. Only three people in London, so far as he knew, were aware that a trip for the prime minister to Washington was even being discussed. Captain Gould now made that four. "Pray do continue" the country's most senior civil servant requested.

As requested, so George Gould continued. "Well, it occurs to me that right now that woman Abigail Fenceville would welcome anything, absolutely anything, which suggests she is, after all, a worthy person to be President, if not perhaps America's Commander-in-Chief.

"There are many in Washington who dispute whether she should be in the White House at all. Suppose, just suppose, we could persuade her to take a Kundalini test, and do so at her own request. We could perhaps show her she had some genuine presidential credentials, which would enormously boost her morale.

"But we could also show her that, just like our friends Messrs Stanley and Brightside, she should stand aside from any speedy military decision-making. She might just go for that and, anyway, she can hardly pick the bits of Kundalini she welcomes, then reject all the rest. It is an indivisible package, not some à la carte menu."

The Cabinet Secretary harrumphed positively at this, the Whitehall stag at bay. His department approved of indivisible packages on principle. They were a way of keeping control. George Gould smiled again and proceeded effortlessly to his coup de grâce. "We then might very well find ourselves in the fortunate position of having someone in charge in Washington who would not only keep her pretty little nose out of defence matters, but even relish that prospect. Once dear Abigail has been Kundalinied, on balance we would then be better off if, far from moving on, she stayed exactly where she is. A totally un-military US president is just what we would surely prefer.

"On the principle that better the devil that you know than the devil you don't, Abigail Fenceville, far from being an appalling woman, now becomes our secret weapon. She becomes the US president who has abdicated the function of Commander-in-Chief. Surely that must be the ultimate dream of America's chiefs of staff.

"Oval Office amateur generals and admirals indulging their favourite pastime of homespun war games are the very last thing the Pentagon wants. Especially when the tempo of global military activity goes from stone cold even as far as mildly lukewarm. It seems to me that if things started to warm up seriously around COTO, Abigail Fenceville is precisely the White House woman power all of us would prefer. Does anyone happen to know the female equivalent of a complete and utter eunuch?" George Gould even smiled slightly at his own spontaneous aphorism.

The meeting had opened in a sprit of dejection. All thanks to the contribution of the ministry's master of military disinformation, it broke up an hour later in the closest such top-level meetings ever came to unbridled joviality.

Chapter Fourteen

Manoeuvres

Washington DC

FRANK SAUCISSON, Attorney-General of the United States, was one of the few members of the Fenceville administration who had not started his career as a used-car salesman in Fillmore, Cheyenne. Or so the Washington Post had worked out. He was instead a wit, whose favourite remoulded motto was "Ich bin ein Frankfurter". Sadly fewer and fewer people realised the saying, or something remarkably similar and equally edible, was over fifty years old. But the Washington Post's headline-writers had understood the multiple joke straight away.

Frank was also a graduate of Yale and a highly successful lawyer. Often when explaining complexities he would use legalese which went straight over the head of America's first lady. Abigail Fenceville had christened this professional patois 'Sanskrit' because Zeke Watchman once told her only Hindu priests ever spoke that obscure language and it was quite meaningless to the ordinary Indians of their day. As a native of the state of Cheyenne herself, Abigail always took sympathy on ordinary Indians no matter which state they came from.

Frank was on his way from a busy morning meeting with chiefs of the defence staff and senior civil servants at the State Department. Abigail Fenceville's appointed Secretary of State Ezekiel Watchman had been totally unaware of the meeting. His civil servants generally found things worked out much more efficiently if he was not involved. Its undeclared agenda had been to discuss moving the US Fifth Fleet from its current base in Bahrain some two thousand five hundred miles east to a new home in Trincomalee, Sri Lanka.

The reason for the relocation was simple. Following the revelation of INA and COTO, the Pentagon no longer felt quite so secure keeping a prime military asset right under the noses of the opposition. "Daniel may well have sauntered into the Lion's Den," explained one of the Pentagon's senior military, "but so far as I am aware even he didn't smear himself all over with top grade lion bait before going in. We are simply asking for it."

Much of the meeting had been spent considering the political repercussions. How much loss of face had it created for the Gulf states in general and Bahrain in particular? How threatened would the Sri Lankans now feel if they were suddenly giving house room to arguably the juiciest military target for several thousand miles? No country wanted their local harbour to become Pearl Harbour Mark II. There were other more positive considerations too. The benefit to the host country of tens of thousands of sailors spending their paychecks, plus the buying power of quartermasters provisioning the fleet, would become a much-prized economic boost in a comparatively poor country such as Sri Lanka.

For all that, the greatest impact was on military strategy. The lawyer from Yale viewed it in a long term historical perspective, and his argument was persuasive. The focus of strategic concern in the Indian Ocean had been moving steadily eastwards for a century. It had begun with the strategic importance of the British sea route to India, enhanced with the opening in 1869 of the Suez Canal. That waterway was the ultimate target of the war fought between Montgomery and Rommel in the western desert in World War Two.

Until 1937 Britain had been content to leave the natural harbour settlement of Aden, as a well-positioned port of call on the Arabian peninsula, to function as a protectorate of India which was where the ships were bound. Then sensing the way the political wind was blowing, and sensing the growing economic dependence on oil transported through the canal, that year Britain detached Aden from India. Instead it now became a full crown colony administered directly from the Commonwealth Office in London. The local sultans were never happy with the arrangement and it survived only until 1967, when Aden was granted independence. That was one major component of a "nothing east of Suez" policy devised and being implemented by a late 1960s government in London.

Frank Saucisson, Yale lawyer and an amateur numerologist with a keen eye for patterns, was much amused by all the sevens. Someone in London had evidently been trusting to luck. Aden had probably been the last British colony to come into existence. The first colony to be granted its independence by Britain was the Gold Coast, which became Ghana in 1957. The last British colony to be handed over was Hong Kong in 1997 in an elaborate ceremony with the Royal Yacht Britannia. Along the road, in 1947 India had been granted its independence. This was the gift of Britain's first-ever majority socialist government, the largest-ever single step in dismantling the old British Empire. King George VI, crowned in 1937, remained Emperor of India for the first ten years of his reign only. The game of sevens apart, by the time of its independence Britain's trade route to India was no longer quite the concern it has been for over a century. Now there was a new strategic game to play instead. And that game was oil, a global cat and mouse exercise colloquially known as the Big Game. The very narrow Straits of Hormuz which joined the Gulf to the open ocean became a serious military concern with the independence of Gulf states such as Iran. Oil was now king, which is why American had based the US Navy's Fifth Fleet permanently in Bahrain.

Yet even that concern was steadily being overshadowed by the strategic importance of the Straits of Malacca. Sandwiched between the Malaysian peninsula of mainland Asia and the island of Sumatra, that narrow waterway commanded the vital sea route between China and the open expanses of the Indian ocean. Trincomalee thus emerged as the obvious choice for relocating America's Fifth Fleet. It offered a large friendly harbour ideal for keeping a handle on that increasingly sensitive maritime link with the Pacific.

Even the US Navy had to move with the times and that had been the outcome of the meeting at the State Department. Once the decision had been taken some advantages immediately became clear. Sri Lanka's naval facilities at Trincomalee would be ideal, especially once they were modernised by the Americans. The base would be located in one of the finest natural harbours in the Indian Ocean. Even better, US Navy personnel would find shore leave around the oriental pleasures of Sri Lanka rather more to their liking than the austere offerings of the Gulf.

At the same time America's nuclear aircraft carriers had been shuffled. The USS Carl Vinson had recently joined the Fifth Fleet and by a substantial margin become the largest warship anywhere in the Indian Ocean. It replaced the pioneering USS Enterprise which was to be retired after fifty years of service. American nuclear aircraft carriers could be as venerable as that.

The Pentagon had been alerted by the British to a new kind of military threat when a brand new Chinese Advance class destroyer tested France's diplomatic tolerance with another visit to Amsterdam Island. It had sailed from Belawan in Indonesia, well within radar range of where the US Fifth Fleet would have been. Suddenly the Pentagon woke up to the prospect that a quite different kind of military challenge was about to unfold. It would no longer be the Fifth Fleet's primary rôle to support land engagements around the oil fields of the Gulf. The arrival of the Chinese destroyer opened up the very different prospect of seaborne engagements for the Fifth Fleet almost anywhere in the Indian Ocean. How should the USA military respond to that?

Thanks to the meeting in the State Department, America's response would be shown to be positive and speedy. Uncle Sam was on the ball, as the Fifth Fleet was to be sent with all despatch on a recreational cruise exploring the strategic stretches of the ocean. It was old-fashioned gunboat diplomacy, only now in a variant which used far more ships. The Pentagon could surely find some plausible excuse for the tour. After all was what they were paid to do. Let Beijing know that even on the opposite side of the globe from its home in Norfolk Virginia, the United States Navy was still a force to be reckoned with.

It had been a fruitful morning's meeting at the State Department and Frank had thoroughly enjoyed himself. But now there was another task in hand, and it necessitated a trip to the White House. One of the State Department civil servants had relayed some interesting intelligence from the department's semi-resident British defence attaché.

It concerned some clever British technology called Kundalini. Apparently this was a whole bag of tricks which measured different sorts of intelligence. Originally designed to assess the capabilities of Britain's front-line military officers, it had subsequently been used to great effect on top brass in the armed forces and also on some very senior British politicians. The general idea was too see whether it would be equally useful on the American side of the Atlantic.

The results in Britain had been most encouraging. The politicians themselves, though wary at first, had found the exercise fascinating and the outcome rewarding. Kundalini confirmed they were the right people to be top politicians, while the very different duties of a battlefield commander could be sensibly left to people with an entirely different mix of abilities. This did open up some new questions. Who, in a tense military situation, should be taking top-level day-by-day, sometimes hour-by-hour decisions? Where was the boundary between political judgement and military expertise now to be drawn? How far should the politicians become involved, if indeed they should be involved at all?

In Whitehall the behind-the-scenes secret testing with Kundalini was regarded as a victory for commonsense, particularly with someone like Alan Stanley in ultimate charge in Downing Street. The State Department, so far without alerting Ezekiel Watchman, could see some interesting possibilities if Kundalini were to be now deployed in the White House as well.

For once, president Abigail Fenceville was ahead of her Attorney-General. "Oh I know all about that Kunda thing already. Alan Stanley told me everything when we met a week ago." Frank Saucisson nodded meekly. Perhaps the filly from Fillmore was not quite so stupid after all. He asked the President for her opinion. "To be honest Frank, it all sounded like a really good idea. Alan said it proved he was a good politician but would have been an unsuccessful battlefield commander. That didn't upset him in the slightest. It simply confirmed he had chosen the right career. He also suggested it might be no bad idea if we did the same thing here in Washington. Now Frank, I realise it was only a first meeting but I do like Alan Stanley and I trust him. He talks my kind of political language.

"So if you are about to suggest we try this, er, what's it called?" "Abby, its called Kundalini." Abigail Fenceville waved a triumphant forearm, complete with clenched fist. "That's right, that's exactly what Alan said, 'Kundalini'. Let's try it out on some of my top people here in Washington. I would be all in favour of that. Just like it did in London it would prove that we are the right people in the right jobs. It would prove I made the right choices for my top team. That would be my final answer to all those sarcastic scribblers at the Washington Post, whatever they say to the contrary. She who laughs last, laughs best."

Frank Saucisson smiled; the President was becoming quite literary minded as her period in office matured. He had also recently read an FBI file on Abigail's recent drinking jaunt to Fillmore, Cheyenne. Just a few weeks ago she had been in the slough of despond. Now it seems the consumption of generous volumes of good bourbon had transformed her morale. She was showing some first signs of actually enjoying her time in the Oval office, being on top of things, even being one jump ahead of her clever Attorney-General. Things were looking up.

*   *   *   *   *

Ministry of National Defence, Beijing

THE SECURE TELEPHONE rang on Zhou Man's desk. The call was from vice-premier Liu Fun, his mentor and guide through the labyrinthine politics of the Forbidden City. "Zhou Man, you've read the reports coming in from the Indian Ocean, of course. Not many people have, but a number of people at high level in the government are extremely irritated by them. It appears the Americans are trying to steal a march on us, and we cannot allow them to get away with it.

"I have been asked to arrange a meeting with our senior officials in defence and colleagues from the Ministry of Foreign Affairs. The Chairman of the Central Military Commission will be present, and the deputy premier also wishes to stay informed. He will probably be there in person. My instructions are we need to draft our nation's response, and also more privately to decide our next moves.

"I suggest you come well prepared to answer questions about our current naval strength in the Indian Ocean, as the West likes to call it, and make sure you are fully briefed on any recent developments in COTO. Today might be you big opportunity. You've worked hard enough for it over the years." Not only was the deputy premier present, he also chaired the meeting. After a suitably decorous tea sipping ceremony, he came quickly to the point.

"Overnight we have received some disturbing reports from one of our warships in the Indian Ocean. Admiral Zhou, please convey the government's gratitude to your officers for informing us so promptly. It is a measure of the high morale in your fleet that its officers do not flinch from reporting the unwelcome news as well as the good. It is very patriotic to do so, whatever all those silly flag-wavers may try to maintain otherwise. I wish I could say the same for all our state agencies.

"Allow me to summarise the position and please, comrades, if there is anything you wish to add do not hesitate to raise it. We are holding this meeting in order to share our thinking and to share our ideas. No one of us, I suspect, has all the answers on his or her own. This is to be a collective effort.

"The Americans have strengthened their Fifth Fleet and, as we now know, are moving its base from Bahrain to Sri Lanka. That is not without significance. A military force which was originally intended to protect their oil supplies from the Gulf is now in a position on the eastern side of the ocean to challenge our own supply routes rather than protect theirs. More than that, they have commenced naval exercises around the Straits of Malacca. That could well be perceived by us as a calculated act of aggression.

"Before I move to the military and global implications of all this, I would first like to say something about its wider political and historical significance. Because today, comrades, we are going to discuss the next great stride in China's Long March. That great advance began in 1949, to repair the damage done in previous times. It has not been an easy march, and it has already taken sixty-seven years, a lifetime. No matter. Here in China we are justifiably proud of our ability to take the long view. Yet although our march has been long, it has always been moving

in the same direction. Unlike our occasional friends beyond Mongolia."
The Chinese deputy premier was now in his element. Traditional
rivalries did not disconcert him at all. He could shuffle the awkward
realities of history with an aplomb which would leave objective historians
gasping with admiration.

As with many of his generation, his power and influence at the
very heart of the Chinese government did not depend on popular votes
through the ballot box, as did the power of his opposite numbers in the
West. His power depended on his intellectual mastery of world history,
on his apparent power to interpret events. It depended on the approval
and admiration of knowledgeable and perceptive colleagues. He was bent
on reconfirming that approval rating today.

The deputy premier could paint an impressive global picture. It
was his party piece. "Let us think for a moment about an even greater
march, the onward march of humanity itself. From the earliest times, the
great power of creating civilisation has always swept westward, always
following the sun. It first arose here in China many millennia go. In our
fertile river valleys we achieved great things, and much later produced
many brilliant inventions. Perhaps we even explored the entire planet.

"But we did so in too much isolation. Maybe because China has
always been so self-sufficient, our forefathers did not need much contact
with the outside world. Instead we were preoccupied with too many
internal wars, a regrettable period in our past. And in the process we
then lost control of the onward march of civilisation.

"The great inventive genius continued to move westward long
before that, on its ceaseless journey towards the sun. It travelled the
dusty roads of Asia and its next resting place was in Mesopotamia.
There it galvanised the peoples who arose from the mud of two rivers
around five thousand years ago. We must remember, comrades, that the
flame of invention and the spirit of adventure must always find both the
stability of earth and the eternal motion of the water in which to flourish.

There are some elements of Western thinking which I sometimes find quite useful. The Mesopotamians became clever. They took the clay of the earth and invented new forms of writing, of arithmetic, of the basis of economic progress. Yet like the early Chinese they could not retain the power they had created. From Mesopotamia the force of new civilisation travelled still further to the West.

"It travelled along the Fertile Crescent to the seagoing Phoenicians and to the over-religious Jews. And from them it travelled to the inventiveness of the Greeks. Their military leader Alexander fought his way back eastwards from Greece as far as India. If his soldiers had not decided that was sufficient exploration, he might even have arrived at the very ramparts of China. Perhaps the Macedonian Alexander should have gone conquering in the opposite direction, following and leading the westward movement of fresh civilisation. He would have found it more profitable."

By this stage the deputy premier was well into his stride, and allowed himself an excursion, a tour de force around great military leaders of history, from Alexander to Julius Caesar to Genghis Khan to Napoleon; to the militaristic adventurers such as Clive of India and Rhodes of Africa who had built the British Empire. His audience loved it. They had studied world history at university too, a compulsory part of top Chinese education, and they were listening to a master of his craft.

"Although Alexander had faltered, his spirit still survives in many places, in many cities named after him. One day a Chinese hero will have that same effect on the world. One day many new cities around the world will have Chinese names. Alexander's tutor was the Greek philosopher Aristotle, a spiritual descendant of the West's greatest philosopher Pythagoras who had devised many new things, acclaimed by many as the father of western civilisation. But let us remember Pythagoras was a precise contemporary of our own great philosopher Confucius, and he devised many new things also. He was the father of our great civilisation. Those two founding fathers created the two most powerful cultural traditions the world has yet known, two cultural traditions which have never been able to live entirely harmoniously side by side. We have been drawn into conflict many times since. Today that conflict is not so much military; it is an intellectual battle and it is a battle for world leadership. It is a battle for the loyalty and obedience of other lands. We are facing that conflict today. That is the intellectual and cultural foundation of this meeting.

"From the inventive Greeks the power of new civilisation was passed to the Romans, as for the first time that power had moved off the land and over the water. The Mediterranean Sea provided the lifeblood which gave strength to the civilisations of the West. It took them over two thousand years. Their historians admire their maritime city states of Venice and Genoa, their cultural centres Florence and Bologna, which became the cradles of their European civilisation. But then they faltered also, under the burden of too much religion.

"From there, the wisdom and enterprise again travelled westward, ever westward, now to the coastal peoples of the Atlantic Ocean. They became the great adventurers, the Portuguese and the Dutch, just as in previous times they had been the Vikings."

At which point the deputy premier smiled, paused and ruminatively sipped his tepid tea. He was thinking of Macao, and Indonesia. Clearly Hong Kong was never far from his mind either. As he generously pointed out, the Rus were just another branch of Vikings and they had founded Kiev, the historic womb of Russia. "It is the same Viking tradition, embedded in their genes, that gives the Russian peoples their greatest strength."

Suitably refreshed, the deputy premier continued. "The real inheritors of the Viking tradition, perhaps their greatest sons, were the British. Either indirectly through rapine and pillaging and a process of infiltration, or through direct military conflict at their unforgotten Battle of Hastings, the Vikings made the leadership of Britain their own. Once they had consolidated their power, it was less than five hundred years before they began to expand.

"As we here in China know only too well, the Viking British created a maritime empire which spanned the globe. They began in the Americas, whose earliest states are named after luminaries of England. New York may be new York, but old York was originally called Yorvik and that was a Viking settlement, the very heart of England's proudest county. In my youth I visited it as a cultural tourist, and then for a year I worked in a Chinese restaurant in Leeds. Believe me I do understand these things at first hand.

"The British followed the Roman pattern and built the world's greatest empire. One of its architects was a Yorkshireman called James Cook, who founded their colony in Australia. We should not be surprised for one moment at that. Once a Viking, always a Viking. And so the British creation was a maritime dominion and because of that it could reach far further than the Roman might ever have dreamt. Here in our Middle Kingdom we can learn much from their British Empire.

"Comrades. As we devise the next great move forward for our Middle Kingdom I want us to bear the maritime strength of the British very much in mind. In their quaintly ceremonial, quaintly religious style the United Kingdom showed the world a new kind of empire. At their height the British controlled a quarter of mankind. Let us not forget that a hundred and fifty years ago the British marched into Beijing. It is time for us to return the compliment. Let us not forget that we Chinese are a fifth of mankind on our own before we even look beyond our shores.

"Let us not forget either that for every Englishman, there are twenty-seven Chinese. We can be twenty-seven times more powerful. Yet the British Empire was irredeemably flawed. It had lost the United States of America at an early stage. But even then in a hundred years, the two Anglo-Saxon races bestriding the Atlantic shifted the power of civilisation from the Mediterranean into one of the great oceans of the world. Let us remember that also. Remember the world's great oceans. Between them, the Anglo-Saxons of the Atlantic devised the incorrect system of western capitalism. Now we have created capitalism with Chinese characteristics, our perfected improvement built on thought and intellect. Their was merely a crude, ramshackle edifice assembled from a succession of economic and financial accidents. That is not the Chinese way. Ours is a superior way, a planned way, a rational way.

"Their imperfect capitalism gave rise to the slaughter of the European wars, those wars which began over a hundred years ago. Because of those wars the creative power of civilisation then ebbed out of Europe again and flowed westward into America. The European races had eventually defeated themselves.

"Instead they sent their huddled masses to the shores of America, to the land of the free as far as they could comprehend liberty. They were very ordinary members of humanity. America built great statues to celebrate their welcome, even if the statues themselves were designed by and provided by the people of France. America was on a mission. It received the poor, it welcomed the tired and it exalted the wretched. The homeless, tempest-tossed impoverished were America's closest brethren.

"Their great woman with a torch in New York Harbour was welcoming someone, anyone, from anywhere, but conquering heroes from the lands of the Vikings they most certainly were not. And within that dichotomy can be discerned the seeds of the inferiority which took root at the very heart of the United States of America. That is not a mental problem we share here in the Middle Kingdom, any more than we share it with the English.

"We have never shared such national inferiority complexes. We may safely leave such self-justifying sentimentality to those who inhabit the far shores of the Pacific. National inferiority complexes are a frequent characteristic, if I may say so within these unrecorded confines of the Forbidden City, of the Americans, sometimes the Russians and indeed the Germans and Japanese. And all for very good reason. They all have much to feel inferior about. It is we, the Chinese, who are the planet's superior race.

"Grasp that, and you begin to understand the two great global wars of the past century. We should try to teach perceptive, not celebratory, history in the universities of this great country. I would have it so myself but there are many of our fellow countrymen who would oppose me. After all, such objectivity is the privilege of the self-confident. And you cannot expect every single one of our billion fellow countrymen to feel that.

"The torch of human ingenuity left the United States quickly. It did not feel at home living in the land of the paper tiger. Across that great self-admiring experiment of the wretched, the United States of America, the power of invention travelled ever westward, always toward the sun. It took temporary refuge in the computer and aviation industries of the American west, once again within sight of the Pacific Ocean. And then the torch crossed those broad waters to become our welcome guest once again in Asia. Our inferior offshore neighbours the Japanese may have been the mere gatekeeper, but we here in the Middle Kingdom have been the principal host at the reception, just as it was always destined to be.

"It has taken seven thousand years for that power of human ingenuity to flow right around the globe, it has flowed through many races and through the seven ages of man. But now the power has carried that fire of invention to raise civilisation to new heights. It has been brought to us on the back of a tiger, many Pacific tigers, back where it belongs, back to its spiritual home, to us, back to China.

"We do not need to imitate the action of a tiger because we are ourselves that tiger. We must stiffen our sinews and summon up our blood. For this time, comrades, we shall not make the same mistake as before. Tomorrow we too face our Agincourt, and this time we shall win." As they were supposed to do, his audience of the wise men of China responded to the deputy premier's manifold thoughts in silence. Some of them who had been educated in England even recognised his Shakespearian references.

Yet what would Abigail Fenceville have made of it all? Or even Alan Stanley? In the West it was essential to find the lowest common denominator. Here in the Forbidden City, in sharp contrast, it was essential to find the highest common factor. Seniority earned respect, even if appropriate references to William Shakespeare would have been lost on most of Beijing's inhabitants. Beijing's teeming inhabitants played no real part in selecting the potentates of the Forbidden City. Perish the very thought.

Among the minority of those present who comprehended the deputy premier perfectly was vice-premier Liu Fun. She had seen a performance of Henry the Fifth many years ago, as well as watched the film. It was one of her favourite Shakespeare plays and she knew its opening lines and its eve of battle speech off by heart. In English. Liu Fun even knew her Emma Lazarus. Like almost every Chinese tourist to New York, she had dutifully taken the boat trip across New York harbour. The comparison between Shakespeare and Lazarus was poignant indeed, something that was revealing and not merely odious. She nodded knowingly at the deputy premier. He smiled back. It was a collection of private insights shared just between the two of them.

As they all pondered his historical panorama, the deputy premier turned to Liu Fun and asked "But I have been speaking of yesterday. Please tell us comrade, what of today? What is your understanding of the world's balance of power? We are in the Year of the Monkey, it is a fire year. It is a time for dynamism, for passion, for energy, aggression and for leadership. Is that the task of the Middle Kingdom today?" Liu Fun swept an imaginary strand of hair from her brow, leaned back in her chair and interlocked her fingers as if creating a puzzle she was about to unravel. She was going to enjoy this opportunity, every second of it. "As you all know, comrades, part of my work is to study the governments of the West. And what can we all see today?

"In America they have chosen an absurd woman called Abigail Fenceville to be their president. Her election tells us so much about the fundamental weaknesses of what the Americans like to call their 'democracy'. The Greeks always considered that to be undesirable rule by the mob, and I agree with the Greeks. Abigail Fenceville is weak, indecisive, a mere pawn in the hands of minor politicians from her home state. None of them begin to understand world politics. The great paper tiger of the eastern Pacific is now grown old, weary and ineffectual. It has rotted into the ground and become an earthworm, and we could not ask for a finer opportunity to pursue our worthy ambitions.

"In the United Kingdom, that birthplace of Atlantic democracy, in that England which still has abounding self-confidence no matter how much misplaced, they have chosen another fool, Alan Stanley, to be their leader. Our researches show him to be a noisy self-admiring cockerel, more or less useless and ready for slaughter. We can simply eat him, provided the particular flavour suits our palate. It may well not.

"It is all very propitious. If this Year of the Monkey is the time for China to take its next great step forward, it can do so walking across the heads of the two leading powers in NATO. I greatly welcome the prospect. We should be most grateful for the natural tide of history."

The deputy premier nodded at Liu Fun in appreciation. He next turned to the man from the navy. "Admiral Zhou Man, what is our military preparedness for our major step forward? It has been your commission for two decades, with the full support of the State Council of the People's Republic. How many ships do we now have, and where can we operate them?" Zhou Man looked around the table with great deference, gauging how much each man present would already know.

"Comrade deputy premier, my news for you is good. Four years ago we launched our first Advance Class destroyer, which bears the name of my illustrious predecessor. Within less than two years she was ready for sea trials and sailing at speed round the waters of Dalian.

"Since then she has explored the Indian Ocean, paying courteous visits to our new allies. And in that time seven more ships of her class have been launched, fitted with their armaments and equipment and put to sea. I have spoken with the military commission and they say our new destroyer fleet could be strengthened with two nuclear attack submarines from our Shang class. Our navy now has ample auxiliary vessels to give it further support.

"Although we have no capital ship yet to match a vessel like the American Carl Vinson aircraft carrier, now we have other ways of dealing with that. Comrade Liu Fun has organised a network of shore bases from which to mount an attack anywhere in the entire ocean at very short notice. In effect, comrades, we now have an entirely new Chinese fleet assembled in our naval base at Sanya in Hainan, and awaiting your orders."

Only a month earlier, Admiral Zhou Man had visited China's most recent centre for naval activity, on the island which marked the southernmost tip of the country. Hainan was tropical, to the south of the Tropic of Cancer. China had a warm-water naval base which openly commanded the seas off its coastline. The very thing Russia had sought unsuccessfully for centuries.

Already the naval base in Hainan was being enjoyed by many patriotic Chinese sailors as they relaxed between duties in their own version of America's Hawaii. The two were in almost exactly the same latitude. Currently, the military facilities on Hainan also marked the furthest limit of Chinese naval and military ambition. But that state of affairs would not last for much longer. The deputy premier smiled. "That is a fine achievement, Admiral Zhou Man. I can see we chose the right man for our task. Tell me Comrade Liu Fun, what is now the position with the shore bases which the Admiral has just mentioned? Do we have sufficient? Have we tested our access to the Islamic ports which were recruited in support our strategy?"

The vice-premier nodded. "Yes we have, comrade deputy premier. Over ten years ago the admiral and I devised our master plan for the Indian Ocean. And today we have full access to Islamic ports in Indonesia, in Pakistan, in Saudi Arabia and in the Yemen. We have access to ports in Africa and in the middle of the ocean we have with the co-operation of the French built a base on an isolated place called Amsterdam island.

"The admiral calculates that we could move one of our new warships anywhere in little more than a day or two. In other words we now have the means to protect our vital shipping routes across a whole ocean, safeguarding our raw material supplies from Africa. The Middle Kingdom can now move out from its homeland to become a global maritime power."

Listening to all this good news, the deputy premier looked down at the table before him and tapped it slowly with his forefinger. Eventually the modern mandarin of Beijing spoke. "My own mind is now made up, comrades. Let me see how many of you agree with it. I think the time has come for China to move well beyond its home waters. If the Americans can maintain naval fleets in distant oceans of the world, then so can we, the peoples of the Middle Kingdom.

"The admiral has described what I now suggest should become our own fourth fleet, an addition to those we already have for the north sea, the south sea and the east sea. The vice-premier has told us we have the bases, the admiral has told us we have the ships. I now propose we base our new fleet in the Indian Ocean, to be commanded by Admiral Zhou Man. There will now be a difference, however. In due course we will announce it is now to be known as The Chinese Ocean. That is our birthright, our cultural destiny. Now is the time to show the independent countries of the world who is its new and greatest power."

It was the Year of the Monkey, it was a time when the western powers were impotent. The deputy premier looked round the table expectantly. There were no signs of dissent. It was decided. Yesterday it had been called the Indian Ocean. Soon it would have a new identity. The world's third largest ocean was now part of China's sphere of influence, it was now under Chinese protection.

Following that jubilant meeting in Beijing's Ministry of National Defence, the world's third largest ocean was destined to become a symbol of the Middle Kingdom's new, much more powerful rôle in the world. The deputy premier drew the meeting to a close. "We will make a formal announcement at the United Nations next month." He smiled.

*　　*　　*　　*　　*

Ministry of Defence, Whitehall, London

"JESUS CHRIST, George, have you seen the overnight reports from the United Nations? Have your read this morning's papers? We are suddenly confronted with sheer effrontery from the Orient." An anxious Peter Storey was on the telephone to George Gould, and he was the closest a Whitehall civil servant could ever come to untrammelled trepidation. Even the telephone shook. The previous day in New York, the Chinese had declared the Indian Ocean was now in their nation's sphere of influence, and had even renamed it 'The Chinese Ocean.' People were simply not allowed to rename oceans.

Peter Storey, a high-raking deputy secretary in the ministry, was almost bursting at the seams. Almost. "George. Are you still there? What are we going to do about it? What are we going to say to the Cabinet Secretary? What is he going to tell the Prime Minister? Do you have any ideas?" George Gould had been thinking about it on and off for at least three hours, ever since he first heard of the Chinese announcement on the morning news.

"Peter. Yes I am here. Yes I have heard the news. Some time ago in fact. Yes it's all very exciting, but let's first ask ourselves 'What *can* we do about it?' The Chinese have caught us with our pants down and they know it. Their timing is impeccable."

Peter Storey asked the seemingly unflappable captain to explain, then changed his mind and invited him into his office. This was a serious matter which merited face-to-face discussion, probably over a cup of tea. With chocolate biscuits. The first rule in Whitehall was never to flap about anything. Flapping was a futile pastime exclusively reserved for politicians.

The civil servant raised an expectant eyebrow while George Gould gratefully munched a couple of the finest delicacies Whitehall had to offer. They were a deputy secretary's privilege. Normally George only got Rich Tea. "The first thing to bear in mind, Peter, is that there is not much we *can* do about it. Let's just take it all a step at a time, starting with ourselves. Britain abandoned East of Suez over fifty years ago, thanks to Harold Wilson and Denis Healey. For half a century we have accepted that the Indian Ocean, or whatever it's called now, is beyond our sphere of influence. A foolish way to save money in my view. That puts us right out of the reckoning for starters.

"Second, the Indians. They have their work cut out as it is, with militant Pakistan in the west, secretive Myanmar in the east and China immediately to the north on the other side of the Himalayas. At least two of those are quite capable of picking a fight with India at any time, while both Pakistan and China are nuclear powers. That would be more than enough to make any of us twitch. The broad expanse of open ocean to their south has until now been the last thing to worry about, and even then they do have a fairly large if somewhat antiquated navy.

"Next the Australians, whose national motto is 'no worries' and has been for years. No worries means no navy either, well nothing to speak of. What naval assets they do have are mainly facing east and north, not west into the Indian Ocean. We both know they have recently seen the light and are rearming as fast as they can, but that's from a very low level, and nothing new is operational yet.

George Gould was ticking off countries with his fingers. "And you can forget about Africa, most of which seems to be caught up in the Chinese sphere of influence already. Apart that is for Somalia which seems to taken up piracy as a national sport. Or the Yemen just across the water where apparently the national sport is international terrorism.

"Then you have Iran which has retreated a long way back from its days as the cuddly land of the Peacock Throne. As for the rest of the countries round this so-called Chinese Ocean, they are virtually all Islamic states tied up with this COTO treaty. Remember we first learnt of the Islamic Naval Alliance unofficially over three years ago now. No-one has denied its existence since.

"That leaves us with the Americans. Just look at a globe. For them, the Indian Ocean is right on the opposite side of he world. It's hardly their back garden. I agree they will have the Fifth Fleet based in Trincomalee, and that is a substantial regional police force. But what they actually do about it all rather depends on the delightful Abigail. Which in practical terms means they will probably do nothing.

"Unfamiliar-sounding places like Mogadishu or the Malacca Straits are much too distant to register on her ultra short-range radar. Instead she keeps them in the bulging Too Difficult drawer of her presidential desk. Abigail Fenceville believes in benign neglect, which is all very well but unfortunately she cannot spot the difference between that and wilful negligence. That's a cross we all have to bear." Peter Storey nodded weakly as George Gould continued his global tour of military intentions. "I'm quite sure the Chinese had all that worked out for themselves long before they made this latest announcement. They spotted a power vacuum, so they manufactured the necessary military assets and sailed into the gap. You can hardly blame them. Here in the West we have simply left the door wide open."

Peter Storey stared at the unflappable captain for a few moments. All that was perfectly true, if rather salutory. The days when Britannia ruled the waves all around the globe were long gone. It was an uncomfortable thought. "I will agree with virtually all of that, George, even if a bit despondently. But it still doesn't answer the question 'What happens next?' Do we simply roll over and let the Chinese sail their warships all over us? It hardly seems British, what with our bulldog spirit and all that."

George Gould had rather expected this. British civil servants were trained to salute the union flag from an early age, and old habits die hard. "Peter, the next thing to remember is that hardly anything has actually happened. Okay, so somewhere on the globe has been given a new name. Happens all the time in Africa. And other places. Mumbai used to be Bombay. Myanmar used to be Burma. America's new friend Sri Lanka used to be called Ceylon when we had it. Bongo Bongo Land used to be, well, admittedly, Bongo Bongo Land. Let's not get too hot under the collar about a new name for a large stretch of empty ocean. More to the point, what are the Chinese going to do about it?"

"I take your point there, George. Even the Chinese can hardly declare war on a flock of globetrotting penguins. Only if someone provokes them, or does something they consider provocative, can anything real start to happen. We don't know of anything, do we? So what does happen next?"

"I think the next thing that happens is you give the gist of all that to the Cabinet Secretary, then let him have a nice chat with the prime minister and the defence secretary. He should play it ice cool. I don't suppose Alan Stanley and Desmond Brightside will be all that concerned anyway. Politicians change the name of things all the time, they're used to it. It makes them feel more significant. Look at the Liberal Party, never the same thing five years running. Labour became New Labour and it's now back to being Real Labour. Don't even ask me about the Department of Trade and Industry. They change its name at least twice every parliament.

"Calling a lot of empty water something different might make old Foreign Office hands leap up and down. Or maybe cause some salt-encrusted admiral to spill his brandy. But let's not go overboard about it." Peter Storey was not entirely convinced. "You're forgetting two things, George. Two different sets of opinion. First our allies. If we do nothing and are seen to do nothing, we begin to look toothless. What kind of ally is that? Second, public opinion. The one thing the British people really detest is johnnie foreigner taking the mickey at our expense.

"So let's see what the opinion polls have to say on the subject. They could be very significant. The British never see the writing on the wall until they have their backs to it, but the public mood can then change very quickly. Whatever his private views may be, and he made them clear enough on COTO during his election campaign, Alan Stanley would have to respond to that."

George Gould agreed about the opinion polls, that was something to await and see, but he had a further suggestion. "One thing we could do to keep our allies and would-be allies entertained would be some timely show of strength. Why don't we arrange a naval exercise in this so-called Chinese Ocean? Do something fairly innocuous, don't let's pretend to have a full-scale naval battle in mid-ocean between the reds and the blues. That would be just a bit too obvious.

"Better to co-operate with the Indians and the Australians to practise an amphibious landing. That's the kind of thing that always goes wrong on the day. Remember "D-Day" should have happened on "C-Day" originally. I've always thanked my lucky stars we didn't plan to go the day before that and have the French laughing themselves silly, at our expense, for going on a bidet." George Gould could never resist his extremely arid Whitehall jokes.

"On the face of it such an exercise could - with complete rationality - be a dress rehearsal for India to deal with Islamic insurgency or unfriendly neighbours, or for Australia to deal with terrorists in the unrulier backwaters of Indonesia. But at least the Chinese could see for themselves we are still capable of organising a few warships in what they now consider to be their private ocean.

"Better still, we could do it all without involving the Americans. Once Abigail Fenceville comes to the party it could all get screwed up. Let's keep it simple. If as I imagine the Australians and the Indians will be knocking on our door here at the Ministry of Defence before the day's out, at least we will be in a position to propose something positive. They'll probably jump at the idea."

And so was born 'Operation Taj Mahal', and it was notionally to take place in September, or as soon as the various fleet commanders could sort out their ships.

* * * * *

Westminster and Whitehall

ALAN STANLEY knew he was confronting a back-bench revolt. Two years earlier his government had been elected on a platform of reducing defence activity and expenditure. Now the newspapers were full of stories about a complete change of heart in Ten Downing Street. They were saying the prime minister had become just as gung-ho as any British general or admiral, and his party colleagues wished to know whether that was true. Many of the members of parliament newly elected in May 2015 had shared all the anti-military enthusiasms Alan Stanley had voiced in opposition, while many party workers around the country were adamantly pacifist. Now they all felt cheated, as was so often the case after the Labour Party came into power. The veteran MP and parliamentary critic Terry Tanner, known to everyone as the Tiger of Tinsley, had been holding forth in Annie's bar. "Every time a new Labour leader gets to Downing Street, the military and the civil service get to him. It never takes them longer than two years. Then it's the turn of the bankers to pollute proper Socialism. Whatever good intentions our party had before the election, they all dissolve into oblivion as soon as we have a Labour prime minister."

The Tiger of Tinsley was possessed of a very long political memory. "It was the same with Blair, it was the same with Wilson, it was the same right back in the days of Attlee. They even argued in favour of the nuclear deterrent, absurd stuff about not wanting to go naked into the negotiating chamber. You can spot the sabre-rattling minds of Whitehall even in the very words our people used."

A meeting of the Parliamentary Labour Party had been called and Prime Minister Stanley instructed to attend. Or else. He arrived with his key supporters, Defence Secretary Desmond Brightside and Foreign Secretary Steve Wilson, to a chorus of cat-calls and boos. How the tables had turned. Less than four years previously, it had been Alan Stanley who was the masterful voice of discontent from the rear of the hall. Now he was party leader, Prime Minister and on the defensive. The party chairman, with as much fairness as he could muster, invited him to the microphone. The Prime Minster was at the top of his form.

"Chair, fellow MPs, fellow supporters of the socialist cause. You have invited me here today, I realise, to explain some stories in the newspapers. Let me say here and now that most of them are untrue, but a few are not. It is true that Desmond and Steven and I have had to advance our views on defence somewhat since we formed this government. I am not the first Prime Minister to do that, nor shall I be the last. Permit me to explain why that is so.

"When we wrote our party's manifesto four years ago, I had not then had the privilege of any briefing from our senior military officers or from senior civil servants. The truth about our military situation is very different from the picture painted in the popular press. For security reasons I cannot explain all of it now. This country is more open than most, but there are some things, especially to do with our defence, which must always remain secret.

"I beg of you to trust me on that, for I can do nothing else." As they had done for years, Desmond Brightside and Steve Wilson both nodded vigorously as Alan Stanley continued: "But now look around you, look at the delegate sitting next to you. All of you, and me included, are in politics to make the world a better place. This Labour Party is built on such political aspirations, on a desire to change the world for the better. It is built, let us be honest, on a political dream.

"There is nothing wrong with political dreams. Without political dreams none of us would have dreamt of coming into politics, none of us would have fought to become MPs. None of us would be here today. But there does come a day when political dreams must give way to political reality. I am still the same Alan Stanley who dreamt those dreams, just as many of you still dream them now.

"But I hope I am also the Alan Stanley who looks the world squarely in the face, who can appreciate the truth even when it is not welcome. When a political leader loses the ability to stare truth in the face, that is the time to replace him. Or her. It would be a sad day when this party routinely sacked its leaders for being realistic. The British public would never forgive this great party for being as foolish as that."

There were still some subdued boos and hisses at the back of the meeting, but they were becoming fewer as Alan Stanley continued, "and it is the British public, the people who elected all of us, I am listening to now. Last month, China announced it was taking over the Indian Ocean. They have even renamed it "The Chinese Ocean". Even if

members in this meeting think that is of no account, that is not the view
taken by the British people. We British are a proud race and we do not
welcome being ordered around by other countries. Many of our fellow
citizens like to think we still rule the waves, even the waves of the Indian
Ocean. Our own party research shows a huge tide of public opinion in
favour of standing up for ourselves, of turning away from peaceful and
supine acceptance of anything and everything that happens in other parts
of the world.

"That is the mark of a coward, not a true Socialist. This country
does not like military bullies and never has, while we in turn as a party
put ourselves in jeopardy if we ignore the will of the people. If there are
still those in this meeting who would reject the nation's views, if they
wish for policies in defiance of what the ordinary people of this country
think, they must ask themselves whether they also reject the principle of
democracy and if not, why not."

As he continued in much the same vein, Alan Stanley continued
to reveal his mastery of the political *non sequitur*. His government
colleagues Desmond Brightside and Steve Wilson were lost in
admiration. They had arrived at the meeting amid cat-calls and boos less
than thirty minutes previously. Now the parliamentary party seemed to
be eating out of Alan Stanley's hand. No wonder he was party leader,
no wonder he was prime minister. They would willingly hitch their
wagon to his star and follow such a man anywhere.

A few hours later two old friends met at an exclusive club in Pall
Mall. It was the sort of place London's top mandarins gathered when in
urgent need of refreshment. Peter Storey was enjoying a drink at the
Athenaeum with the Cabinet Secretary Sir Anthony Pilkington. They
had both been reading the afternoon newspaper reports on what had
happened that morning. Storey tapped a front page story in the
Evening Standard leaked from the meeting of the Parliamentary Labour
Party. "What on earth did you say to the man? What did you do to make

him change his views? This change of heart makes St Paul's conversion on the road to Damascus look like a minor traffic diversion. Your man Alan Stanley used to be a dyed-in-the-wool pacifist, now reading this he sounds just like one of us. Just tell me how you did it. Do let me buy you a double scotch, you deserve it dear boy. Single malt, I presume."

Anthony Pilkington was looking pleased with himself. "Oh, just the usual stuff, Peter, it's one of the best-rehearsed conjuring acts in Whitehall. A secret handed down from father to son, or rather from cabinet secretary to cabinet secretary. You simply hit them where it really hurts. As the man once said so wisely, get them by the balls and their hearts and minds will surely follow.

Never, never overlook the fact that, ultimately, politicians only worry about two things: keeping their seat and, in the case of prime ministers, keeping their parliamentary majority. All you need to do is remind them that the floating vote on which many of their colleagues depend is a vote which methodically follows its wallet, its employment prospects, its jingoistic pride. It never sticks to its political principles because it hasn't got any principles."

"Hmm. How did he take that one? A little below the belt, perhaps." Peter Storey was impressed and took a healthy swig of scotch. He had always suspected that Cabinet secretaries had to be even more astute at electoral arithmetic and voters' motivation than those elected. It was central to their job, if not exactly part of the job description.

"He had to take it because it's true. We have a couple of by-elections coming up and, as luck would have it, they are both in marginal constituencies. Lovely things. The levers of power held in obdurately innocent hands, in the hands of people who simply read the Sun and the Daily Star. People who have never even heard of Hansard. People who are invariably over the moon or down in the dumps. People whose lives are entirely focused on twenty-two men kicking a ball. They read the stargazer columns in their newspapers, that's where they get their ideas about life. So I look upon their's as the political wisdom of the zodiac, a wisdom with all the penetrating insight of popular astrology. In by-elections, the floating vote will swing hither and yon like a weathervane. It all depends on who is blowing the wind. All that business about the Chinese Ocean could not have come at a more opportune moment. Even the floating vote can be upset by something as direct as that. Try to get them to understand the niceties of corporate taxation and you might as well ask them to understand Chinese.

"But ask them to understand the Chinese raising two fingers to John Bull and they understand that perfectly. The great unwashed all start jumping up and down in their cages and increase the sales of newspapers exponentially. It all becomes what they call an election issue, even if there is no actual election in the offing.

"Remarkable stuff, that election issue, an intellectually transparent substance which we in Whitehall can mould into any shape we wish. And because they never have anything better to write about, the newspapers are then filled with idiotic stories along the lines of 'if this result were reproduced in a general election tomorrow, the government would win fifty seats, lose fifty seats, would stay in power, or would lose power, delete whichever does not apply.'

"Neither of them apply because there is not going to be a general election tomorrow, but prime ministers still twitch regardless, in their incurably Pavlovian way. These days I have come to the conclusion our political leaders have a morbid obsession that if they ever fell under the proverbial bus, then political chaos would surely follow, causing serious damage to their place in the history books. And that is the persuasive technique, my dear Peter, which is handed down from cabinet secretary to cabinet secretary."

At this, Peter Storey nodded vigorously. "I can never quite understand why prime ministers worry quite so much about their place in the history books but it does seem to become an obsession with just about all of them eventually. Was it not Enoch Powell who once said that all political careers end in failure? I dunno, Who wants to go down in history as a failure? But since as we know history books are always written by the winning side, it's probably just second nature for political megalomaniacs to seek to get their literary retaliation in first."

Peter Storey turned his attention away from Christmas stocking reading material to the serious matter in hand. "So now we have a political balancing act with two by-elections in the offing: I can see all that. Well done. How did he take to the idea of Operation Taj Mahal?" Peter Storey was wondering about George Gould's bright idea designed to keep Britain's allies happy after the Chinese announcement in July.

"Peter, he just loved it. Perfect fodder for the floating vote. The Romans gave them bread and circuses. We give them ready-made television meals and Operation Taj Mahal. Our malleable Mr Stanley thought it the ideal way to keep our huddled masses content without antagonising anyone else.

"He realised it will not be announced until it is happening, but he would then like maximum television coverage of all our warships sailing around the Indian Ocean. They will probably use Rod Stewart for the backing music, or play patriotic excerpts from The Last Night Of The Proms. Or show the Two Ronnies dancing the sailor's hornpipe. Whatever makes for good television nowadays. But it does seem we now have distinct win-win potential. We keep our allies happy, while he keeps the Colonel Blimps of the British electorate happy. Tell you what, let's treat ourselves to another brace of those malt whiskies."

Yet as they did so and as Anthony Pilkington filled in clues in The Times crossword, Peter Storey could not help reflecting on the modern rôle of prime ministers and cabinet secretaries. It seemed their primary function was to keep other people content in their ignorance, especially the great British electorate and most of all its conviction-free component which simply floated.

Peter Storey rehearsed this perturbing thought with his senior colleague. "It does seem, Tony, that those at the centre nowadays have become slaves to an ephemeral world of knee-jerk reactions, melt in your mouth sound-bites and ill-informed populist opinions. They become mere slaves to the lowest common denominator, one which cannot even count. We have to agree that western democracy has probably taken a turn for the worse.

"This country is being run by people running round in circles. Independent and serious thinking about profound political issues is no longer the pursuit of politicians or even the mandarins of Whitehall. Testing mental gymnastics tasks like that are left instead to desiccated academics amid dreaming spires and to professional recluses like George Gould." It was probably very different in China, both men concluded. No wonder the Chinese had caught the West, in Gould's colourful phrase, with its pants down.

*   *   *   *   *

The Chinese, or Indian, Ocean

THE HELICOPTER from the Australian frigate HMAS Stuart clattered down to the flight deck of HMS Albion. The twelve ships, or rather the visible surface ships, of Operation Taj Mahal were grouping into formation on the equator four hundred miles south of Colombo. As soon as the Australian frigate HMAS Stuart had arrived on station from Freemantle, she had been instructed to send Commander Warwick Sydenham to the British flagship. As he stepped onto Albion's vast helicopter deck and into a stiff breeze he was welcomed aboard by Commander James Heaton.

The two old friends were delighted to see one another. "Hello James. I heard you'd be here. Bit of a change from running naval intelligence in Northwood, isn't it? What's going on exactly? And how is the lovely Violaine?" James Heaton led his old pal out of the wind and into the shelter of his cabin. "First the good news about Violaine. As you already know, our first child was still-born a few years ago now. But I'm delighted to say she is expecting again, and the new baby is due next March. The lass is quite radiant, as you might expect.

"Ever since Malik was killed, Louise has been clucking about becoming a proper grandmother continuously. Although her step-son Hamad has his own children, and Louise loves them dearly, that's not quite the same. That cannot count as dynasty, and in the de Chambon family, dynasty is everything.

"You've met my mother-in-law. As you can imagine our formidable Parisian chatelaine on the Île St Louis has taken total command. Violaine is to spend the final two months in ultimate luxury at a clinic in Harley Street, no expense spared. Nothing is being left to chance this time round, as you would expect." Warwick congratulated James on the delightful news. But then they moved on to discuss the purpose of his trip to the Equator. James explained.

"First, what you are actually going to see is what anyone can see, a tri-nation amphibious fleet about to rehearse landings on the Indian coast. It is all pretty normal stuff, designed to be unconfrontational. Everyone internationally who would expect to be warned about it has been duly advised. Nothing secret about it. The underlying, unstated purpose is to demonstrate that we, the good guys, are still at liberty to sail our warships around the Indian Ocean, no matter what the Chinese now choose to call it. Your ship, the Stuart, will give Australia an ideal vantage point for what's going on.

Warwick nodded. That was his understanding too. "At the same time, James, I am also here to take a very good look at this commando carrier, Albion, when she's in action. Take me on a tour of inspection, please. I gather you can do some pretty nifty things launching very large landing craft out of her stern. One of these days we might well need a capability like that for those troublesome islanders to our north. I know it wasn't on our recent shopping-list for the Royal Australian Navy, but there are some wise heads in Canberra who now think it would be no bad idea if we had a couple of these as well."

James checked the cabin door was properly closed then continued. "And now for the real reason you're here, Warwick. You've done the Kundalini stuff which means you know all about Bijali." His antipodean opposite number raised an eyebrow. "Oh, so that's what it's called. Often wondered." James Heaton continued "the Ministry of Defence back in London thinks it would now be a very good idea if some top brass in the Australian navy learnt about Bijali and encouraged you to fit it to your new Type 45s. In due course you'll find out why we think it is such a good idea, but that's really one for the future.

"Since you seem to be more or less in charge of your new destroyer programme, you were the obvious person to get involved. And I imagine your word will carry considerable weight back in Canberra. We revealed it to the Americans over a couple of years ago. They were so impressed they tested it for themselves out of San Diego and now it's being fitted to principal ships in their Fifth Fleet, over there in Trincomalee. Chris Cunningham came out in person to show them exactly how it all works. When he has to do so, he can speak fluent American and even understands their distinctive logic processes."

Warwick Sydenham was delighted to be back in the middle of advancing technology. Too much of his recent experience had seemed to be in a naval backwater. Now he was on the inside track of the latest naval practice, all thanks to his old friend from Dartmouth. James was pleased for him, and explained: "Put it this way, Warwick. You and I agreed it all at Dartmouth over twenty years ago. You keep me in the picture, I'll keep you in the picture. Given the distance between Britain and Australia, that's a pretty wide screen picture. Your tip-offs about the Chinese Type 45s and various other things have done my career no harm at all in London. Now it's my turn to try and do your career a favour. As you will have realised, Bijali confers a huge military advantage. On the quiet that is one of the other things we shall be testing here in Taj Mahal is Bijali. While this the operation is in progress, I'm going to be on my old ship Daedalus working the magic.

"We're going to be using the Indian ships as guinea pigs while they are all busy landing their commandos. As it just so happens they've been including Bijali in their Ops rooms on refit. Not that anyone of them had the faintest idea they were doing so, of course. Goodness gracious me, no. They don't know the first thing about Bijali in New Delhi, even though technically speaking it is an Indian product. They don't even know it exists. Very few people do. Once the secret gets out the whole thing will become pointless. Right now it's just us and the Americans, and Australia coming to the party will make three."

James Heaton explained that while the amphibious exercise was happening, Warwick's job was to stay in the operations room on Daedelaus and observe what else was going on. Then he could give the full technicolour account to his naval lords and masters back in Canberra. "We also have a British liaison officer on the Indian flagship, the aircraft carrier Viraat you can see over there, just to save them from getting too upset as well. If you recognise the Viraat, well done. She used to be the Hermes in the Royal Navy donkey's years ago.

"I gather the Russians have let the Indians have some of their old stuff too. They have been giving them their old aircraft carrier the Admiral Gorshkov, but it seems there were all kinds of cock-ups. They even had to sack the Indian commander overseeing the deal. Anyway they sorted it out eventually and India now has two secondhand aircraft carriers in its fleet. The Indian navy might not be the newest in this so-called Chinese Ocean, but it is one of the largest." Warwick grimaced. This had been exactly the point of his controversial paper on the navy put into the Australian defence ministry over six years previously.

"For good measure the Indians have also brought along a couple of their Delhi class destroyers, the Mumbai and the Mysore, over there guarding the carrier. They're not a bad piece of kit, relatively new and Indian-built, about the size of a Type 45, but without quite the same level of armament. We rather get the distinct impression New Delhi is very keen to show the Chinese that more than one nation in this part of the world can play their new navy lark."

All commanding officers from the Taj Mahal flotilla were due in a general briefing on board Albion at 15.00 hours. As the British officer commanding the exercise explained, "Taj Mahal is not quite the D-Day landings, but it is definitely one of the larger exercises of its kind. We want to give ourselves plenty of scope to find all the snags, and the Gurkhas have kindly agreed to be the bad guys on land just to make life a bit more interesting for us. You couldn't ask for better bad guys than the Ghurkas. They are out to get us. We need maximum co-operation, maximum military understanding between sailors and commandos. Experience shows that any incomprehension between the two services is generally where things start to go wrong."

Then it was the turn of James Heaton to explain another part of the exercise, a covert part which was being kept well away from view. It was very much off the record, not that much, in a military exercise, was on the record anyway. "Just for your information, gentlemen, although Canberra knows of course, there will be something else going on. I assume you all know Australia has sent one of their Collins Class subs, with one of the best-trained crews they can muster. It is teaming up with one of our nuclear Trafalgar class, ostensibly to monitor the surface fleet exercise; that's just in case anyone spots them and asks.

"In fact we have dreamt up something entirely different. The two submarines are going to be doing just the kind of thing submariners love, apparently. Usually our guys play cat and mouse under the Arctic ice with the opposition. It's an acquired taste. This time they will be playing hide and seek in and around the Sunda Trench. You must know it, even though you and I all avoid places like that on principle. It is that very deep ditch not far out at sea running right along the coast of Sumatra. Just what submariners love, a two thousand mile long hole in the ocean floor. They practically call it home.

"The trench stretches south-east from the Nicobar Islands, they belong to India anyway, all the way to Australia's Christmas Island. So if anyone ever finds us, we do have a half a sensible reason to be there. More to the point, the Sunda Trench runs straight past the brand new Islamic Naval Alliance naval base at Singkil on the Sumatran coast, all part of this Central Ocean Treaty Organisation they keep shouting about.

We first heard about it almost three years ago. Both the Saudis and now it seems the Chinese have forked out for a lot for development and it now shows up beautifully on satellites. Our chaps are rather keen to find out how good they are at detecting submarines. The Chinese have been putting a lot of effort into that as well; we want to know how good at it they have become. Let's find out just how many teeth this mythical COTO creature has got.

"Finally some social news. We are also going to be meeting up with my old chum Xavier de Kerguelen. He's aboard a French frigate, the Dumont d'Urville, which just so happened to be passing by in this part of the world. They have been invited to observe Taj Mahal, which is rapidly turning into a come-as-you-are naval party. But before that they are off to Amsterdam Island, to make an ostensibly routine call at their research base at Martin de Viviès.

"The Dumont d'Urville intends to avail itself of the much-improved docking facilities also built by the Chinese, and drop off supplies and a fresh team of French scientists for the base. Ostensibly they are on some goodwill tour cooked up by the French in Paris, but they are really testing to see whether this Chinese Ocean business has had any real meaning."

Over the next week the multinational amphibious fleet set about Operation Taj Mahal. It was one of the largest naval exercises in the Indian Ocean, or as it now was supposed to be called, the Chinese Ocean, for many years. In accordance with Alan Stanley's wishes, selected reporters from the international media had been invited along to watch and generated much television coverage. The international audience for this maritime extravaganza was almost worldwide. Quite the most interested observers were three thousand miles away in Beijing.

*   *   *   *   *

Central Military Commission, Beijing

A HASTY MEETING had been called by the Ministry of Defence, and Liu Fun was the first to arrive. They were joined by the most senior officers of the Chinese armed forces, two intelligence experts, and some more specialised politicians.   Admiral Zhou Man was also present. Those unaware of the reason for meeting considered it rather precipitate. China, so far as they knew, was not at war, while it was more normal etiquette in Beijing to give somewhat longer notice of such meetings.

It was not long before they learnt the reason for the haste. The minister invited his navy chief to explain. "We have received reports from one of our merchant ships crossing the Chinese Ocean. The amphibious naval exercise which the westerners have told us about on the coast of India proves to be somewhat larger than we were led to believe. As you know, we now equip our most modern container ships with the same radar used on our warships. They can add to our eyes and ears. We have Admiral Zhou Man to thank for that foresight."

Liu Fun asked for precise details, and there was already much information available. The Foreign ministry had been talking to military attachés in several countries, and the full extent of the Taj Mahal exercise had become clear. Most countries ran websites to keep their sailors' families and friends informed when there was nothing secret about operations. There was detail to be had for free about some individual ships involved in Taj Mahal; a multinational naval exercise was the very last thing to try and keep under wraps.

In addition to on-the-spot observations from the Chinese merchant marine, there had been extensive coverage of the exercise on television news in numerous countries. It had not taken Beijing's military analysts very long to confirm from the pictures shown around the world which classes of ship from which of various navies were taking part.

The Defence Minister summed up the situation. "Comrades, this is the largest naval exercise the West has stages for many years in the Indian Ocean, as they call it. We have identified ships from India, from Great Britain, from France, from Australia and from the United States. Such a move so soon after our announcement of the new name can only be construed as deliberately provocative.

"They must have planned this exercise within days of our announcing that ocean is now within the Chinese sphere of influence. The effrontery of it. How would they feel if we organised similar amphibious landings with large numbers of our warships on the coast of, say, Cuba, or perhaps Syria? I need scarcely point out that the effect of this military display could make us a laughing-stock among other countries around the world.

"China must not lose face. Yet our ambassadors have been reporting that while television coverage of military activities in the seas south of Sri Lanka may have not interested the general populace, in the world's chancelleries questions are being asked. Is China just a paper tiger after all? We cannot allow that impression to spread."

Vice-premier Liu Fun took up the theme. "I wonder at what level of authority these things have been arranged? It is not in the character of people like Alan Stanley or Abigail Fenceville to be so military-minded. It must have come from a lower level, from within the military itself. Maybe we can find an opportunity to show them we mean business, before the rest of the world starts to laugh at us. Maybe we can persuade the weakling politicians in those countries to over-rule their over-ambitious military."

The Minister of Defence nodded in agreement, and turned to Admiral Zhou Man. He was more circumspect. The military mind dealt in feasibility, not diplomatic hot air. "Comrades, we perhaps need to remind ourselves the Chinese Ocean is not our private property, however offensive we might consider these particular manoeuvres to be. Ships of other countries, even including their warships, are still entitled to come and go as they please.

"I suggest it will reflect on our global maturity to let them get away with it this time. Tell our ambassadors to explain that Beijing does not regard this brief demonstration of military activity on the coast of India to be anything more than empty sabre-rattling. Tell them to point out that it is us, the Middle Kingdom, which now has naval control of the Chinese Ocean. To over-react in the face of a minor naval provocation would simply look petulant.

"Comrades. Let us bide our time. Although I cannot be absolutely certain yet, I believe a far greater opportunity is coming our way to show the world who are the real masters in the Chinese Ocean. Something which will win us many friends at the United Nations. They say in the West that he who laughs last laughs best. I think that should be our watchword now."

* * * * *

Southampton Docks, England

MEMBERS OF BRITAIN'S security police and some little-known units of Her Majesty's armed forces were guarding Southampton Docks that evening. They intended to be unobtrusive. As they kept their vigil they watched as a steady stream of articulated trucks from various parts of the country, in a carefully–orchestrated operation, were converging on a very large, very fast container ship. The Sydney Constellation was built to take 12,000 standard container units, but on this trip approximately three hundred would contain very unstandard cargo. She was due out of Southampton in the dark of the night on a fast run half way round the world, calling only at Marseilles. She would negotiate the Suez Canal and then take a direct course to Freemantle in Western Australia.

Those three hundred containers amounted to a re-armament kit for the Australian navy. Manufacturers at some of Britain's most advanced engineering, armaments and electronic companies had been working flat out ever since the orders were placed progressively from Spring 2014 onwards. It had taken two years and more to assemble, then test some highly complex systems.

Two naval officers, James Heaton in London and Warwick Sydenham in Australia, had put the orders in place working worked in tandem, orders configured to ensure that nothing was left to chance. The Anglo-Australian plan had been designed so that the jet engines, weaponry and electronic systems would all fit straight into place once they arrived in Australia. Already the hulls of three state-of-the-art destroyers were ready for fitting out at highly-automated Australian shipyards, and more ships were under construction. All in all the undertaking amounted to the greatest peacetime re-armament programme Australia had ever known.

In the UK the programme had been confirmed by the Cameron government in its dying days before the general election of May 2015. Their less sympathetic successors, an incoming Labour government led by the pacifist Alan Stanley, had been persuaded by British trades unions the orders were too advanced and generating far too many valuable jobs to be cancelled. Despite the earlier doctrine of its government, Britain was still in the international arms trade. Labour members of parliament in engineering constituencies had made it plain to their leadership that cancelling the orders would have been disastrous for their local support. In consequence the Australian orders for military hardware had been left unscathed, and in the space of several hours all the containers to deliver it were safely stowed on board.

In the early hours the Sydney Constellation was heading out once again into the Solent, past the derelict watch towers brooding in the seas outside Portsmouth, round the twinkling Isle of Wight and then out into the inky darkness of the English Channel. With her departure, the military vigilance at Southampton Docks could relax. From her appearance, no-one had any reason to imagine the Sydney Constellation's cargo of multicoloured containers differed from those to be seen on a dozen deep-sea container ships sailing out of Southampton, Felixstowe or Liverpool every day of the year.

However it was extremely rare for a container ship to be shadowed by a Type 45 destroyer. As the Sydney Constellation passed Portsmouth, HMS Dragon, the fourth in her class of Type 45 destroyers, took up escort station a discreet ten miles astern. The escort was officially heading for a joint NATO exercise with Italy and Turkey, and was due to make a series of well-publicised courtesy visits around the more democratic regimes of the eastern Mediterranean. Once the container ship had navigated the Suez canal, Dragon would be replaced by her sister ship HMS Daedalus.

The articulated trucks arriving in Southampton Docks throughout the afternoon and evening had been those of well-known commercial hauliers, giving no indication of the factories from which they came. Anonymity was central to the exercise in military logistics. Ships like the Sydney Constellation loaded such containers by the hundred every day.

Yet despite all these sensible precautions the secrets of her cargo were not quite so watertight as the Ministry of Defence would have wished. The sudden arrival of container lorries, in what was immediately apparent to any onlooker a carefully-choreographed operation, had attracted the well-attuned attention of Zhang Turku, an experienced and precisely-briefed Chinese spy.

Zhang Turku was an old hand at watching British docks and shipyards. Over eleven years earlier, he and his father Dheng Turku had been part of a five-man team observing construction of Britain's first Type 45, HMS Daring. On that occasion they had taken mundane jobs in the Scotstoun shipbuilding yard on the River Clyde. Their performance had pleased China's Admiral Zhou Man greatly, and the Uighur-speaking spies had been retained on his most trusted list.

Zhang Turku's ability to blend into the background in the dockland districts of major British ports was second to none. On his previous tour of duty in Scotland, Zhang Turku had developed quite a taste for the lifestyle and the pubs of Britain. He had been delighted when the opportunity arose to serve his country once more with another spying task in a British port.

His exploration of the pubs of Southampton was no more than irregular, however. He had been instructed not to fraternise with the local population any more than was necessary. Better to buy alcohol from supermarkets and drink it at home, watching Chinese television from a satellite and keeping his own company.

Teams of two spies such as Zhang Turku were working in Britain's major container ports, or at least those container ports with a regular run to Australia. Unlike his previous tour of duty in Scotstoun, this time Turku's assignment was a relatively short one. The spies only needed to watch the loading of container ships known to be sailing to ports in that particular country.

Admiral Zhou had guessed, and he had guessed correctly, that the British would not bother to transfer the containers from one ship to another *en route*, which would have made the task of Zhang Turku and his team of fellow spies far more difficult. That would have required putting Chinese spies in a hundred container terminals around the world. On the basis of other intelligence information received, Admiral Zhou Man had also calculated to within a few months when the container shipment or shipments were likely to be made.

Zhang had been briefed on what to look out for, and once again the admiral had been proved right. Most commercial containers arrived at the shore terminal during a period of several few days before sailing, not just in an orchestrated few hours. The Chinese spy was left in little doubt that the cargo stowed on the Sydney Constellation was the one he had been told to look out for.

From an inconspicious Chinese restaurant not a mile from Southampton's waterfront, a coded message was on its way to Beijing within the hour. Within a couple of days it became obvious from follow-up satellite reconnaissance that the Royal Navy was paying the Sydney Constellation an unduly generous degree of attention. It was not difficult to work out that something unusual was going on - and that was all the confirmation Admiral Zhou Man required.

His report was on the desk of vice-premier Liu Fun within a matter of hours. The evidence that Britain was re-arming Australia was manifest, indeed it was all there on display in the cargo manifest of a modern high speed container ship.

Chapter Fifteen

Confrontation

Toulon, French Mediterranean coast

WITH BUNTING FLUTTERING from her rigging, the Dumont d'Urville, a light French stealth frigate of the La Fayette class, sailed out of the main naval base at Toulon. Her commanding officer Xavier de Kerguelen had explained the purpose of her mission to a leading French newspaper, and put up a very capable show on regional television. "It is primarily a courtesy tour round Australia. We have been talking to our good friends in the Royal Navy and in the Royal Australian Navy, and in the present situation it is the appropriate thing to do diplomatically.

"The French Navy and the Royal Navy are the two largest in Europe, while the Royal Australian Navy is the largest in the Southern Hemisphere. All three of us share a sense of being maritime policemen, even within the global balance of power today. Many officers in all three navies enjoy strong personal and professional links - including myself - and they are encouraged. One of my closest friends serves in the Australian navy, and I very much hope to meet up with him as soon as we sail into Sydney harbour.

"Furthermore, Australia is currently showing considerable interest in buying new ships for its navy, and these La Fayettes are just about state of the art in their field. They could be precisely what Australia requires. So in a sense you might even regard this as a kind of French armaments sales trip."

There was some more of the same. Xavier's standing at fleet headquarters as a skilful spokesman for the French Navy rose by the minute. It was all delightful obfuscation to conceal the real reason the Dumont d'Urville was sailing to the Indian Ocean. Several rounds of coded emails between James Heaton, Warwick Sydenham and Xavier himself had sketched out the worthy sentiments with care, albeit with much mutual merriment. As James exhorted the other two: "If Xavier is going to talk utter bollocks, let's ensure it is top quality bollocks."

The French commander mentioned, but only in passing, there was a further albeit minor purpose to the mission. En route across the Indian Ocean the Dumont d'Urville would make a routine call mid-ocean at Martin de Viviès, a French scientific base on Amsterdam Island. The opportunity was being taken to drop off on or two additional scientists and some urgently-needed supplies, main scientific instruments, which had been requested. It would have been uneconomic sending a supply ship all the way just for a small cargo like that.

As ever, there was a hidden agenda. The French military wanted to see for themselves exactly what the Chinese had been doing on the island ever since a deal had been conceded at the United Nations several years previously. Signals from the resident French scientists could explain only so much but they were not military professionals. They also had to be circumspect, not wishing to incur the wrath of their Chinese scientific neighbours now on the island.

When the deal for the Chinese base on Amsterdam Island was originally agreed, the French had been given to understand, very clearly, that China's purpose was entirely scientific, not military. Since then the island had been visited by a new Chinese destroyer of its latest Advance class. That solitary warship put a very different complexion on the phrase 'purely scientific research'. Now France's allies in NATO wanted to know exactly what the authorities in Paris thought they were playing at in agreeing to the deal in the first place. There were even those who suggested the France had been taken for a ride by Oriental duplicity. The matter had been discussed in the French cabinet.

So Commander de Kerguelen had been given some highly secret instructions which no-one else knew anything about. And that was the real purpose, the entirely covert reason why Dumont d'Urville was calling at Amsterdam island. Truth be told, it was the entire purpose of the mission. The courtesy calls around Australia and all the rest were merely a plausible smokescreen. The ingenious graduates of the École National d'Administration, who more or less ran the French defence ministry, were some of the most adept civil servants in the world at devising plausible smokescreens.

That said, George Gould's fingerprints were practically visible in almost every sentence of the brief, albeit top secret, master plan for the Dumont d'Urville's mission. Friend to friend, the entire document required less than two succinct paragraphs. To any independent observer, it was virtually meaningless anyway. Once it got its act together, the undeclared cross-Channel semi-military entente within NATO was second to none. George Gould had enjoyed numerous convivial dinners with his opposite numbers at the Brasserie Lipp. They almost invariably saw aye to aye.

Anglo-French sailors communicated in a patois exclusive to themselves, while the eventual score at the battle of Trafalgar was long since forgotten, not least over a bottle or twain of the finest grand premier cru. It was only a hop, skip and jump by Eurostar from London to the Gare du Nord. George reckoned he could make it door to door in less than four hours. Far removed from the inconsequential rhetoric of politicians, never had an Anglo-French Entente been quite so cordiale, nor even so fruitful. There was much to achieved by shaking hands across La Manche, which was of course much more productive if you rolled your sleeves up first.

So the French frigate Dumont d'Urville, steadfastly keeping up appearances, paid a well-publicised courtesy call in Alexandria before her transit of the Suez Canal. After all, Napoleon had shown an admirable academic and intellectual interest in the cultural treasures of Egypt and why overlook something as convivial as that two centuries later? France had always held the ancient heritage of Egypt in the highest regard. The warship from Toulon was apparently in no great hurry, after all. Except of course that she was.

Once through the canal and out into the Indian Ocean, the light frigate Dumont d'Urville picked up speed. She was more than capable of that. Doing so burnt an exceptional quantity of fuel. It was over four days sailing to Amsterdam Island, and as the ship crossed the equator into the southern hemisphere the weather was delightful and the sea conditions ideal. It was late summer. The ship's company found many opportunities to top up their suntans when they were off-duty.

The call at Martin de Viviès on Amsterdam Island had all the makings of a festive occasion. In true Gallic style the warship's officers threw a splendid party on board for the French scientists on the island, and a day or so later that was followed by a further party on the island itself. The frigate had brought a large marquee for the occasion, and a suitable variety of excellent French food and wine. The event was large enough to invite a number of the senior Chinese scientists on the island to join in.

A thoroughly enjoyable time was had by all. The Chinese scientists spoke better than merely acceptable French. They had all received intensive training in the language before they left home. As the evening progressed, Xavier de Kerguelen casually asked the senior

Chinese scientist whether he could purchase some diesel fuel for his ship; she had burnt more than expected since departing the Gulf of Aden, and it had been agreed with France from the outset the Chinese could hold sizeable stocks on Amsterdam island. Some quick exchanges of messages with Beijing and Paris confirmed the modest deal was acceptable all round.

It was agreed the frigate would come alongside the splendid new jetty the following day for the fuel to be taken on board. Xavier did not disclose NATO knew pretty accurately how much oil was currently in the island's storage tank and that it was running relatively low ahead of imminent replenishment from China. The visit by the Dumont d'Urville had been timed with considerable forethought. George Gould's master plan needed a clear gap between the departure of the Dumont d'Urville and the Chinese tanker's arrival.

The fuel tank was naturally the most prominent man-made landmark on the island and the senior Chinese confirmed it offered a splendid view of the Chinese and French installations. He was pleased to get some exercise and conduct Xavier de Kerguelen to the top. After all, the island was sovereign French territory. It was hardly a request that he could refuse.

From his vantage point the French commander took a number of photographs of the rarely-visited settlement for his personal collection. He was careful to include anything of potential military interest, even if his civilian Chinese host was unaware of that.

Without it being at all apparent Xavier also contrived to leave his expensive Nikon digital reflex camera on a convenient ledge while he sorted out his sunglasses and discussed the principal natural landmarks, such as they were. He then, equally inconspicuously, neglected to collect it for his somewhat precarious return to ground level. It had been agreed the Dumont d'Urville would remain at the jetty until she sailed the following day. In the event her fuel tanks had proved somewhat emptier than anticipated and left a further-depleted stock of fuel in the island's storage tank. The level was now very low, exactly as had been intended from the outset.

Much later that night, when absolutely no-one was around, Xavier went to collect the digital camera he had conveniently forgotten. The Chinese posted no sentries - there was scarce point doing so when the island's only inhabitants were two friendly communities of civilian scientists. Xavier had taken good care to leave his camera close to one of the escape vents on top of the storage tank. It was a matter of a few minutes' work to pour in several litres of a highly concentrated chemical he had brought from France and carried in his large photographic case. The durable plastic containers folded up small once they were empty.

The sophisticated additive has been prepared by one of France's most advanced chemical manufacturers, ostensibly for secret experiments by the French military. In the relatively high concentration Xavier achieved it would serve as a breeding concentrate to ferment throughout the entire tank. Its eventual effect would be to render any fuel contained in the storage tank useless, if not dangerous, for use in high technology gas turbine engines.

His principal mission completed, Xavier de Kerguelen returned to his ship and brandished his Nikon digital reflex camera aloft in triumph to the duty sentry by the gangplank. The following day, her scientific cargo and other domestic supplies duly unloaded, the Dumont d'Urville set sail. Her visit to Martin de Viviès on Amsterdam Island had been a resounding success in every possible sense. Her true destination was not Australia at all, but there was little point alerting the Chinese on Amsterdam Island to the fact.

*   *   *   *   *

Beijing

EVERY CAPITAL CITY has an embassy district, and in Beijing it is clustered near the foreign ministry. The journeys by embassy limousine for the British and Australian ambassadors to their meeting with China's foreign minister were short, almost walking distance in fact. But walking was not appropriate on formal occasions such as this. The meeting had been arranged for noon. Both women spoke fluent Mandarin, nowadays considered an essential proficiency in what had become one of the five most important diplomatic cities in the world.

The meeting was formal and to the point. With only the minimum of diplomatic courtesies beforehand, China drew strong objection to an unwarranted escalation of military activity in the Chinese Ocean. A container ship, the Sydney Constellation, had recently passed through the Suez Canal and, heading southwards, was about to leave the Red Sea. China knew her to be carrying a large consignment of armaments and munitions bound for Australia. She was about to sail close to the port of Aden, a treaty port within the Central Ocean Treaty Organisation. That meant, in Beijing's measured opinion, the ship and her cargo were entering the Chinese sphere of influence. Australia had a long coastline on the Chinese Ocean, and any major rearmament would prejudice a peaceful balance of power.

Neither ambassador had even heard of the ship. Instead they both pointed out that the freight route between Europe and Australia through the Suez Canal had been an accepted artery of world trade for almost a hundred and fifty years. It was the principal means of commerce between their two countries, and container ships had been sailing it for half a century unmolested.

No country along the route imposed a customs barrier decreeing what cargoes could and could not be carried on the high seas. It was all part and parcel of everyday international trade. With further diplomatic courtesy China's foreign minister invited both ambassadors to make further enquiries with their respective governments and to secure an amicable response which would meet the Chinese concerns. Within hours secure communications messages summarised the unprecedented attitude of the Chinese government to London and Canberra, and sought advice on what line to take and what to do next.

*   *   *   *   *

Ministry of Defence, London

LATER THAT SAME DAY Peter Storey sent for George Gould. London's Foreign and Commonwealth Office had forwarded the ambassadorial despatch from Beijing to the Ministry of Defence for immediate response. "What do we know about this container ship, the Sydney Constellation, George, and if I should know anything already, please refresh my memory. And why should the Chinese be getting quite so excited about her?"

George Gould read through the note from Beijing carefully. "In a nutshell, Peter, the Chinese have rumbled us. The Sydney Constellation is carrying about three hundred containers full of military bits and pieces - jet engines, ship parts, advanced equipment and weaponry. As you recall we agreed over two years ago to supply Australia with the kit it needed to jump-start their rearmament project.

"At our end we planned the exercise with great care and we thought we had all the security angles covered. I don't know how the Chinese have found out about it, but it is very clever of them and there is no scope for denying it. The larger question is what we, or they, propose to do about it."

"Well I think it's a damned impertinence challenging our merchant marine on the high seas. The cargo is none of their business." Peter Storey was coming quite close to medium-rise dudgeon. "I think we should send a stiffish reply and ask the Chinese exactly what they want us to do about it. It is all very presumptuous. Do we know who in Beijing is behind the effrontery? I presume they must have some naval muscle deployed in their so-called Chinese Ocean or they wouldn't be rattling their sabres, or whatever sailors rattle. Perhaps they brandish cutlasses; something like that, anyway."

George Gould promised to have a word with the security services, and also with naval intelligence whose job it was to keep an eye on the who's who of senior officers running foreign navies. Peter Storey had another thought. "Let's suppose, just suppose, the Chinese intend to take this seriously; a worst-case scenario. We know China is the new naval power in the Indian Ocean, or whatever they now call it. As said, brandishing their cutlasses.

"If things start to hot up, we could need some quick-thinking military manpower. Suddenly all that Kundalini business starts to make real sense. I think we should also talk to Christopher Cunningham. Can this container ship sail round in circles or something while we determine our next move?"

So it was decided to hold a further meeting the following day, while the Sydney Constellation was requested to drop her speed and make a little less haste into the Indian Ocean. In the meantime there would be time to consult the Australian military in Canberra, and have a word with the Pentagon. As George Gould pointed out "the only worthwhile naval asset we ourselves have in the region is HMS Daedalus, which takes over as escort for the container ship as she leaves the Gulf of Aden. The Australians are sending a frigate to take over as a discreet escort for the Sydney Constellation on her final run into Freemantle, but we don't want to make an ordinary container ship look like the centrepiece of some bloody naval regatta."

The meeting at the Ministry of Defence included Christopher Cunningham of the Sharava Corporation. There was some useful naval intelligence from Northwood. The messenger was James Heaton.

George Gould had cross-checked it with the Chinese desk at the Foreign Office, who confirmed everything. It emerged the person in charge in Beijing was the country's top woman politician, the formidable vice-premier Liu Fun. "No-one underestimates her. She's been behind a lot of Chinese initiatives in recent years, and she's been seen around the United Nations on several occasions. The Foreign office had seen no good reason to mention it before, but their information is categorical."

James Heaton was in agreement. "It wouldn't surprise me in the slightest if the whole of this COTO business has been cooked up by this vice-premier Liu Fun. I didn't put her name in my note on the subject a couple of years back because I wasn't entirely sure, but now we are. And we also believe at Northwood her military sidekick is a chap called Admiral Zhou Man.

I gather from other sources that he popped up in Paris as leader of the team which set up the deal on Amsterdam Island. Ostensibly as a civilian. And it now transpires the Chinese have given him command of their new so-called Chinese Ocean fleet. That makes sense. He was also photographed at the launching ceremony of at least one of their Advance class destroyers."

Christopher Cunningham started at the mention of Zhou Man's name, and said "Hang on a second." He pulled out his mobile phone and dialled his office back in Park Royal. "Antonia, did you once say you knew a man in China called Zhou Man, a big shot in the Chinese navy?"

Antonia Cunningham giggled down the telephone. "I ought to know him, darling. Well before I ever met you, he was my boyfriend, at least my on and off boyfriend, for the best part of fifteen years. It's not an episode of my life I am particularly proud about. Yes, I think we can both agree I knew him pretty well."

"And what about this character Liu Fun. You've mentioned her name before as well, haven't you? Where does she fit in the grand scheme of things?" Antonia now sounded more serious. "Yes I have.

She is the brains behind the whole of the Chinese expansion into Africa and in consequence their extensive presence around the Indian Ocean. The naval thing is only just part of a greater whole. It's officially all to do with protecting the African trade route. It was she who recruited me to that awful job in Lanzhou making jet engines. I only met her a few times but she is definitely a power in the land. Why do you ask?"

Christopher Cunningham explained that he was in a confidential meeting in London and the two names had simply cropped up. Husband and wife exchanged a few ideas on his eating plans for the rest of the day and then rang off. "It seems" he said to the small meeting "we have an inside track on both those Chinese. In her former life, my wife knew one of them pretty well in China, and says the other is definitely Beijing's Mrs Big behind all of this palaver. The whole naval show is really just a part of their African enterprise. It's the same old story. They want to protect their strategic trade routes. We've been there ourselves many times."

George Gould also confirmed the name. "I remember reading some forthright stuff from Liu Fun supplied by our embassy in China when they launched their first Advance class destroyer. Quite a political philosopher on the side. Pretty impressive. It doesn't surprise me at all she is the brains behind this latest activity. If James has also heard about her through his INA contact, and Antonia has met her in charge of things in some previous incarnation of hers in China, it all starts to add up. Gentlemen, I think we now know the complete picture on the lid of the jigsaw puzzle. "

Peter Storey looked round the table at this collective knowledge of the Chinese *dramatis personae*, then tapped it several times with his forefinger and turned to Christopher Cunningham. "Well Chris, may I suggest your wife joins us sharpish. She is fully signed up with the Official Secrets Act, I assume, working for Sharava? She could be the very intelligence asset we need. How much does she know about Bijali?"

Christopher Cunningham briefly explained the careful way Sharava's security proceeded on a very strict 'need to know' basis. Now was perhaps the time to put his wife properly in the picture. It was agreed Peter Storey would urge the Foreign office to give a stalling response to the latest Chinese demands, and to ask exactly what Beijing had in mind. There was no point denying the cargo being carried by the Sydney Constellation. It made much more sense to treat the matter as being beyond China's legitimate concern.

"There's something else." added Peter Storey. "When we find ourselves in a tricky situation like this, I generally reckon it's best to put key manpower near the centre of the action. James, I suggest you and Christopher get yourselves embarked on Daedalus at the first opportunity. I'm sure the RAF can fly you somewhere convenient. That old ship of yours is fully fitted for Bijali, the lot.

"To pay you a professional compliment. More than once you have been ahead of the game as this pantomime has unfolded. I can't think of a better team to run the show should we need to start playing clever games with the Chinese. And Chris, if the Americans will play ball and do something useful with that Fifth Fleet of theirs, perhaps you can rejoin your old friends on the Carl Vinson and give us some eyes and ears there as well."

After they had left, the man from the ministry poured a couple of glasses of scotch. "Well, George, this is a fine pickle. And you within a couple of months of retirement. Definitely a swan song to remember. I can't get over the effrontery of it all. What do the Chinese think they are playing at?"

George Gould held his drink to the light and rotated it slowly. He caught the afterglow of the afternoon sun, a bright ochre light distorting through his glass. Then he slowly put the glass to one side before he started to speak. "You know, Peter, we've all been here before." Peter Storey looked at his old colleague sharply. "How do you mean, we've all been here before? Come off it, George. So far as I am aware the Chinese haven't behaved like this since the Opium Wars."

"I wasn't thinking about the Chinese, Peter. I was thinking about the Russians. Only this time the rôles are reversed. Cast your mind back almost exactly fifty-four years." Peter Storey did some quick calculations on his fingers. "You mean 1962? My God! The Cuban missile crisis. Is that what you have in mind?"

George Gould smiled his private smile of intellectual success, but it was not with any pleasure. "That is exactly what I have in mind, Peter. A shipload of munitions on the high seas. One side determined on arming a friendly country. The other side determined to stop them. Just insert "Australia" for "Cuba". Except this time round, we are the Russians, and this Chinese lady vice-premier Liu Fun is roughly where Jack Kennedy was back then. Meanwhile we are landed with the comedy duo of Stanley and Fenceville playing the part of Nikita Khrushchev."

Peter Storey stared at George Gould for several moments and then said "Christ" very slowly. He even turned it into a two syllable word. "And of course back in 1962, George, it was eventually Khrushchev who blinked first and had to take all his missiles back home. Is that how it is going to pan out this time round? With three-quarters of the United Nations shouting 'sauce for the goose, sauce for the gander!' at the tops of their voices? Do you think the Chinese had this worked out all along? Is that what COTO is really all about? A mirror-image of NATO half a century on? Come to think of it, they as good as told us so two years ago."

It was George Gould's turn to tap the table. "Let's not beat ourselves up on the similarities with the Cuban crisis, Peter. Let's think our way through the many differences. If my guess is right, it's China that might just want to play the 1962 card at the United Nations. It will certainly not be us. For a start, it's less than three years since the Australians started a major re-armament programme. China has been working on this Chinese Ocean strategy of theirs for a lot longer than that. This is not a Chinese response to events in what they suddenly consider to be their own patch, but something larger. It's over four years since they launched their first Advance class destroyer. This latest complaint about the Sydney Constellation isn't the real reason, it's just a convenient excuse for whatever they have in mind.

"Objecting to some unarmed merchant ship was never part of their grand strategy. Second, Cuba is practically in America's back yard. Havana is only about a hundred miles from Key West. It's a little different this time around. Australia is way further than that from the nearest point of the Chinese People's Republic. I reckon the distance from China's Hainan island to the north coast of Australia is the best part of 2,500 miles. First you'd have to cross the South China Sea, and that alone is about half the size of the Mediterranean. Then and you've got the whole of Indonesia in the way as well. And then you've got to cross the Timor Sea. So Australia, entirely unlike Cuba, is not exactly in the Chinese backyard. Totally different.

"So the argument about arming some antagonistic next-door neighbour would be bollocks and I think the Chinese would ill-advised to play the Cuba card. Anyone with an ounce of geography between their ears would just laugh at them. The moral issue might just be comparable, provided you accept their grandiose claims that somehow the Indian Ocean now belongs to them. They're pushing their luck on that one as well. Let's face it, they have not a yard of coastline anywhere near the Indian Ocean. A nearer parallel might be the British claim on the Falkland Islands, but that is sovereign British territory and not one of the Falkland inhabitants wants anything to do with the Argies.

"The next thing is, we do have a key military advantage the Chinese know nothing about. We can use Sharava's clever stuff to read what is being planned on their warships. Chris Cunningham will have the initiator keys for that and it doesn't take long to find out which particular ships they are deploying. Assuming they are using Advance class destroyers, every one has a unique Bijali key, and we can read the Ops room of any of them. It's never been used in anger yet, but there is a first time for everything."

James Heaton smiled. "Tell you what. Why don't we suggest to Norfolk, Virginia that they put Chuck Wellie in the Carl Vinson? He's the Yank who saw our side of things when I demonstrated Bijali. He loved it. But far more to the point, he actually understands it. I'd like to be working with Chuck Wellie again. The last thing we'll want is some uncomprehending American commander who has to try and learn it all afresh from first principles. We simply will not have time for that kind of mid-ocean classroom stuff." George Gould nodded approvingly. His protégé was thinking several steps ahead.

The following day, while James Heaton and Christopher Cunningham flew to the RAF base at Akrotiri in Cyprus, another urgent, more formal meeting was taking place in the Cabinet Secretary's office. Peter Storey and George Gould had both been invited along to Ten Downing Street and they were joined by Britain's ambassador to Washington, Sir Marlow Alderman. The Australian High Commissioner in London, Sir Wesley Latterson, completed the tri-nation team. There was plenty to discuss.

Sir Anthony Pilkington, Cabinet Secretary, explained the overnight position. "We've now had a demand from Beijing. They require the Sydney Constellation to rendevous with one of their warships at a specified point in the Arabian Sea in the approaches to the Gulf of Oman. She is then to be put under Chinese authority..

"From there she will apparently be escorted to one of their treaty ports in the Gulf, we guess that will probably be Dammam, and will be required to discharge her cargo of munitions to be surrendered to the Saudi authorities before continuing on her way. I'd say our Chinese friends are rather over-playing their hand." This latest demand brought an eruption of indignation around the table. "That's nothing more nor less than piracy." Peter Storey exclaimed. "We can't possibly agree to that. Next thing we know, they will be pinching anything they fancy off our container ships as they cross the Indian Ocean."

"The prime minister took much the same view when I spoke to him earlier." explained the Cabinet Secretary, who was now looking rather grim. Wesley Latterson indicated that was exactly the view of the Australian government as well, received a few hours earlier from Canberra. "So there's nothing for it, gentlemen, but to inform the Chinese we reject their demands, that the Sydney Constellation will continue on her legitimate voyage as planned, and we'll all just have to wait and see what happens next."

It was now the turn of the British ambassador from Washington, Sir Marlow Alderman. His news confirmed what James Heaton had guessed the day before. "It's not all bad news. First the Pentagon has woken up to recent events and a substantial task force from their Fifth Fleet is to sail with maximum despatch out of Trincomalee. They are planning to loop round onto the intended course of the Sydney Constellation then sail straight towards her. You might say it's a twenty-first century variant of the Sixth Cavalry.

"I'm also pleased to report this is now considered a purely military decision which does not require clearance from the White House. The Yankee admirals were trying to tell me something about a decoy course for Freemantle, and some smokescreen story about a routine goodwill visit to Australia. They mentioned something about secret British technology which they seemed to think I would know all about, but I didn't and it went straight over my head." George Gould smiled. The Americans were keeping their side of the bargain.

The British Ambassador had not yet finished. "That intelligence test exercise we did with Abigail Fenceville has worked too. I gather it's called Kundalini, or something like that, and that you guys cooked it all up at MoD. Whatever it is it seems to have done the trick. She has made it clear to the Pentagon that she considers the present situation to be purely a matter of military tactics, that it requires quick thinking on the spot, and she is better kept out of it. So our chaps in the Indian Ocean, working with MoD, now seem to be in total command.

The Cabinet Secretary nodded enthusiastically. "Well that's one hurdle we don't have to confront. If I tell the prime minister that's the view from the White House, perhaps he will come to the same conclusion. He didn't do all that well on Kundalini either. The fact of the matter is, we are now playing chess with the Chinese in the middle of an ocean using live ammunition, and the shorter the lines of command the better for everyone. I would much prefer to play this one apart from our politicians, rather than through them."

It was now Peter Storey's turn. "I think, gentlemen we should all remind ourselves we've been here before. George, tell them what you and I were discussing yesterday. Remind them about Cuba." In a few crisp sentences George Gould ran through the parallels between the Cuban missile crisis in 1962 and the situation in the Indian Ocean today.

The Cabinet Secretary buried his head in his hands. "As I recall it was Khrushchev who had to back down. This time it's our turn to be the Russians, as the Chinese will see it. I'm not entirely sure I want us to follow in the footsteps of the shoe-banging Nikita. Our chaps are really going to have their work cut out at the United Nations to talk their way out of that one."

Peter Storey continued, "But it's not all bad news, gentlemen. Apart from the huge geographical differences this time round, we do have certain technology advantages the Chinese don't know about, or we assume they don't know about. Quite unlike the Russians half a century ago, we do have the military upper hand."

* * * * *

The Indian, or Chinese, Ocean

A DAY LATER James Heaton and Christopher Cunningham joined HMS Daedalus in the Indian Ocean, although still some distance from the Sydney Constellation. Large container ships could show a fair turn of speed, even by the standards of warships. A tropical storm in mid-ocean now meant she had changed course to sail round the bad weather. High stacks of containers above decks preferred a smooth crossing whenever possible. There had been some bizarre mishaps in the past.

Daedalus's Signals Officer brought James a small sheaf of messages from London. "I hope this one means something to you, Sir. Someone called Zhou Man? Does that mean anything? Anyway he's a Chinese admiral and he is on board a solitary Advance class destroyer which shares his name. Less than couple of day's sailing away."

James wondered whether it would be possible to patch through to Antonia back in London. The telecoms officer reckoned he could set it up, no problem. It began to look as if they would be hearing quite a lot from Antonia's old boyfriend Zhou Man before too long. James had spent some of the long trip by aircraft and helicopter via Diego Garcia discussing with Christopher exactly what his wife understood about Bijali. Apparently Martin Barraclough would be filling her in to just the level of knowledge she needed, and no further.

Another message on the log for James explained that a small Chinese naval detachment out of Hainan had passed Singapore and was heading into the Indian Ocean. Meantime the American Fifth Fleet was sailing south-east from Trincomalee, watching the Chinese carefully and avoiding contact. Things were clearly warming up.

The Signals Officer continued: "Oh, and someone called George Gould wants an urgent chat with you, Sir. You're to call him on a secure line at MoD. And I was saving this one for last. News has just come from the hospital. Your wife has had a baby boy, mother and son doing just fine. Congratulations, Commander."

James whooped with delight. That news called for immediate celebration, no matter how brief, with the Commanding Officer, Christopher Cunningham and senior officers of Daedalus. There was just time for one quick drink apiece and many words of congratulation for the delighted new father. Then it was back to work.

Naval Intelligence at Northwood told James they were tracking a ship which, given her level of signals traffic, had to be the Chinese destroyer. She was under cloud cover and surveillance satellites were unable to examine her in visual detail. They now reckoned she could be within missile range of the Sydney Constellation in less than twenty-four hours and between times she was heading just about straight through the middle of a tropical storm.

James Heaton wished them well, and commented to the commanding office of Daedalaus "I trust our new friend Admiral Zhou Man has a strong stomach. He'll need it. They're going to be driving through ten metre waves. And those Advance class destroyers are no larger than a Type 45 - in fact they are cloned copy. Bon voyage, guys."

On board his Advance class destroyer Admiral Zhou Man was faring quite well. Like James Heaton, he enjoyed being on the high seas even if it was a bit breezy and a bit rough. She was a fine ship and so far as they could tell she was the only warship in this part of the Chinese Ocean. An unarmed container merchantman posed no threat to a Chinese Advance class destroyer. He was the man in charge, although musing over a most interesting conversation that morning with vice-premier Liu Fun, who seemed to grow more philosophical than ever when adrenalin ran high.

"From what we can see here in Beijing, Admiral, the nearest challenge you face will be from the British, not the Americans. Although the picture is far from clear, they do have a warship to the west of you. It might just be heading for Mombasa. Just remember this, Admiral Zhou. This could be a historical milestone. For over twenty years I have wondered when we would reach this point. So keep an objective mind. Just remember how world politics and world culture work. There are two races on this planet with an all-pervading, unquenchable sense of cultural superiority, and they are the Chinese and the English. So we do live in interesting times after all.

"Remember you are playing to a global audience. Even if we say nothing about it here in China, we must assume that the Western media will be watching our every move and reporting it. We have to face that, no matter how much it may irk us. Your task now is the greater good of the People's Republic, the greater good of humanity, not some localised heroics. Let's hope your British opposite number sees things the same way. You are facing a worthy opponent."

Admiral Zhou was not entirely sure what to make of the vice-premier's cryptic homily, but he did wonder how he would react. It was certainly a long time since the Chinese had confronted the British on the high seas. He would not have long to wait. They were roughly in the same line of longitude as Amsterdam Island when the ship's navigator brought some news. "We now have an exact position for the Sydney Constellation, sir. She's to the south west of us, obviously trying to avoid this storm. We have also picked up a ship, probably a naval vessel heading directly towards her from Australia. We estimate they are heading for a rendesvous. Probably an escort."

On Daedalus, James had managed some fitful sleep. In a succession of telephone conversations the previous evening he had spoken to an overjoyed Violaine at her London clinic. "James. He is absolutely gorgeous. He even looks like you." James knew this to be quite untrue. All new-born babies looked like Winston Churchill.

'Do hurry home, darling. George Gould has called with his congratulations and at least told me where you are. I expect the weather there is good, Come back with a suntan. I hope you're safe. Be careful darling. Please come home safely. Maman told me to send her love.

And I've spoken to your parents and they are absolutely delighted. Your whole family is wanting you home."

James's next conversation was with George Gould. He also offered his family congratulations and then had more serious news. "James. I've been asked to relay a message to you from the Cabinet Office. This contingency at long last means there are very good lines of communications between MoD, Northwood and Number Ten. Everyone is watching you, the Prime Minister even. And the message from here is that you are in full command.

"The PM reckons this is purely a matter of military tactics and split-second decisions. He has agreed exactly that with President Fenceville. They both completely see the point of Kundalini now and both say you need to be the man in sole command. So full military authority rests with you. I know you'll take the right decision when the time comes. The C.O. of Daedalus is fully in the picture."

"It's an interesting thought that with the American Fifth Fleet just over the horizon with your pal Chuck Wellie standing on the poop deck, you in complete charge and the French Navy represented by Xavier Kerguelen in full support, that means we have three permanent members of the United Nations Security Council taking on a fourth. That's quite a party. And to cap it all Commander Warwick Sydenham is somewhere to the east of you quite determined to join in the fun. Welcome to the twenty-first century. All you need now is Judith Durham of the Seekers joining Mick Jagger in a rousing chorus of Rule Britannia. Did you know they are only about three weeks apart in age?

"And Just remember, James, surprise tactics never did any harm. When they realise just how close we really are, that's the time to put the wind up Admiral Zhou Man.

"Good luck James. May the sea gods sail with you." Christopher Cunningham agreed. "Very interesting. The one thing we have never been able to test on Kundalini is what a real-life opposition will think or do once they suddenly discover our intelligence superiority. From a purely intellectual point of view, and after all the testing we did in park Royal and elsewhere, I'm really forward to this."

James Heaton's final conversation had been with Warwick Sydenham on HMAS Stuart, now less than a day's sailing to the east. They were also delighted to learn that the French were now keeping more than a watching eye, and their man on the Dumont d'Urville was none other than Xavier de Kerguelen, looping round from Amsterdam Island. "I tell you, Warwick, it's just like old times. Think Île St Louis.

"Except this time around the French won't be serving the finest food Paris can produce. On the contrary I can assure you that old Xavier has cooked up something distinctly less digestible for the Chinese navy. Again their conversation was deliberately cryptic, but Warwick understood immediately how James was playing his hand. What a surprise it would be to the Chinese admiral when a large slice of the American Fifth Fleet suddenly appeared in a position between his ship and the rest of the Chinese fleet. Like James Heaton he would then be on his own, and may the best man win.

Shortly after dawn, James returned to the Operations room. Today it was his own handpicked crew, for this time the battle was real. Chief Petty Officers were driving fighting consoles which would normally be driven by somewhat more junior ranks. As Commander Heaton had explained at the briefing: "Tomorrow will be one of those days when every one of us in the Ops Room will learn something new; those of you on the consoles and those watching alike."

It was also one of those days which called for older heads on young shoulders, demanding extreme coolth under extreme pressure. The regular trackers were observing their bosses at work with rapt attention. If ever there was a day to learn on the job, this was it. The occasional half sentences from the more senior men showed how warfare tutorials were all in full swing.

Christopher Cunningham was scrutinising the Ops Room of the Zhou Man over the shoulder of the man at the console. As he did so and tried to guess what the Chinese voices were saying. Then James Heaton had a bright idea. "Tell you what, Chris, let's patch through to that wife of yours in London. After all, Antonia does speak perfectly good Chinese. Imagine his surprise if Zhou Man suddenly hears her voice in his Ops room. More than enough to give him acute indigestion. I happen to know we can do that trick using Bijali."

Sure enough, Antonia Cunningham was on the line almost immediately. Christopher gave her a brief summary of what Zhou Man's tracking operators were doing. Apparently there was something close to pandemonium one they realised how close was the British destroyer. The course of HMS Daedalaus toward Mombasa had been a feint.

Suddenly it was decision time aboard China's Advance class destroyer. Antonia was now listening to their conversation. "I think I just picked up something they said about making the weapons ready, James. And they are certainly very busy with their Tracking and Fire Control System. Buzzing around it like bees."

James Heaton reached a spur of the moment decision. "Okay, Antonia, let's see if we can surprise your old boyfriend with something else he was not expecting. I've just asked our Signals Officer to give you an open radio link with the Chinese destroyer. Let's exchange a word or two with Admiral Zhou Man himself. I'm sure he'll recognise your voice. Repeat something you've just heard him say. Let's reveal half our hand. It might just give him pause to think."

The crew in the Operations room on Daedalus listened while Antonia in London held an animated conversation in Mandarin. It was obvious even from the tone of her voice it was not going at all well. Eventually she said her goodbyes and told James he could cut the link. "That's gone and done it. I agree with you, it should have made him calmer. But it's done just the reverse. He cannot get over my voice suddenly talking on his radio, coming out of the blue right into his own Operations room. He has deduced I am spying on him. I've never known him to be so emotional, almost panicking. Quite unlike the onshore naval officer of old. It's made him suspicious of his own shadow. All we can do now is watch to see what he does next."

James remembered his tutor at Dartmouth. No battle plan ever survives first contact with the enemy. The Chief Petty Officer monitoring what was happening on the Zhou Man said she was now targeting the Sydney Constellation. James Heaton said "Right. So here's the plan. The moment he shoots a missile anywhere near our container ship, I want that Chinese missile taken out with a Sea Viper. Make that two, just to be absolutely sure we kiss it goodbye. "Aye, aye, Sir" said the Chief Petty Officer at the Sea Viper console.

"And if he does that, then he's opened fire first and we will retaliate by lobbing a Harpoon in his direction. If it gets through it should blow quite a large hole in the Zhou Man. I understand the Chinese have been working on their own anti-missile system. Let's find out just how good it is. He's on a loser anyway. He must surely have realised by now that a large chunk of Uncle Sam's Fifth Fleet is blockading his way home."

James had rather hoped he could delay matters until the Zhou Man was running low on fuel. Then she would have to take on board some of Xavier's interesting concoction quietly fermenting in the fuel tank on Amsterdam Island. If all else failed, that was Plan B. It was a handy insurance policy to have.

A good naval commander should always have more than one ace up his sleeve. As it was, his main concentration was on putting Daedalaus exactly where he wanted her between the Sydney Constellation and the Zhou Man. James was calculating how long missiles would spend in the air. That's what a good naval weapons officer should be able to do.

Thoughts of his beloved wife and their new baby son, of the world in which his son would grow up, thoughts of his training at Dartmouth - he who hesitates is lost - all flashed through his mind. He was a military officer. He was trained to act while others merely prevaricated. Other people could worry about the politics afterwards.

"Okay, CPO. As soon as the Chinese destroyer launches something in the exact direction of the Sydney Constellation, we'll have to decide on the spur of the moment whether it is just a warning shot or the real McCoy. Either way your job is to knock that Chinese missile right out of the sky. The Chief Petty Officer responded once again with a crisp "Aye, aye, Sir". This was the kind of stuff they had trained to handle for years. Now at long last they were all playing for real.

James next turned to the two CPO's in charge of the two tracking systems. One was running the one on Daedalaus. The more senior, who spoke some Mandarin, was watching and listening what was happening in the Ops Room of the Zhou Man. "Okay guys. Your task is to determine whether the Chinese are just putting the wind up the Sydney Constellation or playing for real. If they were smart they's just put a warning shot across her bows. If he did that we could send him one in return and we could all go home for tea. Somehow I doubt he'll be quite that smart. Right now our friend Admiral Zhou Man appears to be in a state of blind panic."

James next spoke to the man running the Harpoon console. There were no fools among the crew of HMS Daedalaus, and in the mess Chief Petty Officer Duncan Gregory was by common consent one of the cleverest and quickest-thinking. He was a highly experienced sailor with nerves of steel and his eyes were glued to the screen. "Okay, CPO, you are to take your cue from the tracking guys. If they decide Zhou Man is really trying to hit the Sydney Constellation, that's your signal. She's a big enough bloody target after all. There shouldn't be much doubt about it one way or another.

"Even if their missile only takes out a couple of dozen containers, that's still good enough for me. We will then know without a shadow of doubt that the Chinese opened fire first. We can save all the Bijali tapes for the politicians to argue about afterwards. As soon as we are sure about her true intentions - and it should be virtually instantaneous - if they are playing for real then you lob a Harpoon right at the Zhou Man. Stay firmly locked on to her. It will not be a warning shot. Try and put a damn great dent in her pride. I reckon one alone should be sufficient to do the trick. In the process we will discover just how much the Chinese navy have so far learnt about anti-missile technology."

Chief Petty Officer Gregory responded with another crisp 'Aye, aye, Sir'. James rubbed his forehead. "So here we find ourselves, a bit over a century on. Let's look upon this as our very own Sarajevo moment." "Why is that, Sir?" asked HMS Raleigh's finest without taking his calculating gaze from the screen. For a brief moment James was thinking historically, not unlike his Chinese counterpart. "Because, Duncan, either we will have called their bluff, or you are about to fire the very first shot in World War Three."

The Chief Petty Officer allowed himself a quick glance up at his Commander and caught his expression. He and James Heaton knew one other's minds well enough; they had served together before. Then a shout from across the Operations room confirmed a Chinese missile had just been launched directly at the unarmed container ship, and two Sea Vipers were already on their way to intercept. Commander James Heaton RN, the man in full operational command of a rapidly evolving confrontation, had given his orders. The Chief Petty Officer did everything his exhaustive training had taught him to do, made the final checks on his target, and pressed the firing button.

finis

London, November 2014